Tyler Anne Sn[illegible] er
same-named hus[illegible] i
'lions' and a burn[illegible]
superpowers incluc[illegible] uding
cats. When she isn[illegible] g mysteries and
romance, she's readin[illegible] ything she can get her hands
on. How she gets through each day starts and ends with
a big cup of coffee. Visit her at tylerannesnell.com

Kimberly Van Meter wrote her first book at sixteen and finally achieved publication in December 2006. She writes for the Mills & Boon Heroes series. She and her husband of thirty years have three children, two cats, and always a houseful of friends, family and fun.

Also by Tyler Anne Snell

Manhunt
Toxin Alert
Dangerous Recall

Small Town Last Stand

Search for the Truth

The Saving Kelby Creek Series

Surviving the Truth
Accidental Amnesia
Cold Case Captive
Retracing the Investigation

Also by Kimberly Van Meter

Big Sky Justice

Danger in Big Sky Country
Her K-9 Protector
Cold Case Secrets
Cold Case Kidnapping

The Coltons of Owl Creek

Colton's Secret Stalker

The Coltons of Kansas

Colton's Amnesia Target

THE DEPUTY'S SECRET DOUBLE

TYLER ANNE SNELL

COLTON'S REEL DANGER

KIMBERLY VAN METER

MILLS & BOON

First Published in Great Britain 2025
by Mills & Boon, an imprint of HarperCollins*Publishers* Ltd
1 London Bridge Street, London, SE1 9GF

www.harpercollins.co.uk

HarperCollins*Publishers*
Macken House, 39/40 Mayor Street Upper,
Dublin 1, D01 C9W8, Ireland

Special thanks and acknowledgment are given to Kimberly Van Meter for her contribution to *The Coltons of Arizona* series.

ISBN: 978-0-263-39708-6

0425

This book contains FSC™ certified paper and other controlled sources to ensure responsible forest management.

For more information visit: www.harpercollins.co.uk/green

Printed and Bound in the UK using 100% Renewable Electricity at
CPI Group (UK) Ltd, Croydon, CR0 4YY

THE DEPUTY'S SECRET DOUBLE

TYLER ANNE SNELL

This book is for Chelsea M. Without your late-night writing chats, JJ and Price would still be stuck in my head. Thank you. And may you meet your word count always.

Prologue

By all accounts, JJ Shaw was an all-rounder. There wasn't just one thing she was good at. She flourished at a great many things that left her résumé looking like a run-over garden of skill, determination and a little luck.

She was great at math, was a pro at public speaking, won accolades for leadership, never said no to hard work but also never let anyone use her as a doormat. She was fluent in Spanish, had a steel-trap memory, and had spent several summers at STEM retreats that gave her a leg up in any job setting that revolved around computer software or programming. Her degrees—all three of them—were impressive by themselves, never mind together, and when she wasn't contracting out her services to corporate juggernauts across the country to keep her savings account plump and happy, she spent her free time dominating boxing gyms and specialized training camps in various fields.

JJ Shaw wasn't just well-rounded on paper. She was a delight, a wonder and a laugh and a half in person too.

She wasn't just an all-rounder.

She was *the* all-rounder.

Which made the almost-blank piece of paper she slid across the counter hurt just a little.

"I know I don't have much to offer but I can promise you

I'll work hard," she told the woman standing on the opposite side.

The best JJ could guess was that the owner of Twenty-Two Coffee Shop was only a few years older than her thirty. If that. Her name tag read Cassandra and her eyes read hesitance. Her protruding, pregnant belly read an opposing eagerness.

She glanced at the Part-Time Wanted sign taped to the glass front door before settling on prioritizing her needs over her polite Southern concerns.

"I'm not sure if this type of work is something you'll want," she tried. "It's part-time, as you saw, and that really does mean part-time. It won't pay that much and most of the work is cleaning and helping with back-end things until I come back. We have another part-timer already who works after school and on the weekends and then my sister and another full-timer. This is a position that's more for dealing with the things that fall through the cracks when I'm out on maternity leave."

JJ had once spent an entire summer cleaning out horse stalls and pig pens in the middle of the Alabama heat, morning in and morning out. The smells alone were imprinted in her memory forever and it was one of her least favorite jobs. Keeping a coffee shop in the small Georgia town of Seven Roads seemed a much less offensive situation. At the very least it was air-conditioned.

She smiled.

"I don't mind the work, even if it's low on the hours," she assured her. "Honestly, I'm in need of an excuse to get out and about more than anything. I've just come to town and want to see something other than my own walls. Plus, I'd love to have some extra money coming in from somewhere to feel better about the house I just bought."

JJ could see she had piqued Cassandra's interest.

Seven Roads was thimble-sized small. Everyone truly knew everyone. Or, at least, everyone had *heard* about everyone else. Someone always had all the stories, true or not, about every resident.

Old and new.

JJ had been in Seven Roads for over a month and had been careful to only be seen exactly when she wanted to be seen. This was the first time Cassandra had spoken to her and, as far as both women knew, it was the first time the old home on Whatley Bend had been brought up by the newcomer crazy enough to buy it.

Now it was up to Cassandra to take the bait.

She did, though JJ had to admit she was more even keel about it than she thought others might have been.

"You're the one who bought Janice Wilkins's old home? The one over on Whatley Bend?"

JJ nodded.

"I'm working on a plan to renovate it since it's been in such poor condition. I'm staying in a rental near here until then."

Cassandra was impressed.

"That's a lot of work if I remember that house right. You have a lot cut out for yourself." She glanced at the front door sign again. "I'm not sure you'll have the time to be here if you're doing all that."

JJ was quick with a new smile, quicker with a response.

"I'm just overseeing. I won't be doing the work myself," she said. "Plus, you said the hours here were on the low side. I can more than work around that if you give me the chance."

Under normal circumstances, JJ had the feeling the Cassandra might have wondered more about the situation. Yet, she rubbed a hand along her pregnant belly and sighed.

It sure helped JJ's cause that no one else had applied for the job yet.

Cassandra finally relented with a nod.

"If you really don't mind the low hours and the work, let's see if we can figure something out."

JJ made a show of being overjoyed.

"Thank you. You won't be sorry."

Cassandra pulled her résumé across the counter and then motioned JJ to follow her down the hall to the back. She only paused when the bell over the front door rang, and a teenaged girl called a hello.

"That's our other part-timer," she explained to JJ when they were settled in the manager's office. "Even though her daddy can be overprotective sometimes, she's a hoot to have around. I'm sure you'll end up having a good time when she's on shift."

JJ said she was looking forward to that and then they got down to the business side of hiring someone new. When that was done, Cassandra went on a little about some of the regular customers and commented carefully on a few more.

She didn't know it, but JJ was hanging on her every word as she did so.

Then, when a name she was hoping would be said never came, her attention went back to casual.

It made lying easier when the number one question she had been asked since moving to town came.

"So, Miss Shaw, what brought you to Seven Roads?"

JJ smiled once more.

"My dad stayed here for business years ago and I liked the idea of the slower pace when I was trying to figure out where to go next. Also, I think we all hit that urge sometimes for a change. I've just been lucky enough to be able to find a way to make it happen."

Cassandra accepted the answer with a solemn nod.

"I've been there before, for sure," she said. "Sometimes you need space from the bad to realize all of the good still out there."

It was JJ's turn to nod.

Though she felt the strain in her smile.

She couldn't say it—wouldn't say it—but the life JJ had been living before was the good. It was stressful at times, sure, and there were secrets she couldn't touch, but it had been nice and fun and safe.

Now she was JJ Shaw.

She had left that good and jumped right into a past filled with bad.

There was no normal life left for her now that she was in Seven Roads.

She was only there to do one thing and one thing only.

JJ was there to keep a secret, and no one was going to stop her from doing that.

Chapter One

Perry Price Collins already wasn't having the best of days, way before he took the punch to the jaw.

First, as in as soon as he rolled off the couch, his cell phone was buzzing with the sheriff's caller ID.

"I can't promise this in writing, and it definitely won't hold up in court, but I'll pay you everything in my bank account if you could do me a favor." Instead of Liam Weaver, current sheriff of Seven Roads, his wife, Blake, was on the other end of the line, laughing into her own words. But Price could hear she surely wanted the favor.

He rubbed his eyes, grimaced at the slight hangover already beating at his skull and nodded to his empty room.

"You know, I was just out with your husband a few hours ago. Can't this favor take pity on me and wait until later?"

Blake laughed. Or, really, more like cackled. Since marrying the sheriff, she had become more comfortable with teasing him. And especially when he looped in a poor, unsuspecting Price for a "quick drink." That quick drink was now muddy boots in the living room, a bar tab that he couldn't exactly remember and a hangover that he couldn't ignore if he wanted to.

"If you want sympathy, let me remind you who came and picked you two fools up last night. And who fought with some guy for a solid five minutes because he was sure as sure that his keys were back at the bar when they were in fact in his *hand*."

Price squinted, like it would help him back into his memory.

After a moment, he remembered vaguely that the person she was referring to was in fact him.

He sighed, all dramatics.

"Fine, you got me there," he said. "Ask your favor."

Price had known Blake since the two were kids and, between them, they pretty much knew the whole of Seven Roads, Georgia. From Becker Farm to the old popular smoking spot for seniors behind the steel mill, they had both done time in the small town and knew it in and out. Even Blake leaving for a decade or so and then marrying a transplant hadn't thrown off her ability to adapt once again to the town's people and ways.

That went double for her managing the contract work she had been doing for several law enforcement agencies around the state while keeping an eye on the local sheriff's department. She had been a one-woman army before coming back. Now, she had her own troops and was unstoppable when she wanted to be.

However, unlike Blake's life trajectory taking her away from Seven Roads before ultimately coming back to town, Price hadn't left McCoy County for more than a week in total since he'd been born at its hospital.

Nineteen years after that, his daughter had been born in the same hospital. Since then, all thoughts of crossing the county line had come to a halt.

There was some rustling on the other end of the line. Blake must have been moving around. She didn't try to lower her words though.

"Can you go look in Josiah Teller's backyard?"

Price pulled the phone away from his ear and eyed it for a second. He put it back against his ear.

"Say again?"

Blake didn't undercut her request with any more sighs. Now she meant business. He straightened on reflex as her tone shifted completely away from friend to a former sheriff on a mission. Favor or not, the change was no joke.

"Josiah said something dug a hole in his backyard but he's sure it was a human who did it, not an animal," she said. "He called the nonemergency line at the department but, given the case I dealt with back in Alabama with burying things, I have all cases involving any kind of potential burial flagged for me and Liam. He has a press issue to deal with and I have the kids out with me now or else I'd go out there myself."

Blake had built one heck of a résumé before returning to Seven Roads, not to speak to what she'd done since she had been back. Price had followed her career like he had been reading a comic book. He knew about the case that had left an impression with her when it came to burials too.

So he didn't voice his concern that it was Josiah Teller who was the one who had called it in.

"You want me to go make sure it isn't anything fishy," he summarized instead.

"Yeah," Blake replied. "I'd send someone else out there who's on duty, but everyone is tied up. Plus, I trust your judgment."

Price knew he was a likable guy. He was confident enough in himself to claim a good personality. But to have Blake trust in him meant a lot more than simply being liked. His chest swelled with pride at it.

He nodded to the phone.

"I'll head that way in ten. I'll call if it's anything worth mentioning."

Blake said thank-you and didn't keep him on the line past that.

Price went straight to the shower, grabbed some pain meds for his headache when he got out and was at Josiah's front door ten minutes after that. There were pros to living in a town as small as Seven Roads. The commute time was almost always snapping-your-fingers quick.

Price knocked on the front door of the two-story, pulling on a professional smile despite nothing on him being professional at the moment. He was dressed in his jeans, tennis shoes and the worn baseball pin-striped button-up he'd had since he was twenty. He had a hat on to cover his still-wet hair but contemplated taking it off. Just because he was off duty didn't mean he should be too slouched since he was doing a favor for the sheriff.

When no one answered after a minute or so, Price's impatience won over his concern. Instead of leaving, he went around to the backyard. The privacy fence was high, but the side yard gate was open.

"Josiah?"

All the houses in the two-road neighborhood were situated on decent-sized lots. Josiah's was no exception. His yard stretched long and wide. There were no trees, but a hammock was set up between two in-ground posts near the patio.

There was no Josiah.

There was a hole.

Price walked over to the disturbed dirt and looked inside of it.

"That's a hole for sure," he commented aloud.

Price tilted his head to the side.

At first, he had pictured something large enough that a person could be put in, simply for the fact that he'd seen one too many horror movies. Then, he had pictured something half that size. Maybe a hole a dog would dig to hide a bone or a toy. He had only imagined one other potential size and it had been a misshapen thing made by a rooting armadillo or roaming raccoon. Maybe an overzealous squirrel.

But what he was looking at didn't match up with any option he had pictured.

Instead, it just looked like something a small child had done while playing. It was a small hole that a shoebox could fit into and that he guessed was made with a gardening tool instead of someone's bare hands.

Price looked around the yard again.

There were no other holes or disturbed spots around.

"Okay, I'm *slightly* intrigued," Price said aloud. He hooked one thumb through his belt loop to rest his hand and used the other to pull out his phone. He took a picture with it and was about to call the sheriff's department to look for Josiah's number when movement flicked out of the corner of his eye.

A few yards away was the back door with a bank of windows on either side. Those windows were covered by curtains and blinds from the inside. The back door, however, seemed to be open.

"Josiah?" Price called out, walking towards it.

He knew Josiah the same way he knew most of Seven Roads. Everyone in town had a story attached to them that the rest of the residents knew. Josiah was a young guy, smart too, but absolutely strange. He quieted when he should talk and when he should be quiet, he gave a sermon. That had become most apparent when he had gone on a tangent about the difference between air vents and air ducts during Mr. McCall Senior's memorial service. While everyone else was doing the small nods and smaller talk, Josiah had been talking commercial use versus residential grade air-conditioning terms. Not the worst thing a person could do, but it had definitely been a story that had stuck.

Maybe that was why Price didn't think too much about the back door being ajar. Or Josiah not answering his call right away. Price was thinking of the man who had taught him about ductwork and not someone who might have been trouble lurking in his house.

It was an oversight on his part.

One that Price realized quickly.

He pushed the door open. It led up through the middle of the house and alongside the stairs.

"Hey Josiah, it's Price Collins. I was told to come out and—"

The movement that had caught his eye flashed again. This time, it was in the form of someone stepping into the hallway, opposite him.

Price knew he was standing on someone else's property. He knew he hadn't been given permission to come inside, just as he was acutely aware that he had no uniform on, no badge to flash and no service weapons or equipment to defend himself.

What he didn't know was what a person dressed all in black, with a ski mask to boot, was doing in Josiah Teller's house.

But he did know he was about to found out.

THERE ARE A lot of situations where a woman might want to meet an attractive man. Out for a night on the town where you and your girls are feeling pretty and flirty? Yes. Walking through the grocery store on a perfect hair day? Absolutely. Just really wanting to get lost in a daydream while you're sitting at a coffee shop, staring idly through the plate-glass windows? Definitely a situation where running randomly into a good-looking man might be a nice occasion.

However, being caught breaking and entering into a house, dressed like a robber, isn't exactly ideal.

JJ mentally swept her own outfit as she looked the man opposite her up and down.

Her hair was braided tight and tucked tighter beneath her mask; the man's hair was curling out from under the edge of a baseball cap. Her black sweater and joggers were baggy enough to hide her curves; the black undershirt clung in an appealing way against an upper body that she assumed was as fit as his arms. Her stance was perfect for being lithe and fleeing the situation, body tilted slightly toward the living room she was closest to; his stance was like his body—he had walled off the exit behind him and seemed ready to close in on her. JJ knew he couldn't see her dark eyes, slightly panicked; she could see the way his bright gaze wasn't moving an inch from her.

The man was handsome. The man was trouble.

JJ moved fast. One second, she was in the hallway, the next she was in the living room and hightailing it to the front door. Adrenaline filled her veins. Panic filled her feet. Her mind went to opening the door; her feet went the other way.

Pain exploded against her hip as JJ hit the hardwood, mere steps away from the entryway. The man wasn't far behind.

No one has perfect balance. You hit the ground, you use the ground to hit whoever you're going up against.

JJ's godfather's words were old but the directive in them was urgent. Instead of scrambling to her feet and trying to recover, she paused. If her pursuer realized she had stalled, it didn't stop him. He was barking something out as he closed the space between them and reaching for her with clear intention of trapping her in that good-looking gaze.

Too bad JJ wasn't going to let that happen.

The second he was close enough she grabbed his wrist.

Then she pulled him.

The man made a startled noise. It was the only thing he could control. JJ escaped being pinned by his falling body by barely a breath of space. His side connected with the ground and JJ used a childhood filled with gymnastic training to spring to her feet.

It was a spot reversal that clearly gobsmacked the man.

JJ was able to double back and run until she was near the back door before he was on her again. This time, it wasn't her bad luck that allowed an opening. It was the man's apparent passion for baseball. He slid like he was going to home in front of a crowded stadium. And he wasn't concerned about taking the ump with him.

They both hit the ground again. This time, JJ went down without a hope of saving herself. Her adrenaline masked the initial pain, but she knew it hurt. The man's weight didn't help matters. She felt his elbow in her back, his knee against her ankle. The rest of him distributed between the two spots.

All of it was an issue.

One that JJ wasn't going to put up with.

She didn't hear her godfather's words of wisdom or any of her trainers barking instructions in her ear. She didn't think of any manual or video she had studied. She simply moved.

With everything JJ had, she became a whirlwind of movement. She threw her head back until it connected with him. Then the rest of her body followed. Her elbow became a hook; her foot became a pendulum. She wasn't sure what worked but knew she had done something when the weight against her disappeared.

When she heard the cussing, she knew it was now or never.

JJ used the narrow hallway to her advantage. The wall to her left became a springboard to help her pinball herself up and out of the house. Not even the wayward punch the man threw against her side slowed her down.

The second her feet touched the back porch, she was running with everything she had. The man, however, didn't know JJ. He didn't know that, while her fighting skills were good, her ability to escape was better. His yells filled the backyard as he followed her.

But as soon as she cleared the back fence, she knew he didn't stand a chance.

Poor man. It must have taken him a bit longer to realize that too.

JJ could still hear him yelling as she made her way into the woods.

Chapter Two

Josiah Teller's backyard became a lot more interesting as the morning turned into afternoon. He had told them until he was blue in the face that nothing in his house was missing or had been disturbed but that hole in the dirt and grass.

That was the thing that he swore had changed.

Price rubbed his jaw and stared down into the small, unassuming thing and felt more grumble in his chest than the storm in the distance could dare create.

Deputy Rose Little, who had only stopped giving him guff about being hit in said jaw before losing it completely half an hour before, stood at his side with such an uninterested expression it almost made Price laugh.

Almost.

His jaw wasn't the only thing sore about what had happened earlier.

"I'm saying it's unrelated," Rose finally decided. "It makes no sense for someone to get that done up and tussle with the law *and* dig a hole. Plus, Josiah said there should be nothing buried here. He bought the house from Ken and Clarice Weathers. You remember them?"

Price nodded. He did.

Rose went on.

"Ken hated dogs and Clarice hated being outside. Together

they wouldn't have had a dog, and a dog is about the only thing I can think would be the reason anything is buried out here." Rose toed at the raised dirt nearest her. "Josiah is always itching for some excitement. I think he made a mountain out of a molehill, and you just got unlucky enough to take the hits when something worth talking about happened."

She patted Price on the shoulder and turned toward the house.

"I'm going to focus on finding that unlucky thing first," she added. "Why don't you use the time to go get some coffee. Looks like you need it. I'll keep you in the loop."

Price hadn't said much since his initial call to the department, the sheriff and Josiah Teller, who had been called away by work and had hightailed it to the local electronics store while Price had been en route to the house Josiah had left behind.

Josiah had profusely apologized, thinking no one was coming anytime soon to discuss the hole.

That apologizing had only tripled when he realized Price had caught someone breaking and entering.

Now, Price felt all talked out.

Though, he guessed, that was mostly from the frustration.

Whoever had been in that house had outdone him.

He grumbled.

It wouldn't happen again.

"Just go," Rose said after that grumble cleared. She lowered her voice. "You best believe that news of your fight is already making the Seven Roads laps. I suggest you go take that cup of coffee sooner rather than later."

This time, Price let his frustration melt into defeat.

He knew what Rose was saying without her actually saying it.

He needed to go talk to Winnie before the talk got to her.

Sometimes dealing with a masked intruder was less daunting than dealing with a teenage girl.

Downtown Seven Roads was never a busy place. That stayed mostly true for the weekends. There were the regular walkers who made their way in a pattern across the sidewalks and stores, chatting as they went, and then there were the people who worked at the storefronts who walked between the shops. The Twenty-Two Coffee Shop, however, had become its own localized sensation over the last year or so. Mainly because it was the only coffee shop in town, but also for the popularity of the twins who ran it.

Corrie Daniels, the more popular of the two, was behind the counter and all eyes were on him the second he cleared the door. She was smirking before a word even came out of her mouth.

"I was wondering when you would roll in here." She placed the magazine she was reading down on the countertop and, with obvious attention, eyed his jaw. "I wasn't going to say anything if you looked too beat-up, but you seem good enough now to tease a little." She touched a spot on her jaw and then pointed to him. "Let me know if you need some of my makeup to cover that soon-to-be pretty bruise you've got there."

Price had been friends with Corrie since elementary school, though the title of *friends* was used loosely. The two of them had always just been there, around each other growing up in the same small town they had been born in. *Comrades in arms* is what he once described their relationship. Two people who had once dreamed of crossing the county line and never coming back.

Only to still be in town, annoying each other.

Price paused at the counter and didn't reply directly to the comment. Instead, he nodded to the hallway that led back to the main office and break room.

"Is she back there?"

Corrie nodded, her smirk turning back into a look of slight boredom.

"Her break just started, but her phone was blowing up before she even stepped foot away from here. Whoever was around you or Josiah's place sure was talking fast. She got the news before me."

Price sighed.

"And what news was that exactly?" He wanted to hear the gossip version so he could have a defense ready to go.

"Oh, you know how it is with Josiah Teller," she started. "He ticked someone off because he was crying wolf about something again and you wanted to save Little Rose the trouble of going out there. But you got cocky and went out without your badge or gun and got your tush handed to you. Then the mass of muscle ran off before you could even stand straight."

Price stared for a moment.

"That's not what happened," he deadpanned.

Corrie shrugged.

"That's the cinematic version going around," she said. "Which means that it was probably Josiah's neighbor—you know, Tacky Tara—who was the one who started it. Remember her retelling of The Great Divorce of the Youngs when we were in high school? She had the whole town thinking that Mr. Young was some kind of mob boss and Mrs. Young had gone through heaven and *h-e*-double-hockey-sticks to escape his grasp."

Corrie clutched at her chest, all dramatics. Then she rolled her eyes.

"When really Mrs. Young was caught with the literal mailman and all Mr. Young did was pop him once in the eye and then move."

Price remembered the incident, just as he remembered the then-teenage girl Tara who had told anyone who would listen her side of someone else's story.

"In this regard, and this regard only, do I appreciate your brand of nosy," Price had to tell Corrie now. "You at least get the facts straight before you open your mouth."

Corrie smiled sweetly.

"Thank you. I'm glad to be appreciated." She motioned to the hallway. "Now, go set her straight before Tacky Tara's story evolves enough to win an Emmy."

Price nodded.

"Roger that."

The break room was the smallest room in Twenty-Two Coffee Shop but, according to its youngest staff member, that's what made it the coziest. Easy to clean, easy to see and easy to relax in. No matter how stressful the customers became.

Though, *relaxed* isn't the word Price would use to describe what the teenager sitting on the edge of its sofa looked like when he knocked on its open door.

Winnie Collins looked every inch like her mama, but for every single one of those inches, she was Price in personality. Dark eyes narrowed in on him while her mouth thinned into an expression that wasn't a frown, but it wasn't a smile either. It was an in-between look of worry and annoyance.

She stood to her impressive height and closed the distance between them with her index finger outstretched. She didn't poke the skin, but he felt her fingertip hover near his growing bruise.

"Is this the worst of the hits or just the only thing I can see right now?" she asked, instead of giving a greeting.

Price waved her off.

"This was a lucky hit," he said. "I can't even feel it."

Winnie tipped her head to the side and narrowed those eyes again.

"I thought you weren't supposed to be working today. Why were you at Josiah's?"

Price had a rule. He had had it since he brought Winnie home from the hospital and he had kept it during the seventeen years since.

We don't lie to Winnie.

"Your favorite Sheriff Trouble asked me to check out some weird hole dug in Josiah's backyard. I ran into someone who had broken into his house instead. We fought a little, they ran a lot. Lost them out in the woods before Rose showed up." Price smiled. "See? Not as bad as the rumor mill, huh?"

Winnie's eyebrows knitted together. She wasn't upset anymore, but she was confused.

"A hole?"

"That's what I was focusing on too," Price said. "Either way, it's on Little Rose now. I'm only here for some kid, coffee and contemplation."

Winnie didn't look like she wanted to drop the current topic. She opened her mouth to say something, but footsteps made her pause. Price turned to an already-smiling Corrie. He knew what she was going to say before she could even say a word.

She wanted a favor from him.

A gut feeling that proved true with impressive speed.

"Hey, Price, you drove here in your truck, right? Do me a favor and help JJ out?"

Price raised an eyebrow at that.

"JJ?"

"The newest hire," Winnie added from behind him. "Though she isn't new anymore."

Price knew there was a new woman who had been hired part-time, but he only came into the café when Winnie was working. That apparently hadn't synced up with this JJ's schedule yet.

"She's supposed to come in to help me with something in the back, but just called and said she's having car trouble," Corrie said. "She said she could figure something out, but she sounded stressed. Do you think you could swing by and see if you can help her out? Bless her heart, she's a hard worker but I think sometimes she's a little oblivious to things."

Price wanted to point out that the last favor he'd done that day hadn't exactly gone his way, but Winnie thumped his elbow before he could say it.

"Since he's in such a giving mood today, he'll definitely go by and help," she answered for him. "Won't you, Dad?"

Price was still nursing a slight hangover and, despite what he said, his jaw was hurting a little. He also needed to mow the lawn, fix the slow drip in the upstairs bathroom and take a look at the rental property he'd begrudgingly inherited before any more rain came in.

But one thing he had been struggling with since he'd held that little baby in his arms for the first time was another unwritten rule he had become trapped by.

We don't say no to Winnie.

He let out a breath that was mild annoyance and fixed Corrie with an even stare.

"Fine," he said. "But make sure she knows I'm coming. I don't want a Josiah Teller round two surprise today."

Corrie was already pulling out her phone.

"I don't think you have to worry about JJ," she said. "I'm pretty sure that girl is as innocent as they come."

JJ SHOT OUT of the house like the devil was nipping at her heels. She popped the hood of her little Honda and paused as she looked down into the engine bay.

"What can I mess with that will make you not work but not be suspicious?" she asked it out loud. "But also not cost me an arm and a leg to fix?"

She had never been that great at cars. In fact, as far as vehicles went, she only really had a passion for the old motorbike currently hidden in her garage beneath an old sheet and a layer of dust. But there were a few lessons that her godfather had forced her to learn.

JJ mentally scrolled through the reasons she could remember of why a car normally wouldn't start.

"It can't be the battery," she said to herself. "I can't make the alternator or the ignition switch go bad so quickly. I don't know enough about spark plugs to do anything." Her eyes came to a spark plug wire. "Wouldn't that seem suspicious if I unplugged that? I could break a fuse..."

JJ wanted to yell in frustration. She shouldn't have used car trouble as an excuse to not go into the café today. Who would have guessed Corrie would arrange for Winnie's dad to come to the rescue.

"This is ridiculous," she said, exasperated. "No one is as worried about the world as I am. Let's just play it simple."

JJ made the quickest work she could of disconnecting a spark plug wire. Winnie had bragged a few times about her father being capable. He would probably see the problem sooner rather than later then fix it and be on his way. Who was he to be suspicious at all? It wasn't like most people would see JJ and assume she had sabotaged her own car to cover up a lie.

She nodded at her work, shut the hood and hurried back inside.

The pace wasn't a fun one.

She only slowed when she was standing in front of the full-length mirror in her bedroom. Her hair was nice and loose, no longer tight against her head in a braid. Her makeup had been reapplied and she had changed her baggy clothes for a nice, flowy sundress. Her feet were still bare but there was a pair of sandals by the front door that was a far cry from the boots she had been sneaking around in hours beforehand.

As for the bruising, she had gotten lucky.

The man who had fought her had only gotten one good hit in.

One had been enough though.

JJ tenderly touched the spot on her side that she knew for a fact was already bruised.

The light contact made her wince.

That was why she had opted for an excuse to not go into work. It wasn't a normal shift after all. She didn't think she needed much more than a vague car-related issue.

That had been her mistake. JJ had forgotten that she was back in a small town. For better or worse, residents tended to get into everyone's business.

JJ heard a car door shut outside. She gave herself another once-over in the mirror and pulled on a bright, cheery smile.

She would accept Winnie's dad's help, make small talk about the teen and then send him on his way. No muss, no fuss.

Perfect plan.

A knock sounded on the front door.

JJ hid her pain once again and hurried to answer it.

She must have been faster than the man thought she would be. When she opened the door, his head was still turned toward the car in the driveway.

It was the only reason JJ was able to hide the absolute shock that must have gone across her face.

It was clearly the man from Josiah's, even still wearing his baseball shirt.

Had her identity been discovered? Was he there to finish their fight?

But no. His body language was lax, and his attention was clearly on her car.

So, he was Winnie's dad?

But wasn't Winnie's dad a sheriff's deputy?

A cold feeling of unease settled in JJ's gut.

Since coming to Seven Roads, she had been careful not to make any mistakes.

Today, she had not only been caught, she'd been caught by the law.

And now that law was standing in front of her, looking just as good as he had before their fight.

Today really wasn't JJ's day after all.

Chapter Three

Price couldn't say with confidence that he was all that great at understanding the subtleties of women. He didn't have much experience in that department, if he was being honest. Sure, he'd gone on a few dates in the last several years but none of them had exactly panned out.

For one, he wasn't good at being quiet. He was a talker. Had been since he was a kid, would be until he was old and gray. He could probably trace the reason why he loved to chat back to his mother, queen of the talkers. Rest her soul—she wasn't gone but she was constantly driving her second husband up the wall in their home in Las Vegas—she filled every space in a conversation to the brim.

"It's amazing what you end up hearing when you talk too much," she'd always say. "Shows you who people really are when they realize they can't keep you quiet too."

Price had thought the sentiment was ridiculous. Still, he'd managed to pick up the trait.

He listened, sure, but talking was his bread and butter.

That hadn't always been appreciated. Especially on his dates. Though, that also could have had less to do with him dominating the conversation and more that he was dating in Seven Roads. The same place he'd been born. The same place his dates had also been born.

It was hard to connect with someone who knew every little thing about you. From knowing about the unfortunate peeing incident in kindergarten to Jimmy Johnson pantsing you in eighth grade to your grades, fashion choices and tripping during high school graduation. Then there was the fact of holding the single father title at the age of nineteen.

Price was never, not even for one second, ashamed of being a dad. He had never said one bad word about Winnie's mother, and he had never regretted his choices about either one. But he had another rule: if someone spoke about either with any negativity, they were out.

That was why, now in his thirties, he was still single.

It was also why he wasn't as confident as he normally would have been, standing across from JJ Shaw.

First, he didn't know her. A rare occurrence in town.

Second, she did that thing that he believed women had a special power over.

She smiled.

A smile that slowed his mental gears for a moment.

It looked nice but…there was something else there.

Though, maybe that was just Price still off his game from his earlier fight. Or the fact that some strange man was standing at her door.

Price hoped the smile he tugged on was a reassuring one. He took a small step back and jerked his thumb over his shoulder to the car.

"Hey, I'm Winnie's dad," he said in greeting. "I've been sent to help with some car trouble?"

JJ surprised him with a little laugh.

"I was actually about to start googling things. So I'd be lying if I said I wasn't excited at the help." She held out her hand. "I'm JJ. Sorry for the trouble."

Price accepted her hand and shook. There were a few

callouses on her palm. It was an odd contrast to the cheery dress that made his own outfit look dark.

"I'm Price, and it's no trouble," he responded. "There'd really be trouble if I didn't come. Winnie talks highly about you."

JJ stepped back into the house a little to slip on some sandals. They were strappy and made her taller. He had to adjust his gaze a little to meet her eyes again. She averted that gaze quickly as she spoke.

"Oh, that's sweet of her. We haven't had many shifts together yet, but I have to say she's a fun one when we do sync up. And I've definitely heard good things about you. From Corrie too."

She pulled her keys off a hook on the wall and stepped outside. Price made room for her and then some as she walked over to the car in the drive.

"I'm afraid to know what Corrie has to say about me," he admitted. "One time, I accidentally stepped on the back of her shoe and the next day she had the whole school calling me Big Foot. That name stuck for years."

She laughed again but kept her gaze ahead.

"Well, she hasn't been calling you any names around me," she said. "All I hear are stories about your work. You're a sheriff's deputy, right? That must be exciting work."

It hadn't been for years, not until the current sheriff had stumbled upon a homicide after Blake had returned to town. Since then, there had been a shift in the workforce, as with the residents of Seven Roads. It was like they had all been given a wake-up call that said while their town was sleepy, that didn't mean it couldn't also be dangerous.

Price had gotten involved in the last bit of danger, and so had Winnie. It was another reason his earlier scare upset him so much—it worried Winnie. Most likely more than she had admitted.

"It has its moments," he replied.

Where others might have asked more, JJ changed topics to the mission at hand. She gave Price the keys and let him roam around to try and figure out why it wouldn't start.

A few minutes later, he was thankful that he knew enough about cars to notice a spark plug cable had come loose. He put it back, happy with himself, and asked her to try and start the engine.

She obliged but was slow getting into the driver's seat.

When she noticed his attention, she looked a little embarrassed.

"I'm in the middle of renovating a house and it weirdly always makes me sore," she explained.

"You're renovating a house?" He hadn't heard that news.

She paused, a slight wince crossing her face, and nodded. "It's why I came to town."

Where he expected some more, JJ gave him less.

She settled into the driver's seat and started the car. Which succeeded.

Price gave a thumbs-up.

"Looks like that was our issue," he said when she was back out of the car.

JJ was back to the original smile she'd worn when answering the door.

It was polite.

But it felt off, still.

"Thank you so much for helping," she said. "You saved me a lot of trouble and I'm sure Corrie will appreciate it. I'm actually already late helping her."

Her gaze, once again, cut away from him.

Was she shy?

Did he make her nervous?

No matter the answer, Price realized it wasn't his business. Whether he was making her uncomfortable or not, he needed to leave. Instead of forcing them both to make small talk, he decided to give them an out.

"I'm just glad it was something I could help with." He clapped his hands together and took a step back. "If that's all, I'll leave you to it. I have some work to wrap up at the department."

This time, dark eyes swung to his with a quickness that nearly froze him to the spot.

"I didn't realize you were still working right now."

He laughed and pointed to his jaw. JJ might not have been keen to look him in the eye, but he had already seen her sneak a peek at the bruise.

"I have a bone to pick with someone and the sooner I pick it, the better this town will sleep."

JJ's eyes widened. He waved off what must have been concern.

"Don't worry. I know I don't look the most professional but believe you me, I don't suffer an offense long."

He nodded to her, said he hoped she had a good rest of the day and did another little nod when she thanked him again. It was true he was going to look for the meaning behind Josiah's break-in, just as he was going to find the intruder, but for now he was going to go home.

Seven Roads might have been more interesting in the last year or so but that didn't mean it was a hustling, bustling place. He could take his time with this one. Or, at least, take a few hours.

So he fixed JJ Shaw in his rearview mirror and pointed his truck in the direction of Crawley Court, ready to make the five-minute drive home full of music and a few low cusses as he remembered someone had landed a good hit on him.

But no sooner was he out of the neighborhood that he got a call.

It was Rose's number.

Price answered with an annoyed threat.

"If you're calling to rub it in again or make some joke about me being a punching bag, I'm going to hang up."

Rose wasn't.

Her voice was hard. Her words were fast.

"Something happened to Josiah Teller. There's a ton of blood in his house and he's nowhere around."

"What? What do you mean there's blood?"

Price was already mentally switching routes.

There was movement on Rose's side of the call. Someone was talking in the background, but she answered him first.

"I came back to take better pictures of that damn hole of yours and instead found the front door smashed open and enough blood through the bottom floor to tell me someone was fighting for their life." She must have moved the phone. Static pulsed between them for a moment. Then her voice was nothing but cold. "Darius is already out looking for him, but I can't believe, if this was Josiah, that he'll last long wherever he is."

Price gripped the steering wheel. His knuckles went white.

"I'm on my way."

JJ SWITCHED HER high-heeled sandals for flats the second Price Collins was gone.

Deputy Collins.

"How bad is my luck?" she asked the house, grabbing her purse and then locking up behind her.

As far as she could tell, Price, at the very least, hadn't

seemed too suspicious of her. Not of her car troubles, the pain she had been unable to hide or her appearance. She wasn't sure how aware of her height, or eyes for that matter, he had been during their run-in earlier that day, but was glad he had gone when he did.

She didn't like being caught off guard, and she had been twice that day.

And by the same man too.

It was unsettling.

JJ tried to push the feeling off as she started her drive to the café. Like she often did on her way into and out of work, she let her mind wander down a familiar path. The list of five addresses she had memorized before coming back to Seven Roads.

Josiah's house had been low on the list. JJ had only moved it up when she heard about someone digging in his backyard by chance that morning while picking up some milk from the grocery store. Josiah had been wondering to the cashier if he should call the sheriff's department. Apparently, he had.

Their speed and attention had definitely surprised JJ. She should have waited to do her own search until they had come and gone.

But…if anyone *had* been snooping around Josiah's home… Did that mean that it really could be him?

That possibility had lit a fire under her backside. So much so that she had been careless. Price sneaking up on her had been the first and—she vowed—last time she let her guard down.

JJ rolled her window down, put her hand out the window a little and sighed into the humidity that came in. Despite her clumsiness, she believed she'd executed a thorough search. Josiah didn't have a safe, so his official documents had been easy enough to find. Nothing was out of the ordinary or suspicious. Even his personal laptop had been boring, aside from a heavy indication that he was a more than avid gamer. He had a family photo album next to his coffee table and those pictures were of people that JJ didn't recognize at all. Though, she had taken her own picture of some of the faces, just in case.

The only thing she hadn't had a chance to check had been the backyard.

If Josiah had been hiding something, would he have buried it?

And, if he had, then who had dug it up?

Why had Josiah reported it if so?

JJ didn't often drink, but she sure felt the urge as her frustration rose. At the same time, however, she was thankful for it. If she was having this much trouble finding her brother, then hopefully that meant they were too.

She took that thought to heart again and focused on her drive. It wasn't until she was passing the Lawrence Neighborhood entrance sign that she realized she had taken the long way to the café. It was the road that led between Lawrence and Becker Farm. A nice little drive with scenery that opened up to fields and trees on either side. Good for a cluttered mind.

JJ decided that today must have been a coincidence. That Josiah Teller wasn't special, just someone who had made a big deal out of nothing. She would go to the next person on the list in a few days, after her run-in with Price settled down.

Her gaze wandered from the trees at her right to the field on her left. There were no other cars on the road ahead or behind her, so it was a leisurely thing to do.

It was a miracle she saw him at all.

Movement in the field pulled her attention. At first, JJ

wasn't sure what she was seeing. She lifted her foot off the gas pedal and squinted at the thing stumbling toward the road.

When she realized it was a person, stumbling through the tall grass, she put on her hazards and pulled off onto the shoulder.

It wasn't just a person. It was someone who was obviously struggling.

They moved a few steps, fell a little, caught themselves and then kept coming.

It wasn't until she was out of the car, cell phone in hand, that they saw her too.

The man stopped.

He said something but she couldn't hear him.

Then he dropped.

JJ's reflexes had her across the road, over the wire fence and streaking across the distance between them with efficient speed. She was barely out of breath when she made it to the man's side.

She had 9-1-1 up and ringing the moment she saw he was struggling.

He was covered in blood. From head to toe.

His eyes were closed. He didn't move as JJ asked after him.

It was only after the dispatcher answered that JJ made another startling discovery.

It wasn't just a man.

It was Josiah Teller.

Chapter Four

Lane Medical wasn't that bad for a county place. It had serviced locals from Seven Roads nicely through the years and, since it was located closer to the town than the neighboring city, at any one time it housed people who Price knew. Staff, patients, visitors. He hadn't ever visited the hospital without running into someone.

After coming in hot with Rose, he tried to avoid all of the above as he made his way up to the second floor while the deputy was snarled in the emergency room, waiting to talk to the attending doctor.

The surgery ward was an entirely different beast than the general population rooms downstairs. Everything was shining, bright and smelled like disinfectant. Even the resident behind the front desk at the mouth of the main hallway had a neater look to her that those battling in the ER below didn't have the luxury to maintain.

This face was familiar and unavoidable.

Thankfully, that wasn't exactly a bad thing.

"Deputy Price!"

Lily Ernest was one of those people that slightly skewed Price's perception of time. She was the legendary medical examiner Doc Ernest's eldest daughter, but Price still remembered her as a baby, as a kid and then as a teenager who was only a few years older than Winnie. Now? It bowled him over how adult she looked in scrubs. The image clashed with the memories of her toddling around her mother.

It made Price think of Winnie. He still paused on occasion by the growth chart he'd notched into the doorframe of her bedroom at home.

But, just as quickly as he thought of his daughter and how kids never kept, Price reminded himself that he wasn't there for a social visit. He buttoned up his parental awe and gave Lily a polite but curt nod.

"Hey there, Lily. You doing okay?"

Lily tapped her name tag.

"It's nice to be on rotation here, I won't lie. Mom's a bit disappointed I'm not in with her though." She pointed down, meaning the morgue in the hospital's basement. "One day she'll realize I really have no plan to work below sea level."

Her little laugh was kind.

It was also gone quickly. Her gaze dropped to where his badge would usually be, and she added a thought in a much lower voice.

"If you're here to talk to a surgeon, our very best is currently in an emergency surgery. I'm not sure I can help with anything else."

Lily knew she couldn't openly talk about a patient, especially to the law without consent. That probably went double for someone not even in uniform. So, she'd given him what he wanted to know without saying it directly.

She was definitely her mother's daughter.

"If I wanted to wait for the surgery to end, could I do that in the lobby?" Price jerked his thumb over his shoulder and down the hall to the surgery suite's lobby. He'd only had to wait there twice in his Seven Roads life. If the Good Samaritan was still around, they would be there.

Lily nodded and confirmed his hope.

"Yes. There's only one other person in there at the moment so it won't be crowded."

Price gave the girl a genuine smile.

"I'll go do that then. Thanks."

Price followed the hallway through two turns and stepped into the surgery suit's lobby with a growing fire in him. He was angry that Josiah had gone from being fine that morning to needing emergency surgery that afternoon. It also pricked at Price's guilt. Had he caught the masked man earlier, would this have happened?

It was a what if that he was trying to push aside to focus on getting as much information from the Good Samaritan as possible. They needed to catch who did this to Josiah now.

Not later.

Unlike the emergency room lobby, this one was small and closed in with only one door for guests, one door for staff that led in the opposite direction and one door to the bathroom. The two rows of uncomfortable-looking chairs were empty but that last door opened right as Price stepped inside.

He had already teed up several questions for the Good Samaritan, ready to be fast and to the point. However, he stopped short when the person in question caught his eye.

"JJ?"

JJ Shaw was still wearing her summer dress but, this time, it was stained crimson. Still, she managed another smile that took in Price's attention and whirled it around all at once.

FLY UNDER THE RADAR, my butt.

"Deputy Collins," JJ said in greeting.

She didn't know what else to say past that. The moment she found Josiah she had known she would be talking to

McCoy County law enforcement and, yet, she hadn't thought it would be him.

Wasn't he off duty?

"Twice in one day," he said. "We should get a bingo card going."

Three times, she thought, but who was counting?

Price's gaze dropped to her body. JJ resisted the urge to cover up. He hadn't been the only person to stare at the blood on her dress since she'd arrived. If the cotton was on the other foot, she would have done the same.

"It's not mine," she assured him. JJ waved her hand over the parts of her dress most stained. "A few of the emergency staff tried to wrangle me into a room but, like I told them, this belongs to that poor man." She paused. "I'm assuming that's why you're here? I'm the one who found the man in the field."

Price's gaze was still on her dress. He nodded absently then held up a finger.

"Hey, I need to ask you some questions, but could you give me one second?"

JJ blinked.

"Um, of course. Yeah."

He spun on his heel and was out of the room in a flash. If he wasn't such an easy man to read, she would have been worried that he'd put two and two together. That standing there in her flats, she was the same height and relative size as the person he had fought with that morning. That common sense would make her the top suspect in what had happened to Josiah.

But JJ wasn't getting the impression that Deputy Collins was ready to bust her.

Still, she decided to keep standing just in case. If he did

come back in, cuffs out and accusations flying, she wasn't just going to stay put.

The houses left on her list could be searched without a backstory or a pleasant smile and a part-time job at a café. Sure, if her cover was blown then it would make things harder. Not impossible, just more complicated.

JJ didn't need to be JJ Shaw to find her brother.

She was plenty enough, name or no name.

The thought stayed her nerves. She loosened the new tension in her shoulders but made sure not to seem too relaxed. She marveled at the fact that, once again, she had gone from a plan of staying under the radar in Seven Roads to meeting the law three times in one day.

The *same* man too.

Deputy Collins was back in the lobby in less than five minutes. He came in apologizing for the delay and holding a plastic bag, not cuffs, in his hand.

"Don't let this make you think you're going to be here all day or anything, but I thought, no matter how long, you probably don't want to just be sitting in that."

It took JJ a second to realize what he meant.

He passed the bag over. She peeked inside.

It was a set of scrubs.

His gaze went to her dress again. He pointed to the bag.

"A friend of mine works here and she seems about your size," he added. "I figured wearing this would be more comfortable."

JJ hadn't expected that.

"Oh, I couldn't accept this," she tried. "I'm okay, really."

Price waved his hand, and the thought, off.

"Think of it this way. This is just as much for the rest of us as it is for you," he said. "I'm not sure I can hold a conversation without staring. I'm thinking that the rest of the hospital probably isn't going to let you leave without doing the same."

He was right, of course.

Her walking around covered in blood wasn't helping the whole beneath-the-radar thing either.

JJ smiled.

"I guess you're right. I'll—I'll change then. Thank you."

There he went, waving her off again.

"Here in Seven Roads, we watch out for each other. It's no big deal." He dropped into a seat near the door. "Take your time. I'll be here."

She bowed a little, went to the bathroom and found herself slowing as she did just that. There really was a lot of blood, the more she looked at her reflection. There had been no way to get Josiah to her car and avoid it. It was a fact she had come to terms with quickly once Josiah had stopped moving. When he went limp, that had been when she had decided to completely commit to not caring about avoiding the mess. JJ had pulled him through the field, put him in her car and driven with speed to the hospital.

The attending doctor had told her the time she had saved instead of waiting for an ambulance had probably saved his life.

He hadn't known that her reasoning behind the move had nothing to do with the man and everything to do with the simple reason that she hadn't wanted her call to be registered at the sheriff's department.

That was a trail she couldn't easily cover up.

JJ looked at her hands. They were stained but clean.

It should have thrown her. It should have made her feel something like sadness or panic or worry.

Instead, she was trying to calculate the possibilities that had led Josiah from his house to that field.

There hadn't been a lot of blood on the ground where she had first found him. Not enough to show that he'd been attacked in the immediate area but then again, she hadn't had time to search either. His house had been a few miles away but surely he couldn't have walked like that in the same condition. Did that mean he'd been attacked in the distance between?

And by who?

Josiah wasn't her brother. He had an adoption record, sure, but he'd been adopted as a toddler, not a baby. That struck him from her list.

So had what happened to him been just bad timing on her part?

Her search put Josiah in the spotlight but someone else had already planned on fighting with him?

There was no way to know until she got more information. JJ removed her dress and started to put on the green scrubs. She made sure not to look in the mirror as her bare back came into view. The scar was small, but the memory tied to it was better left out of sight.

Maybe that's why Josiah hadn't affected her so much.

It wasn't the first time she had seen something like that.

JJ folded her dress, placed it in the bag and straightened her new clothes. The scrubs fit her nicely.

Price had a good eye.

Well, at least for clothes.

He still had no idea she was the masked person from that morning.

She was going to have to work hard to keep that from happening.

She went back into the lobby to tell him thank you but hesitated before she could say a word. Like in Josiah's house that morning, JJ could with absolute sincerity say that Price was a good catch. Attractive, attentive and as far as she knew from talk around town and knowing Winnie, a good dad too. There was also a calm about him. He seemed more collected than she would have thought was normal.

He was a good man, most likely.

Probably a good deputy also.

Too bad for him his luck ran out when he met her.

Chapter Five

The field had been for sale since the late nineties. No one had bought it in the years between then and now. What was more, no one would buy it in the future. It wasn't Old Man Becker's land, but it might as well have been.

"No one wants to be next to Old Man Becker's land, so it's been sitting empty for years," Price told JJ. He pointed toward the trees that lined the field in the distance. "There's an access road there that technically cuts the Becker land off from this but, well, it's usually only used by the workers and teens off doing something their parents don't want them knowing about. You said Josiah was coming from that way, toward the county road?"

JJ had put her hair up in a ponytail. It swished from side to side as she turned to the direction Josiah had come.

"I can't for sure say where he started but he definitely was coming from that direction."

They had already run down everything that JJ had seen and done since Price had left her house. Then she had said it all again to Rose when she had come upstairs to the surgery suite's lobby. JJ had been the one nice enough to offer to take them out to the exact place she had found Josiah before Rose had brought it up herself.

Then Price had been the one to offer her the ride.

"Winnie'll have my head if she knows I'm not being as courteous as ever," he had defended himself to Rose's eyebrow raise. "Plus, it's not like we have a lot of manpower to push off everything on you and Darius. I'll get the story from her, take some pics, mark with a flag and wait for y'all to come out."

Rose must have been more stressed than usual. She dropped the subject with a quick thanks. Then she'd gone to talk to Lily, who had gone wide-eyed at the actual appearance of a uniform and badge.

Now, the field in front of Price and JJ was hot, bare and sporting a trail of blood that led him right to the tree line and back to the access road. There the trail stopped altogether. JJ followed but kept her eyes to the ground. She didn't speak until she was at his side.

"There's not enough blood here," she said after a moment. She ran her finger, pointing down at the ground and back toward where she had originally found Josiah. "There's more back there because he stopped but there's only some spots leading back to here." She nodded to the road. "And since it ends at the road, I'm guessing that means he definitely didn't get his injuries out here. He was either dumped here by car or escaped from one."

Price felt his eyes widen. A half smile tugged up the corner of his lips. JJ saw the change and immediately shook her hands in defense.

"I watch a lot of crime series," she said hurriedly. "There was an episode like this on an old show I watched. The woman escaped her kidnappers, and we spent half of the episode trying to figure out where the original attack took place."

Price nodded.

"Well, however you got there, you're not wrong." He put

his hands on his hips and looked down at the last drop of blood in the area. "It definitely seems like Josiah exited a vehicle here."

But had anyone followed him?

"Why didn't anyone stop him from going through the field?"

Price turned back to JJ again.

Her brow was drawn in.

"I mean, I guess if someone was after him, they could have been hidden in the tree line while I saw to Josiah," she said. "That could have been his good luck out of all of this. I showed up when I did and spooked whoever did that to him."

Price nodded. He hadn't told JJ about how they had found Josiah's house. It was part of an ongoing investigation and, even though he had no quarrels with JJ, he didn't see the need to inform her of it. She had already done more than enough.

"Seven Roads might be small, but our Detective Williams is mighty," he said. "We'll get this figured out in no time."

JJ straightened her back. She nodded but didn't respond past that. Instead, she pulled her cell phone from her pocket and read a text in silence. Price used that time to mark the area. When he was done, JJ looked apologetic.

"If there's nothing else you need me for, could I go home?" She motioned to her clothes. "The scrubs are nice, but I wouldn't mind a quick shower."

Price felt bad he hadn't suggested it first. He walked her back through the field, both minding to step on the path they had carefully made before, and stopped by the hood of her car.

"Just so you know, this isn't exactly the natural speed of Seven Roads," he said. "It's usually a quiet place. Well, minus the gossip."

He grinned.

JJ opened her car door and let her hand rest on the top of the door.

There was some dried blood near her wrist.

"Don't worry, I've seen worse." Her frown went deep. Then it swirled into a small smile of explanation. "I've lived in a few big cities before coming here. This place is silent compared to those." She patted the top of the door. "Let me know if you need anything else from me. You have my number and know where I live. And, I guess, where I work too."

Price confirmed he did.

Before she could slide into her seat though, he reached out to stop her. Their hands didn't touch but it was enough to make JJ pause. She gave him a questioning look.

"Sorry," he said, pulling back. "But do you think you could do me a favor? Could you not tell Winnie about any of this until I talk to her first? The news will probably still get to her before I can but just in case it's slow today, I'd like to try."

JJ smiled.

"Don't worry. The most I'll do today is text Corrie to reschedule. If she needs more, I'll cite car trouble again. After that, I'm staying myself right on my couch."

JJ BROKE INTO the house in complete silence. No alarm beeps, no indoor chatter, no breaking glass or scraping metal. Nothing came before she slipped into the back door and nothing came after she closed it back up tight behind her.

The Alberts were on vacation and had never been a fan of digital security systems. They were from an older generation and had lived in Seven Roads since the seventies. If it wasn't for their kids probably insisting they lock their doors, they seemed to believe that their neighbors should be trusted no matter what.

That was probably why they barely made an effort to hide their spare key beneath the mat on the back porch.

Good for them, better for JJ.

She made her way across the hardwood until she turned into what looked like a guest bedroom. It was easy to navigate with the light from outside peeking through the small gaps between the curtains.

It was even easier when JJ used a gloved hand to make a bigger gap in the opening.

There were two people still milling around Josiah's house. Crime scene tape was on the front door and from her vantage point, she could see one of the uniformed men was making use of the back door. He wore gloves and, she bet, booties. One of the two also had a camera bag slung across his shoulder as he stood there.

So Josiah's attack had most likely occurred in his house.

The same house she had been searching hours before.

Which was bad for two different reasons.

One, it meant that whoever had done the deed had missed her and Price. Which would explain why Price was so obviously invested in the case, despite being off duty.

He probably felt some kind of misplaced guilt for not being able to protect Josiah.

Because he most likely thought that the masked person he had tussled with that morning was the very same person who had landed Josiah in such a state.

Which brought on the second, not-so-great problem.

The search for the masked person was now the top priority of the department.

JJ rubbed the side of her index finger with her thumb. The glove was smooth at both spots. She knew she didn't leave any evidence behind during her search of Josiah's home…

but that sureness had rested on the fact that no one would be doing an in-depth search of the place behind her.

Had she made any mistakes in covering her tracks?

Was there anything in there that could tie her to the crime scene?

"No," she whispered to herself.

Still, she couldn't feel completely at ease about it.

This was the second person on her list who she had crossed off and she'd managed to get into not one but two things of hot water alongside of her goal.

JJ decided then and there she would cool off her search for a bit.

She wanted to find her brother but, more than anything, she *needed* to find him.

And she needed to find him before *they* did.

JJ stayed in the Alberts' home until eventually all law enforcement left. If they found anything tying her to the scene, she never got a call or visit once she returned home. It should have made her rest easier but falling asleep that night was more difficult than she thought it would be.

She thought about Josiah falling in the field.

She thought about the blood on their clothes.

She thought about waiting alone in the lobby as he was rushed past to surgery.

JJ wondered if he was doing better. She wondered if he was alone.

Then, because her life had had moments of intense cruelty woven into its fabric, her thoughts slid even further back in time.

She saw her dark hair hanging down, reaching toward the roof of the car. There was glass everywhere. There was blood too.

There was no use in JJ squeezing her eyes shut. Then,

or now. The image was there, and it would stay there for a while. So she embraced the pain and let her eyes lose focus on the ceiling above her now.

Like she'd told Price earlier, she had seen much, much worse than Josiah Teller in that field.

Chapter Six

Josiah Teller survived his surgery. A week later, he was recovering well in a suite in Lane Medical.

"He remembers someone knocking on his front door, but after that he said he can't recall a thing." Detective Williams had his arms crossed over his chest. Outsiders might think he was being nonchalant, but Price knew him well enough to understand he was brimming with anger.

An entire week had gone by and not one stitch of evidence or a lead had been found about Josiah's attacker.

And now he was having to admit that to their newly returned Sheriff Weaver.

Liam sat at the head of the meeting table, fiddling absently with his wedding band. He tilted his chin to the side a little in thought.

"The doc says it could be a trauma response given how violent the attack seemed to be," he said. "That or the very real possibility that the physical injury was too much. Either way, I don't think we can bank on Josiah remembering anytime soon."

Price's coffee mug between his hands was empty. He'd finished part of a patrol before joining the recap and was starting to feel the lack of caffeine now. He had already been feeling frustration way before Sheriff Weaver had entered the building.

"I've been visiting Josiah and each time we talk, we always find our way back to the fact that Josiah really can't figure out why anyone would attack him or go through his house," Price added.

"It could have been random," Rose offered. She was standing in the doorway of the meeting room, paperwork in her hand. She was on the other side dealing with a public intoxication arrest near the county line. She pointed in the direction of the area of the sheriff's department that housed the two holding cells. "My drunk friend earlier was willing to fight anyone and everyone just because they were there. It could have been kind of the same thing. Our attacker did what they did simply because Josiah opened the door."

"But then what about their stint in the house that morning?" Darius asked. He turned his attention to Price. "The guy you fought came back. Whether that was for an object in Josiah's house or Josiah himself, it doesn't read as random. They came to Josiah for a reason."

That was the sticky part. If one of the two events hadn't happened it would have made more sense, but with the two it was tripping them all up. And it wasn't like they could simply make it all clear. That didn't mean they would stop trying to though. Darius was still the detective of the department, and he was still putting in his best. Price, guilt aside, had returned to his normal daily routines.

At least in body.

In mind, he was still in his fight against the masked man in Josiah's house.

If he had subdued him, then would Josiah have almost died?

Price let go of the *what-ifs* as the meeting concluded. He

finished out his shift and found himself driving in the direction of the only coffee shop in town. It was just after four and Winnie had arrived right before him from school.

"Don't tell me you're going for another coffee," Winnie said in greeting from behind the counter. "You're too old to have one this late." She had a textbook open, a highlighter in one hand.

The sight warmed him.

Price had never been the greatest at school. There was something about putting pencil to paper that had never worked well for him. That and he'd spent most of his academic career talking and playing around instead of focusing on the task at hand. Winnie's mother had been different. Her attention had always been on studying. It had been the people part of school she hadn't been a fan of at all.

Winnie?

She was split between the two.

She brought home *A*s, studied religiously and had won two spelling bees in her time. She also was good at the talking bits. People liked being around her. Price had often gotten compliments about how polite she was too. He had been rabble-rousing then, and now his kid was soothing the old annoyances he'd left behind.

It made him proud.

It also made him sure of one thing: Winnie Collins was going places.

And, when she finally went to those places?

He was gone too.

Price reached across the space between them and gave her a light thump on the forehead.

"I'll remind you that you called me old when you're my age," he said. "I bet you won't joke about it then."

Winnie didn't dodge the little hit but brushed it off. She

didn't give up her highlighter though. Instead, she used it to point toward the back.

"I can make you the normal but fair warning, Corrie just got a call and she got that face she normally does when something exciting just happened."

Price glanced in that direction.

"Something exciting?"

Winnie sighed.

"I suspect she'll tell you all about it once she sees you."

Price was already angling his body toward the door.

"You know, you might be right," he said. "I think I should cut down on the caffcinc. I'll just come back to grab you after shift. I'll stay in the car though."

Winnie laughed. Price might have liked to talk a lot, but gossip was a double-edged sword he'd been cut by plenty of times since becoming a young father. He didn't like indulging in it unless he had to. Winnie was more or less the same. She'd often rolled her eyes at Corrie's need to tell her everyone else's business.

Not to Corrie's face though. Winnie was, once again, the polite Collins.

She waved bye and Price was back in his truck.

It felt too early to go home, but he wasn't about to go back to the department. Price scanned the parking lot. It took him a few beats to realize he was looking for JJ's car. She must have gotten off work earlier.

He wondered how she was doing. Josiah had said she had visited him once in the hospital since he'd gotten out of surgery, but that had been when Price was on duty.

Word had traveled around that she'd been the one to find Josiah in the field, but Winnie had assured him that while a few more people had come to the coffee shop looking for her, JJ had seemed to stay out of the way of most people's rapid-fire questioning. That was good, he'd decided. She probably needed some peace after everything she'd seen.

Price nodded to his own thoughts and went back to trying to figure out his next destination when the door to the coffee shop swung open. Corrie was indeed excited about something. She was visibly bouncing when Price made eye contact with her through the windshield.

She made a stop motion and was at his truck door all within what seemed like one quick movement.

Corrie wasn't smiling but she wasn't frowning either. Her voice however was sweet with the syrup of a favor.

"Hey there, Price," she said. "This sure is fate catching you here."

Price's eyebrow rose at that.

"You do know my daughter works here, right?" he deadpanned.

She waved that off and dove in.

"I mean, when I need a really big favor, you just so happen to be around. It's kismet!"

During high school, Price wouldn't have called his relationship with Corrie Daniels that much more than an acquaintance that *sometimes* bordered on a casual friendship. Now, in their thirties, he was starting to realize somewhere along the line that had changed. Corrie was now someone who looked after Winnie, teased him about his lack of a dating life, questioned his choices and, apparently, had no hesitation in asking for favors.

Price wasn't sure if he liked this change.

Just as he wasn't sure he'd like a favor that had her this animated.

He narrowed his eyes, suspicious.

"Fate *and* kismet," he repeated. "If you say *destiny* next, I'm out before I hear your ask."

Corrie was unperturbed. Her question didn't come with the fancy buzzword though.

"How do you feel about going to a fun little party tomorrow night as our plus-one?"

That surprised him. He didn't know which point to land on first.

"Party? Our?"

She jerked her thumb back at the coffee shop.

"It's a business bureau thing in the city, mainly meant to network. Originally, it was supposed to be Cassandra going but she can't with the baby. Then I was going to go but, well, something just came up that I need to do instead."

"And so you're asking *me* to go? You know I don't work here, right?"

Corrie rolled her eyes.

"I'm asking *you* to be the plus-one to *JJ*, who's been nice enough to agree to go and schmooze a little on our behalf."

Price was less sarcastic in his response.

"JJ's going?"

She nodded.

"I'd send you with Winnie but it's an adult soiree with drinks and the like. Plus, I figured since your social life could use a boost, it might be good for you to go too. That and I feel bad sending our quiet JJ out to battle alone." Corrie slapped her hands together. "Y'all only have to fake nice and chat for an hour. You'll have my gratitude for life. What do you say?"

Price didn't have to think about it long.

"What's the dress code?"

JJ ENDED HER call with Corrie and left her cell phone on the coffee table. She left her house soon after.

The sun wasn't setting but the heat wasn't as high as it had been during the day. A fact that made her exercise clothes less stifling. Even the small bag she was wearing across her chest wasn't as uncomfortable as it would have been had they been in the thralls of a southern summer. She adjusted it as she drove to the park near Main Street. She adjusted it again once she was outside and walking the beginning of the path.

Seven Roads wasn't that difficult of a place.

It was small but spread out enough that not everyone who lived within the town limits was on top of each other all of the time. Which meant she could do something as innocuous as jogging to get her close to Jamie Bell's home without raising any suspicion.

JJ started her run slow.

Her leg muscles thanked her for the act of mercy.

Since her fight and run-in with Deputy Collins, her ribs had let her know quickly that any exercise was a no-go for a while. The forced break from working out had also bled into her search. She had taken the last week to be as normal as possible instead. Partly, she was waiting for the potential other shoe to drop from her break-in at Josiah's. Partly, because even without anyone pointing fingers at her, the town's attention had slightly turned her way.

So, she had waited.

Then she'd heard that Jamie Bell was about to leave town on a three-month-long business trip.

Which meant searching his house was now or—three months later.

While JJ was good at playing house by herself for a week, three months was too long. That didn't mean she was going to make the same mistake as she did going into Josiah's home. This time, she was going to scout the place longer, only going in when she was sure no one else was around.

And if she found proof that he was the one she'd been looking for?

Then you'll what? she thought to herself, not for the first time. *Tell him that you're his biological sister who isn't actually dead and that you're back in town to make sure the people who almost killed you don't try and kill him?*

JJ picked up her pace. She shook her head slightly at how ridiculous it all sounded.

However, that didn't mean it wasn't true.

That's why she had to be careful, even when she needed to be fast.

The park around her was replaced by the neighborhood that shared a sidewalk with it. Trees were sparse, manicured yards were not. There was a homeowners association. The only one in all of Seven Roads.

Jamie Bell was making decent money as a travel writer.

If he ended up being her brother, JJ made a mental note to be proud.

Until then, she passed by his house at a slow clip and took in as many details as she could.

Two-story. Twelve hundred or so square feet. No visible security cameras or a doorbell camera. The garage was single-car and closed. A vehicle was in the driveway, but it didn't match the SUV he usually drove. JJ had heard he had a boyfriend but didn't know what kind of car he used, only that he lived across town and lived with and took care of his grandfather.

They were probably preparing for him to leave the next day.

She kept on jogging until she was well past the house. An old frustration welled up inside of her as the concrete passed beneath her feet with each new step. She was looking for a needle in a stack of needles…while pretending she wasn't.

All while racing against someone else looking for the same needle.

She wished it was easier.

She knew why it couldn't be.

She—

"JJ?"

JJ stopped in her tracks. She'd been so focused on Jamie's house in the distance, she had let her guard down to the street behind her. A truck was idling on the other side of the two-lane road.

The man smiling at her through his open truck windows could not have surprised her more.

"Deputy Collins?"

Price looked like he was about to say something clever but in another unforeseen twist of fate, JJ's plans of staying beneath everyone's radar went up in smoke.

Literally.

A small explosion tore through the small neighborhood around them.

JJ covered herself in reflex.

It was only after Price was out of the truck and yelling at her that she realized whatever had happened was far enough off that she was fine.

But the same couldn't be said for the two-story home five houses away from them.

JJ couldn't believe it, even as she saw the newly erupted flames at its side.

It wasn't just someone's house.

It was Jamie Bell's.

Chapter Seven

Something blew up. Not large enough to destroy the house but enough that flames were already lapping at the wall on one side.

Price had felt the impact in his truck. At JJ's side, he could easily see the chaos.

"Are you okay?" He used one hand to pat her back and arm, even as she nodded. That was all the confirmation he needed. Price pushed his phone in her hand and started to run.

"Call this in and get back," he yelled over his shoulder.

He didn't know if she responded. There was no time to talk about anything.

A car was in the driveway of the affected house.

Someone was probably home.

The heat from the fire met Price as his feet hit the driveway. The front porch wasn't on fire, but it was close enough that Price didn't slow down until he was rounding the side yard and tearing through the back. He tripped in his haste but started yelling out for the homeowners before he was at the back door.

"Sheriff's department," he yelled in reflex. "Is anyone inside?"

Glass was breaking somewhere, probably from the heat,

but no other sound came through. Price tried the door. It was locked. He called out again but nothing. He took a few steps back and checked the only window next to him. It was also locked.

He was going to have to break either the door or the window.

Price ran the fastest math he could and decided the window would be the best option. No sooner than he went for the flowerpot he intended to use to break it did someone push past him.

JJ had something in her hands and set to the door without a word.

"What are you doing?" he yelled out. "You need to lea—"

The door opened. JJ cut him off with her own shout.

"Jamie Bell and his boyfriend might be in here!"

Then she turned and ran right into the house.

Price's lack of time, once again, kept him from reacting the way he wanted to. Instead, he followed her.

The layout of the house was nearly the same as Price's. The back half of the house had a small bathroom, a dining room and a kitchen opposite the living room. Stairs ran between the latter two.

The explosion had originated in the kitchen. Heat and smoke radiated into the hallway with intensity. Price placed an arm over his mouth and peered into the destruction.

No bodies as far as he could see.

JJ must have concluded the same. She was already running up the stairs.

Price followed, skipping two steps at a time.

Once they were at the landing, they split up. JJ went to one of the doors on the left and Price went right.

It was a bedroom and, thankfully, there wasn't much to it either. A bed, dresser, and nightstands.

No Jamie Bell or his boyfriend.

Maybe the car Price had run by in the driveway had been left behind and there was no one in the—

A scream came from somewhere else on the second floor.

It was JJ.

Price backtracked faster than he had run into the bedroom and went to the room opposite. It was a lot less simple.

The bedroom was twice as large, had more furniture cluttering the open space, and had, not one, but three people in it.

One was a man on the ground.

One was a man in a hooded jacket.

One was JJ and she had her hands on the jacket of the latter while standing over the former.

"Price," she yelled.

There was no directive in it, but he understood the assignment, even if he didn't have the context. He closed the space between them, just as the man in question threw out a punch to get JJ off him.

It was a hit that didn't land. At least not against JJ.

The man's fist connected with Price's open palm right before Price sent out his own hit. The man staggered as the punch landed against his jaw. The sudden imbalance knocked JJ off the hooded man's jacket.

But she wasn't done.

Price watched as she launched an all-out attack.

An attack that wasn't bad at all.

The second she was in striking distance, she struck.

When the man dodged and returned a hit, she dropped down.

Before Price could intervene, she swept her leg out.

The hooded man fell to the floor.

Price would have congratulated her, but his reactions were doing their very best to catch up as it was. He grabbed the strap of the bag across her chest and with a good amount of force, he slung her back toward the door.

"Leave now," he yelled.

Price watched a range of emotions pass over her face amid the growing smoke eking in. It was the only reason he knew about the incoming attack before he saw it.

Price whirled around, arms up in defense, and blocked the baseball bat as best he could. Pain slammed into his forearm. Price couldn't help but yell from it.

The pain and yelling cost him another reaction.

Not JJ.

Without a sound, JJ was back in the fray.

And boy did she make it flashy.

In one fluid movement she seemed to climb the hooded man like a dang tree. Then she slung herself around until she was on his back, arm around his throat. The man didn't like that one bit.

He dropped the bat. Price grabbed it, ready to use it to end their distraction from escaping the smoke and, no doubt, growing fire.

Like the entire scene that had played out since spotting JJ on her run, Price was once again utterly surprised.

With smoke above their heads, a man unconscious near them on the floor and a siren starting up in the distance, Price watched as the hooded man propelled himself backward with noticeable force.

That alone wouldn't have been that interesting of a turn of events.

Yet, he wasn't alone.

Price lunged toward them just as JJ's body connected against the wall next to the bedroom window.

The sound of the impact was loud enough to hear over the chaos around them.

But JJ didn't make a sound.

Instead, she went limp.

Her body slid like a rag doll off the hooded man as he threw himself clear of Price's lunge forward.

"JJ!"

The only thing Price managed to do was catch her head before it could hit the ground.

It wasn't until he had her securely against him that he realized one problem had just jumped the other.

The fight with the hooded man had ended. He ran out of the bedroom door without a look back.

The fire, however, was just getting started.

STRAWBERRY SHAMPOO.

At first, it was a joke. It smelled so much like an actual strawberry that it was more distracting than refreshing. There they would be, sitting around the dining-room table eating or lounging on the couch watching TV, and the smell of strawberries would mingle in between them. Even in public, the smell was noticeable.

"Who's eating fruit at a football game?" the man sitting behind them at the stadium had asked once.

It was a poignant scent.

Then, one day, it became a part of their family's fabric.

Elle Ortiz was the smell of strawberries, and her husband and daughter began to love strawberries all the more for it.

So that night years ago, JJ didn't need to open her eyes to know her mother was near her. She smelled the strawberries before she smelled the smoke and blood. Before she opened her eyes and screamed. Before she realized her entire life had stopped and she'd never see her parents again.

Strawberries.

It had been nice.

Now, with her eyes closed, she smelled them again.

It's Mom, JJ thought. *She's near me.*

She was pressed against warmth. Moving with their breaths in and out, rumbling against her body as they spoke.

And strawberries.

There was no denying that's what she smelled.

JJ almost smiled.

But then the pain started. It pounded against her skull and radiated down her back. Her elbow ached. Her throat hurt.

Was she back in that car?

She couldn't have been. That had been years ago. It had been raining, it had been night and her godfather had been so loud. Yelling, *screaming* at her to get out. To leave her parents behind. To run and never look back.

Now the sounds were different.

There was a man, but he wasn't yelling. He wasn't trying to scare a little girl into safety.

He wasn't trying to save his best friend's daughter.

Instead, the warmth against JJ had a low rumble. One that was almost soothing.

If she hadn't smelled the strawberries, she might have stayed wondering.

Still, there was enough of a hope that JJ opened her eyes slowly.

The car was supposed to be upside down, her hair and arms were supposed to be hanging down toward the ground, glass and blood across bent metal. The glow from the headlights bouncing off a tree was supposed to show her the outlines of her very still parents and the terrifying and growing cloud of smoke from the engine bay.

However, the world was right side up.

A seat belt wasn't holding her, it was a man. He had her cradled against him like a father would a child, an arm beneath her legs and an arm fastening her upper body to his. He wasn't eerily still like her parents, and he wasn't yelling at her like her godfather. He was speaking softly to someone, somewhere around them.

It was daytime too. Warm even.

There was smoke but it was a good distance off, eating at a house, and not an ominous growing cloud a few feet away.

But.

There *was* the smell of strawberries.

It just wasn't Elle Ortiz's shampoo.

The ache that ran wide and deep, unimaginable in size and depth, filled with a tidal wave of sorrow.

"It's my hair," she said aloud.

JJ's head swam. The body she was attached to moved. Not enough to jostle her but enough to bring her attention to the face peering down at her.

Price Collins was all concern in his eyes.

He didn't understand.

How could he?

She didn't mean to, but the finishing thought slipped out while looking into those eyes.

"It's my shampoo," she said. "Not hers."

Then it was over for JJ.

She placed her head back against his chest and closed her eyes. She was crying next.

"It's okay," Price said. "You're okay. You're okay."

JJ's head swam. She felt nauseous.

The sun overhead bothered her.

She turned her head into Price's shirt and balled her fist into the fabric next to her eye.

He didn't talk to her for a long time or, maybe, it wasn't that long at all. The world felt fuzzy. She felt hungover. She felt drained.

It wasn't until sometime later that Price notably lowered his voice.

"The ambulance is here," he said. "You need to go in it. Who do you want me to call to meet you at the hospital?"

JJ didn't open her eyes. She answered honestly. Her voice had a rasp to it.

"There's no one to call," she said. "I can go alone."

Price made a noise of confirmation. She was about to tell him to let her down, but he started walking.

It wasn't until the ambulance siren was closer that JJ started to come back to the world around them.

"Where's Jamie?" she asked with a start. "Is he okay?"

JJ opened her eyes and found Price's gaze was back on hers.

He searched her expression.

He didn't avoid the question, but his answer was tight.

"He's fine."

JJ's eyebrow rose at the way he said it. The small movement made the pain in her head flare. She winced.

"You worry about getting seen to," he added. "Let me worry about everything else."

JJ hadn't known Price long at all.

Yet, for the first time in ages she felt something surprising.

Relief.

Maybe it was because her head was pounding, her elbow hurt something good or she had a sneaking suspicion her back was already black-and-blue, but JJ simply accepted his words.

For now, at least.

Once she found out if Jamie Bell was her brother, then the real work would start for her. And bright eyes or not, she wasn't going to let Price Collins come near the chaos that would come after that.

Chapter Eight

Jamie Bell didn't sustain any injuries from the fire.

Because Jamie Bell wasn't even in Seven Roads.

"He had to change his schedule around last second and go to his new jobsite early to set something up. He was set to come back in the morning before leaving again in a few days."

Price was leaning against the outside wall of the hospital, arms crossed over his chest and nothing but focus on Deputy Little. She had come off patrol duty already but was still hands-on despite the fact that her stomach was growling, and the sun had long since gone down.

But that's just what you had to do when you worked at a department that had less than a football team's worth of employees.

You stepped up because there was space you needed to fill.

"His poor boyfriend Georgie up there was helping him pack up some things when—well, all heck broke loose," Rose said.

This wasn't news to Price. Once they had verified that Georgie Reynolds had been the unconscious man on the floor, Jamie had been called. He'd answered the phone quickly and completely shocked. The brand-new information to Price was the reason behind Jamie being out of town sooner than he'd apparently told others.

"I know you and Miss Shaw left early but I have to say, the fire chief was mighty intimidating at the scene," she added after a moment. "He said we still have to wait for an official report, but he seemed confident, and angry for it, that the gas stove was tampered with to go kaboom. He was surprised there wasn't more damage."

"Something we already suspected, considering there was a whole damn man upstairs ready to fight," Price said. He shook his head. He was angry too. "The way he had Georgie already laid out, it's easy to make the jump that he wanted the fire to spread. We just came in too fast."

Rose nodded. This had been a conversation that they had also already had. The potential plan of the man in the hood and what his motives might have been.

"That's another thing I meant to tell you earlier." Rose snapped her fingers and then pointed at him with a finger gun. "The fire chief made a point to praise your rescue efforts. You managed to get two unconscious adults out of a burning house with little to no injuries yourself." She smirked. "He even said if you're tired of flashing a badge, he'd gladly welcome you into his station."

Rose was trying to lighten the mood. Price knew it and he suspected that she knew that *he* knew it too, because they'd both been present after the ER doctor had sent JJ up for a CAT scan.

To say Price had been angry was an understatement.

He was filled with rage. And not just rage, but rage tinged with guilt.

As smoke had filled the bedroom and neither JJ nor Georgie had moved an inch, Price had known instantly that he wouldn't be able to save both at once. In fact, there was a very good chance that just taking one of them out of the house would be a difficult feat. In his mind, he knew to save one was to most likely damn the other.

He'd already been picking JJ up as the thought blared in his mind.

He carried her through the burning home without hesitation, right out until he was in the backyard and far enough away from the house.

Then, he'd been incredibly lucky to get Georgie out before the fire consumed the walkways and before Price couldn't take the smoke anymore.

By the time he was outside again, some neighbors had converged and were quick to lend a hand. Some took Georgie across the street to wait for the ambulance while the others hurried to make sure neighboring houses were empty, just in case.

One man tried to help with JJ, but Price didn't give him the room.

The second Georgie left his arms, JJ took his place.

Price carried her to the other side of the street as sirens blared in the distance. He kept her there while coworkers and fire fighters converged. He only relinquished his hold once they were loaded into the back of an ambulance.

Now that guilt sat there, reminding him of that split second when Price had thought he was choosing between JJ and Georgie.

It wasn't regret at choosing to take JJ out first. Instead, it was guilt at realizing something he hadn't said aloud.

Once JJ had gone limp against the wall, Price had forgotten entirely that anyone else had existed. Georgie had become an afterthought.

And it shouldn't have been that way.

It was a grating realization. One that was still bothering him.

Rose must have seen the feeling pop up on his expression. She might not have known the exact reason for it but she tried to console him regardless.

"Hey, you did good work today," she said, patting his shoulder twice. "Georgie is going to recover from his fight and our favorite Good Samaritan is too. So try not to worry too much. Instead, do like the sheriff said and get some rest. I know you've gotta be tired."

Price was. His body hurt and the adrenaline had worn off long ago.

But he wasn't going home.

Rose didn't need to know that.

He gave her what he hoped was a nice smile and nodded.

"I'll leave in a bit," he lied. "Let me know if you hear anything, okay?"

Rose said she would, but paused before turning away completely.

"The guy you fought today…do you really think it's the same guy in the mask you fought at Josiah's?" It was a good question. He answered it the same as before.

"The size felt off," he admitted. "But, just because it might not have been the same guy, doesn't mean they aren't working together. The actions are the same at least."

Rose sighed.

"Two violent break-ins and attacks from masked and hooded suspects." She shook her head. Then her gaze went up to the building behind him. "And you and our Good Samaritan JJ have the bad luck to get thrown into the middle of both of them."

She tilted her head a little and let out a brief but heartfelt laugh.

"I gotta say though, that woman up there sure knows how to hold her own," she continued. "If you ever decide to take up the fire chief's job offer, maybe we should ask JJ Shaw to replace you."

Rose said her goodbyes and Price watched her go before walking back into the hospital lobby.

It wasn't until he was in the elevator and pressing the second-floor button that he thought about Jamie Bell's locked back door.

How had JJ opened it so quickly?

JJ DIDN'T HATE HOSPITALS. She just wasn't used to them. At least, not being in them as a patient.

She set herself up on the small couch next to the hospital bed and eyed her IV pole with annoyance. If she hadn't gotten sick in the ambulance—or passed out before—she wouldn't be in this mess. Something she'd already scolded herself for. What was the use of spending half of her life training to withstand almost every hardship, only to be taken out by a wall?

And a man.

Her stomach turned a little. It wasn't because of her confirmed concussion.

Josiah had been attacked.

Jamie Bell's home had been attacked.

Two of the five men who were on JJ's list were coming to, or were already in, the hospital.

It wasn't a coincidence to her anymore.

That meant that JJ had been too slow.

They were finally in town, and they were looking for her brother too.

The question now was: How much did they know?

Had they gone after Jamie Bell because they knew who

he was? Or had they heard that he was about to leave town too and acted like JJ had?

JJ balled her hand into a fist. She made sure not to push down too harshly on her right palm. Along with the scar on her back, there was another just there. Small, but a heavy reminder.

She had been too slow—too careful—in her search for her brother since coming to Seven Roads. It was clear that she wasn't racing against time anymore. She was racing against them.

Him.

And she couldn't lose this time.

JJ's thoughts hyperfocused on everything she knew about her mission. So much so that she almost missed the knock at her door. She must have still looked out of it after inviting them in.

Price's eyebrows drew in, concerned as he walked inside.

JJ mentally pulled herself together, along with the imaginary mask she had been wearing in public since moving to Seven Roads.

She held up her hand to stop his words before he could say what she guessed he would inevitably say.

"Some people don't like hospital food—I don't like hospital beds." She narrowed her eyes at the bed, untouched since she'd been moved out of the ER. "Downstairs, I understood the need to be in one but now I see no point. Especially since I have this handy-dandy rolling IV."

Price's expression of concern turned into a laugh. He wasn't shy about going over to that same bed and patting it.

"Then you won't be offended if I take a load off here for a bit, right?"

He didn't wait for an answer and sat down at the foot of the bed. His long legs nearly reached the ground, but there was a small enough gap between his shoes and the floor that it made for a humorous image. When he swung them a little, JJ felt the urge to smile.

Instead, she took a really good look at the man.

Price had not only ridden with her to the hospital, but he'd also stayed with her in the room she'd been assigned in the ER. Not only had he stayed by her side, he'd done more than just stand there idly.

In the ambulance, he'd held her hair back as she'd gotten sick. In the ER lobby, he had spoken to the front desk clerk to get her checked in. In the room, he'd talked to the attending nurse and doctor, asking more questions than even she had about her own condition.

Price had only left her after she'd been sent to the second floor and *that*, she thought, had mostly been because of her insistence that she was fine and he had more important things to do than babysit her.

It had only been in his absence that she'd felt an itch of disappointment that he wasn't standing next to her.

That itch she'd decided to scratch a second after that thought had come into her head. Staying beneath the radar might have proven useless in the last week or so but she could at least try to stay off Price Collins.

But there he was, swinging his feet while sitting on the edge of her hospital bed, no more than a few feet from her and her IV pole.

He was his usual smiling self.

However, the rest of him seemed to be lagging a bit.

JJ hurt from her fight with the unknown man. She couldn't imagine fighting him and then having to carry two people from a burning house.

He must have been tired and hurting.

She doubted he'd admit it though, just like she doubted she could convince him to leave her alone again.

Maybe if she went a different route this time…

JJ pointed a finger down at his shirt. It was slightly destroyed from the earlier hustle and bustle.

"You know, it might not be a bad idea for you to head home and change into something less almost–flame broiled. I know you said you have a friend who works here, but I've worn her scrubs before, and I don't think they'll fit you."

Price was unfazed. He plucked at his ruined shirt and then shrugged.

"I think this could be a new style trend. Like those jeans with the holes all in the knees that Winnie said was all the new rage. It even has a nice, outdoorsy smell built right in."

He grinned.

JJ retroactively felt bad, once again, for hitting him the week before.

She caught herself from grinning right back.

Instead, she made sure to harden her expression, letting the jolly man know she was serious.

"Listen, I appreciate everything you've done, but you've already done enough. You saved my life—and Georgie's—today. You don't have to hang out with me after. I'm fine."

JJ thought she had finally done it—finally convinced Price Collins to leave—but no sooner had his grin fallen than a look she could only describe as mock offended animated his features.

He even put a hand to his chest in a classic Scarlett O'Hara dramatic move.

"You might be fine, but have you ever wondered about me? What if I'm the one who's not fine?"

JJ opened her mouth. Then she closed it again.

Heat started to crawl up her neck and seep into her cheeks.

Had—had she thought she was special to the deputy? Was his constant consideration only because of his role as law enforcement and not because he cared about her as a—

A friend?

A fellow local?

An acquaintance who had fought alongside him?

JJ didn't know what she would describe their relationship as, and suddenly it left her stumped and in silence.

Thankfully, Price took mercy on her.

He dropped his dramatic pose and gave off a hearty laugh that seemed to fill the room.

"Don't worry, I'm fine too," he said. "I'm just waiting for Winnie and Deputy Gavin to drive my truck here. Then we'll get out of your hair so you can rest."

More than an itch of disappointment moved beneath her skin at that. JJ tried to recover with her own little laugh.

"Well, good then," she said. "I guess waiting in here is nicer than staying in the lobby."

Price's expression did another little change that JJ couldn't track. It was like he had his own mask on, and it slipped enough to see what he was really thinking.

But even that JJ couldn't place.

She wondered if it was simply him being tired.

His next words, however, didn't sound at all like a man in need of his own bed.

He sounded so sure of himself that JJ sat a little straighter as he spoke.

"Staying with you has nothing to do with the lobby downstairs being nice or not. I'm here because you're here."

In all her years of training her emotions to stay hidden, JJ found herself struggling the most right then.

Price Collins might not be dangerous to most, but for her, he was downright a problem.

Chapter Nine

Something was wrong with JJ.

Price knew it—knew it in his bones—but had no right to confront her about it. To ask her what was bothering her. To say he had his finger on *something* but he wasn't sure what. It wasn't just her being uncomfortable in a hospital room. It was *something* else.

But he couldn't say anything of that. All he could do was go along with the plan he'd unknowingly already made the second JJ had admitted she had no one to call to the hospital.

He was going to make sure she wasn't alone.

Not after what she'd just been through.

Which meant another Collins had to be brought into the fold.

"You sure you're okay with this?" Price asked. "You can say no and I won't kick up a fuss."

Winnie had her book bag slung over her shoulder and put on a look that was slightly annoyed.

"I already told you I don't mind," she said. "But if you keep asking me, I'm going to start."

She shook the pillow she had under her arm. He knew there was a blanket and a change of clothes in her book bag too. Winnie handed him the keys to his truck. She kept her voice low as she continued, both trying not to let anyone in the hospital hallway hear their conversation.

Especially not the woman they were talking about in the room behind them.

"I don't mind keeping JJ company while you go home. I like her, remember? So this will be kind of like a sleepover. So don't worry about it."

Price still hesitated.

"I'd stay with her, but I don't think she's comfortable with the idea," he explained again.

Winnie snorted.

"Have you smelled you? I wouldn't want you just chilling in my room while I'm trying to sleep either."

"She's probably not going to be quiet about you staying either," he pointed out. "You might have to do that stubborn thing you do sometimes."

Winnie rolled her eyes and swiped a hand dramatically beneath her chin.

"She was against *you* being here," she said. "Me? I'm a delight."

Price couldn't help but smile.

After he'd gotten to the hospital, he'd made sure to call Winnie's cell and let her know that he and JJ were okay. It was the only part of his job that he'd never liked—worrying her then hearing her try to pretend it didn't.

Even now, between her small jabs, he could see she was straining a little. Just as her hug after arriving had been more tight than normal.

"You're a delight," Price repeated. He meant it.

Winnie dropped her teasing with a nod of her head.

Her expression became serious.

"Go take care of yourself for a change, Dad. We'll be okay."

Price knew enough about himself to understand he would

never not worry about Winnie but, in the moment, he accepted that it was time for him to step aside.

At least, for a little while.

That didn't mean he liked it.

"Call me if anything happens," he said. "And regardless, call me in the morning when you're up."

Price didn't say goodbye to JJ for a second time and instead took his truck straight home. There, he did as all three ladies he'd talked to in the last few hours had instructed: he showered.

The water was hot, and it beat against his back without mercy.

It distracted him from his past conversations with Detective Williams and Rose and the sheriff. Then the loop of what-ifs and whys they all had been asking since Josiah Teller's attack. After that, he landed on Good Samaritan JJ, as Rose had started to call her.

There after, and then during, the last two attacks.

Blood on her clothes for both.

A hospital visit after too.

The shower ended and Price wrapped himself in a towel and perched on the edge of his bed.

His back hurt. His whole body hurt.

His ankle hurt too.

If his trip in Jamie Bell's backyard had been worse, it could have been a lot harder to get JJ and Georgie out of that house.

Price tipped backward onto the bed. The intention was to stretch out the soreness radiating through him, then get back up, get dressed and head back to the hospital to wait in the lobby for the morning.

But his intention passed by his follow-through like ships in the night.

Then exhaustion pulled them both under.

PRICE WOKE UP THIRSTY, confused and still in his towel.

It took him several minutes to realize that, not only had he fallen asleep, he had managed to stay asleep for hours. His cell phone's clock let him know it was almost five-thirty in the morning, and no texts from anyone let him know that if anything exciting had happened since his slumber, it wasn't being reported to him.

Price sat up and put his head in his hands. He took a few breaths to try and wake up some more. Instead, he got the nasty reminder that his body had done some more extreme exercises than usual the day before.

He got up and went straight to the bathroom counter. He took two ibuprofen, dressed as fast as he could stand, made some coffee and was headed back to the hospital before five forty-five had rolled around. He was riding the elevator up to the second floor a few minutes later.

And, before six a.m. had a chance to grace Seven Roads, Price was standing outside of a hospital door, looking with concern at JJ Shaw.

The interesting part, however, was the placement of JJ in relation to the hospital door. Instead of being asleep inside of her room, she was standing in the hallway, hovering next to the door. A door that didn't actually lead to her room.

Price gave her a quick once-over—she was still in her hospital gown but no longer attached to an IV pole—before clearing his throat as quietly, but noticeably, as possible.

The noise came through quiet but clear.

JJ whirled around, eyes wide and fists balled.

Price raised his eyebrow at the move. He smiled too.

"I know you said you don't like hospital beds, but staying in hospital hallways is a little extreme, don't you think?"

JJ surprised him with an eye roll. He was glad to see at the same time that she lost some of the tension in her. The fists she had balled opened. She also took a small step toward him and got right to the point before he could ask about it.

"Jamie Bell came in a few minutes ago." She pointed to the door she had been slinking around outside of. "I saw him go in after talking to the doctor, but I couldn't hear what they said."

Price was no longer in a teasing mood.

He stood straighter.

"He hasn't come out yet?" he asked.

JJ shook her head.

"I was hoping to bump into him to ask how Georgie was doing but, well, it hasn't—"

The door they were staring at started to open. JJ was faster. She went from being next to it to next to Price's side. On reflex, he angled in front of her.

They went from looking like eavesdroppers to looking like they were simply going back to her room.

Not that Jamie Bell seemed to mind either way.

The second he caught sight of them, his attention was locked on who they were, not where they were. Once the door clicked shut behind him, he was talking fast.

"Deputy Collins, I was going to try to find you later this morning." He didn't leave JJ out. His gaze shifted to her. "And you? You're JJ, right? They said you'd been admitted but I didn't want to bother you or your daughter until everyone was awake."

Price mentally stumbled over the mention of daughter, then realized that Jamie must have been talking about Winnie.

JJ didn't skip a beat though.

She put a hand on Price's elbow and took a step forward.

Her voice changed as she spoke. It was, for lack of a better description, more syrupy.

"We're the ones who didn't want to disturb you." She nodded to the door he'd just come through. "How's Georgie doing?"

Jamie looked like he hadn't slept at all in the last twenty-four hours. His face was haggard.

"He'll make a full recovery. He should be able to go home in the next few days." He paused. A look Price had seen a few times before passed over his expression. Anguish. He met Price's gaze again. "He's my home. Losing the house is hard but losing him would have been…" He shook his head. "Thank you. Both of you for what you did."

Price waved off the gratitude, but JJ answered before he could.

"We're happy to have helped," she said. "And we're glad that Georgie is going to be okay. The whole situation was scary enough without adding a long hospital stay. Speaking of, would you like to grab a quick coffee in the cafeteria with us? They should be open now."

Price was surprised by that but, just as quickly, he was on board.

He knew that Detective Williams had already talked to Jamie, and probably would again now that he was in town, but Price hadn't had the pleasure yet.

And he was mighty curious about a few things.

"It'll be my treat," Price added on. "I'm sure you could use a pick-me-up."

Jamie looked between them and then nodded.

"I wouldn't mind a cup, if I'm being honest."

THE HOSPITAL CAFETERIA was small but there was enough seating that the three of them settled near the entrance to the only public patio. It gave them a big window and a nice view of the sun still rising.

It also helped show that Jamie Bell was, in fact, in deep need of a caffeine boost.

Price felt bad for his plan to pry into the man's already-chaotic affairs.

Jamie, however, dove in first.

"I still can't get over all of this," he said, hands wrapped around his Styrofoam cup as soon as they were seated. "I had just talked to Georgie half an hour before I got the call from the department. Everything had been fine and then suddenly he was unconscious in the hospital and my house had burned down." He shook his head again. "And this guy? The one who broke in? I don't understand it."

Price knew the story of events from Georgie's retelling after he'd regained consciousness an hour after the attack. He had been packing up some things in the upstairs bedroom when the man in the hood had come into the room.

He'd instantly fought with Georgie, and it had been vicious. Georgie hadn't stood a chance and had been laid out quickly.

"I can't even tell if anything was taken," he added. "The house was a total loss."

"And Georgie didn't recognize the man at all?" Price asked.

Jamie shook his head.

"Never seen him a day in his life. And if Georgie hasn't seen him, there's a good chance I haven't either. Other than work, our social circles are the same. And even when it comes to work, I'm a remote worker so the people I interact with are usually not even in state."

There was a sketch artist coming into the department later that day. Price would be giving his account of the man who had attacked them in lieu of Georgie and JJ. He had managed to see just as much of him as the other two. Possibly more, considering he had been fortunate enough to avoid being knocked out.

"So, if this man had picked your house because of you, you wouldn't know why," Price guessed.

"Right," Jamie said.

"Maybe they knew you were out of town and wanted to take something?" JJ offered. She had a small cup of coffee and sat right at his side. Looking down at her, Price couldn't help but feel she resembled a detective at an interrogation table taking on the job of good cop.

Her eyebrows were even drawn together in concentration.

Jamie didn't seem to mind.

"I've already talked about that with Georgie. There's nothing we can think of worth enough for someone to break in and be as vicious as that guy. Definitely not something worth trying to burn my house down over." Jamie looked to Price. "My only valuables are the personal things I usually keep locked up in the closet and, thankfully, Georgie had already moved them to his car before all of this happened."

"Personal things?" Price asked.

Jamie nodded.

"My social security card and birth certificate, a few family and sentimental trinkets, my favorite book signed by the author. Some other odds and ends."

Price felt his eyebrow raise at that.

"You move all of that every time you leave town for work?"

That seemed excessive.

Jamie put on a sheepish look.

"You're not the first person to ask about that." He readjusted the Styrofoam cup between his hands. "I spent some time in foster care when I was a kid, and after being taken from a few homes with little to no notice and nothing but a trash bag to hold everything I owned…well, I've kind of gotten into the habit of taking my most valuables with me when I leave home for too long." He shrugged. "Some people buy safes. I just carry around a cardboard box."

Price felt for the man's past experiences. He was about to point out that it was a trauma response that, at the very least, probably saved his most precious items from the fire, but JJ spoke up.

Her voice was still filled with syrup but surprisingly blunt.

"How long were you in foster care?"

Both men turned to her. She didn't back down.

If Jamie minded past his initial hesitation, he didn't voice it.

"Not as long as a lot of the kids I knew, but from four until around ten. My mom passed and then I was lucky enough to be placed with the Bells, even though I was in a different county."

"I didn't realize that," Price admitted. He knew of the Bells, and had for years. He was older though, never having gone to school at the same time as Jamie.

"Not a lot of people knew at the time, since my parents traveled so much for their work," Jamie said. "It wasn't until I had settled in that they both changed jobs so they were always home." He smiled. He was tired but it was warm. "They made sure to find ways to support me, and even as an adult they still ask for monthly updates on my local adoptees group. I don't have the heart to tell them that we stopped meeting years ago."

"Local adoptees?" There JJ went again. The question was harmless, but Price couldn't help his gut from questioning the tone it came in. It didn't fit but he didn't know how.

Jamie nodded.

"There's a few of us in town still who've been adopted.

The Baptist church put the group together when I was in high school. A few of us from it still keep in touch." He addressed Price next. "Josiah Teller was a part of it back in the day too. Him and Nancy Hernandez's sister. The three of us used to be really close."

Price knew Nancy Hernandez.

He knew her sister, Portia, too.

He didn't know Portia had been adopted.

He also didn't care.

Because he had stuck on one thing and one thing only.

Josiah Teller.

Price expected JJ to ask another straight-to-the-point question about Josiah—a man previously attacked after his home was broken into—having a connection with Jamie, a man whose home was broken into and the person inside attacked.

Instead, she didn't say a word.

Price glanced her way.

JJ Shaw wasn't just quiet.

She also wasn't surprised.

It was right then and there that Price felt more than sure of something than he had before.

JJ Shaw was hiding something.

And he had a feeling it might be the reason she was in Seven Roads.

Chapter Ten

They parted ways in the same spot that they'd met. Jamie thanked them a few more times and then went into Georgie's room, yawning despite his coffee.

JJ watched him go.

He wasn't her brother, but she felt sympathy for him.

One moment, his life was going exactly the way he wanted, and in the next, he'd become the man with only a box of valuables left. Though, that sympathy evened out quickly for JJ.

As Jamie said himself, the person he loved would be fine so he would be too.

It was a warming thought that moved through JJ while watching the door close behind him.

That warmth was still there when she turned to Price.

Then it grew cold.

Price wasn't just looking at her. He was staring.

There was a difference.

JJ took a small step back, hunching ever so slightly so her height changed. She also averted her eyes. Hers were a dime a dozen in color but that didn't mean Price couldn't use them to realize she was the one he fought at Josiah Teller's home.

"I'm really glad they'll be okay," she said, swinging her

gaze back to the door behind them. "It definitely could have been a lot worse."

Out of her periphery she saw Price nod. She doubled down on sincerity.

"Speaking of being okay, I really was last night, but I have to say it was nice having someone around. Thanks for getting Winnie to keep me company."

JJ chanced a look at the man.

She could have sighed in relief. He was back to his usual smiling self.

"Hey, I didn't have to force anyone to do anything." He held up his hands in defense. "After you helped me with that man yesterday, she said our family owed you." He shrugged. "And I don't make the rules. I just follow them."

Just as she knew Winnie was a good kid, JJ knew that Price had been the first one to come up with the idea to have someone keep her company. After all, hadn't she admitted to him that she had no one to call?

That didn't seem to be something Price Collins would let sit still.

Friend or not. Acquaintance or not. Whatever-they-could-be-called or not.

Regardless, she had been begrudgingly comforted to have someone to talk to.

Plus, Winnie wasn't like other people in Seven Roads. Her gossip meter seemed to be turned off. That included the power of prying. The teenager didn't ask any questions unless JJ led her to them. Even then, she didn't drill into a topic too long.

It let JJ do something she hadn't done in a while.

She had let down her guard a little.

Now, she remembered that she wasn't dealing with the youngest Collins anymore.

She was back with the big one.

JJ mentally buttoned herself up. She returned his smile.

"I'm also thankful she isn't a snorer," JJ added. "Though she definitely seems to be a deep sleeper. When the nurses did their rounds earlier, she didn't budge."

Price snorted.

"You should see her in the car. If the trip lasts more than ten minutes, she's already been asleep for five."

They quieted as they went into the room, but Winnie was already awake. She had changed out of her pajamas and was making the hospital bed.

"Did you sleep there?" her father asked her.

Winnie immediately pointed to JJ.

"She made me! I told her I'd take the couch, but she was all weird about not liking the bed!"

It was JJ's turn to put her hands up in self-defense.

"I told you I didn't like hospital beds."

Price actually rolled his eyes. The effect was such a drastic softening from the stare she'd just been given. It made JJ wonder if she was being overly paranoid.

It was true that she had been around both break-ins and attacks, but hardly anyone could accuse her of being involved. Only two groups seemed to know the possible connection between Josiah and Jamie.

And it seemed that they had already ruled both men out.

Which meant Marty Goldman might be next.

That's why, instead of staying beneath the Seven Roads radar, JJ had accepted the favor asked of her by Corrie. Marty Goldman would be at the small business networking event that night.

Another reason why JJ was more than ready to leave the hospital, and its beds, behind. Winnie, having already talked about the event the night before, waved her cell phone at JJ and tapped its screen. She was already on the same page.

"I'll text you the hair tutorial link that I talked about when I find it again," she said. "I'm pretty sure it's deep in my Pinterest board but I'll find it before you have to leave tonight. And, again, if Janie from third period can do it by herself and look like she did at last year's homecoming dance, I'm sure you'll really nail it."

JJ smiled at that.

"Much appreciated." She touched her hair. It still smelled softly of smoke. "I'm sure my hair could use the confidence boost."

"Before you leave tonight? You're still going?"

They turned to Price. His carefree attitude was gone again. She had a feeling he was about to give her a speech about taking it easy or more resting, but Winnie stepped in with the assist.

"We already talked about it and decided that JJ could use a little fun after the last week or so," she said. "Plus, it's also for work kind of and if she doesn't go then you'll have to take me and I don't want to be my dad's plus-one. So don't try to talk her out of it."

"The doctor also cleared me during the last round," JJ added in. "He said I'll probably be sore but nothing some Icy Hot or some ibuprofen can't help."

JJ and Winnie were standing almost shoulder to shoulder across from Price now. His gaze moved between them, slow. JJ was momentarily reminded of her own father. She oddly felt like she was also waiting for his approval.

Then, she remembered it wasn't all about her.

Before the fire had broken out, Corrie had changed the plans yet again to include Price as JJ's plus-one to the event. Mostly because he had been unlucky enough to walk inside of the coffee shop after needing a substitute partygoer. Partly because Price seemed to be a man who liked to help out, especially when it was within the realm of his daughter's life.

Since then, neither had had a chance to speak about it though.

JJ felt guilt pulse through her.

"But I definitely understand if you're not feeling up to going," JJ said hurriedly. "You probably are hurting more than me and, well, I guess might need to work overtime? I really don't mind going alone. It's not that far and—"

"I'm going."

Price's words were undeniably concrete.

Three syllables that held power.

Not even his daughter made a quip about it.

Instead, JJ simply nodded.

The rest of their time in the hospital room consisted of packing, going over their schedules for each other and then signing JJ out. There was enough time to take Winnie to school and even a spare twenty minutes to drop JJ off at home before Price had to go to work.

There, in her driveway, Price confirmed his pickup time for that night.

Then, as she was opening the passenger's side door, he threw her off one last time.

"By the way, were you adopted?"

The question came out of nowhere. Normally, that wouldn't matter. JJ had spent years learning how to control her surprise.

Yet, right then and there, she faltered.

"Am I adopted?" she repeated.

Price didn't backtrack the somewhat invasive question. Instead, he explained.

"Yeah. I only ask because you seemed really interested

about Jamie being adopted." A beat went by, then he added, "And Josiah. So, I was just thinking that maybe you might be too."

JJ was lagging.

She felt her smile slide, but she couldn't decide if it seemed natural or not.

She had an entire backstory, locked and loaded for JJ Shaw.

Adopted as a baby by her godfather.

Grew up with him, happy and healthy.

After he married a nice, decent woman and moved up north, JJ decided to come here for a slower pace of life than the city.

She knew what to say and had said it all before.

But there was just something about Price that pulled at her in a way that was wholly uncomfortable.

She wanted to lie; she wanted to tell the truth.

And, for the first time in a long time, she couldn't stop herself from doing both.

"I wasn't, but my brother was."

Price looked like he wanted to say something more, but JJ needed to end the conversation there. So, she did.

"I'll see you tonight, Price."

And with that, she walked away without looking back. If Price wanted more, he didn't get it.

WINNIE TOOK MORE pictures of Price than he had taken of her before the last school dance.

"You're in a suit," she'd said after batting away his complaints. "If I don't document this, then how will future generations know that you had clothes other than your uniform and jeans?"

She'd posed him in front of the fireplace, the bookcase

his father had built by hand, on the front-porch stairs, and—his favorite—looking all dramatic getting into his truck. When he rolled the window down after the photo shoot had ended, she prescolded him for not taking a picture with JJ at the actual event.

"I know you aren't going to do it, but you need to," she had said, finger pointing with purpose. "She already sent me a picture of her hair—which she absolutely nailed—but I want to see the full thing. You two being fancy and awkward at a social event neither one of you wanted to go to."

Price would have normally laughed—said something snarky about being awkward—but he'd spent most of the day at work tired and growing even more so.

The department was frustrated. Price especially.

The sketch artist had come in that morning and done a workup on the man in the hood at Jamie Bell's.

No one had recognized him and, as of that afternoon, nothing had popped in any of their law enforcement databases for him.

Detective Williams had said he had a potential lead, but hadn't been back to the department all day.

Then there was the part of Price that had branched off during his idle time and done a little digging himself.

Both Jamie and Josiah had in fact been adopted. Though, at different ages and in different circumstances. Before, during and after the legal paperwork had been done, they had seemingly led completely separate lives other than the occasional support group meeting.

That, and their attacks, would have been enough to draw his attention.

But then Price had seen another similarity that he couldn't ignore.

Josiah Teller and Jamie Bell were the same age.

"That was one reason our parents really wanted us to see each other," Josiah had said on the phone earlier. Price had called to check up on him but also to mention his conversation with Jamie the day before. "They thought we could relate more to each other since we were in the same grade too. Everyone else in the group was younger or older by a few years."

After that, Price couldn't help but pivot to JJ.

Her social media presence was barely there and, of the accounts, there were no family ones attached. Price started to put her name into a more involved search but stopped himself again.

Just because JJ was hiding something didn't mean it was his business.

It didn't mean it was bad.

Price held onto that thought with new resolve. He held it fast as he parked at the curb outside of her house and then went to the front door to knock. He held it true as he waited for her to open the door.

Then he didn't have to work hard at all to keep his thoughts from wandering.

Price didn't know much about hair tutorials or fashion, but he believed in that moment that JJ Shaw had indeed nailed it.

The dress code for the event was cocktail; JJ Shaw was devastating.

She wore a black dress that cut above the knees, dipped down the chest and matched up nice with a pair of ankle boots. There was a small leather jacket hung over one of her bare arms, and the purse she wore across her body had a gold chain the same color as the hoops in her ears.

As far as hair went, his daughter had pulled through. Half of it was pinned back in a braid, the rest curled and falling across her shoulders like some kind of movie star readying for a premiere.

JJ caught his reaction easy enough.

She smiled uncertainly.

There was no recovering.

"I think I might be underdressed."

JJ waved her hand at him.

"Stop it. Don't go making me feel any more self-conscious than I already do. Corrie already made me video chat while I was getting ready and that was enough to make me rethink going at all." Price stepped back as she started to shut the door behind her. She stopped and patted at where a pocket might have been had her dress had one. "Ugh. Speaking of, I left my phone in my room. Let me grab it really quick."

She turned, jacket still over her arm, and stepped back into the house.

That's when he saw it.

A scar shone across a stretch of JJ's back, uncovered by her hair that had parted just so.

Scars were nothing new to Price. He'd seen his fair share—big and small and everything in between—and even had a few of his own.

Yet, maybe it was because he'd already felt off about the woman, this scar seemed different.

It seemed angrier than most he'd seen before.

And he had a feeling JJ hadn't wanted him to see it.

Her jacket was on when she came back but Price took extra care not to glance down regardless. He also worked to keep their small talk on the drive to the venue in the city away from any topics that were less than ideal. A move that she also seemed okay with following.

They talked about the coffee shop, about Corrie and her sister Cassandra, and touched on some fun stories about

Winnie as a little kid. No one went deeper than that and talk about the recent violent attacks stayed out of the cab of the truck entirely.

When they parked across the street in the public lot from the venue, that small talk went to a plan of action for them to do their best at networking for the Twenty-Two Coffee Shop.

"Are you ready?" Price asked, holding his arm out once they had made their way to the outside of the building. There were a few other guests coming up behind them, also dressed to impress. He could also hear the consistent chatter of several people inside.

JJ nodded.

There were no nerves showing from her.

Instead, she seemed oddly focused.

If Price had known that the next time he'd come back through the doors, everything would be different, he might have changed his mind.

But there was no way to know.

So, he held onto JJ and went inside with a smile, oblivious to the domino effect they were about to set in motion.

Chapter Eleven

The gathering was a lot more upscale than JJ had originally thought it would be. Business owners, operators, investors and some leading industry-specific professionals all mingled around a ballroom while waiters and waitresses moved in-between with actual trays of drinks and appetizers balanced on their hands.

JJ was immensely glad that she had listened to Corrie, who had suggested she go dressier rather than the blouse and slacks she had originally intended to wear. She wasn't the only one.

Price lowered his chin over her shoulder. His name tag brushed against her jacket. She could feel his breath at her ear.

"Remind me to give Winnie a raise in her allowance next month. I would have worn jeans if it wasn't for her."

JJ stilled herself from reacting to the closeness. She did smile though.

"Sounds good to me. I owe her for the hair anyway."

Price pulled two drinks from a waiter as they glided by and stood tall at her side once distributing them. He took in a deep breath and then nodded.

"Okay, so the plan is to find the florist lady Cassandra

and Corrie want to get in good with, right? And then rub elbows with the local event lady."

He bobbed his head around. It wasn't as noticeable as it might have been had the room not been filled with tables, chairs, standing decorations and enough guests that the live music at the back of the room was competing with their chatter.

"Robertson. Maggie Robertson," JJ reminded him. "Cassandra wants to start hosting events at the coffee shop and thought if we were friendly enough with her, we could do some kind of partnership deal in the future."

Price nodded. His eyes continued to scan the room.

JJ was doing more of the same.

However, she wasn't looking for Maggie Robertson or the head of the local event scene.

She was looking for Marty Goldman.

"The picture Corrie gave you isn't helping me here," Price said after a moment. "We need to move around so I can start reading name tags too."

JJ felt a small pressure at her lower back as Price gently placed his hand there. He pushed a little. It put JJ in step beside him.

Once again, JJ struggled to rein in her focus.

"I'll let you start the conversations, but let me know if you get tired of schmoozing and I'll jump in," he whispered, oblivious to her mental stumble. "Or I can help you escape if you need instead. I'm really good at diverting conversational attention."

Somehow, JJ didn't doubt that. With one hand and a slight push, he'd managed to divert her attention and scatter her thoughts.

If Price Collins put his mind to actively being distracting?

JJ let out a little laugh.

"Pick a code word and I'll be sure to say it."

Price nodded. She glanced over to see a smile had tugged up the corner of his lips.

"Let me think on it a bit. It has to be a good one."

For the next half hour, they weaved in and out of partygoers, stepping into ongoing conversations and then starting their own. Everyone had business cards and together JJ and Price became a well-oiled machine in presenting the one from the coffee shop and accepting cards from the people they were networking with. Price also took it upon himself to put each in the pockets of his suit. It was a move that JJ found oddly touching.

They ebbed and flowed like that in a comfortable rhythm, despite not sighting either one of their targets, including Marty Goldman.

"Maybe they're some of those people who like to be fashionably late or just have to make a dramatic appearance," Price reasoned as they took a water break next to one of the caterer tables. "We can keep schmoozing around until we see one of them or try to get someone more exciting on our side."

He looked absolutely mischievous as he openly scanned the crowd near them. He was covert when he nodded toward the group of people milling closer to the band.

"That guy there? The one with the brown suit and lady half his age on his arm? I'm pretty sure that's the guy who runs the courier service the art lady we talked to last said was a good person to know. Why don't we go accidentally bump into him?"

JJ agreed but, as they started walking that way, she had to scold him a little.

"What is it with you and not learning names? I'm not sure I've heard you say a name other than *that man* and *that lady*."

Price fell back a little as a group walking by forced him

to slow down. It put JJ a few steps ahead of him. Still, she imagined his expression. He was probably smiling, laughing a little and ready to lob a cheeky remark back. JJ realized she was almost looking forward to turning to him once there was more room to see if she was right.

But she didn't get the chance.

She had found something familiar in the ballroom.

Her feet kept going a few steps, unsure if her eyes really were seeing what they thought they were.

Who they thought they were.

There was no way, absolutely no way that her old life was here.

Not like this.

Not with the two of them.

The men were in suits, standing on the outskirts of the group of people watching the live band play. One wore a comfortable-looking fit, dark blue and complimenting his blond hair. The other had a suit that was classic. Black, white button-up, a tie that was plain but no doubt expensive. His hair was copper. His resting smile was sharp.

While both men were together in the same space, sharing a conversation, they were light-years from each other.

One was Marty Goldman, suit blue.

The other was the son of the man who had killed JJ's family.

Her instincts tore themselves apart. JJ took another step forward and then stopped.

If it had been anyone else at Marty's side…

Was he here for Marty?

Surely, he was.

Why else would he be talking to him of all people…

Was this the first time they had met?

What was his plan next?

Did that mean Marty was her brother?

The ballroom seemed to become silent around her. Then it was an echo chamber of nothing but questions. None of them she could answer.

Then those questions came to a screeching halt as a sight that truly terrified her took place.

The two men started to walk away from the crowd, heading in the direction of side doors that led deeper into the building.

Josiah Teller had been viciously attacked in his own home, driven away and then dumped in a field. Jamie Bell's house had been partially blown up, then absolutely destroyed all while the sole occupant had been beaten and left to the same fire.

What would happen to Marty Goldman if he wasn't the son of Able Ortiz?

What would happen if he was?

"The last dance I went to was the father-daughter one for Winnie when she was in middle school, but I'm sure I can pull out a few moves that won't embarrass you too badly."

Price's voice filled the terrifying silence that had wrapped around her. She hadn't realized they had made it to the small stretch of dance floor other guests were currently using. A couple moved smoothly past them, but JJ was still eyes on Marty, moving farther and farther away.

JJ didn't have time to wonder why she did what she did next.

Instead, all of her seemed to come up with a new plan right on the spot.

One that finally included another person.

JJ spun around and took Price's hand in hers. When she spoke, her voice was low but had years of pain, anger and determination powering through every word.

"I'm about to give you a lot of information and there's no time to ask questions about it, but I promise I'll explain more later. Right now, I need your help."

Price had been smiling.

That smile disappeared.

She didn't wait for the go-ahead.

She went for the jugular instead.

"My real name is Lydia Ortiz, and I moved to Seven Roads to try and find my biological brother before the people who killed my parents find him." She touched her chest with her free hand. "I'm the person you fought in Josiah Teller's house, but I am not the one who hurt him, and I am not working with the man who hurt Georgie. The man who most likely did is walking away with Marty Goldman right now."

She moved her hand so she was pointing to Marty's retreating back.

The doors were already closing behind him. She couldn't even see the black suit his companion wore anymore.

It pulled her anxiety as high as it could go.

She had run out of time.

If Price wasn't going to help, she hoped he wasn't going to stop—

"What do you need from me?"

His words came out calm and even. His expression was impassive.

JJ didn't question either.

"I need you to be a distraction."

THE SOUNDPROOFING OF the doors was impressive. As soon as they closed behind Price, it was like he had stepped into an entirely different world.

It was quiet, for one. Not even the thump of the music behind him penetrated through. The same went for those chatting inside. Instead, Price only heard lowered voices and footfalls from the few guests who were walking to and from their destinations.

No one was stopping to chat.

That went double for Marty Goldman and the man in the black suit.

They weren't wasting time to get to wherever they were going. Price was surprised at the distance between him and the two already.

He wasn't the only one.

JJ had followed him into the hallway. He couldn't see her but felt her tucked back at his flank.

JJ.

Lydia.

Price didn't have time to sort out the bombshell she'd just dropped on him.

The only truth he knew and accepted was her belief that Marty Goldman was in danger and that the man in the black suit was the danger.

He wasn't going to let that instinct go simply because he couldn't see the whole picture he was apparently now a part of.

It helped that the more he closed the distance between him and the two men, the more he could tell something was wrong with them.

Marty, a man he knew by name and had seen a few times around town, was walking like a man who'd had too much to drink. There was an unevenness to it. A tilt. Barely there but like his body and brain couldn't decide what either were supposed to do.

Go fast? Slow down? Stop? Run?

The man at his side, though, was the complete opposite.

He knew where he was going and just how he was getting there.

His gait was smooth, his clip even.

But where were they headed?

The hallway stretched the length of the building, only turning right into the rest of the paths and rooms in the convention center. Straight ahead, the hallway dead-ended into a window that stretched from floor to the two-story-high ceiling.

Was there another event happening deeper inside?

Or were they taking the exit to the outdoor area?

Maybe they were going to the bathrooms instead?

JJ slipped her hand into Price's, pulling his attention enough to include her in it.

Her voice was a whisper next to his shoulder.

"Marty is panicking. Look at his shoulders."

Price had been so focused on Marty's walk that he hadn't taken in the set of his shoulders.

She was right. They were stiff as a board, held high and rigid.

Not the look of someone who had had too many drinks and was being helped to the bathroom.

Then the first turn into a hallway happened. The men turned but had to step around an elderly couple walking in the opposite direction. It gave the man in the suit enough space to cut his gaze their way.

JJ's hand disappeared from Price's grasp.

"He can't see me," she said urgently.

Price didn't think she had to worry about that.

The man in the suit made eye contact with Price and Price alone.

And they both held the gaze longer than they should have.

"Don't follow us," Price ordered, body already tensing in anticipation.

"What?"

Price undid the button holding his suit jacket closed.

"We've got a runner."

JJ repeated the question, but the man proved Price right.

He ran, disappearing completely from view.

Price was right behind him.

Chapter Twelve

Marty Goldman slid into JJ's view as Price disappeared from it.

JJ ran to the man she could see, stopping next to Marty with her hands flitting around the air above him in worry.

"Are you okay?" she yelled at him.

Marty looked the part. Sure, he was disheveled and seemed panicked, but there were no obvious signs of trauma or blood.

He confirmed with a nod.

"Yeah, I'm—"

JJ spun around on her heel and was charging after Price before he could finish his sentence.

The hallway wasn't as long as the previous one. Instead, it branched off several times before coming to its end. JJ had already lost sight of Price by the time she skidded to a stop at the last option to turn. She listened for a few beats.

Then she heard a door slam somewhere in the distance.

JJ backtracked and followed the echo to what seemed to be the main hallway. There was an elevator at its end, another door for the stairwell next to it. JJ didn't have to open it to know that's where they had gone. She could hear the loud footfalls hitting what must have been metal and concrete.

JJ did some quick math.

They were probably ahead of her by one flight. If she ran in after them, not only would she be unable to catch up, she would be in danger of exposing herself as involved.

What would the man in the black suit do?

Would he get off at the first floor he could, or try to put more distance between Price and himself?

There was no time to sit and wonder.

So, she left it up to fate.

JJ smashed the up button for the elevator. If the doors opened in the next few seconds…

They opened immediately.

JJ tucked inside and decided to press the second floor. Her painted fingernail was backlit by the lit up Two but her mind was already in planning mode a floor above. If she was fast enough, maybe she could catch sight of them if they had left the stairwell. If not, she would go up another floor.

The sound of someone coming made her move her finger on reflex to the close-door button. However, the person was faster. He swept into the elevator and turned to face the doors in one fluid move.

JJ was about to stumble her way through, making an excuse that would get him to leave, when she realized who exactly he was.

JJ didn't know why she even made plans.

Fate sure didn't let her keep them.

Lawson Cole wore his black suit well. There was no doubt about it. Up close, she could see that it was also, in fact, tailored specifically to him. Like a second set of skin. It didn't look like he was a man who had been asked to dress up and attend an event. Instead, he looked like a man the event had been thrown for.

It was infuriating to see him doing so well.

It was terrifying to see him so close.

And it was worrying that Price didn't come into view as the elevator doors closed in front of them.

JJ assessed the situation as fast as she could. Lawson wasn't making any quick movements. He hadn't grabbed her or said her name or even, it seemed, looked at her.

Had he not seen her running behind him and Price?

Maybe he thought she was just some partygoer who was exploring or a staff member on business?

JJ took a tentative step back.

The doors might have opened quickly, but she had severely misjudged the speed of the actual elevator. It hadn't even started rising yet.

If Lawson hadn't recognized her, would it be suspicious for a normal person to just stand there motionless without speaking?

Or this is the time, a thought said, skittering across her mind. *You could confront him now and end this.*

But it wouldn't end this, would it?

Could it be that simple?

And where was Price?

She couldn't simply expose herself, attack Lawson and expect the deputy to be okay with it all.

The elevator finally started to rise.

JJ decided to feign innocence.

"Oh, I'm sorry. Which floor did you want?" She didn't turn her face toward him but instead motioned to the panel. "I have a phobia of elevators and kind of forget to be present when I'm in them."

She did a little laugh. Polite, self-deprecating.

Lawson surprised her by doing more of the same.

"The second floor works for me too," he replied with a laugh.

JJ assumed he hadn't seen her running. She assumed *he*

assumed that she hadn't seen him running either. She could play this off until they parted ways.

Then she could follow him.

From there she could make a new plan.

From there she could—

"Elevatophobia."

JJ inclined her head a little.

The rising had slowed. The doors still weren't open though.

"Huh?"

"That's the name for it," Lawson said. "The phobia of elevators is *elevatophobia*."

The hit that came next was brutal, and JJ couldn't dodge even a fraction of its power.

One second they were facing the front of the elevator, and the next she was pressed against the back of it, a hand around her neck.

JJ's own hands flew to Lawson's in an attempt to cut off the contact. But Lawson's grip was phenomenal. JJ coughed as he squeezed.

"If you didn't like elevators, you shouldn't have gotten into this one." It came out as an almost-purr. To match, his grin became catlike. "You're here to help the deputy, and now you're going to help me instead."

JJ could move her body fine but the force he had on her neck had her completely at his mercy with no plan to counterattack.

She curled her fingernails into his skin, but Lawson looked as if he'd already lost interest in her. He turned his head to look behind him.

"I thought he might be around here."

He moved enough that JJ was able to see that the elevator doors had finally opened. A small open area gave way to a hallway that looked to run between several rooms. Half of the lights were turned off.

Movement came out of one of those areas, heading straight for them at a slow but even clip.

JJ met Price's eye.

The sound of a grin was still in Lawson's words.

"Stop or I'll break her," he said.

To show he meant it, he tightened his grip. JJ couldn't help but let out a strangling cough.

Price stopped dead in his tracks.

He wasn't grinning but his words were just as sinister.

"Let her go or I'll break *you*."

Lawson must have believed him. His grip didn't detract but it did loosen.

"Prove to your date that you can breathe," he ordered. "Say something."

Your date.

Lawson was referring to her as Price's date.

Not as Lydia Ortiz.

He didn't recognize her.

He didn't know her.

That meant he couldn't *really* use her.

Every fear, every hesitation that JJ had fallen prey to since the reappearance of Lawson Cole felt like it dripped down from his hand and melted into a puddle on the floor.

If he didn't know her, then he'd already underestimated her.

JJ's face must have given away her change in mindset. Price's brow drew in together.

She complied with Lawson's order and spoke to him.

It just wasn't what either man had apparently been expecting.

"I'm actually really good at fighting."

Price's eyebrow rose and Lawson started to turn to face her.

JJ was already moving.

THE WOMAN DROPPED her body weight out of nowhere.

Lawson caught a glimpse of her smile before he had to release his hold on her neck. That glimpse lasted as long as a blink. There was no time to do anything but defend after that.

Now in a low crouch, she threw an elbow that buried deep within his side. It was a biting, sharp pain that made him stagger back into the corner of the elevator. His hand hit the panel to try and steady himself. He only had a split second to decide to use the misstep to his advantage.

He pressed one of the upper floor's numbers along with the close-door button.

Then the woman was back on him.

He caught a punch she was throwing only to take a kick in its place. It went into his hip but not his groin. That would have spelled disaster. Especially with the deputy on the outskirts.

Lawson needed to at least keep him away from the fray.

He took the woman's hand still in his grip and slung her against the opposite wall. It gave him a small window to deal with the approaching brawn of the deputy.

In a hit that felt movie-worthy, he connected a powerful blow against Deputy Collins's chest. If it had connected with his head, it would have been a knockout. Instead, all it could do was literally knock the man back.

He tried to catch himself, but he hit the floor hard.

The doors started to close. He wasn't going to make it.

But his date?

She was an absolute nuisance.

"Fifth floor," she yelled out.

Then the doors closed.

Lawson managed to move as the woman used the wall to push herself at him like a spring. She ducked as he swung out and got him again in the side. Before he could recover, she swept out with one leg and nearly pulled one of his along with it.

But they were in a small area, and he was a tall man.

He used the walls to his advantage to keep himself upright.

The momentary win let him switch to offense.

When the woman came at him again, he returned the side jab with one of his own.

It landed.

She let out a yell of pain and stopped her onslaught, trying to backpedal.

He wasn't going to let her.

Lawson struck out again, this time aiming to get her in a chokehold where he would certainly apply more pressure than before.

Yet, the woman surprised him once more.

Instead of the attack landing or her avoiding it all together, she used it.

Catching his wrist with one hand, she used the other to send a hit to the outside of his elbow. The pressure applied the wrong way to the bend of his arm was shockingly painful. Lawson forgot his earlier plan of attack and yelled as his reflexes had him trying to get more to his right to ease the pain.

The move created a perfect opening for the woman.

He heard her heel connect with the metal of the elevator wall while she jumped up and moved around and onto his back. Her hold went from a hand on his wrist to her arm around his neck.

Now he was the one in a chokehold.

It was impressive, objectively speaking.

It might have worked had it been someone else.

But Lawson wasn't afraid so there was no reason to panic.

He coughed as his air supply was cut off but kept the rest of his body in motion.

He reached back and grabbed the woman's jacket.

Then he yanked her off and slung her away like a wet shirt.

Skills were nice but his size wasn't something she could ignore.

The woman made a noise as she hit the floor.

He knew by that sound that it had hurt.

"I don't think your guy is worth all of this," he grunted out to her, rubbing at his neck.

Lawson had to give it to the woman. She had spirit.

She scrambled to her feet and hurried backward so she was opposite him, the corner behind her. Despite being in a dress that didn't seem too comfortable and boots with a noticeable height, she fell into another fighting stance.

The elevator was slowing.

He had no doubt Deputy Collins would meet them when those doors opened.

Lawson couldn't go another round with this woman or her date.

He needed to finish what he'd come to do. Seeing the deputy had already been a complication. He didn't need any more than he already had.

So Lawson pulled out the knife that security had missed.

It was small, thin, but undeniably effective.

And the woman must have realized it. Her stance went from attack to defense, her forearms raising slightly so she could cover her face if she needed to quickly.

Something Lawson wasn't keen on testing at the moment.

He spelled it all out for her.

"You might be able to get some hits in on me, but with this, no matter how good you are, I'll be able to return the favor." He shook the knife. "And this will hurt a whole lot more than fists."

The woman didn't say he was wrong.

She also didn't test his theory. She stood there in silence as the elevator doors opened again.

"Good to see you again, Deputy," Lawson said in greeting to the panting deputy outside of the doors.

He eyed the weapon and then glanced at his date.

Lawson didn't want to waste any more time. He pointed to the woman.

"Get out," he growled. "Or I'll shred both of you."

If looks could kill, Lawson believed his time would have come to an end right then and there. Yet, the woman didn't have the power. Instead, she shared a look with the deputy.

He nodded.

Only then did she slowly move along the wall and out of the elevator. Not one moment of that did she break eye contact with Lawson.

He had to hand it to her. She had been an interesting opponent.

Lawson turned the knife out and stood just inside of the elevator doors. The deputy moved but only to put himself in front of his date.

His stare was just as unrelenting as Lawson pressed the button for the first floor and then the close-door one next to it.

Lawson was glad to see that the deputy had enough sense to keep his position as the doors slowly started to close, but there was obviously something he wanted to say.

It just wasn't at all what Lawson had expected.

"Marty Goldman was born from an affair. His parents lied. He isn't adopted."

Lawson's head tilted in question just as the doors closed.

The ride to the first floor was faster than it had been on the way up.

Lawson made quick work of exiting it, and the building, without any issues.

It wasn't until he was being driven away that he let himself sit with his thoughts.

After a few minutes he turned to the man sitting beside him in the back seat.

"Marty Goldman might not be adopted. It might have been a lie his parents told to cover up an affair."

"Is that why you didn't grab him?" the man asked.

Lawson didn't want to go into detail.

"Find out if it's true."

The man nodded. He wasn't in a position to ask too many questions. It was his fault Lawson had gone into public in the first place after his botched attempt to get Josiah Teller.

Lawson ran a hand through his hair.

He spied a rip in his suit jacket's sleeve.

He'd already not been a fan of Deputy Collins since his involvement in their Jamie Bell search. And now? Now he was around Marty Goldman?

It looked like the deputy had caught on to their common thread.

Not that he was too surprised. It wasn't like there were that many men from Seven Roads of the same age and adopted.

Still, the deputy sure had become surprisingly annoying.

Not to mention his woman.

Lawson noted the various pains she had inflicted on him.

He decided then and there that before this was over, he would teach them both a lesson.

And his mantra?

Ladies first.

Lawson pulled the name tag that had fallen off inside of the elevator out of his pocket and handed it to the man next to him.

"I also want you to find out everything you can on JJ Shaw."

Chapter Thirteen

Lawson was nowhere to be found. Security didn't see him and the cameras around the convention center were of no help. The fact that there had been none in the area where they had fought Lawson definitely was a blow to Price's mood.

As was Marty Goldman's apparent lack of information about the man.

"He said he was one of the investors from a group I've been trying to get in touch with," he'd told JJ and Price once they confirmed he was absolutely fine. "He said he could get me into his higher ups' good graces if I could pitch my newest idea to them here. I—I didn't have any of my notes or information, but I couldn't pass up the opportunity."

So the panicked Marty they had seen had been because of business, not safety.

He wasn't JJ's brother, but she couldn't help but feel sisterly and scold him.

"Next time a stranger asks you to come with him to a secluded place, don't," she'd said.

Marty, to his credit, looked sorrowful for his error in judgment. He made another one as he accepted her lie that she believed the man had been a scammer, ready to take his money.

Price, in hearing this, followed up with such a serious warning that both she and Marty had snapped to attention.

"If you ever see or hear from him again, immediately call me."

Marty had agreed to the terms and JJ had lightly suggested he keep what happened quiet. Since he had been the one to wander off with a stranger and, in his mind, nearly get robbed, it was a concession he was more than willing to make.

After that, Price had simply turned to JJ and said four words that zipped her mouth shut tight.

"We're going home now."

The drive back took place in stony silence.

JJ didn't know how she should break it. Or, really, what she should break it with. Price not enlisting the authorities for Lawson had been a surprise. Him not driving her directly to the department once they were back in Seven Roads? Also a surprise.

One she was glad to meet as they parked in the driveway.

Price's driveway.

"Winnie is staying the night at a friend's house," he announced. "Let's go."

His tone was sharp but not particularly loud. JJ didn't like the change from the happy-go-lucky man she had grown used to seeing. Then again, she had been the reason for the change.

She watched him exit the truck and walk around the hood.

He didn't even look back at her as he went and started to unlock the front door.

I could run right now, JJ thought. *There's only two more names and now I know Lawson's here. I don't have to keep playing pretend. I can just hide.*

JJ opened her door and then closed it softly behind her.

He may know who I am but if I wanted to, I could disappear from his life forever.

She walked up the sidewalk and paused as he opened the door.

I can do all of this alone. I don't need him.

JJ followed Price into his home.

She didn't have the mental bandwidth at the moment to think about why, for the first time ever, she was deciding to trust someone.

Instead, she let her instincts take over.

And, for whatever reason, they were at ease around Price Collins.

"Are you hurt anywhere?"

Price's voice broke through her thoughts with a start.

JJ shook her head.

"Nothing but bruising." She tapped her side. "He only landed one hit and, thankfully, it was this side." JJ stopped herself from adding that it was a lucky hit, considering she had just recovered from Price's rib shot during their fight at Josiah's. She cleared her throat and motioned to his chest.

"What about you? He slugged you pretty good from what I saw."

Price's face was impassive. She couldn't read a thing on it.

"I'm fine," he answered. "Want some water?"

"I'm good," she said.

"Good."

He walked off like the conversation was over. JJ couldn't help but raise an eyebrow as she followed him into the living room to the right. Its decor was rustic and warm, covered in knickknacks and walls with framed pictures of Winnie and him through the years. If she had been there under different circumstances, JJ would have liked to have taken a closer look at everything.

Instead, Price motioned to the couch.

No sooner was JJ sitting then he brought over a dining

room chair. He sat it opposite her, a small coffee table between them, and then settled onto its seat.

Then those bright eyes of his were zeroed in on only her. "It's time you explain."

JJ didn't know what she expected.

Still, she found herself tamping down the urge to sigh.

Price had saved her life in the fire. At bare minimum he deserved her respect.

So, she started at the beginning without any more hesitation.

"My dad used to work for the FBI, dealing with white-collar crime cases in the South. *His* father had been conned out of all their family savings when he was a kid and, because of it, they had a lot of rough years." JJ adjusted in her seat. She hadn't told this story to anyone and now, even though she was okay to tell Price, she felt wholly uncomfortable for it. "But that made my dad work all the harder to help others avoid the same fate. So, he didn't just do his work. He made sure he was really good at it."

JJ wanted to smile for her father reaching his life's dream. She only stopped herself because of the nightmare that had followed.

"When I was really little, there was this anonymous group of men in suits that fit the kind of criminal my dad went after. They cropped up in Tennessee and really started becoming a problem. That wasn't my dad's jurisdiction, but he followed the case like a football fan might follow a team's schedule until eventually he met a man named Riker Shaw, an agent working the case. They became fast friends and, eventually, Riker became my godfather."

Price didn't stop her here, like she thought he might.

Instead, he kept listening with obvious rapt attention.

JJ continued, not exactly wanting to say what happened next but knowing she needed to do it all the same.

"A few years later, a branch of that anonymous group had popped up around Georgia and, finally, in my dad's jurisdiction. By that point, he and Riker had become almost experts on the group, so Dad was the point person here."

JJ smiled a little. She pointed to the wall behind Price but envisioned the city they had just come from.

"We actually didn't live too far from Seven Roads when I was a kid," she said. "In fact, before everything, I had been here a few times with my mom. She had a few friends we would occasionally visit. It was when I was younger though. And it was before the accident."

JJ let out a quick breath.

Price's bright eyes kept on shining on her.

"My dad was apparently finally able to get enough information on the group that he wasn't just about to shut down the branch, but cut down the entire tree," she continued. "It was big news. News that he and Riker realized had reached the wrong people. So, one night, Dad loaded me and Mom up and had us racing to a safe house where Riker was going to meet us. We didn't make it."

The small moon-shaped scar on her palm felt hot. JJ knew it wasn't. She knew the mark her fingernails had bit into her hand were old and worn.

Still, she had to fight the urge to rub at it. To try and smooth it away.

Because the ache in her definitely wasn't going anywhere.

"A man chased us down and drove us off the road. It was raining so the accident, which might not have been so bad, was fatal."

She could see Price; she could see her parents hanging motionless upside down in front her.

"I was the only one who woke up," she said, keeping her voice as even as possible. "I had no idea what was going on but then there was Riker, yelling at me to get out."

JJ couldn't help but pause here.

She admitted something to him that she truly had never wanted to say aloud before.

"I'll never forget the face he made after he checked on my parents and then looked back at me. I knew it then. They were gone. They were gone but it also wasn't done. The bad guys were still coming."

JJ took in a breath. She didn't pause anymore.

"Riker didn't get me too far, despite his best efforts. We were caught by two men, and, weirdly enough, we were lucky that one of them was the actual leader of the group. A man named Jonathan Cole."

Price's eyebrows pulled together.

"Any relation to our friend Lawson Cole from the elevator?" he asked.

She nodded.

"Jonathan was his father. And, let it be known right now, Lawson is nothing like his father." She leaned forward a little and held up two fingers. "Jonathan had only two rules that he made sure no one broke, no matter what scheme or activity they were running. That was you don't hurt women, and you don't hurt children. No matter what."

"Chivalrous," Price commented.

She nodded.

"And the only reason why the Ortiz children are alive." JJ put the fingers down and started to rub at her palm. "Jonathan struck up a deal with Riker right then and there. If Riker didn't release the evidence, Jonathan would keep the secret that not everyone had died in the car accident. He would also cover our tracks until we could leave our lives behind and start new ones. Riker, a single man who had never dreamed of having a family and then suddenly had a ten-year-old to look after, took the deal. We left, got new identities, and have lived as father and daughter ever since with no trouble ever coming our way.

"I had a good childhood with Riker. I really did. He gave me the world and really did become a second dad to me. He also helped me work through a lot of emotions that I struggled with, about knowing my dad's killers were just out there. I even thought for a bit that I had moved on as much as I could. But then Jonathan Cole himself visited me last year."

This was where JJ's emotions fluctuated a bit.

This part was new.

Price's eyebrow rose. JJ still couldn't forget her own surprise when she had seen the old man for the first time since she was a kid.

"Apparently, he had known for a while where I was but had kept his promise through the years. He'd worked hard to not let anyone know that there had been survivors in the accident. He saved a life to pay for his man taking a life, is what he'd said. The only problem was, he'd kept the secret too well. He didn't even tell us that my mother had also survived. So we had no idea that she was pregnant."

This part undeniably hurt. JJ had to speak in facts not emotions or she'd be crying soon. Telling Price had been hard enough. Losing it on his couch…that would be too much.

And she couldn't afford that right now.

Her words came out cold for her effort. She muscled through them the best she could.

"Jonathan said he never told her that I had survived either and so, thinking she lost her entire family, she accepted the protection he gave her and hid away from the world throughout her pregnancy. Then, when the time came to give birth, she had several complications. They continued to be an issue months after my brother was born and she passed away before he turned one."

Despite her best efforts, a lump formed in JJ's throat.

She would never know the end of her mother's life, and it tore at her soul to think of her going through everything by herself.

It was one reason finding her brother had become everything to her.

JJ clenched her hand into a fist. She eased it out in the next moment.

"Jonathan said he purposely lost track of my brother after that, thinking that knowing anything more than a general location would put him in danger. All he knew was the town he had gone to live in, nothing else. And that's when he told me about Seven Roads. And that's why I came."

Price's brow was still drawn in together.

"But why did he tell you at all? Why did he reach out after all of these years?"

"Because the old man was dying and I was the last stop on his attempt-at-redemption tour," she said.

"He felt guilty," Price guessed.

JJ shook her head. She laughed. It was unkind.

"No. He even told me he didn't regret what he did. What he *did* regret was what he believed would happen once he was gone."

"You mean after he died?"

JJ nodded.

"Apparently, word got around their organization that he had let evidence disappear that could destroy all of them. Then, after some digging, they found out that he'd not only let it go, but he'd let it go with a surprise survivor from the accident. Able Ortiz's flesh-and-blood child. The only problem was, they thought it was the wrong one."

"Your brother."

"My brother, someone I didn't even know existed until that moment."

"That's why Lawson is looking for him," Price realized. "He thinks your brother has access to this all-destroying evidence?"

She nodded.

"Jonathan said he was holding off any moves the best he could but, after he died, he knew his son would use finding and officially dealing with the evidence and our family as a way to vie for the new leader of the group, instead of Jonathan's right-hand man."

"He's going to use it as a power play."

JJ nodded again.

"Jonathan told me he couldn't outright stop his son because, at the end of the day, it was his son, but that he could give me a fighting chance to maybe save my brother." JJ opened her arms wide and motioned around them. "I thought I was faster than Lawson but, apparently, he's moving just as quick."

She could have stopped there. Price wouldn't know that she'd held back.

Yet, those bright eyes kept looking at her like she was as normal as she had been when he'd picked her up earlier that night.

And that meant something to her.

That meant a lot to her, actually.

So, JJ added one last thing to her life's worth of chaos.

"What Jonathan Cole and his son *don't* know is that Riker and I have our own secret about that night too."

Price's eyebrow rose again.

JJ bit the bullet.

"We never had Dad's evidence to take them down. We bluffed."

Chapter Fourteen

Sunlight came home two hours before Winnie did. Price had expected her, and unlocked the door minutes before she was coming through it.

She had never ever been a fan of spending the night at other people's houses. She'd have fun, sure, but as soon as she could get someone to take her, she was back to the house looking hungover despite not having a drop to drink.

Her friend Abagail had an early riser for a mother, so Price had expected her.

If his mind wasn't working through a case in the background, he would have smiled at the predictability.

He did smile at her, though, as she trudged into the kitchen and dropped her bag next to the breakfast bar. She settled on one of the stools and reached her hands out with a pout.

"If you make me an egg bowl right now, I promise I won't complain *as much* next time we have to rake the ungodly amount of leaves in the backyard."

Price snorted and stepped to the side of the stove.

He had just finished scrambling one of his famous egg bowls.

"Remember you said that."

Winnie dropped her head in defeat but didn't complain.

"I'll have no regrets as long as I can eat something in the

next minute," she said. "I love Abagail, I really do, but her family doesn't believe in snacks. The last time I ate was yesterday at like six. Not to be dramatic, but I think I could eat even Corrie's cooking at this point."

Price grabbed her a bowl and started to fill it.

"Not to be dramatic, but I think I'd rather go hungry than chance Corrie's cooking," he said. "Remember when she tried to get the coffee shop to eat that weird turkey dinner thing she made for Thanksgiving?" He pretended to shiver. "I'll take no-snacks Abagail's house over that any day."

Winnie agreed and took the bowl with a low bow and several thanks.

Price returned the gesture with a laugh and then started on the second of three bowls he'd planned on making.

"Did you at least get some sleep?" he asked over his shoulder.

Winnie said she did around a mouthful of food.

"We watched a few movies and I fell asleep toward the end of the second one. She might not have snacks, but her bed is super comfy. It also helped that her little brother was staying over at his friend's house too. He wasn't around to annoy us like usual."

Price paused, spatula in midair for a moment.

Less than eight hours ago, Price had learned everything there was to know about JJ Shaw.

Lydia Ortiz.

She had gone from the quiet, unassuming part-timer trying her hand at a slower pace of life…to a woman living a double life, hell-bent on scorching the earth to find her little brother.

"So it was you who I fought in Josiah's house that morning," Price had asked once her story had finished.

JJ had looked apologetic at that.

"Josiah fit the description, age and circumstances to possibly be my brother. I was keeping an eye on him, trying to figure out how to go about finding proof that he was when I heard about his call to the department about the suspicious hole. I thought the department brushed him off and, when he rushed off to work, I decided to go head and check it out. That's when you showed up. To be fair, I tried to leave without fighting you. You were just, well, in the way."

She'd given him a little smile at that.

Price had remembered her moves then. Not only had she hurt him, she'd been faster than him too.

"After that, though, I decided to lie low," she'd added. "Then I found Josiah."

They assumed Lawson, for whatever reason, had one of his men come in after her. It had only been a coincidence that she had seen him walking through the field.

"You were casing Jamie Bell's house after you heard he was leaving town for a few months," Price had guessed next.

JJ had nodded.

"I'm assuming Lawson heard the same news I did and, well, we decided to act sooner rather than later."

It had made sense then. What she had been doing to the door.

"Let me guess. One of your sneaky skills is lock picking," he'd said.

JJ didn't even try to hide it.

She'd put three fingers in the air.

"Scouts honor I only use it for good, not bad."

After that, she had promised that her behind-the-scenes sleuthing hadn't included any other questionable activities. She had also been adamant that no one else knew about her existence and she hoped to keep it that way.

"I'm only here to find my brother and then figure out a

way to keep him out of all of this long enough to find Dad's evidence, or at least figure out a way to take Lawson and his group down permanently."

Price had fixed her then with a searching look.

"If you find him, he might not want to stay out of it," he'd pointed out.

At that, JJ's expression had hardened. Her words had been just as hard.

"I don't plan on telling him who I am."

"What do you mean? You're not going to tell your brother that you're, well, his sister?"

JJ had shaken her head.

"I'm dangerous to him, with or without Lawson out of the picture. Besides him, there's still people in the organization who hate my dad. If I can't keep my brother from being targeted, I might have to put myself in their sights instead. And if that happens, I can't have any link to him. No one can know that Able and Elle Ortiz had two children."

Price had been struck silent at that.

Now, scrambling eggs in his kitchen while his daughter sighed into her food, he still couldn't find the words.

Only anger.

Rage.

And it all went to Lawson Cole.

He had already proven to be a problem at the convention center.

Now, in Price's eyes, he was the only problem.

Price placed the newest batch of eggs into a bowl and started on the last one.

Winnie's voice cut through his thoughts, bringing him fully back into the present.

"I guess I'm not the only one who was really hungry. I don't think I've ever seen you put down two egg bowls before. I'm not sure it's the best idea. Doesn't the bacon give you heartburn? You're going to need some TUMS."

Price rolled his eyes and waved her off with his free hand. "While your concern is truly touching, for your information *this* is for JJ."

"Oh, you're doing food delivery to her house now? Last night must have been fun."

Price heard the footsteps echoing from the hallway behind them. He turned as Winnie made a sound between a cough and a sputter.

"Is that JJ? She spent the night?"

Before Price could answer, the woman in question came into view.

She had her hands up in a defensive gesture.

"I did but don't get any ideas," she told Winnie. "It was a stressful night, and we came here to talk about it after and, well, apparently that stress sent me straight to sleep. On the couch."

She pointed in the direction of the living room.

JJ wasn't entirely lying. Night had turned to early morning as they talked, so JJ had asked if she could stay on the couch until they reached a more acceptable hour to be potentially seen going home by her neighbors. Price, knowing her neighbors, doubted they would be awake but on the off chance they were, he agreed avoiding that gossip would be nice.

That, and the simple fact that Price hadn't actually wanted JJ to leave.

Sure, she had stuck around to tell him her story but that didn't mean she would continue to stick with him to see the rest of it through.

He had already thought she would run into the night after

they had first gotten to his house and he'd left her in the truck alone.

Would he have tried to stop her if she had?

Would he go after her and tell the department what was going on?

Would he *still* tell the department what was going on?

Price believed JJ's story. He believed in her without any hard evidence, he had already realized.

Yet, that didn't mean he wanted to let her out of his sight now.

She was a person of interest.

He just wasn't sure what to do about that next.

Price handed the egg bowl over to JJ. Winnie was doing her best to change her expression from shock to belief. Price had to admit, this was the first time in her years of living that he'd had a woman spend the night.

He gave her some room to collect herself and took his food to the breakfast bar too. JJ settled down on the last of the three stools on the other side of her.

If this had been the JJ of yesterday afternoon, he wondered if she would have played shy and apologetic on repeat. Instead, she seemed oddly at ease.

"Corrie would have loved the party," she said after a few bites of her food. "We schmoozed with a lot of people we didn't even need to, but your dad here was a talking machine. I don't think there was a person we met who escaped his conversation."

That made Winnie jump in surprise. She laughed.

"Deputy Little says that Dad is a bad guy's worst nightmare. He can just talk them into the ground if he needs to."

Price rolled his eyes.

"The goal of last night *was* talking," he reminded the ladies. "And, may I point out, Miss Shaw, that you never gave me a code word to help get you *out* of a conversation. So, I didn't see a reason to limit my abilities."

"Hey, I'm not upset at your chatter," JJ said. "It meant less work for me."

Price said he was glad to assist and, unlike the night before, Price simply listened as the two of them dove into small talk.

It was comfortable.

It made their small fight the night before feel like a dream.

"Lawson is clearly playing with fire—his man actually blew up half of a home—so don't you think we should too? With the department on your side, you'd have more firepower yourself."

JJ's reaction had been immediate.

She'd been frowning so deeply that it seemed to pull her entire face down with it.

"The department has rules. Lawson has already shown that he isn't playing by any. I'm not going to either." That frown had managed to deepen somehow. "If you really want to help me, by association you're also breaking the rules. And, if something happens to my brother, or me, it could all come back to haunt you. So, you really need to think about wanting to help me before you agree to follow me into what might happen next."

JJ had told him to sleep on it. He'd followed her request and had.

It was simple math, really.

He was the law; JJ had been breaking it.

Lawson had done bad; JJ wanted vengeance.

An innocent man was being targeted; an innocent woman was gunning for the one doing the targeting.

Seven Roads was in danger; JJ Shaw had become a ghost to try and fight against it.

A brother was in trouble; his big sister had sacrificed herself to save him.

No matter which way Price ran the numbers, it had always come back to him feeling sympathy and anger.

He didn't have siblings, but he did have a daughter and there wasn't a part of him that wouldn't burn the entire world to save her. Thinking about JJ's parents having their children's futures taken from them was hard enough, but now to know that their nightmare hadn't ended? Now to know that their daughter was shouldering it all alone to try and end it for them?

Price wasn't sure which thought put more fire within him.

He'd told JJ the night before that he would think about it—really consider helping her while also keeping it a secret from everyone he knew—but the truth was, he hadn't considered it all.

Because Price had already decided the moment he'd seen Lawson Cole's hand around JJ's neck in that elevator.

She wasn't going to be alone ever again.

Not while he was around.

Chapter Fifteen

They dropped Winnie off for her shift at the coffee shop but didn't go in. They had other plans. Plans that included JJ letting Price into her home.

"It's pretty standard," she said after coming into the house from the garage. They had already shut his truck inside, hoping to keep his being there on the down-low. It wasn't in the middle of the night and not even early morning anymore, but still, JJ wanted to err on the side of discretion.

"The house, I mean," she tacked on. "It was already furnished when I bought it. I think most of this comes from a show house, to be honest. It's a very furniture storeroom floor kind of vibe. But it works."

JJ felt a flash of nerves at having the deputy in her personal space. Then again, she had just insisted that she sleep on his couch the night before. It didn't seem right to shoo him away from her house, especially since it wasn't exactly special.

There was only one room that held any kind of sentiment for her, and she still needed to hype herself up for that.

"I don't think it's standard," Price replied, politely. He motioned around the living room. "It's neat. Unlike my vibe of an explosion at a yard sale. You've seen how many little things I have collecting dust."

JJ remembered all the family and friends in pictures that he had framed and displayed.

She had only a handful and, of those, they had all been carefully curated to uphold her backstory if anyone ever visited. As for little knickknacks and collectibles, she had none. JJ had spent the better part of her life building skills, not hobbies. Fun memories? Those were few and far between.

It hadn't bothered her before. Yet now she couldn't help but feel self-conscious about it. Like they had just left a warm room filled with music and stepped into a cold expanse of silence.

Just to cut through it, she fumbled with the TV remote and turned the flat-screen TV on.

"Make yourself at home while I run and take a quick shower." She tossed him the remote. "I'll be back in a jiffy."

JJ hurried to her bedroom, threw together a fresh change of clothes and was in the shower before the water could even heat the rest of the way up.

Price Collins was in her home and not just for a visit. He was there to talk about her brother, Lawson Cole and how to deal with both. It made her feel jittery, but not necessarily in an uncomfortable way.

If JJ was being honest with herself, she was excited.

Not just to have someone to help, but to have Price's help.

He had surprised her, more than once, since meeting him. He seemed like a good, charming guy who was quick with a joke, easy for a smile. He was a great father, evident in how close he and Winnie were. A good friend too, based on the fact that even Corrie couldn't disparage the man.

But that wasn't the end of it.

JJ had seen it while she was in the elevator. She'd seen it fighting with the man in the hood at Jamie Bell's. She'd seen it while fighting him herself at Josiah's.

Price had an edge to him.

A sharpness that could split.

It was the same sharpness she had seen when he had pulled her aside after breakfast.

"I'm in."

Two words.

Simple, but even as she showered, they made her stomach flutter.

"Pull yourself together," she told herself in between the shower's streams of water.

Lawson and his group weren't just a what-if anymore.

They were real and they were already here.

JJ didn't dillydally after that. She dressed in a pair of jeans and a simple tee, braided her wet hair and only applied light makeup. She had grown used to not putting perfume on, afraid that she would make herself *too* memorable while trying to stay beneath the radar, though she paused next to her jewelry box.

There were simple things in it. A few necklaces, rings and earrings that also weren't all that memorable. JJ picked up the only thing inside with color.

It was blue, square and had an almost-worn-away flower painted on its surface. Two smaller circle beads sat on top and beneath the square. It was a hanging earring, dangling the beads on a silver wire, clumsily knotted and glued at its end.

There was only one.

JJ was feeling nostalgic. She slipped it in her right ear and smiled.

Then she was down to business.

She wasn't the only one.

Price had his hands on his hips and was staring down at the dining room table when she found him. He wasn't in a suit, but his profile screamed that he was definitely a man who took a few trips to the gym. She remembered landing a hit against those same muscles at Josiah's. She wondered what he would feel like in a more ideal position.

A butterfly dislodged in her stomach.

That butterfly went back and grabbed a friend.

Price turned to her, brows drawn together and oblivious to the encroaching blush pushing up her neck.

"I'm guessing you're not the kind of person to write down important information you want to keep secret, huh?"

JJ tucked her chin a little and went around to stand opposite him. He had a piece of paper and pen on the table. It had three names on it: Josiah Teller, Jamie Bell and Marty Goldman.

She tapped her temple.

"I don't like leaving a trail, no," she said. "Riker used to joke that I would make a good super villain if I ever felt so inclined. I tend to do everything as analog or off-the-books as possible. Ironic, considering I'm going after a group who employs some of the same values."

Price waved a hand dismissively through the air between them.

"But you're using your powers for good, not evil, so I'll say it evens out." He pointed to the list of names. "Me? I need to see some ink to think. And, yes, I know that rhymed."

JJ held in a smile. Price's expression had gone sharp again.

He wasn't trying to be charming.

He was trying to work.

"Okay, so you found these guys through adoption records you may or may not have used your computer powers to get," he kept on. "You said there's two more names you found that fit the bill? The same age, adopted, and living in Seven

Roads? I'm honestly surprised there's more than one with that description, let alone five."

JJ took the paper and pen and spun both around.

"Well, apparently, Marty Goldman didn't count," she reminded him. "As you were smart enough to throw out to Lawson—even though you had no idea what was going on, by the way—Marty's adoption was a lie. One his parents came up with after realizing his mother had an affair and then ended up working it out and staying together. His record of adoption was less a record and more a collection of posts I found mentioning it." She tapped Josiah and Jamie's names. "These are the only two I actually found official documents for, though I couldn't find the specifics like when they were adopted. That's why I needed to get into their homes to see their official paperwork. Or something that might convince me they were my brother."

She wrote down two more names.

"These last names are *mostly* based on hearsay and, I had been hoping, two names I wouldn't have to check in person yet."

Price leaned over.

She watched his eyes widen at one of them.

"Before you say it, I know," she said. "Connor Clark. He's going to be a problem."

Price shook his head. He tapped the other name.

"No, Anthony Boyd is going to be the problem. He needs to be the last person we look at, and really hope we don't have to. Connor Clark? He's actually doable."

"You know both?"

He shrugged.

"Connor is a high school teacher, or has been, for a few years now. He spoke at Winnie's freshmen orientation before she started school. And I *only* remember who he is so clearly because every single mom in there was drooling. He's a looker."

In the most casual way possible, Price brought his gaze up to hers. Then it roamed across her before he nodded.

"I guess you'd have that in common if he really is your brother."

Price's attention went right back to the paper.

JJ was glad for the break because every inch of her face felt like it was on fire.

"I don't know where he lives, but I do know it's somewhere near the school," he continued. "As for any family, adoptive or otherwise, I haven't heard anything. How did you end up flagging him?"

JJ cleared her throat as discretely as possible before she answered.

"Uh, there's an online fostering and adoption Facebook group for the state. He commented on a post where someone was asking advice on when they should tell their child that they had been adopted as a baby."

"What did he say?"

"'Being adopted isn't something that is embarrassing or should be kept hidden. Normalizing it as part of the child's story will only help them realize that it is normal.' Something to that effect at least. He also liked several comments that suggested they tell their child when they're old enough to understand and to mention it often."

"Which might not be enough to put him on your list but I'm assuming he's also the same age?"

JJ nodded.

"He also lived here when he was a kid before leaving for college."

"And how did you get Boyd on here?" Price asked. He didn't sound as enthused anymore.

"Anthony Boyd was adopted by his stepmother when he was a baby. I couldn't find any pictures of his biological mother on any searches I ran. I didn't want to rule him out as a possibility until I could find out if his father had any pictures of his mother around or talk to him about her. The problem is with that—"

"That Anthony Boyd's father passed when he was a teen, his stepmom remarried and moved, and currently he lives and works on my least favorite place in Seven Roads. The Becker Farm, run by the meanest and nosiest old man I ever met."

JJ felt her eyebrow go up.

"Price Collins has someone he doesn't like that much?" she had to ask.

Price grumbled.

"More like Becker doesn't like me. You get caught *once* fooling around in his barn in high school and he holds a grudge like a hamster holds food in his cheeks." He sobered. "Have you asked Corrie about these guys? She's a gossip magnet. Even if she doesn't know the backstory herself, she could probably get it for you."

JJ had already considered that avenue, but the fact of the matter was, she'd already used it three times.

"I learned a lot from her about the first three names on the list. I don't want to push my luck. Or hers." Now that Lawson was around, she didn't need him hearing about a woman asking after two names he might or might not have already.

Price seemed to pick up on that thought.

"So what's the plan, then?" he asked after a moment. "What do you want to do?"

She believed that Price had accepted her story, but JJ was on edge about her next steps.

Price was the law. Would he really help her break it if she needed to?

JJ cleared her throat. This time it wasn't because he'd made her blush.

"We try to talk to them to see if we can figure out where they came from."

Price must have picked up on her change in worries.

His bright eyes raised to hers.

"And if talking doesn't work?" he asked.

JJ kept her voice just as strong.

"Then we improvise."

LAWSON SLAMMED HIS fist on the tabletop. He was frustrated; he was energized.

"There's one last name we could think of that might have a tie to the Ortiz child," the man across from his said. "I have someone going out there to check on it. But—"

"But that deputy just went with that woman of his to the farm," he finished, rehashing the information he had just been given himself.

The man nodded.

"I don't know how much Deputy Collins knows about what we're doing, but since he's been at the last three scenes, I don't think it's too much of a stretch to say he's tangled up with us."

Lawson hit the tabletop again. Now he was just frustrated.

"Dad said he made a deal with Ortiz's partner all those years ago to keep it a secret. Who's to say they didn't loop in any more law enforcement? Or maybe the son himself could have if he realized who his dad was." He clenched his fist. "This. This is why my father was a fool. We have no idea what to expect with this supposed evidence floating around out there. That's why we need to destroy it once and for all. And anyone who's even remotely related to it."

The man nodded.

Lawson grumbled.

"What about the deputy's woman?" he asked after a moment. "Can we use her?"

"Normal. Southern polite, works at the coffee shop in town alongside the deputy's daughter. I'm guessing that's how they met."

Lawson sat up straight.

"Wait. Did you say that Deputy Collins has a daughter?"

"Yep. Seventeen-year-old girl."

Lawson's mind starting spinning. He smiled after a moment.

"Does she go to the high school?"

The man nodded again.

Lawson's smile turned into a smirk.

He was back to energized.

"Send someone to this farm and keep an eye on the deputy and his awful woman."

The man tilted his head in question.

"What about our lead? The teacher?"

Lawson was nothing but smug now.

"I think we might have just found a way to kill a lot of birds with only one, very effective stone."

Chapter Sixteen

Improvising came quicker than either of them expected.

"When I offered to help, this wasn't what I thought you meant."

Price was ducked down, one shoulder tucked against a wall, the other facing an open field. JJ was in front of him in the same stance. Instead of turning to address him, though, she swung her hand back. It wasn't a slap, but it hit her mark.

Her hand covered his mouth.

"You wanted to be here so hush."

The sudden contact threw him off, but he still smiled against her palm. The sweet image of JJ Shaw had been one he'd already found interesting. Once the act had dropped? Well, he was finding this JJ to be entirely entertaining.

Even when she had them doing something that wasn't exactly on the up-and-up.

JJ dropped her hand and used it to point ahead of them.

"Your friend said Boyd lived in the barn, right? That's the new one?"

By his friend, she was referring to the son of the owner of Becker Farm. Instead of willy-nilly breaking and entering, he had tried to use casual conversation to get information on Anthony Boyd's whereabouts. It had made for a slightly awkward conversation in the beginning, but Price had saved it by an excuse of potentially needing help with future home renovations. Anthony Boyd's strength was well known, considering that had been one of the main reasons a grump like Old Man Becker had hired someone not from his bloodline.

"He's not in town, though," the junior Becker had told Price over the phone. "He and Dad are in Alabama for a livestock auction. They won't be back until Monday. Want me to get Boyd to call you then?"

Price had thanked him for the offer and said he'd reach out again himself.

That had green-lit JJ Shaw, who was currently sneaking her way across the back of one of the storage buildings on the Becker Farm.

"If no one's home, this might be the easiest and quickest way we have to look at what we need," JJ had said, coaxing him outside of the western gate of the farm. "If it's not Boyd? Then no one will ever know we were looking for anything. No one gets suspicious and no one's in potential danger. It's a win-win."

Now she waved an impatient hand back at him.

"He said new barn, right?" she repeated. "Is that the one right up there?"

Price hadn't seen the new barn in person, but he definitely knew where the old one was. He nodded and pointed.

"We should see it once we turn the corner."

True enough, the moment they rounded the storage building they had a straight sight line to a structure that Price hadn't seen before. It was all traditional on the outside—red and white, stall doors tall and wide, and all types of tools and equipment parked on the dirt patch outside—but the junior Becker had taken the time to talk about how it was unlike any of the buildings on the farm.

He'd been proud to say that he had approved Boyd's living quarters, located as an apartment on the second floor.

"I'm assuming those stairs lead right up to the apartment." Price pointed to the stairs on the outside of the barn. JJ bobbed her head this way and that for a moment.

"I don't see any security cameras mounted anywhere."

Price snorted.

"And you won't find any on the property," he said. "Old Man Becker likes his privacy. Even from himself. He'd sooner do rounds every hour on the hour than let electronics and the internet do it for him."

JJ nodded and didn't talk after that. She led the way across the open land with surprising speed. Though, maybe it wasn't that surprising to Price anymore. She *had* been the one in the mask who had managed to outrun him at Josiah's.

The same person he had fought.

The same person who he'd managed to hit pretty decently.

Then, a few hours later, he had been helping her with her car like nothing had happened.

Price mentally paused.

A new thought occurred to him, but he kept it quiet for the moment.

They took the stairs careful but quick. JJ already had her handy-dandy bag opened and her lock-picking tools out. Price snaked a hand past her and tried the doorknob first.

It turned with ease.

"I thought you said he wasn't home," JJ whispered in a rush.

Price opened the door.

"He's not, but I'd bet living on this land gives you a false sense of security," he said. "Because who would be reckless enough to tempt fate when it comes to ticking off the Becker patriarch?"

He went past her and into the dark space. When he flicked the light switch on, he was already impressed.

The apartment above the barn was indeed an apartment. Small, but nice. There was a full kitchen that opened into the living room and a small nook beside it that housed a desk and chair for a workspace. Two doors were open at the back wall, showing the bedroom and the bathroom, respectfully.

No one jumped out and yelled at their intrusion.

Nothing but them moved at all.

"This is nice," Price had to comment aloud. "Good for Boyd."

JJ lightly pushed him deeper into the room so she could turn and shut the door behind them. He heard the deadbolt slide across behind him.

"Go ahead and take it in so we can start taking it apart," she said. "Let's see if we can find where he keeps his important documents first."

Price wasn't a fan of going through someone else's private things, but he had to admit that JJ's method of searching was…different than what he had expected.

She was like a surgeon, but a surgeon who didn't know which type of surgery they would be performing yet. There was a precision to her, a methodology she was adhering to that was clearly in her head. Her eyes were sharp, her gloved fingers nimble. She was taking in the details but at the same time, it felt like she was discarding them the second she realized they were of no use to her.

It still wasn't right what they were doing, but of the *not* rightness it wasn't bad.

Or you're only okay with it because she's JJ.

The thought pushed itself to the top of his mind in a flash.

It caught him off guard enough to physically wave his hand through the air like he was clearing it out.

JJ caught the motion.

"What's wrong?" she asked.

Price sidestepped a real answer and got to the other thought he'd pushed aside earlier.

"So you were doing this when I came to Josiah's, right?"

"I was actually on my second round, worried I missed something," she said with a nod. "I would have tried to restrain you to do it but thought better of it since I'd already done a thorough search. Plus, you ended up being a pain."

There was a hint of humor in her voice.

"A pain who showed up on your doorstep a few hours later." Price eyed a collection of books near them. None looked to fit the bill of what they were looking for. "Which, now that I think about it, I'm realizing your car breaking down was probably an excuse you told Corrie to get out of working."

He saw the corner of her lips turn up. She put the papers she had been looking through back on the desktop.

"Let's go see if there's a safe or something similar in the bedroom," she suggested.

Price put his head back and chuckled.

"Wow," he breathed out. "How did I not notice it was you? And here I thought I was observant."

"To be fair, I don't think most people would have thought it was me behind the mask. I also put on heels."

He followed her into the bedroom.

"Heels?"

She nodded.

"When I realized who you were when you came to my house, I put on heels so I was taller than when we fought. I was worried too many similarities might really push my luck."

Price remembered her sandals and their wedged height

when he'd first officially met her that day. They had looked nice with her dress.

Turns out they were specifically to keep his suspicions at bay.

Price shook his head.

"You sure are something, Miss Shaw."

She was already at the side of the bed, opening the nightstand.

"I'll take that as a compliment, Deputy Collins."

They spent the next few minutes searching in silence. Anthony Boyd didn't have a safe or any kind of area that had a collection of seemingly important things. He was a spartan guy, all things considered. The pictures he had displayed were no exception.

"He put up all of the typical events," JJ observed. "Graduation, birthdays and a few candids of who looked like friends. Have you seen any pictures of his dad, though?"

Price tapped one on the dresser next to the bed.

"Here. It's the only one though."

JJ sidled up to him. She peered down at the picture.

"He might just not be good at pictures," Price noted. "Just because he doesn't have a lot with his parents, doesn't necessarily mean there's anything there."

JJ sighed.

Price thought back to her home from earlier that morning.

Maybe *home* wasn't the right word. It was a house. A place where she slept and ate but living? It had reaffirmed the description that he'd come up with for the woman already.

Ghost.

She was going through the motions of living while trying to stay detached from the very same people.

What if she did find her brother? What if she did take down Lawson and his group?

Would she really not tell her brother who she was?

Would she just disappear from his life?

From Seven Roads?

From Price?

Her hand startled his thoughts. The fabric of her gloves curled into his palm.

If her expression hadn't changed so drastically, Price might have mistaken the move as something else. Instead, she was facing the open door, tense.

"Did you hear that?"

No sooner than she asked, he heard the front door rattling.

He shared a quick look with JJ. Her eyes were wide.

Someone was coming in.

THEY JUST TRIED the doorknob. When the door didn't give, the movement stopped. Price didn't. He took JJ by the waist, she assumed to shuttle them into the closet or under the bed to hide next, but then stayed himself.

His hand rested on her hip while his gaze was glued to the door.

She wasn't doing anything differently.

JJ watched as the doorknob shook a few more times then went still.

There were only three options now: unlock the door, break the lock to open the door or walk away.

She knew which option she preferred. It was one thing for her to be caught in Anthony Boyd's apartment. It was an entirely different matter for a deputy of the law to be caught. That was without all the messy questions of why they were together too.

Maybe she could distract whoever came in while Price hid.

Maybe they both could hide.

Maybe—

"They're walking back down the stairs." Price's voice was low.

JJ strained to listen.

It was faint but he was right. She could hear retreating footfalls against the wooden stairs outside.

"Why would they leave?" she asked, more to herself than him.

They shared a look.

Then they were moving in tandem to the only window that lined the left wall. JJ was nimble in moving the simple curtain over the kitchen sink just enough to get a view of the side yard below. She couldn't see the end of the stairs, but the two men were easy targets as they walked across toward the front of the barn.

Adrenaline shot through JJ faster than lighting to a rod deep in a storm cloud.

She couldn't get a good view of the face of the shorter man, but the one in dark joggers and tennis shoes had a face she wouldn't forget.

"He's the one we fought at Jamie Bell's," she said, voice pitching higher than she meant to. "Why are they here? Are they following us?"

Price's expression went razor-sharp.

"Let's find out."

Chapter Seventeen

JJ didn't like regrets. But, well, she was big enough to admit that she had a few.

Pain seared up her leg, her elbow throbbed and something felt like it was in her eye. The only thing that didn't have any complaints on her happened to be her head. Which was nice, considering she'd had a concussion not that long ago.

Did she regret her almost year-long journey to trying to quietly and calmly find her brother? No.

Did she regret breaking the law, fighting off bad guys and going up against Lawson by herself? No.

Did she regret sharing her life story and current plan with Price Collins, charming deputy with an easy smile and warm hands? Not at all.

Did she slightly, a little, maybe kind of regret not listening to him back at the barn and chasing one of the men all the way into the woods while he dealt with the other, only to fall down a rather steep hill, making herself an easy target for said man? Well, she couldn't say she *didn't* regret it.

She didn't recognize this man, but made the assumption that he might have been the one who had attacked Josiah Teller after she had left his house.

And that jump in conclusion happened all thanks to the

knife he had in his hand as he backtracked to the spot at the bottom of the hill where she was currently struggling.

All the training and skills she had accumulated through the years took a back seat while she scrambled to pull air back into her lungs. The impact of the fall had done more than a number on her.

"Your hands go into your pockets at all, and I cut them off." The man's voice came out strong and full of oxygen. He was a few yards away but closing that distance fast.

JJ put her hands up in defense. Her leg muscles worked double-time to push her to stand.

"Un-unarmed," she managed to say.

The man kept coming.

JJ hadn't seen the state of Josiah's house after his attack, but she had seen the man. The cuts, the blood… She could fight against a knife but, the truth was, knives scared her simply for the fact that she could imagine what a cut felt like. The pain and sting. It was all too easy to imagine what the man could do without having it actually happen.

"Stop—stop," she said around a cough.

He still didn't.

So JJ took a lesson out of her godfather's page of parenting.

"Chicken—chicken wings!"

Her voice had found some more of its strength. The man she'd just yelled at heard what she said loud and clear.

And it made him slow.

"What?" he asked.

JJ took a tentative step backward.

If she hadn't fallen, she could have cut off his attempt to pull his knife out. Now? She needed help. Preferably her partner with the gun. JJ, at least, assumed Price had his service weapon on him.

Either way, two people against one very sharp-looking knife sure sounded more strategic than one.

"Spaghetti!" JJ yelled, this time louder than before. "Fruit Roll-Ups, hummus, Pringles!"

The man's eyebrow rose but the rest of him paused.

She had confused him enough to have him stop in his tracks.

The second he stalled, she went into gear.

JJ spun around and ran along the bottom of the hill, hoping for an easier way up than the tumultuous path she had taken down. The man cussed behind her. She wasn't going to be a damsel from a movie and look back. Instead, she tucked her chin and made fast work of searching out more even ground. She couldn't have been that far away from Price. Once she was at the top of the slope, she could probably see where he was detaining the man from Jamie Bell's house.

"Winnie Collins!"

JJ came to an almost instant halt.

She whirled around, utterly confused.

The man with the knife also stopped but he kept his knife pointed out at her.

"See? I can yell stuff too." He moved the aim of his knife to a spot in the distance. "But I'm guessing you don't have spaghetti or chicken tied up in your car, do you? That's where our things are different."

JJ's stomach dropped past her feet.

Maybe she hadn't heard him properly?

"Who?"

The man looked fragile by himself. There were wrinkles along his face, a scar at the side of his jaw, and a slight lean to him, like he had an injury somewhere along his leg or back?

Had Josiah managed to wound him during their fight?

The knife, however, was the line in the sand between them.

That was, until he said Winnie's name.

He said it again too.

"Winnie Collins. Your boyfriend's little girl." He smirked. "What? You think we were following you just for fun? I'm here to trade. I can do that with you while my friend deals with dear Dad Deputy."

The knife didn't seem so bad anymore.

It was maybe five inches long, some of that the metal hilt. The blade wasn't serrated and didn't retract. If she could stay on the back of it, she could handle it.

"She's in your car? Where's that? We didn't see any cars when we came in."

The man's smirk was simmering. He thought he had her.

"We hid ours with yours, of course. Since you two seem to be so good at being so sneaky. Too bad the girl didn't have your stealth."

Price's truck was at the western gate of the Becker Farm. The walk to the barn had been around two minutes. They hadn't gone into the woods but instead skirted them, careful to stay somewhat within the tree line.

JJ pointed in the direction he had.

"You want to trade me for Winnie?" she asked.

He nodded.

"Why?"

Did they know who she was, or had she become a pawn to use against Price?

The man's smirk melted away at that.

He was impatient.

It probably didn't help that his friend hadn't rejoined him. The last they had seen of their partners had been Price wrestling cuffs on the other man.

"We'll talk at the car," he growled. "Get going or you and the girl will be sorry."

JJ didn't weigh her options. She knew what she needed to do.

She nodded and started in the direction of the western gate. She kept her hands up. The man didn't hesitate. She could hear his shoes crunching over the leaves behind her.

Then he changed the game yet again.

"You sure acted better than that girl when we grabbed her," he added. "She was still blubbering when we left."

JJ stumbled. It slowed her down two steps. The man moved diagonally just behind her.

"She cried that much?" JJ ventured.

The man snorted.

"Buckets. But I guess most girls would lose it when they know they're in danger. Why? You can't believe your kid doesn't have the stones to not make a peep?"

That cinched it.

"No," she said. "She just doesn't seem the type."

THE MAN HAD some moves, Price would give him that. He got his cuffs out and on one wrist before the man was a snake in the grass. He slithered this way and that until Price lost his grip.

The second the man realized he was free, he was off and running.

It surprised Price. He thought the man he'd fought in Jamie Bell's house would have more, well, fight in him. Especially without the threat of fighting against the speed of a fire. But the man turned into a rabbit and made quick time of leaving the land next to the barn and running right along the tree line like it was nothing.

Part of Price wanted to change direction and chase after JJ and the other man. The other part wanted to keep up with his suspect *for* JJ. He was a part of her family's trouble. Which meant he could help lead them to a way to solve it.

He couldn't let that lead go.

Not when he was this close.

I'm actually really good at fighting.

JJ's words from the elevator echoed in his head as he made the final decision to track his guy. Then it was an all-out race.

Price put everything he had into each step. His lungs burned. His muscles complained. The service weapon in its holster at his hip beneath his jacket bumped along for the ride. He wasn't going to pull it out.

Not yet.

Not when all he had to do was—

They were moving along the curve of the tree line when the open land between the woods and the western gate came into view.

Instead of a big nothing, Price nearly lost his footing when he saw a whole someone trucking it in the same direction as the gate.

It was a woman.

"JJ?" he yelled out, voice strong despite his running.

Thankfully, it carried.

He could see her head turn their way.

But she didn't stop.

If anything, she picked up speed toward the gate.

It was unsettling.

It also was distracting.

The man he was chasing had slowed.

It cost him the lead.

Price grabbed hold of the back of his jacket and pulled him to stop. They were both going too fast. The move threw off their respective balances and they hit the ground. Price was ready for it though. The man was not.

He yelled out as the ground was unkind to him.

Pain pulsed into Price's knees and palms, but he was in control right after.

He took the cuffs still attached to the man's wrist and finished the job.

"Don't—don't move," Price said through clenched teeth.

The man didn't try. He was making a noise between a whimper and a groan. Price didn't wait to see if he was hurt or not. He was staring into the distance.

JJ had made it to the gate, but he couldn't see what she was doing.

Then she switched direction and was coming back at him.

Like a moth drawn to a flame, Price's feet had him running toward her before he even realized what he was doing.

That run became feral as he realized two things.

One, JJ wasn't just running. She was running and holding herself. He couldn't see where it was coming from, but blood stained her shirt. And not just a little.

Two, she was yelling something, and it was a desperate yell. Fear seemed to be seeping from her face right into her words.

And, when she was close enough, that fear went from her and exploded within him.

"Call Winnie!" she yelled.

Price collided with JJ, stopping them both. JJ kept yelling despite being tucked into his chest.

"Call Winnie now!"

All the blood in Price's body seemed to freeze. He didn't question her. It didn't feel like there was time. He pulled his cell phone out of his pocket and fumbled to unlock it. He had Winnie's caller ID up and the call started within the space of a terrified heartbeat.

JJ angled herself against him, so her face was pressed

against his, phone between both of their ears. Her breathing was ragged. Price would later realize his was too. In that moment though, every fiber of his being was agonizing through a ringback tone that seemed to last forever.

However, it only really lasted two rings.

"Hey, Dad." Winnie's voice came through loud and clear.

"Are you okay?" he asked.

"I'm bored at work but yeah. Why?"

JJ deflated against him. Price had to reinforce his hold around her. She kept her face against his and spoke into the phone before he could respond.

"Winnie, go give your phone to Corrie," she rasped out. "I—I need to talk to her."

JJ reached up and took the phone as Winnie said an unsure okay. She pushed off Price and dug into the bag she had been wearing across her chest. It was covered in blood. She unzipped it and took her own cell phone out. She handed it over.

Corrie answered the phone before she could explain.

"Corrie? This is JJ. I need you to close the coffee shop and drive Winnie to the sheriff's department. Right now. Don't stop for anyone or anything. Got me?"

Price had never heard JJ sound so cold.

She met his eye.

"I'll stay on the line with you until you get there."

Price understood her phone now.

She wanted him to call the department.

Something bad must have happened. Something more than the blood on her.

Not only had he never heard her sound so cold, Price hadn't seen JJ look so scared.

He nodded.

Then he called the sheriff directly.

Liam answered quickly.

Price didn't waste either of their time.

"I need two cars and an ambulance over at the Becker Farm. But, Sheriff, I need you to stay at the department. I'm sending my daughter your way."

Price shared another long look with JJ.

He didn't know what was going on but, in that moment, he trusted no one more than the woman who had been leading a double life.

Chapter Eighteen

The world had a funny way of still turning, no matter what JJ was feeling.

She could be confused, happy, healthy, bleeding, disgusted, enraged, missing her mama, craving ice cream, thinking about that one smell of disinfectant that only ever seemed to exist in the hospital hallway…

She could be in a plane, on a couch, wearing a fancy dress or hanging upside down in car drenched in rain with a sea of glass beneath her hair…

And it just didn't seem to matter to the world at large.

It kept turning. It kept going.

It kept leaving JJ in its dust to figure it all out so she could catch up before the next swing got her.

She was standing behind a two-way glass, staring into an interrogation room and looking at a man handcuffed to the table. His world had him angry, frustrated, defiant. All three were written on his face and spelled out clear in how he fought everyone tooth and nail since he'd been arrested.

"He wouldn't give us a name and we can't find him in any database." Sheriff Weaver's badge was shining on his belt. He seemed to be handling his world in stride. Ever since the call with Price, he hadn't taken a step he didn't want to take.

Not even when it had come to Price explaining that they couldn't give answers to everything just yet.

That *just yet* wasn't going to extend that much further, though, if JJ had to guess.

Especially since she was about to show the man in charge that she wasn't just some bystander.

Instead of being helpless at the window, JJ sighed.

"I think we need to talk now, if you don't mind."

A few minutes later and JJ's world brought her to a small room with a big table. The sheriff sat in a chair at its side, Price stood near its head and JJ felt lost in between. Her arm hurt, her leg was already bruising, and everything she had worked for felt like it had already crumbled.

The best she could do now was hope to be standing again when the next swing around came for her.

JJ started by tapping her cell phone on the top of the table.

"I can find out who that man is, most likely, but I need to ask for something first." She started in the last place she meant to. Bartering with the head of the law when she was in no position to do so.

Sheriff Weaver, to his credit, didn't immediately shut her down.

"I would really appreciate if we could not connect me with any of what's happened," she continued. "Any mention of my name in reports or posts or interviews. I'm not saying make it where Price was alone during everything, but just don't put JJ Shaw in any kind of writing. Ideally, call in the people who saw me today and ask them to keep my name out of their mouths too."

Sheriff Weaver tilted his head a little. He'd been rumored to be a quiet, loner of a man until he had met his now-wife, just as he was also rumored to be a no-nonsense man when it came to his job. JJ could see that no-nonsense man coming through now. He spoke right to the point.

"My people don't talk idly. I don't either. That said, I don't think a person in this town could promise that your name won't come up one way or the other."

JJ sighed again.

"But we can slow talk down, at least," she said. "It could give me time to…adjust."

Price took a step closer to JJ so that he was facing the sheriff more directly at her side.

"I've already talked to everyone who saw her. They said they won't say anything."

JJ cast a quick look at Price.

How long had they been separated that he had that time?

He had been with her when the EMT had bandaged her arm. He had been with her when Detective Williams and Deputy Little had shown up. He had been with her when they had found the man she'd fought.

When had he left her side?

She had seen how tightly he'd hugged Winnie when they made it to the department. How all of him had dragged down in relief that she was really okay.

Was she missing time in between?

JJ didn't ask. The sheriff looked between them. She couldn't read his expression.

Was she even trying to?

JJ's phone sat on the table between them.

She didn't want to use it; she knew she would.

"I know someone who might be able to find out who that man is," she went on. "But before I do, I have to warn you that he's a source I need to protect. I would *like* for my name to stay out of all of this, but I *need* his to stay absolutely clear of it. Will that be okay?"

She added the last part to feel more polite but, the truth was, even she heard the lack of wiggle room in what she phrased as a request.

Sheriff Weaver didn't kick up a fuss.

"I'll respect your terms as long as it doesn't run the risk of harming anyone. Yourself included."

That wasn't a quick no.

That wasn't a permanent yes.

JJ had little room to ask for more.

"Let me make the call and then I'll tell you everything," she added. "I'll be right back."

The sheriff okayed the move. JJ wasn't sure what she would have done had he not. She felt like the world definitely wasn't slowing down as her feet led her to the only room in the department that she thought would keep her shielded from the growing anxiety in her chest.

The ladies' room had two stalls inside, and both were empty. JJ felt a tinge of disappointment. She didn't have to pretend to be okay for a little longer. She didn't have to play her role as calm and mysterious.

She didn't have to pretend that she wasn't spiraling.

Instead, she was faced with her reflection.

The bandage along her arm was long. She had been lucky to only get the long cut. Lucky that it hadn't needed stitches. Her shirt was ruined, stained beyond saving, but it was her phone that pulled at her attention like a beacon in the darkness.

She went to her contacts, but couldn't go past the first name on the list.

Dad.

A wallop of anguish slammed into JJ's chest. She didn't want to see herself anymore. She grabbed the sink with one hand and clutched the phone to her chest with the other as she moved out of the mirror's scope. Her back hit the tiled wall between the sink and the wall with a painful thud. She closed her eyes as a lump formed in her throat.

She smelled her strawberry shampoo.

The sound of the door opening made her open her eyes.

JJ could feel the part of her used to putting on a mask try its hardest to bring up a polite smile and a reasonable excuse for why she was all but crying in the corner of the bathroom, covered in blood and clutching her phone.

But then she saw who had come inside.

She watched as Price turned around, shut the door and locked it.

She watched as he walked slowly to the spot in front of her.

She watched as he fixed her with a look that was as quiet as velvet.

Then he took her face in his hands.

"Thank you." His words were soft but genuine. That confused her even more.

"For what?" she asked.

Price ran one hand down so his index finger and thumb could hold her chin.

"You've spent so much time trying to stay out of the spotlight as much as possible but, today, you didn't hesitate to put yourself in the middle of it. For Winnie." He sighed. A small smile turned up the corner of his lips. "That was a mighty move, Miss Shaw."

JJ expected another thank you. Instead, she got something else entirely.

Price pressed his lips against hers in a kiss that was gentle. Quiet. Velvet.

It was only when he broke it that JJ realized she had broken first.

All the stress of the last few hours, the last few days, the last few years, pushed JJ down into Price's chest. She was crying soon after.

Price was simple with his actions as he was with his kiss. He wrapped his arms around her and didn't say a word.

"I'D SAY WHAT you did was make some dang questionable choices but, I guess, at the end of the day I might have done the same."

The sheriff ran a hand down his face. They were in his office, but neither was sitting down. Liam was leaning against the corner of his desk and Price was leaning against the wall. Both had their bodies tilted toward the door. They didn't want to be overheard and had already buttoned up once when Winnie had come in asking for money for the vending machines.

Now they were alone again to circle the same drain they had been circling the last half hour.

"I would have looped you in had I thought it would do more good than harm," Price admitted. "I thought we still had time."

It was a sticky situation, no matter who had done the sticking. After JJ had made the call to her source, she had sat down and told her story to Liam while Price sat at her side. Her telling the sheriff had been a different experience from when she had told him. She'd been completely detached. Maybe because she was tired. Maybe because she was hurt. Either way, it came out as if being read off a teleprompter by a newscaster finishing off a twelve-hour shift.

It had been a far cry from the woman he had held in his arms in the bathroom.

"Up until now, there's been nothing to grab on to either," Price pointed out. "We were already looking for Josiah's and Georgie's attackers. All I got a day before you was the backstory."

Sheriff Weaver actually snorted.

"I have a feeling you have a few more details than me. Miss Shaw in there might have given me her story, but don't think I didn't notice the few nudges you sent her way."

He wasn't wrong.

When JJ had been about to mention her break-in and subsequent fight with Price at Josiah Teller's, Price had put pressure against her. He trusted the sheriff and knew he was a lot more lenient when it came to going off the books in certain situations but, in that moment, Price had found himself oddly protective.

JJ had gotten the hint and left the search out as well as her intention to conduct one at Jamie Bell's house. Instead, she had simply stated her findings as definitive "They aren't my brother" statements for each.

Marty Goldman's adventure had been a bit different.

Just as Lawson Cole's name and attack had changed the game for the sheriff while Winnie's mention had changed the players.

What Price had told JJ in the bathroom had been true. He recognized what she had done, even if the others didn't. When the man in the woods had lied about having Winnie, he had unknowingly forced JJ to pick her anonymity or the immediate action of making sure his daughter had been, and would continue to be, okay.

Price hadn't been in those woods. He hadn't seen her have to decide, but the best he could guess was that she had made the decision in record time.

Not only that, she had gone up against an armed man with nothing more than her hands to try and get to Winnie as fast as possible.

JJ Shaw had already sacrificed a normal life to try and save a man in secret. Now, she had sacrificed her identity at just the possibility that his daughter was in danger.

The least Price could do was protect as much of that identity as possible, even if that meant withholding from his friend, his boss and his colleagues.

JJ Shaw had told the truth to help him.

Lying to protect her?

Price had decided that was the least he could do.

Now he fixed his friend with an apologetic smile but didn't tell him he was wrong.

Sheriff Weaver, to his surprise, returned his own smile.

"I know it might be a strange thing to say, but sometimes you remind me of my wife," he said.

Price placed a hand to his chest.

"Considering your wife's nickname is Sheriff Trouble, and she's one of the most epic people I've ever met? I'm honored."

The sheriff rolled his eyes.

"While she is those things, I meant the whole calculations thing." Liam tapped his head. "You're talking to me, but your numbers are running all around the people you're trying to keep safe. I'm even guessing you already have a plan to try and do that, with or without any of our help."

He wasn't wrong.

Since he had seen that Winnie was alright, Price had already started putting together a list of what happened next. Some of the items on that list had been dependent on how the sheriff would react to their news.

And how Lawson Cole would react to two of his lackeys being in custody.

"My main priority is making sure that Knife Guy's bluff of having Winnie doesn't ever become a reality," he pointed out. "If we can do that while running down Lawson Cole and his group while keeping JJ and her brother out of harm's way, I'd be counting my blessings every day for the rest of my life."

The sheriff nodded. Any teasing friendship disappeared. He was nothing but the sheriff when he spoke again.

"We'll hope that JJ's source comes through and can tell us who our man in custody is. Ideally, they'll know who the guy she sent to the hospital is too. Though, we won't be able to see him for a good while. Last I heard he might not make it."

They hadn't talked about it yet, but the fact was that JJ hadn't just fought against the man in the woods. She'd nearly killed him. Though he had gotten his licks in on her before she had gotten the upper hand. Price had spent the better part of an hour trying to convince her to go to the hospital. The only reason he hadn't been more forceful about it was thanks to the EMT who had taken a good look at the cut before bandaging it.

"As for Anthony Boyd and Connor Clark, I'm reading Darius in on the bare-bone facts when he gets back," Liam continued. "Between the two of us, we can try to figure out where they came from."

This was a point of contention.

The urge to protect JJ flared again.

The sheriff must have sensed it. He held up his hand in a stop motion.

"Your lady isn't the only one who can be clever when she wants to be," he added. "We'll keep everything low profile as well as keeping JJ's name away from all of this. Trust me."

The tension in Price's shoulders lessened but only minimally.

Liam's seemed to tighten.

His voice came out with undeniable command.

"Don't think though for one moment I'm letting you continue running around this town playing detective without a badge for it," he said. "It's time for you to leave. As of right now, Price Collins, you are officially benched."

Chapter Nineteen

Price stood shoulder to shoulder with Winnie. Each had a bag at their sides. Both were staring at the house behind JJ with grade A poker faces.

"I know it doesn't look like much, but the inside isn't as bad as, well, this." She motioned back to the work-in-progress two-story that she had purchased before coming to Seven Roads.

"It's…charming," Winnie tried, smiling as she did so. "Right? Kind of like one of those nice older homes you see on HGTV that everyone ends up wanting."

She not so subtly elbowed her dad's side when he didn't immediately respond.

Price took the hint. With his duffel bag held up by his hand over his shoulder and wearing his baseball shirt and jeans, he reminded JJ of a college student coming home after a long week at school. Young, carefree and ready to eat.

It wasn't a bad look.

In fact, it was almost nice to feel like he wasn't the same man who kept having to change his life around to deal with her problems.

Even now, he brought out that charm that JJ had begun to crave.

This time, it came out with some teasing.

"You definitely can't buy character like this much anymore." He grinned. "That's for sure."

"*Dad*," Winnie scolded in a not-so-quiet whisper. She sent another elbow to his ribs. He laughed and looked at JJ.

"As a former part-time home renovator, I understand that burden of the *before*. I ended up selling my fixer-upper to the sheriff's mother-in-law and haven't looked back." His words softened. "Don't stress about us. We're fine."

JJ wasn't so sure about that.

She said as much while leading them to the front porch.

"Let's remember you said that."

The old home off Whatley Bend was the center of JJ's cover story. She had purchased it as the reason for coming to Seven Roads, as well as the blueprint for her future. It had been chattered about in the gossip mill for a while when she had first come to town, but when no progress had been visibly made, that chatter had died down. It helped that Janice Wilkins's former home was less than accessible and not near any locations or public areas remotely interesting.

If anything, it felt like an outsider to JJ.

A part of the town but not, at the same time.

Maybe that's why she liked it, despite never having had any experience or desire to buy and renovate a house.

JJ bypassed the urge to explain why the siding was warped in places, wood was rotted off others and the landscaping could use a few—if not several—helping hands, and led them into the foyer. Winnie slipped off her shoes, but Price kept his and the duffel bag on. He had work to do, but he stayed long enough to listen to the two-bit tour.

"Everything in here works, but just isn't that nice-looking yet," she said, sweeping her arms toward the stairs just off the space. "This goes to two bedrooms, one bonus room that looks like a wasteland where supplies and tools have gone to die, and two bathrooms that *look* like they should also be in the wasteland. But I swear, everything is clean."

JJ went on to explain the bottom floor's layout, make a few excuses for her utter lack of progress on the house again and then showed Winnie to the bedroom.

"Is all this furniture yours? I thought it might be empty here." Winnie eyed the guest bedroom's yellow-painted iron-rod bed covered in a paisley bedspread.

JJ laughed a little at that.

"A few things are mine, but most of what you see came from Janice Wilkins," JJ answered. "Since she was downsizing and wanted to move quickly, she offered the furnishings and I agreed. It seemed like less hassle on my part at the time."

Price had fallen behind a little, but JJ could see him across the hall, peeking into the bonus room.

JJ's face flushed with heat.

"She even told me to keep a few things I didn't need," she said hurriedly. "Including a set of rusted dumbbells, a crib and a small collection of cow saltshakers."

Price had no doubt seen at least the first two of those items standing visible in the bonus room. The dumbbells were surprisingly compact. The crib was not.

Suddenly, JJ felt more self-conscious.

Thankfully, Price didn't hover.

He filled the doorframe and tapped his duffel bag.

"I'm curious about that saltshaker cow-thing, but first, let's get set up."

The next hour or so, Price did what Winnie had called a security reset. Security cameras and motion lights that he had brought were mounted outside in strategic places, new locks were installed on the front and back doors and sensors were placed along the seals of the windows on the first floor.

JJ was in awe of how thorough he was being. Though she wasn't sure it was necessary. Sheriff Weaver, Price and JJ had put their heads together for where they should lie low for a little while on the off chance that Lawson and his remaining men decided to strike again. His house was out of the question, the safe house the sheriff had used before had been taken off the market and JJ's house had also been put on the do-not-chance list. When the sheriff had realized that not even he knew where exactly JJ's work-in-progress home was, it convinced the three of them that Janice Wilkins's old home was the ticket.

"We don't know if Lawson, or whoever, even knows you were a part of what happened on the Becker Farm. But considering you went head-to-head with him at the convention center, I'm sure you're someone of interest to them," the sheriff had pointed out to her. "They may not make a move now that there's been a big fuss with two of their guys, but keeping the two people they'd probably use against Price *with* as far out of the way as we can is the best we can do."

Another one of those butterflies had fluttered its way around JJ's stomach at the mention of her being important to Price. She tried to remind herself that he was simply a good guy and proximity alone had gotten her the honor.

Still, she found herself fighting another wave of heat as he peeked his head around the kitchen door when he was finishing up and called her name.

"I could use your expertise real quick if you don't mind," he said. "Follow me outside."

JJ did. Each step after him she tried to remember what it felt like to wear the mask that had hidden her emotions as best she could.

That imaginary mask fell right back off when he took her by the shoulders and spun her back around to face the house. His hands were warm. She could feel them through the fabric of her shirt.

"Okay, Miss Sneak," he said. "Let's say you want to break into this bad boy. Show me all the ways you would so I can adjust my defenses if I need to."

JJ laughed.

"Wait? Is this what you think my expertise is? Sneaking?"

Price shrugged. He moved his hold from her shoulders to draping one arm around them, moving his body to her side. He was still facing the house.

"I'd actually say that your expertise is being surprising," he said. "Part of that charm just so happens to be getting into places with locked doors."

JJ was glad that his attention was elsewhere. There was no way her face wasn't the color of a stop sign.

"I think your expertise is making people with not-so-ordinary lives feel normal," she offered. "I once let it slip to my ex that I could theoretically hack into our university's website if I wanted, and it inspired a meltdown from him."

"Why?"

It was JJ's turn to shrug.

"I guess I ruined his image of me. Which is wild to me, considering the JJ Shaw he knew was a lot less reserved than the JJ Shaw in Seven Roads."

Price let out a sigh. It moved her body too.

"What can I say? Some people freak out a little when they realize they aren't the most interesting person in the room. That's why I always tell Winnie to never settle for someone who doesn't keep you guessing."

JJ already knew that Price was single. She had known for a while, even before they had been thrown together. Yet her curiosity soared to the forefront and her question came out before she could think to censor it.

"Was her mom like that? Always keeping you guessing?"

Forget the stop-sign red. JJ felt like her face had gone directly into fire. She hadn't meant to overstep that far. She tried to backtrack in a flash.

"Sorry, that's too personal. I just haven't heard you or her or even Corrie talk about her, so I was just curious."

She glanced over to see the corner of Price's lips turn up.

"Don't apologize. I'd wonder too," he said. "As smart as Winnie's mom was, she was just as fun. Straight *A*s and straight chaos. She'd be the cool, calm, collected student at school and then would rope us into so many different kinds of shenanigans that not a day went by with her that I didn't feel like I was in some kind of sitcom." The smile didn't leave. It simply softened. "But then she got pregnant, and we had to really sit down and think about things. She's a good woman, but she never wanted to be a mom. That used to drive me up the wall, but now that I'm older and I've seen some things, I respect the resolve she had back then. She knew what she wanted, what she was capable of, and stuck to her guns. Then, on top of that, she gave me room to do the same. She never once pushed me to be a dad."

He patted himself on the chest in a teasing way, but JJ had a feeling he was being genuine.

"I chose that job myself. Pay's bad but I don't mind the work." His smile amped right back on up. "She still reaches out and emails with Winnie on occasion, but as far as interesting to me now, it's just not there. Not many people have had me on swivel either since we parted ways. Though I did date a lady who had a doll collection that took up *two* of her bedrooms a few years back. I bet she'd get a kick out of that cow shaker collection Ms. Wilkins left you."

Price laughed at his own comment. His arm was still around her. It was comfortable. *He* was comfortable.

And, apparently, to him JJ was interesting.

The thought warmed her.

It also saddened her.

She couldn't afford to be interesting anymore. Not until she could find her brother, stop Lawson and get herself into a position to keep the last of her family safe. No one could ever find out that Elle and Able Ortiz's children were alive.

Which was why JJ had decided long ago that she didn't have the luxury of a life for just her.

Interesting or not.

NIGHT FELL AND no one from the department or elsewhere made a peep. JJ and Winnie had put together an easy supper from what they had taken from their house and the three of them had enjoyed it while watching an HGTV show on Winnie's phone.

Price forgot for a bit that them being there wasn't exactly in their plans. It just felt nice and relaxing.

JJ fit in and that was nice.

It was also something that Winnie commented on after she had gotten ready for bed. Price sat on the ugly paisley duvet cover and watched as his daughter tried to find the right words.

"I know you told me that you aren't going to lie to me, but you aren't going to tell me the entire truth either. I just want to say, I hope whatever is going on with JJ that you help her fix it. I don't know what did it, but something about her is different. Like she isn't trying as hard anymore in general. And it's not like a bad thing. I actually like this version of her more." Winnie made a frustrated noise. "I guess what I'm trying to say is that I'd like to see more of this JJ, and I hope whatever had her so pinned up before gets straightened out. And that you're the one to help her do that."

Price's eyebrow rose sky-high at that.

"Me? Why me?"

At this, Winnie shrugged.

"Because you two are a good team."

It was a simple answer but one that sank heavy against Price. He told his daughter good-night and spent the next hour alone downstairs. It wasn't until he heard footfalls from the main bedroom that he decided that feeling needed some clarification.

He needed some clarification.

He took the stairs one at a time, but there was a new anxiousness in him. It was still there as he went past his daughter's closed door and still there when he lightly knocked on JJ's. Even after JJ opened the door and came into view, that feeling was still moving around there in his chest.

"We need to talk," he said.

There was no hope in the world for him, he'd realize later, after JJ nodded and then stepped aside.

"Come in."

Chapter Twenty

Price still had on his baseball shirt and jeans, but the look he was sporting now wasn't at all what JJ would describe as carefree. She stepped back another step after he closed the door behind him. He locked it too.

"What's wrong?" she asked, worried that she had somehow missed something and an attack was imminent.

Yet, the only target in his sights was her.

Price closed most of the distance between them in one clean stride. She noticed stubble along his jaw. She could smell some kind of spice from his skin. JJ had to tip her chin back a little just to look up into his eyes.

Why was he this close?

Did he think Winnie would overhear him and was trying for privacy?

She was at the other end of the hall with thick walls between her and them. Surely shutting the door had been enough.

Then again, maybe privacy wasn't at all on his mind.

When he spoke, his words were loud and clear.

"What about us?"

The volume and delivery might have been decisive, but JJ was as confused as ever.

"What about us?" she repeated.

Price gave one nod and brought his index finger to her shoulder. The small amount of pressure he placed there was brief but it sure did radiate after he pulled it back. He tapped himself next.

"You've got all of these plans on what to do to find your brother, what to do with Lawson and his group, and you even said you know what you want after it's all said and done, right?"

JJ nodded slowly.

"Yes. I don't want anyone to know my connection to him, to my parents."

"But you'll stay here? In Seven Roads, right?"

She nodded again.

"I don't think I could leave him after everything my parents went through."

"So, Seven Roads is settled then. You—this house?—is where you'll stay."

JJ was following the words, but she couldn't hang on to the feeling behind them. It felt…angry.

"That's the plan. Why? What's wrong?"

Price put his hands on his hips. It might have looked humorous had she understood what had inspired the now-obvious frustration.

"Winnie said something earlier and it got me thinking that…all these heavy things we've talked about, we never really hammered out the details of the *after*. I mean the brother thing, not wanting to reveal yourself, I get that. Though, to be honest, I was already trying to think of ways to persuade *you* to maybe rethink that too. But, that aside, I started thinking about all of these conversations with you. Then I started remembering your looks and then things that are *there* but not really there for you."

JJ knew her eyes had widened. He paused and searched

her face. Then he ran a hand down his own and dropped the other from his hip. She watched him turn around, take a few steps away, blow out a breath and come right back to the same spot so close to her.

"You smile, you say the words, but there's this—this space between them all," he continued. "You have convinced yourself that you *need* to keep up the life of the JJ Shaw who first came to Seven Roads to try and find her brother, but then I think you feel the *want* of actually living a life of this JJ Shaw. Of the woman who can hack into websites, fight close combat in elevators, make my kid laugh and fit right into my everyday life without so much as lifting a finger to try."

JJ didn't dare move.

Not even a blush stirred.

Price took another breath in but didn't walk away this time.

Instead, he shook his head.

"I realized just now that I think I know what you're going to do once we find your brother, and I'm hoping I'm wrong. So I'm asking again. What about us? What about me? What do you feel like you need to do if everything works out with Lawson and your brother? And, what about if it doesn't? Because, I'll be honest. I'm not like you, JJ. There's no space between I'm getting lost in. I know what I want, and I know what I need and it's one and the same."

His gaze dropped to her lips.

He watched her ask the only response she could manage in the moment.

"And what's that?"

He put his hand against her cheek. His eyes didn't leave her lips.

"You."

They hadn't talked about their first kiss even once after

it happened in the department bathroom. A part of JJ had wanted to. A part hadn't. It had been an intense day and emotions were running high and he had comforted her. That was it, right?

She had needed that answer.

She hadn't wanted it.

Price was right. There was that space in between the two lives she had been living.

Price was also warm.

His lips connected for another kiss. There was no denying this time everything was different.

Price pressed his body flush against hers. He tilted her head back slightly and paused. JJ realized he was waiting for her to accept him or reject him.

There was no getting lost in between for her anymore.

JJ applied her own pressure against his lips, against his body. That was all the man needed. His tongue parted her lips, and their kiss went from a solitary instance to an all-consuming constant. JJ's hands wound their way up his neck and tangled in his hair. Price's hands cradled and roamed until they were no longer standing.

The bed in the main room was firm. It didn't give as Price laid her down its middle, it didn't cave as he started to take off their clothes and it didn't buckle as she arched against his fingers sliding between her underwear and skin. He maneuvered inside of her with one hand and adjusted her against him with the other.

JJ moved against his mouth.

He held her close, working until she couldn't take it anymore.

Then he adjusted again.

This time JJ helped.

She returned in kind and stripped him until there was nothing between their bodies but heat and sweat.

Price had already made it clear that he was a fan but feeling him against her was an experience that excited her to no end. When they were done with the appetizers, he devoured the main course. She used the last of her willpower to not call out as he pushed deep inside of her.

There was no space between them at all after that.

PRICE WOKE UP feeling good.

Well, not all good. He was sore in spots from his fight the day before and from the party, but who cared about some bruises and pulled muscles? He felt good on good, and he knew exactly why.

He rolled over, ready to cuddle up to a Miss JJ Shaw. Instead, he grabbed at a whole bunch of empty space.

Price popped up like a daisy in spring.

He palmed his phone on the nightstand, hoping there were no security alerts that he had somehow slept through, but heard an explanation for the lack of JJ.

He heard water sloshing from the bedroom's attached bathroom and let out a breath of relief.

Then he got to smiling again.

Price rolled out of bed and went to knock on the bathroom door.

"Yeah?" JJ called.

"Can I come in?" he asked, hand already on the doorknob. He waited though as she took a beat to respond.

"Um, sure."

The bathroom was full of steam. The bathtub was full of JJ and bubbles.

Price eyed both with a grin.

JJ's face was already flushed from the heat, but he thought

he might have seen it turn a deeper shade of red. She collected an island of bubbles and pulled them closer to her chest.

"I know we showered last night but, well, I felt like I needed this too."

Price laughed and put his hands up in defense.

"Hey, I'm not judging your need to soak. In fact, the idea doesn't sound half bad…"

He nodded to the spot opposite her.

She shook her head but laughed.

"I don't think so, sir. You're just going to have to wait your turn. I'm a one-person bath kind of woman. Especially when this woman is in desperate need of Icy Hot on several places." That blush seemed to flare to life again. She lowered her voice a little. "Plus, I'm not pushing my luck with Winnie being around. I don't know about you, but I'm not that eager to scar a teenager like that."

Price laughed.

"I guess you're not wrong there," he said. "Can I at least chat with you while you soak?"

JJ looked surprised.

"Chat with me?"

"Yeah. Like you said, I like talking. I especially like talking to you. Can I sit?"

That surprise was still there but she nodded.

"Just don't try any funny business. This is a casual, platonic soak."

Price pulled his towel off of the rack and folded it into a seat next to her on the tile. It made him a good height to lean his elbow on the lip of the tub. He put his head on his hand and stared across the water at said casual, platonic soaker.

JJ rolled her eyes.

"Maybe saying yes was a bad idea," she commented.

Price shrugged.

"I'm just admiring the view, is all. Can't blame a guy for that."

Where he thought she might complain once more, JJ simply rolled her eyes again. A small smile played at her lips though.

It was nice to see her like this.

Not the naked part, not the vulnerable part.

It was the trusting that had him feeling all types of ways.

JJ Shaw had opened up to him about her past, she had let him into her bed, but neither was a promise to let anything else happen past that. He'd asked her about them, about her future plans, but he hadn't gotten an answer. Not a verbal one at least.

Her letting him sit there now meant more to him than she knew.

Because the choices she was making now had nothing to do with Lawson Cole, the search for her brother or keeping her secret identity safe.

It was just a woman soaking in a bubble bath, talking to a man who had fallen for her all while sitting on damp tile in his boxers.

Because, while he hadn't spelled it out to a tee, Price had also realized that he had fallen for JJ Shaw.

Straight to the bottom of the bottom.

Did JJ return his feelings?

He wasn't sure how much.

He also decided not to push her right now to ask.

Especially after catching sight of something he'd already seen in bed the night before.

It was the same scar he had seen before they had left for the party. Angry, shining, and most likely undeniably painful when it had first happened.

A scar from the accident.

It sobered Price a bit, though he made sure to keep a small smile on.

Maybe it wasn't enough.

JJ went from bantering and dove right into the complicated world outside of the bathroom walls around them.

"You never asked who my source was," she said. "I feel wrong somehow not telling you, now with everything we've been through."

"You don't have to," he pointed out.

She didn't hesitate.

"It's Riker. My godfather. I can't remember if I told you or not, but when I went off to college, he married a really nice woman who ended up needing to take care of her parents. So they moved out of state and they're still out there being all cute and happy." She sighed. It moved some of the bubbles nearest her mouth. "It's why I never told Riker about Mr. Cole coming to see me. Why I never told him about Mom surviving and having my brother. Why I never told him the real reason I left the city for a small town I'd only visited once or twice. He just—he just has a lot of guilt for what happened, a lot of regrets. I know, because we both tried to work on our feelings about everything through the years. He eventually said he found peace, but I know it eats him up that we never got the justice my parents deserved."

She started to swirl some of the bubbles around. Her eyes stayed on them as she continued.

"I didn't want to tell him what I'd been up to until I had it all sorted. I wanted to keep him in his peace as much as possible. But, if anyone could identify someone from the group, or know a different source that could, it's him. And since they might try and use Winnie against you, I didn't want to just wait and hope. So, yesterday I sent him pictures and described the men. Said they were working for Lawson Cole and asked if he could help."

"What did he say?"

She kept swirling.

"He had a lot of questions, but I told him I didn't have the time. That I was okay, and I'd explain everything once he got back to me. I told him I needed it fast. Then he said fine, he loved me and to stay safe." She sighed again. "A part of me wanted to keep him out of this forever because I know once he finds out about Mom still being alive…he's going to run himself into the ground with guilt, even though I don't think anyone would blame him for what happened."

"Just remind him that he saved a hurt, terrified kid and bluffed a powerful man into giving that girl a safe life to live. He did good."

JJ nodded.

"He did. But the second he finds out about my brother, he won't just keep living the life he has now. He'll rush back here and join the fight. He'll leave his happy, safe life and, well, that hurts my heart if I'm being honest."

Price reached his hand out and took JJ's in his. He let it sink a little in the warm water. Her dark eyes found his and sunk there too.

"You don't need to worry about everything and everyone all at once," he said. "You also can't control or predict how people will feel. Let's work with what we have, let's deal with the now, and I promise you what comes next, I'll help you with. Okay?"

With his other hand, he tapped the bottom of her chin and smiled.

"Soak in the tub, not in what-ifs."

It took a few moments, but JJ cracked a smile.

"That was incredibly cheesy, Deputy Collins."

He shrugged.

"Doesn't mean it wasn't true."

She admitted he was right, and their conversation went to the bathroom around them, then the house renovations as a whole. It was normal and comfortable. JJ also held his hand the entire time.

It wasn't until she was finished, dried and dressed that Price made his way down to the kitchen to start breakfast. Winnie was just waking up and JJ stopped in her room to chat. He smiled as he descended the stairs to the sound of them talking in the background.

That smile was still playing at his lips when an alert on his phone and a text came in at the same time.

It was the sheriff. He was outside and wanted to talk.

Price didn't waste time. He threw on his boots and was at the sheriff's truck in a flash.

Liam looked like he hadn't slept much. He had a sandwich bag in his hand and threw it to Price when he was close enough.

"I went to Josiah's to have another look around to see if there was anything we might have missed. I found that in his room. I saw its partner yesterday or else I wouldn't have thought anything about it."

Price knew instantly what the small item inside the bag was.

An earring.

A blue one. Identical to the one JJ had on the day before. Price had meant to ask her where the missing one had gone but so much had already been happening.

Including Price's decision to keep JJ's search through Josiah Teller's house a secret.

He opened his mouth now to say *something*, but the sheriff cut him off.

"I'm not here to talk about that. I'm here to talk about the man who JJ fought in the woods." He let out a long, dragging breath. That tired came out strong with it. "He succumbed to his injuries late last night."

Price felt cold.

"He died," he said bluntly.

The sheriff nodded.

"That in itself would be a lot, especially for JJ, even though it was self-defense, but something else happened."

Price's already-bad feeling only deepened.

Hearing the words only added anger into it.

"Your neighbors called in about half an hour ago. Someone tore up your house, Price. And they left a message behind."

Price was seeing red, but he managed to read the note from the picture Liam held up for him.

He read it aloud, fire and ice in his veins.

"'A life for a life. Your daughter's next.'"

Chapter Twenty-One

Life got fast. Real fast.

Deputy Little and Deputy Gavin came out to the house and then the former Sheriff Trouble, Liam's wife, came too. It was one thing to bluff about having Winnie Collins. It was another to threaten her.

Price was at the helm of their meetings that took place in the dining room. JJ took part at first, but she had found herself in the bonus room, idly staring. It was only when Winnie came in after a while that JJ realized she had made a decision.

It wasn't a want.

It wasn't a need.

It was a *must*.

Still, JJ's feet were slow about it.

Maybe it was that space in between again that Price had talked about. She was getting lost in it.

She couldn't keep that going for too long though.

Seeing Winnie pretend to not be scared was a good reminder of that.

"Did you get kicked out too?" The teenager pointed down at the floor. The kitchen wasn't far off from their spot above. "I tried to join, and Dad used his cop voice on me. I appreciate that he never lies to me, but it still feels like I'm missing out on some things I might need to know."

Winnie came to a stop next to JJ. She was standing next to the crib of all things. Winnie peered over the edge and at the cow saltshaker collection that was resting inside. She didn't seem to need JJ to respond. She went on, just like her father did.

"This isn't the first time that he's been nervous, but I think that's when Dad really shines. I know he can be lame and goofy and sometimes just won't leave you alone, but he's also really good at his job. He's really good at keeping people safe. So, I wouldn't worry too much. He'll figure it all out."

JJ's heart tore.

She looked over at the girl, who was light-years ahead of her age.

There she was, trying to comfort JJ when it was JJ's fault she was the one being threatened.

A life for a life.

JJ had no doubt that it had been Lawson behind that message, using his father's old adage and twisting it for revenge.

Because the man *she* had fought in the woods had died.

No matter which way JJ looked at the situation, she was the cause of the trouble now in Seven Roads.

She was the reason Price's daughter—the person he loved most in the world—had gotten a death threat by the same people who had killed her father. Who had tried to kill her. Who now wanted to kill her brother.

JJ didn't ball her hand into a fist because she didn't want to damage what was resting on her palm. Instead, she looked at it for what felt like the hundredth time since Price had slyly given it to her without a second thought.

Winnie inclined her head to look.

"Oh, that's pretty," she said.

JJ smiled. It was one of the few she truly felt.

"Isn't it? My mom actually made it for me all by herself." She laughed. "This was actually the third attempt. My mom was really, really not a crafty person. It was a rule in my house that me and Dad wrapped all the presents and made the birthday banners and did anything that included tape, glue or having to deal with a billion little pieces."

JJ moved the earring closer so Winnie could see it better.

"So when she gave these to me for my tenth birthday, I really understood how special they were," she continued. "Then, when my dad let me know that she had been trying to make the perfect pair for weeks, I decided right then and there that *these* were my favorite pair of earrings that I'd ever own."

She ran a finger over the scratch mark that split the worn flower painted on the side.

"You see this scratch?" she asked. "Dad told me that she almost threw the whole thing away because she thought it ruined it. But Dad, knowing just how to make my mom feel better about anything, convinced her that *this* scratch is what makes these earrings so valuable. 'It's an Elle exclusive. The rarest of rare. No one else in the entire world will ever have this.'"

That smile started to slip away.

Winnie didn't notice.

Instead, she was impressed.

"I can't believe you still have them after all these years. Dad got me a pearl bracelet last Christmas and I still haven't been able to find where I lost it in my room."

JJ stopped rubbing the side of the earring.

Despite herself, despite her resolve, JJ told Winnie Collins something that no one else in the entire world knew. Not even her father.

"I actually did lose this," she said. "I was wearing them when I was in a car accident when I was ten. The other one, I still wear when I'm missing my mom. It wasn't until today that I got this one back."

Winnie's eyebrow rose.

"How?"

JJ's smile was gone.

"My best guess is that Mom wanted it to find me again."

JJ had been looking for a sign, for a lead, for anything that would lead her to the truth. To her family.

She thought it only fitting that, in the end, it was her mom who would lead her to her brother.

JJ took the other earring out of her ear. She pulled on one last smile and turned to Winnie.

"I'm really awful at keeping track of things. Do you think you could hold on to these for me until your dad has everything taken care of? It would help me feel less nervous knowing they're somewhere safe."

Thankfully, Winnie didn't know the full extent of what was going on. She didn't question the request. Instead, she looked suddenly determined.

"Don't worry. I won't lose them like the pearls. You can count on me."

JJ ran her finger over the scratch one last time before handing both earrings over.

"I'm actually going to go lie down for a little bit," JJ said once they were in Winnie's hand. "I didn't get much sleep last night. Do you think if your dad comes up here, you could tell him I'm sorry?"

Winnie snorted, eyes on the earrings.

"Sorry for what? Napping? Don't worry. Dad has definitely taken his fair share of naps. Plus, if he's not going to let us in on the talks downstairs, what else can we do?" She waved the concern off. "Go nap. I got you."

JJ wavered right then and there.

She wanted to say more, but knew too much might make the girl suspicious.

So, JJ went to her bedroom and shut the door behind her.

A MANHUNT TURNED Seven Roads upside down. Still, as it became afternoon, no one could find Lawson Cole. It was frustrating. It was enraging.

It finally made Price feel like he had done enough for the moment to deserve a break to check on JJ. Since giving her the news that the man she had fought had died, he'd seen a change in her so drastic that he had done the only thing he could in a time like that.

He had given her space.

Now he wanted that space to disappear. He wanted to check on her, he wanted to be near her. He wanted to sit next to her, hold her hand and talk out the situation. Then he wanted to make her and Winnie something good to eat. After that? They could figure out their next steps.

He told his friends downstairs that he would be right back and went to Winnie's room first. She had her door open and was sprawled out on her bed, reading a book. Price paused to take in the sight. He remembered when she was half that size, begging him to read her favorite kids' book about learning numbers by counting sheep.

Price was about to say just that when he noticed something lying next to the book.

"Are those JJ's earrings?" he asked instead.

Winnie jumped in surprise but recovered with a scowl on her face. She scooped the earrings up and dramatically placed them against her chest.

"They are and, before you say anything, I already promised to keep them safe. And that this isn't the same as the pearl situation so before you say anything—"

"Keep them safe?" he interrupted. "She asked you to keep them safe?"

Winnie nodded.

"Her mom made them for her and, well, she didn't say it, but I think her mom is gone so they mean a lot." She held one out to him and pointed to something across its surface. "She said her mom handmade them for her, but she lost one in an accident. *Then* she found this one today. Now she's worried in all of this going on that she might lose them again."

Price had been about to take the one held out to him.

He paused the move midair.

"What?" was all he could manage.

Winnie saw the change in him. Her answer was slower but still she didn't understand.

"I think she gave them to me because she's trying to keep me distracted," she admitted. "She didn't really seem that stressed when we talked earlier. Maybe she thought I was."

Price started to backtrack through the door. He stared down the hall.

JJ's bedroom door was closed.

Adrenaline poured through him as he took each step closer to it.

He heard Winnie follow him. She whisper-yelled out.

"Don't wake her up! She said she was going to nap."

Price shook his head.

He already knew what he would find once he opened the door.

Or, rather, who he wouldn't.

Still, he held out some hope.

That hope didn't last.

Once the door was open, it was easy to see the room was empty.

Winnie bumped into him.

"What else did she say?" he asked, striding across the room to the bathroom, just in case.

It was also empty.

Winnie looked confused.

"Nothing. She said she was going to take a nap and that she was sorry."

Price turned at that.

"She was sorry?"

Winnie nodded.

"She told me to tell you she was sorry..." Winnie's confusion started to turn to realization that she had missed something important. "I—I thought she meant she was sorry that she was going to take a nap."

Price cussed low and checked the room for anything that might tell him that he was wrong. When he couldn't find anything, he pulled out his phone and started to call JJ.

"Dad!"

Price hurried to the bathroom. Winnie pointed into the trash can as the call went to voicemail immediately.

He didn't have to wonder why.

In the trash can was JJ's phone.

Smashed to pieces.

That was the last nail in the coffin.

Price didn't stay still after that.

He ran down the stairs, Winnie right behind him.

Once he got everyone's attention in the dining room, he whirled around and looked his daughter right in the eye.

"I love you, but I have to go and help JJ right now," he told her.

Fear etched itself into Winnie's expression. Price hated it.

He knocked her forehead twice with a gentle rap.

"I wouldn't leave you if I thought you were in danger. But, JJ is. And, like you said, she and I are a really good team. When I'm in trouble, she saves me. When she's in trouble, I save her. Those are the rules. Okay?"

Before she could say anything, he turned to Liam's wife, Blake. She stood between Deputy Gavin and Rose.

"I don't think Lawson will come after us anymore, but just in case, can you please keep my daughter safe?"

Blake, mother to three and fierce protector to any and all of those in need, nodded on reflex.

"Update Liam in the car," she ordered instead of questioning him. "We're good here."

He nodded, grateful.

He turned back to Winnie.

Price would never forget the first time he ever saw his daughter. She was impossibly small, and he was incredibly afraid. Now, she was almost an adult. Still, that fear always stayed.

In that moment, though, his daughter gave him something else. Something that he realized he needed from her before he could go.

She gave him permission to leave her.

"Go save the day, Dad."

He didn't need anything more. Price was in his truck and flying down the road in what felt like one fluid movement. He put the sheriff on speaker just as he was tearing out of the neighborhood.

"Lawson Cole doesn't need to use Winnie anymore."

The sheriff didn't make him repeat it.

"Why?" he asked instead. "What happened?"

Price thought of the earrings. The blue one with a scratch. He thought of her telling Winnie she was sorry to him.

He slammed his hands on the steering wheel as he answered.

"Because JJ is making a mighty move and turning herself in to him."

The sheriff was all alarm. It had nothing on the storm of emotions raging within Price.

"Why would she do that?" Liam asked.

Price cussed low.

"Because she finally found her brother," he said. "It's Josiah Teller."

He had no doubt that now JJ knew, she was going to sacrifice herself to keep Josiah safe.

And Price couldn't—wouldn't—let that happen.

Chapter Twenty-Two

JJ had exactly two cards left to play.

The first was the obvious one. The card she knew she would most likely play in the end.

Josiah Teller was her brother. She had found him all thanks to the earring her mother must have left with him before she passed. JJ didn't need any more proof. She didn't need to see him again, to talk to him. She had been lucky enough to already share a few conversations with him during the week he had been in the hospital.

She also took to heart the fact that without meaning to, she had already saved her brother when she had found him in the field. Everything after had been bonus.

It also made her heart soften a little more to realize that the man seemed to have had a happy life before trouble had found him. She had been through his house—though maybe not as thoroughly as she would have liked—and seen a life well-lived through the years.

Pictures of people smiling, hugging and celebrating. He had hobbies. Art supplies had filled his guest bedroom, something that now made JJ smile. It would have tickled their mother to know that despite her lack of patience with arts and crafts, her son seemed to thrive at it. He also seemed to be a fan of reading, something their father had been avid at. She hadn't been able to search all the books, but it looked like he tended to gravitate toward science fiction. Something that JJ actually loved herself.

It was a small thing, but it felt like a lot at the same time.

Josiah was a little bit of all of them, even if he didn't know.

JJ took that solace with her to play that first card.

Like Riker before her, she would try to make a deal with a Cole to keep the people she loved out of harm's way. Winnie, to be exact. Price by extension.

No one would ever need to know that Elle and Able Ortiz had had two children. Once JJ gave herself up, that was it.

Price wouldn't be happy but she was confident that, no matter what, he would keep Josiah a secret too. He would look out for him as well. Maybe that was why JJ had told Winnie the story of the earrings. She wanted to leave a breadcrumb or two so Price would find his way to her brother.

He's going to be so mad at you, JJ thought.

But JJ had already decided to play the second card, and once she did, there was no turning back.

JJ walked up to the Colt Bar and Grill's front door. They weren't open yet but the sign on the door said they would be in two months. There was a grand opening party being planned too.

JJ took a quick look around the building and parking lot. It wasn't remote but the establishments closest to them was a gas station and a Subway that faced the opposite direction. Two cars were in the lot. She had snuck out of her house with a bike she'd kept in the back. That bike she looked at once more before she knocked on the tinted door.

It wasn't long before that door opened.

A man she had never seen before gruffly told her that they were closed.

She sighed.

"I need to talk to Lawson Cole," she said. "If he's here, let him know that JJ Shaw has some information."

The burly man wasn't a talker. He also didn't need her to keep prying. He disappeared behind the door for a minute or two before opening back up. This time, he stepped aside to let her in.

The building was surprisingly open for what it was. JJ wasn't a pro at renovations, but she had to believe no progress had been made to the structure in years. The bones of a restaurant were there but everything was worn, covered in dust and in obvious disuse. She was surprised this was where Lawson was holed up. Though, when the burly man took her down a hallway and into a room at the back, she admitted to herself that this fit him in a way.

Potential on the outside but rotted on the inside.

At least the storage room seemed to have been dusted. It was also set up to look more like a lounge. There were still shelving with boxes and plastic tubs close to the back wall, but the rest of the space had tables and chairs, two couches, and an area that looked like it had been used to make simple meals. There were two other doors at the end of the room, but both were closed. JJ didn't have the time or the mental bandwidth to wonder about what was behind them. Her attention went right to the man sitting at the table in the center of everything.

Lawson Cole had his head tilted a little in smug curiosity. Like the cat had been delivered his mouse. It was only icing on the cake that the mouse had delivered itself. He leaned forward. He was wearing a suit.

She wasn't a fan.

"JJ Shaw, I almost didn't recognize you without you bouncing around an elevator." He looked to the burly guy behind her but addressed her still. "Should I be expecting our Deputy Collins and the sheriff department soon, or are they already lurking around outside?"

Based on the lack of fear in him, JJ assumed he had an exit strategy just in case. Or maybe he had more people hidden in the building, waiting for his word. Either way, he was too calm for her liking.

Though, maybe that was his ego.

If someone thought they were untouchable long enough, they probably couldn't help but believe they were.

"It's just me," JJ assured him. "No one even knows I'm here, especially not Deputy Collins."

The burly man must have shown that she was, it appeared, alone.

Lawson smiled. It was all snake.

"Then, I have to ask a few questions, first—"

JJ raised her hands and turned around to face the burly man.

"Check me," she ordered. "No weapons, no phone, no wire. No anything."

The man really was a simple guy. He did as she said without comment. Lawson had stopped though. His eyebrow was high. JJ's patience was low. When his lackey was done and gave the thumbs-up, JJ walked over and took the seat opposite Lawson at the table. It put them only a few feet apart.

The closer proximity made her feel sick with disgust.

She cut to the chase.

"You're going to ask how I found you next and then why I'm here, I'm sure," she started. "So let me answer," JJ held up her index finger. "The man who attacked me in the woods wasn't identified but I figured someone from your group had to have confirmed his death to give you the whole *life for a life* excuse and escalation for Deputy Collins and his daughter. So I hacked into the hospital's security system and, in what I can only say is a disappointing lack of self-awareness on his part, found a man sneaking into the morgue in the basement. I took a leap of faith and tracked him to the parking lot where I was able to find out that he had taken a cab, of all things, here. I'm not sure what you're paying these guys, but may I suggest in the future going the extra mile for a vehicle that isn't as easy to track."

She held up a second finger and continued to back talk the man as much as she could.

"Which brings me to say I want to make a deal and I want to make it fast before someone else figures out you're here."

Lawson's smile had dropped a little. He was irritated.

"A deal?" he asked. "Let me guess. You want me to back off your dear deputy and his daughter? What could you even offer me to make that remotely enticing?"

There was no reason to beat around the bush.

JJ dove right in.

"I'm offering you me." She held up her hand to stop his, no doubt, snarky remark. "And before you turn that down, I should let you know that I know you're looking for Able Ortiz's son."

It was a complete and utter change.

Lawson really had had no clue that JJ was involved.

No more snake smile.

"But, I have to say, you got one thing wrong about this entire thing," she added before he could cut in. JJ touched her chest. "Your father not only kept it a secret, he kept *me* a secret. I'm the daughter you're looking for. Able and Elle Ortiz never produced a son."

His eyes widened.

"Their daughter died in the car accident," he said. "The mother survived with an unborn child."

"That's what you've *heard*, but have you ever seen proof?

Or do you think it was something your father said to try and cover for me one last time before he died?"

That's when JJ finally knew what she suspected all this time to be true.

Lawson Cole truly had no proof that her mother had survived and had a child. It had been a rumor, a rumor that had been the truth, but nothing he could have verified.

So JJ's plan was going to work.

She could cover up the existence of Josiah once and for all right here. She leaned into it to make sure the job was done well.

"I came back here to live a nice life in a place my mother used to love and then, one day, I see you bouncing around here and suddenly men who would have been the same age as that unborn child—with adoption stories to boot—start getting into trouble." She shook her head. "I guess I'm like my dad. I couldn't just let that sit. I thought I could finish what he started."

She sighed. It wasn't an act.

"But then you put me in a tough spot and went for an innocent girl. I realized that I wasn't willing to bet her life on the fact that I could win against you. If only for the logistics."

Lawson's voice was tight.

"Logistics?" he repeated.

JJ nodded.

"You have more people than me. Plain and simple. So, I'm here to take the loss instead of dragging anyone else through this mess. So, let's end this now."

To his credit, Lawson seemed to be taking the news in stride.

He recovered faster than she thought he would.

"If all of this is true, what kind of deal are you offering? Your life for the deputy's daughter's?"

This was the part that would lead to her end.

If there was more time, if she had been more sure of his numbers and what information he did and didn't have, JJ might not have given in as easily.

But she believed she had finally hit a dead end she couldn't come back from.

JJ thought about her mother, all alone before she died. She thought about her father, dedicating his entire life to helping others. She thought about Riker, giving up his everything to keep her safe and loved and happy. She thought of Josiah, happy that their family would live on no matter what happened to her. She thought of Winnie, holding her mother's earrings.

She thought of Price, holding her hand in the middle of bubbles.

JJ smiled.

Lawson leaned in just a little more. He was all ears.

Which was good. She needed him to really believe her. So she told her last lies, her last truths and the last deal she would ever make.

"I am the evidence against your group. I am the only one in existence that knows enough about you to destroy you. So, once you deal with me, there's no reason for you to ever come back here again. There's no reason for you to hurt or harass anyone else here, because all it will end up doing is putting a brand-new target on your back. And, if you really want to be the new boss calling all the shots, getting all that new attention would only make your cousin seem all the stronger. Dealing with me? That will cement your spot against him. And isn't that what you really want?"

That was it.

JJ closed her mouth.

The deed was done.

And, by the look on Lawson's face, he had already made his decision well before he said it out loud.

"I guess it's only fair to accept," he said. "A life for a life, after all."

Chapter Twenty-Three

Lawson might have accepted the deal but that didn't mean he was ready to button it up and call it a day. He turned his head and shouted toward one of the closed doors with notable glee.

"Boys? Why don't you come out so we can all chat." Lawson turned back to her, his eyebrow raised again. "Wait. I do have a question you didn't answer in that way-too-wordy speech you just gave."

He pointed at his face and made a disgusting pout to seem cute.

"How exactly did you know about me when you saw me at the party? I'm fairly certain your father's intel didn't include me yet. Like you, my father also kept me hidden until I was older."

JJ knew it wasn't the time or place, but what else did she have to lose?

She smirked and was about to tell him another secret she had guarded well through the years.

But, behind him, the world shifted.

The door he had called out to opened.

However, the boys he had been calling weren't the ones who appeared.

JJ tried her very best to keep her face the exact same it had been before she recognized the two men. She might not have kept talking had she not realized that the burly man, who she believed to have been behind her, had been gone for a bit.

So, to stall, she continued.

"When I was sixteen, I found your father and then tracked him to a funeral he was attending for someone in your group. I stayed on the outskirts, trying to figure out how many of you there were and realized we were sorely outmatched. Then I saw you, standing at his side in a suit even then."

JJ felt the old anger from the past flare anew.

"After that, I made sure every plan I made included ways to destroy you too. But I was told to take a breath by a godfather who wanted a much better life for me."

That anger washed away. JJ felt a different kind of warmth in its place. One born from patience, love and understanding.

"Honestly, I guess he's the reason you and I are both here right now," JJ added. She turned to one of the men behind Lawson. He was the older of the two, weathered but not worn.

"Does a life for a life apply here?" she asked him.

Riker smiled.

"That's definitely something we should talk about."

All hell broke loose within the next minute.

The burly man came back and stayed as simple as before. He ran right at the first person he could, just as Lawson reminded them that he did indeed have *some* skill. He threw himself backward and started fighting Riker, a blessing in itself since the fight would have already been over had Riker had a good shot.

JJ couldn't track that line of the fight too long. Her attention diverted to her immediate problem. The burly man was back and unavoidable. She braced herself for an impact that would at the very least break some bones.

It never came.

The man was stopped in his tracks by a hit that was so loud it seemed to vibrate through the space around them.

And Price kept going.

Hits were doled out in an impressive flurry against the bigger man, making Price look like a man possessed. They targeted his chest, side, and finished with a one-two wallop against the man's head. JJ could only watch in awe as Mr. Burly went from as formidable as a wall to as placid as a doormat.

JJ watched as Price's bloodied knuckles brushed against the man's collar while checking to see if he was faking it or really unconscious.

The man was liquid.

He was out.

Price's gaze swiveled to hers in the next instant but there wasn't time to say a thing.

Lawson had gotten out of Riker's reach, and it was clear he had a new target in mind.

JJ went from bracing against a potential attack from the burly man to barely being able to lift her forearms up against the new frightening attacker.

Unlike the man before, Lawson was going to make it to her.

JJ saw his fist incoming and knew there was enough torque behind it to do an unsettling amount of damage. He was already upon her as she gritted her teeth.

But so was Price.

Large, quick hands wrapped around her biceps and pulled her backwards just as Lawson's hit landed against her forearm. Pain lit across her, but she knew the quick movement back had saved her from absorbing the entire force. JJ, never a woman to let go of control, melted into Price's plan with absolutely no fight.

She let herself be slung back even further while Price replaced her position between him and Lawson with nothing but righteous anger. JJ stumbled several steps away from the new match up.

There she watched the man she had fallen in love with deliver a bone-crunching punch to the man she had spent years hating. Lawson let out a scream that gurgled as blood gushed from his nose.

That's when she saw the gun in his other hand.

This is what JJ would think back on later as the downfall of Lawson Cole. A perfect example of his unchecked ego.

Riker hadn't been able to take his gun away.

She definitely hadn't had the chance either.

So, why hadn't he used it against her when the opening had been there? Why, instead, had he come at her with his fists?

Was it out of anger?

Did he want to feel her hurt personally?

Or had he simply forgotten in the rush of the fighting that he had had a trump card that would have ended her?

JJ would never know and, in the moment she clocked the gun, she wouldn't have the time to wonder.

Instead, only fear had taken over.

Not for her, but for Price standing between them.

JJ wanted to yell, to do something to stop the quick aiming of Lawson's gun, but there was no time.

Thankfully, Riker had been forgotten.

And he was right on time.

Instead of using his gun to end the man who had given them such grief, JJ's godfather used his weapon as a bat. He swung the handgun down with the strength of a man who had been waiting over a decade to get justice.

There was nothing any of them could do but watch it happen.

And watch JJ did.

Lawson Cole crumpled to the ground, blood across his face from Price, and a hit from Riker that might have killed him.

His suit, always immaculate, was stained red.

JJ found her footing again, easier this time. Her forearms hurt and the burly man near her wasn't moving at all. Riker was heaving in breaths, his eyebrow busted and part of his shirt torn.

Price's knuckles were busted and bloodied, but he used one of those hands to give her a thumbs up with a surprisingly cheeky smile. Amongst the chaos and adrenaline-filled people still standing, he delivered a one-liner that pulled a genuine laugh from her.

"I don't think I ever told you, but I'm also actually really good at fighting."

Chapter Twenty-Four

Four months later and Price was still mad.

"I already said I was sorry. *And* that I won't ever do it again."

JJ was sitting shotgun in his parked truck, wearing a dress with daisies on it and a look of reproach that matched the expression of the girl sitting behind her.

"Yeah, Dad. She's already apologized a ton," Winnie added. "Also, you have to remember she only sacrificed herself because she wanted to make super sure that you and me were safe. And her brother. Her *only family left after her tragedy.*"

Winnie was overly dramatic with the last part, but his girlfriend in the passenger's seat really ate it up.

She gave him the big doe eyes and nodded.

"Next time I feel outnumbered by an anonymous criminal organization trying to find and destroy everyone I love, I won't sacrifice myself," she said. "At least, not without checking with you first. Okay?"

Price narrowed his eyes but couldn't deny that he liked hearing JJ put him and Winnie on the list of people she loved.

He also couldn't fully blame her for what she had done, especially since they realized their situation had been a lot more dire than originally believed.

Lawson Cole's nameless organization hadn't just been one branch on a small tree. His ego had been somewhat warranted. Aside from the men Price had fought alongside Riker, there had been more lying in wait. It wasn't until Lawson himself started turning on his group that everyone realized just how outnumbered they had been.

Still, that didn't mean Price would ever fully be okay with JJ going off into danger alone.

Though, to be fair, she hadn't so much as left his side or Winnie's for more than a few hours since then. They had gone from partners to a unit of three.

Well, three plus the occasional fourth.

"Alright, alright, I guess as long as you check with me, I'll try not to bring it up every time we come here," Price said now, motioning to the house past his windshield.

"That would be nice, considering we come here every Sunday for dinner," Winnie said.

Price let out a long sigh.

"If you two keep ganging up on me, I'm going to have to rethink our futures. Specifically, this whole *combining households* thing. You two against me *and* a house renovation? I don't think I can take it."

Winnie rolled her eyes and opened the truck door. She patted him on the shoulder before jumping out.

"Don't act like you don't love it, Dad."

She was off in a flash, running up Josiah's driveway with a laugh.

JJ stayed in her seat. Price did too. He could tell she was nervous about the day they had ahead of them. He simply waited for her to say so. She did after a moment.

"I guess it doesn't feel real sometimes. Being here, being able to do this with them."

Price knew what she meant. Being at Josiah's was nothing new, at least not in the last four months. Ever since Price and Riker had convinced her to talk to Josiah. To tell him about his biological family.

She had asked for Price to be with her when she sat Josiah down, and that was how he became the second person to realize that Lawson Cole had been right. The key to finding Able Ortiz's evidence against his group had been his son all along.

But, it had been Elle Ortiz who had been the one to lead them to it.

Josiah's adoptive parents hadn't simply been strangers that had wound up with him. Instead, his adoptive mother had been a nurse at a scared Elle Ortiz's hospital bedside as her health declined. In the little time she had left, she had convinced the young couple to not only adopt her son, but to keep his origins a secret. Then, with the money given to her in guilt by Lawson Cole's father, she had orchestrated an airtight paper trail that would purposely throw off anyone who might come looking.

But, her last and most heartfelt request had been kept in a small wooden box with a few keepsakes she was promised would stay with her son.

The first had been Able Ortiz's wedding band.

The second had been Elle Ortiz's engagement ring.

The third had been Lydia Ortiz's earring.

The fourth had been a key. She hadn't known what it belonged to but had believed it was important.

And it had been, but only one person had been able to figure out where it led.

Riker Shaw hadn't been able to save his best friend or his wife, but he had been the one to figure out Able Ortiz's makeshift hiding place for all the evidence against the Coles' organization. It had taken a month to track down, but he had done it. Not only was the group being dismantled, the growth that had happened after Able's passing had been halted by the fact that Lawson was giving everyone's secrets away for his attempt at a lighter sentence.

JJ had mused one night that, in the end, he had become the most destructive evidence against himself.

She wasn't wrong.

The investigation was still ongoing but the fear that they would become targets had gone. That was largely thanks to a deal struck to keep the Ortiz family's and Riker's names out of everything attached to it. The last deal that Riker Shaw made for his best friend's family.

JJ had admitted she was okay with keeping the name JJ instead of changing back to Lydia.

"As much as I love the name my parents gave me, I wouldn't be where I am without JJ," she'd said. "It feels more wrong than right to give her up."

Price was wondering how she would feel becoming a Collins, but had decided to wait until after he proposed. Which he planned on doing in the near future. With the same ring that had belonged to her mother.

"I know I can't remember her, but I feel like Mom would have wanted JJ to have this," Josiah had told him when it had become evident to everyone just how much Price had fallen for JJ. He'd pulled him aside one Sunday dinner and handed the engagement ring over. "I'd like to keep Dad's ring, though, if you don't mind. Whether I wear it or pass it down to my kids, I'd like to hang on to him a bit longer."

Price had thought that was an idea that the late Ortiz parents would enjoy.

It also gave Riker an opening to pull him aside and officially give the father-in-law speech to him.

"You've seen her fight, you've seen her think, so I don't

have to tell you that you'll be sorry if you ever wrong her," Riker had said. "But, on the off chance that isn't enough, let me tell you that if you ever hurt that little girl of mine, you'll have to deal with me right after."

His words had been nothing but intimidating—and accepted.

Though, six months later when Riker would walk JJ down the aisle at their wedding, he'd be blubbering like a baby.

But now, sitting in his truck, Price's wandering thoughts wandered right into the hand he took in his.

"If you think this is a dream, then let me show you it isn't."

Price leaned over and kissed the woman he loved. He felt her smile into it. When he broke the kiss, he was smiling too.

"Satisfied now?" he asked.

JJ surprised him with a laugh and a shrug.

"I guess," she said. "Though, I wouldn't say no to you trying to convince me a little more later tonight."

Price let out a bite of laughter.

"That, I can do."

* * * * *

COLTON'S REEL DANGER

KIMBERLY VAN METER

Chapter One

CJ Knight's arrival in Arizona felt like walking into a mirage, the lines between reality and nightmare blurring under the relentless sun. The last place he wanted to be was in the heart of memories he didn't trust anymore.

Yet here he was, dragging his feet across the tarmac, a sense of duty overriding his dread.

What he wouldn't give to be back in LA poolside, drowning the shock beneath a waterfall of rum and Coke, but Hollywood didn't care about your personal trauma unless they could sell it for a buck.

God only knew how long it would take for someone to try and sell his situation to a streaming service. People loved sordid stories attached to celebrities, ate 'em up like candy from a bowl.

Three months ago, the news had hit him like a desert storm: his manager, Doug DeGraw, a murderer. The man he had trusted implicitly, confided in and called a friend, now a headline in every tabloid.

CJ's world had spun off its axis, leaving him grappling with a betrayal that cut deep. He and Doug had been close—or so he'd thought. Now, in the aftermath, he was forced to question if he'd ever known the man at all because he never would've thought Doug capable of murdering anyone, much less a woman in a fit of rage.

But the facts were hard to ignore. Doug was a cruel, worthless piece of trash who'd tried to cover up a horrific crime without so much as a blink of conscience until he'd gotten caught.

And CJ was left to find a new manager.

Not to make it all about him, but the search had been less than productive, something he'd complained about with his buddy Landon Rollins, another actor still waiting for his big shot.

"Man, what the hell? You didn't have a clue about DeGraw?" he asked, flabbergasted, lathering sunscreen on while soaking up some rays poolside at CJ's place a few days before CJ left.

Landon often house-sat for CJ when he was on location, which worked out for him because he was perennially broke and usually couch-surfed.

CJ shot Landon an aggrieved look. "It's not like he acted like a stone-cold killer around me. He was, like, normal. *Trust me, I've been questioning everything I thought I knew about the guy, but the bigger issue right now is I'm without a manager."*

"Yeah, that's rough," Landon quipped derisively. "You still scheduled for that Arizona shoot? Did you know I tested for that part, too?"

Yeah, sure you did, buddy. *CJ suppressed a groan and the urge to roll his eyes, but it was too late to get out of that commitment. "Shooting starts in a week. I'm leaving for the airport in a few days. Are you still good to watch the house?"*

"I'm here for you. You know that."

"Thanks," CJ said, although he wasn't stupid. The minute he was gone, Landon would act like he owned the place,

throw parties and probably break something in the process that CJ would have to fix when he returned.

But even with that said, CJ trusted Landon to keep things mostly under control until he returned. Landon might've liked playing "Lord of the Manor," but he was a pit bull about keeping out thieves and troublemakers, and that was worth the cost of a party cleanup.

"You shouldn't have a problem finding a new manager," Landon said confidently, settling against the chaise lounge as he adjusted his sunglasses with a sigh. "You're, like, box-office gold. Everyone wants a piece of CJ Knight."

Box-office gold. Ka-ching *was all they heard when CJ was part of the conversation. And the minute news had hit that Doug had been busted and was out of the game, the sharks had scented blood and started to circle.*

The whole thing made him sick and made him feel covered in grime, even though he hadn't done anything wrong.

"In the meantime, chill, man. Enjoy the rays, get some vitamin D and rest up before you have to get back to work."

CJ chuckled wryly at Landon giving him advice about anything remotely adult-ish. Landon was a giant kid who refused to grow up, but he sure knew how to capitalize on his strengths. Too bad he was a terrible actor and didn't take anything seriously enough to improve his craft.

"Where in Arizona?" Landon asked.

"Back to Sedona."

"Mmm...hot chicks in Sedona."

There was only one hot chick in Sedona who remained stubbornly set in his memory, and it was the one woman who would probably set him on fire if he so much as looked her way.

Probably not unwarranted, either. He'd really screwed up any chance of making anything of that connection.

So, no big surprise that hiding out in his Hollywood Hills home was more palatable than leaving his sanctuary to return to Sedona, Arizona, to film another project.

But when the job rang, you answered—because an actor without a ringing phone was an actor without a future.

Still didn't make the doing any easier.

AMAZING HOW SOMETHING so beautiful could suddenly change in the blink of an eye. Whereas the last time he'd been here he'd been in awe of the towering red rocks, now he just felt the oppressive heat trying to squeeze the air from his lungs.

The vast open skies, once a canvas of freedom, now felt like an unending void.

Dramatic much? Yeah, but he wouldn't be an actor if he couldn't feel all the feelings, right?

He walked, his steps echoing the turmoil within, a discordant rhythm to the usual airport hustle.

It was easy to let his mind run away with him because he was already uncomfortable in his surroundings.

Times like these, his mind was merciless.

With every step, his mind replayed the revelations, the lies unraveling like a film strip gone haywire. How had he not seen it? The signs, the oddities? Doug's charming facade had masked a darkness that CJ could barely comprehend.

He had been so blind, so naive. It gnawed at him, this gnarled knot of guilt and anger, coiling tighter with each thought.

He had almost made it through the terminal, his thoughts a whirlwind, when he saw her. *Ahhh, crap. I don't need this right now.* And suddenly, the urge to spin on his heel and run in the opposite direction was hard to fight.

Erica Pike.

The universe had a sick sense of humor.

Good God, the woman was hot. The sight of her was like a jolt, snapping him back to a reality he wasn't prepared to face.

It'd only been three months, but it felt like a lifetime ago that he'd been the recipient of her dazzling smile, and the taste of her kiss lingered in his mind.

Except what could've been fantastic between them—well, he screwed that up in royal fashion.

And now, judging by the chill emanating from her moss-green eyes, a happy reunion was not in their future.

However, if *awkward* reunions were an Olympic sport, this moment would win gold.

Why was she here? The last time he'd seen her at the airport, she'd been picking someone up, a lawyer or something? But she locked eyes with him, and it felt purposeful, as if she'd been waiting for him, and if that didn't make his insides get all wobbly, nothing else would.

Ahh, crap, he realized. She was his ride.

But he was an actor, right? If he couldn't fake a pleasant, civil exchange and act like all was well, he needed to hand in his SAG card.

"Uhh, hey, Erica. We gotta stop meeting like this." He tried making light of the fact that he'd essentially ghosted her after they'd had sex. It hadn't been intentional, but his life had imploded, so Erica's feelings hadn't exactly been the top priority. When she failed to oblige him with an obligatory chuckle, he went for the compliment. "Man, you look great. Your hair… I love it like that." He gestured to the loose bun of dark hair spun on top of her head, loose tendrils teasing her soft jaw.

She wore a gauzy white linen pantsuit that looked effortlessly classy and yet sensual. With those long legs, Erica had a model-like gait that lent an air of sophistication everywhere she went—and people always turned to stare, wondering if she was famous.

But she might as well have been a robot for all the emotion she was showing. In fact, the subtle twist of her lips at his compliment barely qualified as a smile as her gaze raked him up and down, responding coolly, "You look…comfortable."

Yeah, he probably deserved that. He looked like he had rolled out of bed, finger-combed his wavy hair, pulled on a pair of jeans and grabbed the first thing his fingers could find that was relatively clean, which, in this case, had turned out to be a classic-rock tee.

Because that was exactly what'd happened.

Was he wearing deodorant? He resisted the urge to take a discreet sniff, wishing he'd taken the time to shower before catching his flight from LA.

And why hadn't he paid better attention to his travel itinerary?

He hadn't even noticed where the production company had booked his lodgings; otherwise he would've balked at staying at the resort where Erica was the executive assistant.

Erica delivered a frosty but professional smile, her hands clasped in front of her. "Hello, Mr. Knight. I'm here to pick you up and take you to the resort. We have a car waiting to take you to the heliport. Did you check luggage?"

There was nothing rude about her delivery, but the chill coming from her eyes could've rivaled the Antarctic.

Mr. Knight. Ouch. CJ hefted the small carry-on bag. "Just this. I like to pack light."

"Very good. This way, please."

Say something. Anything, a voice urged, but his lips remained sealed shut as he followed her through the busy terminal to the awaiting town car.

"So…how'd you pick the short straw to come get me?" he asked, trying for humor. When all else failed, shoot for the joke.

"I always handle our VIP guests," she answered without missing a beat or humoring him with an obligatory chuckle. They exited the terminal, going straight to the sleek black car idling at the pickup curb.

Erica opened his door for him, which felt weird, and after he'd slid in, he started to offer a seat beside him, but she closed the door and went to the passenger-side front seat to ride with the driver—leaving him alone.

Most people climbed all over themselves to spend a little one-on-one time with CJ.

Not her, though.

Do you blame her? That judgy voice was getting on his nerves, but the censure was warranted. He owed Erica an apology for how he'd handled their…thing. It wasn't like they'd been dating, but…there'd been a spark. Definitely something between them that'd felt different.

Until he'd bailed.

But to be fair, all hell had been breaking loose and his life had imploded. That had to warrant some leeway, right?

CJ released a long sigh, leaning back against the plush leather, rubbing his palms along his jeans as sweat prickled his temple. It was only May, but the temperature was already kissing the backside of the nineties and the car air felt stale.

He tapped the darkened window separating the front from the back, and the divider went down, revealing Erica with a blandly expectant expression. "Yes?"

"Uh, it's kinda hot back here. Can you adjust the air?"

"Of course, Mr. Knight," she said with a short smile, hitting the button and disappearing again.

The air changed minutely, and CJ realized with a chuckle that Erica was purposefully keeping the air less than crisp.

He supposed he deserved that.

Hopefully it wasn't a long ride to the helipad.

ERICA HAD INDEED drawn the short straw when she'd realized it would fall to her to squire CJ Knight from the airport to the resort.

As the executive assistant at Mariposa Resort and Spa, her duties included managing all VIP guest relations.

There was a reason Mariposa had gained a reputation for catering to exclusive clientele. She wasn't about to let their reputation slide just to save herself from seeing the man who'd left her feeling like a wadded-up piece of scratch paper.

But it wasn't the professional obligation that gnawed at her; it was the personal sting. That night with CJ had felt like something more than just a fleeting connection. How wrong she'd been. He'd vanished, leaving her with a mix of embarrassment and bitterness. Not even a text or phone call—just silence—as if she'd meant nothing and didn't warrant his attention after he'd gotten what he'd wanted.

Argh! The red-hot button of rage in her heart was something she wasn't accustomed to dealing with because she never allowed herself to be in these kinds of situations.

She wasn't the one to get awestruck by celebrities—if anything, she found Hollywood types too cliché in their perceived self-importance, but CJ had seemed different, and that was where she'd screwed up.

It wasn't just that he was good-looking. Sure, he wasn't hard on the eyes, but it was something else, something in him she'd thought was sweet and kind. But then it had all turned out to be bullshit, and the mortification of being played was something that ate at her on the daily.

He was just another Hollywood player, and she'd been foolish enough to think otherwise.

She'd spent a week prior to this moment preparing herself for the inevitable rush of feelings upon seeing CJ again, but it was one thing to write a plan on paper, entirely another when it was time to put the plan in action.

The car rolled to a stop at the private helipad owned by the resort and put her mask of professional distance back in play. *You can do this*, she told herself. *He's just another entitled rich guy who thinks he can do whatever he wants.* She had plenty of experience dealing with that type.

Erica opened the door and gestured for him to follow—her fake smile felt painted on, but at least she wasn't snarling.

The helicopter's blades whirred into life, filling the cabin with a relentless buzz that drowned out most sounds. Erica sat opposite CJ, her expression a mask of professionalism. She noticed CJ's lips moving, obviously trying to strike up a conversation. This was her moment to play ignorant.

"Yeah, so, Arizona, huh? Quite the place," CJ shouted over the noise, attempting to bridge the awkward silence. His words were mostly swallowed by the rotor's din, but his expression was unmistakably one of forced casualness.

Erica glanced at him, her face blank. She tapped her earphones and shook her head, mouthing, *Can't hear you!*

CJ leaned forward, raising his voice. "I said, Arizona's quite something!"

Again, Erica shrugged, pointing to her earphones and feigning a frustrated frown. She couldn't suppress a smirk as she turned her gaze out the window, secretly relishing in thwarting his attempt at small talk.

He leaned back, defeated, and they spent the rest of the

flight in silence. CJ would occasionally try to say something, gesturing wildly to be heard, only to be met with Erica's exaggerated shrugs and pointed taps at her earphones.

There was nothing wrong with her earphones—Mariposa always made sure anything attached to the resort was state of the art, but CJ didn't know that, and she didn't want to waste the energy listening to the sound of his voice.

By the time they landed, Erica was almost impressed with CJ's persistence. The humor of the situation didn't escape her, but she kept her amusement firmly locked away. This was business, after all, and CJ Knight was just another guest. It was her job to see that they were delivered safely—not engage in chitchat.

As they disembarked, Erica kept her demeanor cool and detached. She showed CJ to his room with practiced efficiency, her tone polite but distant. "If you need anything, Mr. Knight, don't hesitate to ask," she said crisply and turned to leave, but CJ tried again to talk.

"Erica, wait..."

She turned, mildly irritated. "Yes?"

"Are we going to talk about—"

She cut him off with a quick "If you have a preference for breakfast, please let our staff know, and we'll make sure to accommodate your needs" and then left him and his question behind.

Her heart was thundering in her chest, a reminder that she wasn't as emotionally removed as she'd like to pretend.

Did she want to talk about why he'd ghosted her after their night together? No, not really. She wasn't going to trot after the man, begging for a reason. Her mother always used to say, *When people show you their true colors, it's wise to believe them*, and CJ had shown who he truly was when the cameras weren't making him into a screen hero.

No, CJ would find that she wasn't like the women he was used to having around, and she had zero interest in being part of his adoring fan club of empty-headed fame chasers.

Drawing a deep breath, she smoothed nonexistent wrinkles from her linen suit and kept walking, punting thoughts of CJ into a mental waste basket, where he would stay.

Chapter Two

CJ knew what he ought to do—study his lines, immerse himself in his character and adhere to his meticulous pre-shoot routine before being summoned to the set in a few days.

That was the professional thing, the expected thing.

But it wasn't what he *wanted* to do. His mind was stuck on thoughts of Erica, a conundrum that felt more complex than any role he had ever played.

He couldn't fathom why her opinion suddenly held such sway over him, especially after he'd left without a whisper the last time they'd met.

It was an enigma that kept him restless, pacing the confines of his luxurious room at Mariposa.

This resort, an oasis of opulence in the scorching expanse of Arizona, endeavored to be paradise on Earth. Yet amid its grandeur, CJ felt displaced, his thoughts orbiting around Erica.

He tossed his script onto the bed, its pages landing in a disheveled heap, and left his room.

As he navigated the lushly landscaped grounds, his eyes scoured every corner, every hidden nook where Erica might've been hiding.

The resort was vast, a labyrinth of exclusivity and secrets, but suddenly he had tunnel vision. He had to talk to her and smooth things over. Why? He wasn't exactly sure, but the urge compelled him like no other.

But as he continued to wander without seeing her, his frustration grew. Had she vanished into thin air?

If he could just explain how the chaos of DeGraw's crime had upended his life, she'd understand.

And then what? What was he hoping for? He hadn't thought that far, but he wasn't used to working so hard for someone's forgiveness, and the effort felt clumsy and foreign.

Maybe it was the challenge that drew him. Erica was certainly that.

His fame had been of no consequence to her, and while she hadn't been overtly rude, she hadn't been easily charmed, either. Yeah, the chase had intrigued him, but it was more than that. Erica had been different, and he'd liked that about her.

He rounded the corner and nearly ran smack into her as she talked with maintenance personnel.

"Erica," he called out, hoping he sounded chill and not needy.

Her expression, ever the mask of professionalism, betrayed none of her inner thoughts as she excused herself from the conversation and approached him. "Mr. Knight. How can I assist you?" Her tone was cordial yet distant.

But now that he had her attention, that driving need deserted him, leaving him tongue-tied. Worse, the audience of her staff made things ten times worse.

CJ hesitated, his gaze flitting around the area. "Can we go somewhere private to talk?" he asked.

Erica glanced at her watch, her brow furrowing slightly.

"I'm sorry—I'm on a tight schedule. Is there something wrong with the room?"

"The room is fine. I want to talk to you about the last time we saw each other."

Erica's expression remained impassive, though her lips tightened subtly. "That's not necessary, Mr. Knight."

Enough with the *Mr. Knight* bullshit. He'd seen her naked, twisted into positions that would make a notable entry in the Kama Sutra, and she was treating him like they were strangers. Of course, she was doing it on purpose. He hadn't taken her for the passive-aggressive type.

He gestured for her to follow him for more privacy. She relented with a barely suppressed look of annoyance.

"C'mon, Erica, I know what you're doing," CJ said once they were out of earshot. "Is it really necessary? We're both adults, right?"

"And what am I doing?" Erica's question was calm, her hands clasped in front, a posture reminiscent of a concierge dealing with a difficult guest.

CJ gave her a look, not buying her fake robotic act. "I get it, you're a great executive assistant. Top marks. If I needed help with the accommodations, you'd no doubt fix things without blinking an eye and I'd appreciate your efficiency, but...we've got history, and your *Mr. Knight* bull is obviously a passive-aggressive dig at me. Maybe I deserve it, but can't we talk things out?"

"As I see it, there's nothing to talk about."

"Let me, at least, apologize," he said.

"An apology isn't necessary," Erica interjected, her professional mask slipping for a fleeting second to reveal a glimpse of underlying hurt.

"I disagree. I know I hurt your feelings—"

Her breath hitched, but she shook her head. "Your apology is noted, Mr. Knight. Is there anything else?"

No, he wasn't going to let her ignore his attempt at apologizing. She wanted him to play the villain, but he wasn't going to make it easy for her.

"There's this tension between us. I want to clear the air."

Erica's demeanor shifted, a hint of steel entering her voice. "Mr. Knight, I assure you any personal issues will not affect my professional duties."

"I know that," CJ insisted, his patience wearing thin. "I'm trying to make amends, Erica. I genuinely regret how I left things. I should've been more considerate."

"Considerate?" Erica's composure cracked, a flash of anger crossing her face in a rare appearance as if that single word had punctured the professional reserve she clung to. "You *disappeared* without a word, CJ. You made me feel like garbage after getting what you wanted. You pretended to be a different person so I would sleep with you. That's more than being inconsiderate—that's slimy and gross. And now you expect forgiveness? A clean slate? Sorry—I don't hand out clean slates to people with dirty fingers."

Her words were a knife to his ego, but he couldn't deny their truth. Damn, she really wasn't pulling any punches. "So that's it? You're not even willing to hear my side?"

"Why should I? It's not necessary, CJ," she cut him off, her tone rising. "You have your work, I have mine. Let's keep it professional."

Flabbergasted by her rigid stance, he admitted, "I didn't think you'd react like this."

"Like what? A woman who demands more respect from the people she sleeps with?"

CJ's cheeks burned. Maybe he'd become too immersed in LA culture. One-night stands were common, and no one blinked an eye or called anyone out for not sending a text afterward. But standing there before Erica, her censure made him feel small, even though he was a few inches taller than she was.

Erica forced a hollow and fleeting smile. "All right, well, if you're finished with what you needed to say… I have work to do."

"How about we start over?"

"No."

The finality in her answer left CJ with nothing more to say. He wasn't about to chase after her, to grovel for her attention. He was used to adulation, not rejection.

As Erica walked away, CJ stood rooted, the weight of their exchange pressing down on him.

He had hoped to bridge the gap between them, but he had only widened it. Watching her retreat, he grappled with the unfamiliar sting of rejection. He had always prided himself on being grounded, unaffected by the trappings of Hollywood fame, but now he was forced to confront a harsh truth—Erica saw him as just another self-absorbed celebrity.

Was she right? No, not even close. She had no clue who he truly was, and it was rude of her to assume she knew the measure of his character based on one situation.

If she'd just listen to him…

The notion spurred a fleeting desire to chase after her, to prove he was different. But Erica was unlike the women he usually encountered, unsettling his confidence and sense of self.

She believed he had disrespected her, a perspective he struggled to understand, but something bothered him.

Yes, a crisis had upended his life, but would he have reached out to her otherwise? The thought was unsettling. He enjoyed his freedom and his lack of commitment, but

Erica… Erica was different. There had been a spark, something genuine and unfamiliar.

C'mon, man, this is a waste of time. Let her go.

He had lines to memorize, a character to embody. He couldn't afford to be sidetracked by a brief connection, by a possibility that had no place in his current trajectory.

With a final, resigned glance at Erica's disappearing figure, CJ turned and returned to his room. The door closed behind him with a sense of finality. His focus needed to be on his career, not on a spa resort manager who couldn't accept an apology, no matter how heartfelt.

ERICA WATCHED CJ walk away, his retreating figure a silhouette of unfulfilled intentions and lingering regret. The corridor, usually bustling with the quiet efficiency of the resort staff, now seemed oppressively silent, echoing the chaos inside her head.

Despite her poised exterior, Erica's thoughts churned with conflicting feelings, and that wasn't like her.

His unexpectedly sincere apology bothered her more than she wanted to admit.

So, he'd apologized. What did that mean? Did he expect they could just be buddies after he'd humiliated her?

Start anew on a different, more honest footing? *Oh, hell no.* The idea scraped against her dignity, reminding her of the vulnerability she had exposed that night they'd spent together.

Under normal circumstances, she wasn't the type to slide into bed with just anyone. But CJ had seemed different—their connection had been mesmerizing.

Nope, correction—none of it had been real, remember?

Embarrassment surged at the memory, a reminder of how

she had allowed herself to be swept away under what now felt like false pretenses.

She had believed in the connection, the spark between them, only to wake up to an empty bed and, later, zero communication.

Her pride, wounded by that abandonment, refused to bend, to give him the benefit of the doubt that part of her yearned to offer.

Screw him and his attempt at smoothing things over.

Recalibrating her thoughts, she forced CJ from her head and busied herself with the usual duties required of her position.

It was all good until she had a breather, a quiet moment between crises, and Erica found her mind replaying their brief encounter.

The warmth of his touch, the intensity in his eyes, the way he had made her feel both desired and understood—these memories burned with a vividness that she couldn't seem to purge. It was irritating how such a brief moment could leave such indelible marks on her psyche.

Objectively, the sex had been good. Probably better than just good—but it hadn't been mind-shattering, she thought, purposefully dredging up a college memory with her ex-boyfriend, Denzel, that still had the power to leave her blushing.

Except, in all fairness, Denzel had never made her feel seen or heard like CJ had. The emotional connection between them had left her spinning into the ether, amazed at how they'd seemed connected in ways that went beyond physical.

And that was why she was still mad—it'd all been fake.

Argh! Stop thinking about CJ, and move on.

She'd be so happy when CJ Knight was no longer her

problem. *It's only for a few days*, she consoled herself as she dove into her work responsibilities.

Laura Colton, one of the owners and assistant manager of Mariposa, hustled over to Erica, motioning for her to wait up.

She smiled, genuinely happy to see Laura, practically glowing with the love of a smitten woman—Noah Steele was a lucky man—and waited for her to catch up.

Cheeks pinked, Laura laughed breathlessly at how winded she was from the quick jog. "I knew I shouldn't have canceled my gym membership. If I keep declining at this pace, I won't be able to stay on top of all the activity around here."

"Hush—you're in no danger of that," Erica disagreed, shaking her head. The woman was drop-dead gorgeous and always looked like a movie star, but she was a consummate professional and always knew what was happening around the resort. "What's up?"

Back to business, Laura said, "I saw the actor CJ Knight was on the VIP guest list. Are you okay with that? I can take over for you if you want."

Erica hated being considered weak, and Laura's offer to step in only made her feel like some fragile bird needing shelter—and that wasn't Erica. She forced a bright smile. "Goodness, no, you have enough on your plate without adding my responsibilities to the pile. I'm fine. Honestly, I don't even care." At Laura's dubious expression, Erica doubled down, saying, "Seriously, totally fine. Please—stop looking at me like that. I'm perfectly capable of separating personal from professional."

"Oh! I know you are," Laura exclaimed, as if worried she'd inadvertently insulted Erica. "I was just… I don't know…actors are such…well, they can be a lot and…"

Erica saved her boss from continuing to stumble on her words, gently letting her off the hook. "You have a wedding to plan and a resort to run—please, let me handle CJ Knight. Besides, it's just for a few days here, and then he'll be someone else's problem. I heard they're shooting on location somewhere in Sedona."

"That's true," Laura said, biting her lip. "I'm sorry—I'm scatterbrained right now. Of course you can handle whatever comes your way. I'm just overthinking things."

"Understandable."

"Well, please let me know if you need any help," Laura said before heading to the next item on her to-do list.

Even though Laura was a sweetheart, Erica wished she hadn't shared what'd happened between her and CJ during a pity party moment. Erica liked to keep her personal life private—messy personal details had no place in her professional life—but she was human, too. And CJ had really hurt her feelings.

The hardest part was acknowledging that a part of her, a part she fiercely repressed, wanted to forgive him, to explore the what-ifs that haunted her quiet moments.

But she couldn't. She wouldn't.

Her pride, her sense of self-worth wouldn't allow it. She had built her life on being strong and independent, not the kind of woman who succumbed to charming actors with mouths full of pretty lies.

As the day wore on, Erica became increasingly distracted, her thoughts returning to CJ and the unresolved tension between them. It was more than just wounded pride. It was a battle between her rational mind, which admonished her for even considering forgiveness and the part of her that longed to rewrite their story, to give it a different ending.

She ended the day feeling drained, and the emotional turmoil left her mentally exhausted.

By the time she put Mariposa out of her mind to go home, she was worn out and irritated that CJ's presence was dominating so many of her thoughts.

Mostly because it was unlikely that CJ was thinking of her at all.

Chapter Three

True to her word, Erica was completely professional whenever they had to suffer each other's presence, but by the time CJ was called to set, he was grateful to leave the uncomfortable situation with Erica behind.

It shouldn't have been this hard to put someone in his rearview mirror, but something about Erica nagged at him, refusing to let him move on.

During an unhinged moment, he'd considered having flowers delivered to her desk—something big and ostentatious and something she couldn't ignore—but then he'd come to his senses and realized he'd have better luck getting her attention if he flushed money down the toilet and clogged the septic.

It was a relief to return to something he understood—the chaos of a film set.

"Caroline Briggs, first assistant director. Welcome to base camp," said the harried woman with a wild spray of graying hair springing from her hastily pulled-back bun. She unabashedly gushed, "Mr. Knight, I love your work. Forgive me for fangirling for a minute, but I absolutely jumped at the chance to work on this film because I'd heard you were signed on. Seriously, you're, like, a legend."

It was unusual for an AD to be awestruck by a celebrity. They were usually too overworked and crushed by the weight of their enormous responsibilities to bother with celebrity stuff, but after Erica's cold shoulder, it felt good to be liked again.

"The pleasure's all mine," he said, smiling.

"Your trailer is stocked per your rider, and if there's anything you need, please don't hesitate to grab me. Here's my personal cell. A driver will come to transport you to set, which is a few miles down the road." She handed him a business card, gesturing to the luxury set trailer reserved for him. "If you could report to makeup in an hour, that would be great."

He smiled, familiar with the drill. "Got it." He pocketed the card and headed for his trailer. Stepping inside, he nodded with approval. The small table was filled with fresh fruit, containers of assorted nuts and his one indulgence—sour gummy bears—which were hard to come by when he was on a strict meal plan during shooting. He liked to keep his body and mind sharp when filming, which meant cutting out many processed foods, but a man couldn't live on chicken and broccoli alone. Even though his nutritionist balked, he insisted on the gummy bears—they were sometimes integral to his sanity.

This film—a Western period piece—was bound to be grueling due to the location, the heat and the fact that period pieces always had so many more moving parts to consider when filming.

Base camp, a cluster of trailers that formed a makeshift community, was a hodgepodge of craft services, equipment rigs and the star trailers a few miles from the set so as not to disrupt any of the filming. Still, sound carried in a place like Arizona, so signs were everywhere to remind people to keep the noise to a minimum.

He watched as a special dirt hauler trundled down the road toward the location.

Special dirt for the main set was hauled in and meticulously combed to look organic to the area. However, it was specially made to create little to no dust, which could create continuity problems later.

But then, someone had to manage all that "movie dirt" so it was ready for the next shot.

The business of make-believe was a robust business, and everyone wanted a piece of the pie.

He remembered the first time he'd stepped on location for his first real gig. He'd been overwhelmed by the sheer scope of the operation. It was a mini mobile town with its own heartbeat and community. It was easy to understand how people fell in love with their coworkers or costars during shooting when they lived in a manufactured bubble of altered reality.

Hell, he'd even made that mistake—falling for his costar—and he'd stubbornly believed she was The One. But while Mimi Watson was ethereal on-screen, she was a headache in real life. He'd learned real quick that he'd fallen for the illusion of Mimi, not the petulant, spoiled brat that she was when the cameras were off.

The first time she'd snapped at a waitress for a small mistake had been the moment he'd realized they weren't compatible.

After that, he'd made it a point to keep a professional distance from his costars or anyone he worked with.

Maybe that was why Erica's judgment felt so wrong. He wasn't the guy she believed him to be, and it stuck in his craw that she wouldn't budge in her opinion.

Let it go, Knight. He sighed and exited the trailer to report to makeup.

He grinned with true pleasure when he saw his favorite makeup artist waiting for him.

"There he is," said Julian Reed, the best in the business and the world's biggest gossip. "Come here and give me some sugar."

CJ bent forward for the expected air kiss that Julian demanded and dropped into the makeup chair while Julian fussed around him. "Feels like a hundred degrees already, and it's not even eight a.m. yet," he groused. "Thank God you have your trailer set to frigid."

"Honey, I can't have my babies sweating off all my hard work," Julian said, adjusting the many bangles on his wrist. "Now, tell me what's new? I mean, aside from the whole murder thing with your manager, Dougie DeGraw. That's something you don't hear every day."

CJ didn't want to talk about Doug, but he liked Julian and supposed he could indulge his curiosity. He shrugged, admitting, "Your guess is as good as mine. I've been hiding in my house since the news broke. I wouldn't know if the second coming of Jesus was happening and tickets for the event were being sold for the Hollywood Bowl."

"Oh, honey, that would be something, wouldn't it?" Julian clucked his tongue and finger-combed CJ's hair, pursing his lips. "Who has been cutting this mop? This is a disgrace. You should pop into the stylist's trailer before going on camera."

"Jules, it's a Western period piece, I doubt anyone's going to notice if my ends are a little off-point."

"Fair," Julian admitted. "But just so you know, this kind of thing gives me hives. Anyway—" He pulled two wet wipes and thrust them at CJ. "Wipe your face so I can start the magic. Your pores look big enough to require their own zip code. Good lord, have mercy!"

CJ laughed, shaking his head. "You're the expert."

"Indeed. Now, give me the good stuff. What the actual hell… Did you know that Dougie was a murdering psycho?"

And here it goes.

He supposed he ought to get used to that question but didn't know how he ever would.

Erica sighed in relief, knowing CJ was finally out of the resort. For days, she'd worked overtime to avoid interacting with the man, but she'd invariably catch a glimpse of him in the hallway or, worse, coming from the pool.

That memory, in particular, seemed stuck in her brain.

She'd sucked in a wild breath at the shocking sight of CJ, a thick towel wrapped around his torso, his abs glistening, his wild mop of hair adorably mussed—and that brief flicker in his eyes when he'd seen her had nearly caused her to miss a step.

She'd quickly ducked into a storage room, acting as if she'd purposefully been heading that way, when in fact she'd simply been waiting for the coast to clear.

So much for acting like a responsible adult, her inner voice had quipped as she'd leaned morosely against the stacked linen tower. *You're literally hiding in a closet.*

Not hiding, she'd corrected, her gaze roaming the small room, *doing inventory.*

Aha! Her sharp gaze had caught a small gap in supplies. *See?* Erica would need to ask Martha to order more shampoo bottles from that cute boutique shop in town. Feeling slightly less stupid, she'd straightened her blouse and stepped boldly from the storage room with a purposeful stride but had been secretly disappointed that CJ hadn't been standing outside the door waiting for her.

Argh. That's some twisted logic.

So, yes, CJ checking out was a blessing. Now life could return to normal.

Bella, one of the younger maids, found her. "I saw that Mr. Knight checked out. So he's not returning to the resort?" she asked.

"No, he's not. Is there a problem?" Erica asked, perplexed. Had CJ trashed the room or something?

"Oh, no—no problem. I was doing my end-stay cleanup routine and found something he must've left behind by accident," she clarified. "I didn't know if he might want it back. I mean, I figure he probably will, though. It's kind of expensive."

Bella produced an electronic tablet, and Erica wanted to groan. "Yes, thank you, Bella," she said, accepting the device with a quick smile. "I'll see to it that his property is returned."

Bella's smile warmed Erica's heart—the girl had been horrifically assaulted but had emerged the other side stronger and braver than anyone she'd ever known. "Awesome. He's so nice. I'd hate to see him stressed out over losing it," Bella said, leaving Erica to finish her shift.

Erica stared at the tablet and fought the urge to swear beneath her breath. She could send it by courier but ran the risk of it getting damaged, which would make the resort liable for its replacement.

Or she could just run it over to the production and drop it off, ensuring that it was intact when it left her possession.

What were the chances she'd run into CJ? Pretty slim.

She could take those odds.

Holding the electronic to her chest, she resigned herself to hand-delivering CJ's property.

After detouring to her office to get the secret production

location and the contact information, she popped into Laura's office to let her know where she was going and why.

With an apologetic grimace, Laura looked conflicted, saying, "I wish I could take it for you, but I'm supposed to meet with the florist in about forty-five minutes and I'll never make it back in time."

"Oh, don't worry about it." Erica waved away her concern, hating that her boss thought she was incapable of making a delivery. "I'll drop it off with the production office and head back. It should be a quick trip."

"You're a rock star," Laura said with relief before glancing at her watch. "Oh! Damn it, I forgot I have to go over those carpet swatches before the carpet rep returns later this afternoon."

Erica chuckled, leaving her boss to her chaos, and headed for her car.

The resort flew in the guests, but there was a small road the staff used to take them in and out.

Wiping away a bead of sweat, she climbed into her car and immediately turned on the AC. Arizona heat was relentless, even in late spring.

It was no wonder CJ had been in the pool so much while he'd stayed at the resort. She shook her head, immediately irritated at herself for dredging up that memory again.

Deliver the item. Leave. Forget CJ Knight.

Stick to the plan.

The production was filming on a private ranch in Sedona. When she rolled up to the gate, she found two production assistants monitoring the flow of traffic into the location.

She rolled her window down with a smile, showing her ID badge from the resort. "Hi, I'm Erica Pike, executive assistant at Mariposa Resort. CJ Knight just checked out, but he left behind his tablet," she explained, gesturing to the tablet on the passenger-side seat. "Thought he might like it back."

The assistant nodded. "The trailer camp is just up the road. You can't miss it. The AD's mobile office is the first one on the left."

Erica thanked the assistant with a smile and rolled on.

This would be quick and easy—no different than any delivery.

So why was her heart rate fluttering?

Chapter Four

Erica scanned the bustling base camp, her eyes drawn to a large trailer with the words Assistant Director written in bold black letters. She approached and knocked on the door, but there was no answer. As she waited, her gaze wandered the organized chaos of equipment, props and people rushing about.

As a seasoned executive assistant at Mariposa Resort, Erica was used to seeing high levels of organization and efficiency. But this world was on a whole other level. It reminded her of the behind-the-scenes operations at Mariposa, where everything ran like a well-oiled machine to provide guests with seamless luxury and the guests never caught sight of the chaos behind the curtain.

Lost in thought, Erica didn't notice when a production assistant stopped beside her. "Can I help you?" he asked.

Smiling, Erica stepped down the metal steps and introduced herself. "I'm Erica Pike from Mariposa. I called ahead to let the assistant director know that we found some property belonging to CJ Knight in his room after he checked out this morning."

"The AD is on set—something about the horse wrangler not showing up this morning. I can take you there if you want."

"Oh, that's not necessary. I can leave it with you if that works," Erica said, starting to hand the tablet over, but the man vehemently shook his head.

"Sorry—I can't accept personal property. It has to go through the AD, or it'll be my head. Jump into the Jeep, and I'll drive you over. It's a few miles away, so you definitely don't want to try and walk there in this heat."

She resisted the urge to groan when she realized she'd likely see CJ—a prospect that made her palms sweat.

"I don't want to interfere with your work," she hedged, wondering if anyone else could accept the property.

"Don't worry about it," he assured her as he reached out to shake her hand. "Caroline can be pretty strict about protocol on this high-value production. Rocko Bellini—it's a pleasure to meet you."

"Only if it's no trouble," Erica replied with a smile. She could tell from his demeanor that Rocko probably had his own Hollywood dreams. Without hearing his whole story, Erica guessed he was working his way up while hoping for his big break.

"Rocko Bellini…that's a great name," she commented, trying to make conversation as they drove.

Rocko laughed, navigating the newly paved road stretching into the horizon. "Actually, my name's Eric Jones, but that's not exactly a name that rolls off the tongue. Besides, there was already an Eric Jones listed with SAG, so I figured, why not pick a name that really says something? Something with old-school class and charm? And then one day, I woke up and the name *Rocko Bellini* just jumped into my head like it was divine intervention or something. I figured that's a sign from the universe, so I went down to the SAG office that day and officially became a new man."

Erica hid her amusement, nodding. "Sounds like it was

a sign, definitely. Have you been on any productions I might know?"

"Well, just some small parts, but I did have a speaking part on *Grimm*—do you remember that show? Great show. I was hoping for a recurring gig, but the series ended, and it was back to California. It was filmed in Portland, Oregon—did you know that?"

"I didn't. I actually didn't watch the show. Not much of a supernatural fan. I prefer crime dramas, stuff like that."

"Yeah, that's cool. Well, since then, it's been small parts here and there—enough to keep my SAG card active, but not enough to pay the bills. My cousin got me this gig as a production assistant and it's been pretty dope, but I'm ready to get my shot. Someday it'll be me above the line."

Erica chuckled, enjoying his enthusiasm. "I hope you get there."

"Oh, I will. Mark my words. Hey, if you get the chance, watch episode four, season six of *Grimm.* I'm in the coffee shop scene. I had some funny lines—not laugh-out-loud kind of lines but kinda dark humor, you know? I think I delivered."

Erica nodded, offering a half-hearted promise to check out Rocko's suggestion. In reality, she knew she wouldn't. But for now, Rocko's charismatic energy was enough to distract her from the looming prospect of running into CJ.

They pulled off a safe distance from the filming area, and Rocko apologized with a charming smile. "We'll have to walk from here. The sound guys get grumpy if there's any unwanted noise in their ears."

"I understand," Erica replied, stepping out of the vehicle. The warm Arizona sun kissed her skin as she took in the scenery around her.

The desert landscape was surprisingly beautiful, with its

rolling hills and vibrant wildflowers scattered throughout. Despite being so close to her own resort, Erica had forgotten how stunning Arizona could be.

"Watch for snakes," Rocko warned, gesturing for her to follow.

Erica nodded, her eyes scanning the ground. She wasn't particularly fond of snakes, but she was determined not to let her fear get the best of her. Rocko led the way, navigating the rugged terrain like he'd been born to the area and not an LA-Hollywood type.

Erica couldn't suppress the nervous energy tickling her insides as they walked. The distant sound of voices directing actors became louder as they approached the filming area.

Finally they reached the edge of the set, concealed behind a curtain of tall saguaro cacti. Erica's heart raced as she caught her first glimpse of the action. A group of actors dressed in old Western attire stood in a dusty street lined with weathered wooden buildings. A saloon sign swung lazily in the desert breeze.

"This entire set was built for this production," Rocko whispered, motioning toward the "Main Street," which looked plucked straight out of the movie *Tombstone*.

"Impressive," she murmured as her gaze searched for CJ among the cast.

Her heart skipped a beat. There, near the makeshift hitching post, his dark hair hidden beneath a worn cowboy hat, CJ leaned casually against the wooden post, laughing and joking with his costars, looking like a Western snack.

Even dressed like a dusty old cowboy, he was nice to look at. He exuded an air of confidence and charm as if he'd been born to be a star. Okay, so objectively he was hot, she allowed, folding her arms across her chest, but his character was as ugly as they came.

Still, Erica's breath caught in her throat as she watched him. Memories of their one-night stand came flooding back. Stolen glances from across the crowded building, playful banter at the bar and then one unforgettable night when they had shared a dance under a star-filled sky before heading back to his hotel room.

Heat flooded her cheeks as she pushed the memories away. Rocko nudged Erica gently, pointing toward a small tent adjacent to the set. "That's where you'll find Caroline," he whispered. "She should be able to assist you from this point forward. Nice to meet you." He tipped an imaginary hat and headed off toward his next assignment.

Erica tore her gaze away from CJ, forcing herself to focus. She approached the small tent where Caroline, the assistant director, was frantically pacing back and forth while talking on the phone.

"What do you mean you don't know where he's at? We need that wrangler here now!" Caroline's voice crackled with frustration as she continued her conversation. She glanced up briefly and offered Erica an apologetic smile before returning her attention to the call.

Stepping inside the tent, Erica waited patiently, understanding the stress that the assistant director must've been under. Stacks of production paperwork cluttered the table, scripts lay open on every available surface and a large corkboard was covered in colored sticky notes that seemed to represent the intricate web of scenes and shots for the film.

This was where the magic happened, where dreams were brought to life on the silver screen. She sighed, wondering what it must've been like to live this kind of life. She'd never been the creative type—more of a linear thinker—but she admired anyone who could make something out of nothing. Give Erica a spreadsheet over a right-brained task any day.

Caroline finally hung up the phone and let out a weary sigh. "Sorry about that," she said with a harried smile. "Welcome to the madness."

Erica returned the smile. "Thank you. I totally understand." She produced a business card from her linen pocket. "Erica Pike, executive assistant at Mariposa Resort. We spoke on the phone."

"Yes, something about a tablet CJ left behind at your resort?"

Erica quickly produced the tablet. "Yes, here it is. The resort takes a hands-on approach to personal items of value left behind by VIP guests. I didn't feel comfortable sending it by courier given that it's an electronic device. You never know how it might be handled."

Caroline agreed. "Lord knows that's true. I ordered a replacement phone, and it was delivered looking like it'd traveled through a tsunami. Ended up being broken and had to exchange it at the local store. Totally frustrating."

"Well, I see that you're dealing with your own crises, so I'll let you get back to it. Do you know where Rocko went? I'll just catch a ride back to base camp where I'm parked."

Caroline grimaced. "I'm sorry, I know it's asking a lot, but would you mind hanging out for a bit? I can't really spare Rocko right now. We've been struggling with some setbacks lately, and it's an all-hands-on-deck situation."

Erica hid her alarm—not only because she had things to do back at the resort but also because hanging around could mean more unfortunate time spent with CJ. But what could she do but agree? "I don't want to create any problems," Erica said. "I'm happy to wait."

"Thank you." Caroline breathed a sigh of relief. "You don't by any chance know any horse wranglers in the area that might be willing to work for scale on short notice?"

"Off the top of my head, no, but I could probably find someone for you back at the resort. One of my bosses, Joshua Colton, might know someone."

"Good to know," Caroline said. "I'll keep that in my back pocket as a viable Plan B. Go ahead and grab something from craft services. Help yourself. We're dead in the water until we find that damn wrangler—or someone to replace him. God, what I wouldn't do for a margarita right now. Or maybe we'll move the shooting schedule around," Caroline left, muttering to herself as she grabbed her cell phone. "Damn that wrangler."

Erica hesitated, unsure if she should leave or wait as Caroline suggested. However, she sensed that Caroline needed some privacy for her next round of phone calls, and out of professional courtesy, Erica decided to leave.

She found her way to craft services, ordered an iced coffee with a protein bar and found a quiet place in the shade to wait.

With some luck, CJ wouldn't even notice she was there.

However, as CJ somehow swiveled his stare her way at precisely the right moment, their stares locked, and Erica knew luck wasn't on her side today.

CJ COULDN'T BELIEVE his eyes—was that Erica over there at craft services? An unbidden thrill nearly coaxed a surprised smile from his lips, but he managed to stop it from forming. Should he go over there and say hello? She was on his turf now. Wouldn't it be rude to ignore her?

But Erica had made it clear she didn't want anything to do with him. So, did he stay put and pretend he hadn't seen her?

They'd locked stares—pretending that he hadn't seen her seemed out of the question.

She already thought he was a toad; he didn't want to do anything to cement that belief.

Excusing himself, he took a chance and walked over to craft services, acknowledging Erica as he grabbed a blueberry muffin. "Fancy meeting you here, miss," he drawled, going for humor in the face of a potentially awkward encounter. "Begs the question…did you miss me or…do you harbor a secret desire to find yourself on the silver screen?"

"Neither," she answered, sipping her iced coffee. "You forgot your tablet at the resort. I'm simply returning it."

CJ realized with a start he hadn't even realized his tablet was gone, but he was grateful it had been returned. Quickly sobering, he said, "Thanks. I appreciate that. I have pictures on my tablet that I would've been really upset to lose."

"Careful—pictures of Hollywood parties can get you into trouble," she quipped, clearly assuming he had pics of a dirty nature.

He chuckled, correcting her quietly: "No, actually, I have pictures of my grandfather before he died last year of pancreatic cancer. I used to visit him in hospice, and we'd use the tablet to play games. When I was there, I showed him how the camera worked, and he thought it was the coolest thing. He'd always been fascinated by gadgets. So, I'd wheel him around the garden area, and he'd use my tablet to snap pics. Used to make him happy, and seeing him happy…well, it made me happy."

Erica's expression faltered, and she looked embarrassed that she'd taken such a left turn in her assumption. "I'm sorry. I… That was crappy of me." Humbled, she said, "I'm glad I was able to return your tablet safely."

"Me, too."

"I'm just waiting for my ride," she blurted when a beat of silence hung on for too long, explaining, "Your AD is working on finding someone to take me back to base camp. She said I could get something from craft services." She lifted her coffee. "This is really good. The crew is well taken care of in the food department."

CJ nodded, a flicker of relief passing through him at the change in subject. He hadn't meant to make her feel like an ingrown toenail. "Yeah, they do a decent job here. Keeps us going during the long hours." He glanced around, adding, "Also helps keep tempers in check if you keep people fed well. Today's shooting schedule is a mess. Everyone's starting to get antsy."

"Yes, I heard something about that. Your wrangler didn't show up to set?"

"Yeah, we can't do any work with the horses without the wrangler present. Union rules. And because today's shooting schedule was slated with the horses, we're stuck twiddling our thumbs in this heat while we wait for direction."

"Your AD is working hard to get someone here," Erica shared. "But she looks pretty stressed out."

"Yeah, I don't blame her. When things go wrong, the AD takes the heat from all the upper-level people."

"Meanwhile, the stars get to enjoy pastries and iced lattes," Erica said in a faintly teasing tone.

Was that the tiniest sign Erica was thawing in her attitude toward him? He hoped so.

"Would you like a tour?"

A glimmer of interest flashed in her eyes, but she seemed reluctant to accept his offer. "I don't want to distract you," she said.

"You're not distracting me—you're keeping me from losing my mind from boredom," he said. "C'mon, I'll show you the cool stuff. Maybe it'll take your mind off the fact that you hate me."

“I don’t hate you, CJ,” she said, exasperated. “I… Never mind. If you’d like to give me a tour, that would be a nice treat.”

“Great.” He grinned, tossing his half-eaten muffin. “Follow me for the grand tour of Main Street in Dry Gulch—a town where the West wasn’t exactly won, but it was a place to wet your whistle and stock up supplies before moving onto bigger and better.”

The fact that Erica laughed with genuine amusement gave him more than a spurt of hope. Let’s face it: he was charming, and if given half the chance, he’d show Erica he wasn’t the bad guy she thought he was.

Or at least, she might leave the set willing to hear his side of the story.

Maybe even let him take her to dinner to make amends.

Okay, maybe that was a tall order, but a man could dream, right?

Chapter Five

Erica probably should've declined CJ's offer, but she couldn't resist the opportunity to experience the behind-the-scenes of an actual Hollywood film.

It wasn't that she was awestruck by the celebrities—it was the sheer amount of work and expertise she saw at work to make movie magic happen.

And CJ seemed to understand that.

"Are you sure you're not needed?" Erica asked, following a quick tour through the wardrobe tent, which the costume director had temporarily set up for wardrobes changes or emergency costume fixes.

"It's fine," he assured her. "From what I heard, our entire shooting schedule has to be reworked, and we're already losing daylight. Likely the whole day of shooting will be lost because of the missing wrangler."

"I don't quite understand why a wrangler needs to be on set for the horses," Erica said.

"Union rules. It's a safety issue for both the actors and the horses. Just to make sure everyone is doing things by the book and cautiously. Horses can be dangerous to work with if you're not careful."

"Can you ride?" Erica asked.

"Enough to look convincing on camera," he answered with a wink. "But I wouldn't call myself an actual rider."

She appreciated his honesty. He could've just as easily lied to try and seem impressive. The simplicity in his admission, the absence of pretense struck a chord within her. "I can't ride, either," she admitted. "I'm a little afraid of horses, actually. I had a bad experience when I was a kid that stuck with me."

"What happened?"

Erica hesitated, not sure she ought to share anything so personal. The vulnerability of the moment was palpable, a rare opportunity to share a piece of her past that she usually kept hidden. "Well, I was at a friend's birthday party, and the parents had paid for a company to bring horses to offer free pony rides. Except they weren't ponies—they were actual horses that the company had purchased at an auction. I suppose the upside was that they were saved from the glue factory, but the downside was that they were surly and totally ill-suited to working at a children's party. Several of us were bitten—some badly enough to break skin." She reluctantly slipped her linen blouse down to reveal her shoulder, unveiling the thin white line on her shoulder. "I was one of the kids who needed stitches."

CJ's brow furrowed as he peered at the faint scar. His expression softened, a mix of empathy and concern washing over his features. "I'm sorry," he said. The sincerity in his voice was unexpected, almost disarming. "That must've been terrifying."

Erica forced a short laugh, admitting, "It was. I haven't gone near a horse since. I mean, I think they're beautiful, majestic creatures, but I have zero interest in being next to one ever again." The laugh didn't quite mask the lingering shadow of that childhood fear.

"I wasn't bitten by a horse, but one time I was scratched by my grandmother's cat and got cat scratch fever. I ended up in the hospital overnight for high-power antibiotics."

"I've never heard of anyone getting sick from a cat scratch."

"Yeah, it can happen. Now I'm religious about washing my hands anytime I handle an animal, just in case."

"Did the experience make you scared of cats?" Erica asked, thinking of her own cat, Mitzy, at home.

"No, but it did give me a healthy appreciation of good old-fashioned soap and water. The doc told me if I'd washed out the scratch right when it happened, I probably wouldn't have gotten sick."

A reluctant smile found her lips even as she tried to stop it. This easy energy between them…it was unnerving, given their history, yet impossible to ignore when he was this genuine, this disarmingly real.

As they continued their stroll through the bustling set, Erica couldn't help but notice a commotion near the stables. Crew members were frantically whispering to each other and casting worried glances in that direction.

Curiosity piqued, she tugged at CJ's sleeve. "What's going on over there? Is everything all right?" she asked, concerned.

CJ turned toward the stables with an unsure frown. "I don't know, but it doesn't sound good."

"Do you think it has something to do with your missing wrangler?"

"There's one way to find out," CJ said, gesturing for her to follow, but she held back until CJ slipped his hand into hers, assuring her everything would be fine.

She should've pulled her hand free, but there was something about the warmth of CJ's hand in hers that calmed her apprehension.

CJ hailed one of the production assistants assigned to the area where the horses were corralled, and the assistant, immediately recognizing the movie's star, hustled over.

"Is everything okay?" CJ asked.

"Sorry, Mr. Knight—one of the horses got loose, and we don't have anyone qualified to go after it. I mean, I used to ride horses at my grandparents' ranch, but I haven't sat a horse in almost twenty years."

"You haven't worked with horses in twenty years, but you're working with the horses?" Erica asked, confused.

"Ma'am, no disrespect, but when someone in production asks if you can ride a horse, you say yes and figure it out later. A job's a job in this business."

Didn't seem very safe, but Erica kept her feelings to herself. Her professional instincts bristled at the cavalier attitude, a stark contrast to the meticulous standards she upheld at the resort. She would never run Mariposa like this, but it wasn't her operation, so it was best to keep quiet.

For his part, CJ seemed to understand, commiserating, "I once said I was bilingual just to get a part."

"Are you bilingual?" Erica asked, curious.

"Hell, no. I can barely manage decent English most days," CJ replied without any shame. "But this business is hard. Nothing more terrifying than a closed door to opportunity."

The sound of hooves on the ground, thundering against the hard earth, echoed through the set as a massive quarter horse, bucking and rearing in excitement or fear—it was impossible to tell which, crashed through the flimsy wall divider aimed at keeping the animals shielded from production.

Erica shrieked in fear, her childhood memory rearing its ugly head. Her heart raced, the old terror surging back as the horse's muscled body shone with sweat in the midmorning sunlight and its eyes were wild with unbridled energy.

CJ jumped into action, putting himself between Erica and the horse, using a soft and calming voice to soothe the animal.

"He's scared and in an unfamiliar place," CJ explained smoothly, his hands up to keep the horse at bay. "Horses respond to energy. Everyone needs to stay calm. Whoa there, buddy, you're okay, but you're scaring everyone. C'mon now, it's okay," he said, in a gentle tone while slowly gesturing for the production assistant to hand him a carrot.

The production assistant grabbed a carrot from a bucket and inched his way over to CJ to hand him the vegetable and then quickly backed away.

"There, there, buddy, see? It's not all bad," he said, allowing the animal to sniff at the offered vegetable, assessing the situation. The horse whickered and snuffed but accepted the carrot, crunching loudly. "Pretty good, huh?" CJ said, gently running his hands along the strong neck while surreptitiously securing the lead on the halter. "There you go. All better, right?" He motioned toward the production assistants watching in awe as the calmed horse walked easily behind CJ, possibly hoping for more treats, while CJ secured the horse inside the makeshift corral, locking it securely. He fished another carrot from the bucket and gave it to the horse with one final rub on his forelock.

Erica stared, her breath still caught in her chest, but not out of fear. The sight of CJ, so unexpectedly capable and gentle, stirred something in her, a flutter of admiration she hadn't anticipated. Maybe it was a little dramatic, but had CJ just saved her?

It felt that way.

And she didn't know how she felt about that.

AFTER THE COMMOTION settled and the quarter horse calmed, CJ's first thought was of Erica. The incident had unfolded so quickly, yet her shriek of fear, raw and piercing, still echoed in his ears.

He turned to her, searching her face for signs of distress. "Are you okay?" he asked, his voice laced with concern. The fear he'd seen flash in her eyes was something he hadn't anticipated facing today, yet here they were, her vulnerability laid bare by the runaway horse.

Erica nodded, her breath still uneven. "Yes, I think so," she managed, attempting a brave smile that didn't quite reach her eyes. The encounter had clearly shaken her, bringing forth memories she'd rather have kept buried.

CJ felt a twinge of guilt for having exposed her to this, even though the circumstances had been beyond his control.

The fear slowly leached from her gaze as she recovered, commenting, "You were amazing with that horse. I thought you said you weren't a good rider."

"I'm not, but I never said I wasn't good with animals," CJ teased, clarifying. "Every summer I used to work for an old neighbor who had a couple of horses. For a few bucks an hour I'd muck the stalls and throw out the hay. The old man was too frail to do the job himself, but he wasn't willing to rehome the horses. I helped him out so he could keep them. He couldn't teach me to ride, but he taught me a few things about how to calm an agitated animal."

Erica's expression softened with reluctant marvel. "Every time I think I have you figured out, you go and do something that makes me question everything I thought I knew."

"I'll take that as a good sign, given our history," he said.

She blushed and grudgingly nodded. "Maybe so."

His concern for Erica momentarily pushed aside the myriad of questions swirling in his mind about the loose horse.

However, as the immediate worry for her well-being subsided, his thoughts returned to the situation at hand. It was highly unusual for a horse, especially one as well-trained as those on set, to break loose in such a dramatic fashion.

Someone had to have unlocked the gate, an act that seemed too intentional to be a mere oversight.

"What's wrong?" Erica asked, catching his expression.

"Something's not right. Someone would've had to unlock that gate and spook the horse to send it running like that."

"I'm sure it was an accident," Erica said, but she seemed to share his concern. "Should you tell the assistant director?"

"Yeah, probably."

But the production assistant, a young man named Alex, overheard them and hustled over, anxiety etched on his face. "Please don't tell Caroline. It was my job to watch the gate, and I left for a few minutes to grab a bite to eat at craft services. I swear I was only gone for ten minutes tops, and when I came back the horse was out, but it's all good now, right? No harm, no foul."

CJ nodded, appreciating the young man's candor and understanding his anxiety. "I get it, Alex. It's important to acknowledge when we've slipped up. But tell me, what exactly happened?"

Alex took a deep breath, too nervous to lie effectively. "I left to grab a quick snack—I hadn't eaten all day and thought it would be a quick trip. But that's no excuse. I was responsible for monitoring the gate, and someone must have unlocked it."

Erica, observing Alex's earnest demeanor, softened slightly. "It's good of you to come forward, but why didn't you report this immediately? The situation could have been much worse. Someone could've been really hurt."

Alex's shoulders slumped, the weight of the potential consequences hitting him. "I was scared," he admitted. "Scared of the repercussions, of being blamed for putting the production and everyone here at risk. I mean, this is my first gig, and I didn't want to jeopardize the chance of getting hired on another production."

But CJ understood the guy's anxiety. No one wanted to take the blame for anything going wrong on a multimillion-dollar production. "Look, I've got some pull. I'll make sure you're good. Just make sure it doesn't happen again, okay?"

Alex bobbed a nod, and CJ motioned for Erica to follow him toward Caroline's tent.

The missing wrangler's absence now seemed more suspicious than unfortunate. "Do you think the horse being let loose has anything to do with the missing wrangler?" CJ mused aloud, more to himself than Erica. The idea that someone might've been trying to sabotage the movie set seemed far-fetched, but in an industry rife with competition and envy, it wasn't entirely out of the question.

Erica followed his line of thought. "It does seem oddly coincidental, doesn't it? Both the missing wrangler and now this." She hesitated but asked with a subtle cringe, "Do you think someone on the crew could be responsible?"

CJ frowned, considering the possibility. "I don't want to jump to conclusions, but something doesn't feel right. I've been on plenty of productions, and this is the first time I've felt this black cloud at my back."

Maybe it was because of what'd happened with Doug, but CJ's sense of security was tilted on its axis—a feeling he wasn't accustomed to.

"You were pretty incredible," Erica admitted, glancing his way, catching his gaze. "I mean, I can't believe how scared I was. I felt like a little kid all over again and about to pee my pants with fear."

The idea of Erica—Miss Professional—wetting her drawers in fear because he'd encouraged her to come and see the horses made him feel ten times worse. "I'm so sorry for putting you in a position where you felt unsafe."

"It's not your fault. You couldn't have known that was going to happen," she said, letting him off the hook. "I'm just glad you were there to handle the situation the way you did. The upside of all this might be if your movie career doesn't pan out, you've always got an in as a horse wrangler."

He chuckled, but he couldn't shake the feeling that this was no accident. They arrived at Caroline's tent only to find it empty. "Damn," CJ muttered, but then caught sight of the production manager walking past.

"Hey, man, can I talk to you for a minute?" he called out.

The man, immediately recognizing CJ, stopped and waited. "Everything okay?"

CJ made quick work of sharing what'd happened, making sure not to point fingers at anyone, least of all the poor production assistant who was probably crapping himself with fear over potentially losing his job.

"The guy stepped away to grab a bite to eat, and then the horse was let out. It's probably a poorly thought-out prank, but I thought someone ought to know, given the fact that the wrangler didn't show up to set today."

He didn't want to say the word *sabotage*, but it clung to his thoughts.

"We'll look into it," the production manager assured CJ, his expression perplexed. "Looks like we might need to install security cameras to make sure this kind of thing doesn't happen again." He rubbed his forehead as if the very thought of adding one more item to his to-do list gave him an instant migraine. His cell phone chirped, and he whipped it out to read the message. "Hey, looks like they're looking for you on set. Caroline got the shot list changed."

"Thanks, man," CJ said, watching as the man jogged a way to handle another crisis. Turning to Erica, he said, "Want to watch me in action?"

She blushed, and he realized too late the sexual innuendo was too big to swerve. He chuckled, clearing his throat and clarifying, "I mean, watch me in the next scene. Could be entertaining."

Erica smiled, shrugging. "Seeing as I'm stuck here until I can catch a ride back to base camp, sure—as long as it's not a scene with horses."

He chuckled. "You're safe with me," he said, adding with a wink, "I promise."

But even as he smiled and seemed chill about the situation, deep down, he was still troubled. Someone had compromised the set. He could feel it in his bones. He wasn't a detective by any means, but his gut instinct told him that horse getting loose had been no accident.

The question was, why?

The incident had not only threatened the film's production but had also endangered Erica, something he found he could not forgive or forget. She hadn't asked for his protection, but she was going to get it anyway.

Maybe if someone had looked out for Allison Brewer, the yoga instructor Doug had killed at Mariposa, she'd still be here.

Maybe if he'd seen some kind of sign that his manager was a murderer…

Shake it off, man. Time to work.

Chapter Six

After her unexpected adventure by the horses, Erica found herself being gently ushered toward the heart of the film set. The director, a woman known for her sharp eye and even sharper wit named Anna Wilson, greeted Erica with a warm, if somewhat distracted, welcome. "Any friend of CJ's is welcome to hang out with us," she said. "I'm just annoyed that of all days to visit the set, it would have to be one where all hell is breaking loose. Sorry, but we're not usually this chaotic."

"Sometimes things are out of our control," Erica commiserated. "I'm the executive assistant at Mariposa Resort. Usually we say that if it can, it will go wrong, and we just have to pivot to accommodate."

Anna barked a short laugh and popped an antacid. "Amen to that. Okay, places, people. We're behind, and we're losing daylight."

Caroline, the assistant director, echoed Anna's direction, and the whir of activity started as people took their appropriate places in the production.

"This next scene is crucial," Anna shared. "We weren't scheduled to shoot this scene until a few days from now, but we adapt when we can—all because of one damn horse wrangler. I knew we should've planned for two instead of relying on one person."

Sitting beside the director, Erica felt a flutter of excitement mixed with nerves. She was about to watch a movie being made from the inside, an experience far removed from her day-to-day life at the resort.

As the preparations for the next take were finalized, Erica's gaze found CJ. He stood apart, his focus inward as he morphed before her eyes into someone entirely different.

The transformation was startling, a testament to his skill as an actor. But this shift, this ability to become someone else so convincingly, stirred a discomfort within her.

This was how it felt when he'd ghosted her after spending the night curled in each other's arms. *Jarring* wasn't the word for how it had felt in the aftermath.

The scene began, and Erica watched, captivated, as CJ and the actor playing the antagonist squared off. The tension between them was palpable, even from a distance, their exchange laden with threats and underlying danger.

CJ's character was a far cry from the man she knew—or thought she knew. He was intense, his presence dominating the scene, his voice carrying a weight that seemed to pull the very air tight around them.

Erica found herself enthralled by the performance, by the sheer talent it took to bring such a character to life. Yet this admiration was tempered by a nagging reminder of the role CJ had played off-screen.

The man who had charmed and lied, who had used his skills as an actor not for art but to manipulate her. The contrast between CJ's heroism with the horse and his deceit in their personal encounter left Erica wrestling with conflicting emotions. His actions earlier had shown a care and concern that had felt genuine, a stark contrast to the manipulation she'd experienced at his hands. But which version of CJ was real?

As the director called "Cut" and the tension on set dissolved into a bustle of movement and conversation, Erica remained seated, lost in thought. She was amazed by CJ's talent yet troubled by the duality of his character. How much of what she'd seen in those moments of crisis had been the real CJ and how much was just another role he played effortlessly?

The director turned to her, a knowing look in her eye. "Impressive, isn't he?" she asked, clearly proud of her leading man.

"Yes, very," Erica managed, her voice neutral. "He's very talented."

But her compliment felt hollow, overshadowed by the complexity of her feelings. The director, oblivious to anything but her film, returned her attention to the monitors.

Erica's thoughts drifted back to the scene she'd just witnessed, to the palpable tension and the undeniable charisma CJ brought to his character. It was a performance, yes, but one that highlighted the fine line between reality and pretense.

So, swallow your damn pride and just have a conversation with the man, a voice in her head counseled with enough hint of exasperation to make her wonder whose side the voice was on.

The conflict within her remained unresolved as the director called for a break, and Erica found herself standing, almost mechanically, her applause for the scene automatic.

She was caught in the dichotomy of CJ's world, where fiction and reality blurred, leaving her unsure of her footing—and that was an unfamiliar feeling for Erica.

She preferred much more straightforward situations where there was clearly a right or wrong answer. Checking her watch, she tried not to fidget as time continued to slip through the hourglass. Let this serve as a lesson to never leave her cell phone behind under any circumstances. She supposed she could ask to borrow someone's phone, but she already felt like a burden when there was so much chaos all around her.

Anna motioned for CJ to come to her, and he obliged, moving swiftly, his expression still locked in his character. Erica swallowed a shiver of awareness as her heart rate fluttered at the intensity in his energy. How did someone change their vibe so effortlessly?

"CJ, doing a good job, but I have some quick notes."

"I'm all ears."

"Okay, so you know when you deliver the line 'I know you were at the Buford Homestead the night Clarissa was killed'…?" At CJ's quick nod, she instructed, "I really need you to deliver that line as if it's taking every ounce of strength in you not to shoot him in the head. Like, you want to so bad, but you can't because you're the sheriff in a lawless town, trying to make a difference. Got it?"

"Yeah, got it." He wiped at the sweat beneath his worn cowboy hat, returning to his mark but not before cutting her a short glance with a subtle hint of a smile that sent butterflies rioting through her stomach.

Unfortunately, the director caught that look too and chuckled, warning, "Careful—that man's been known to break a few hearts on set."

Erica's cheeks flushed as she fought the fluster from her voice. "Oh, no worries of that. We're not even… I mean, we barely know each other. Actually, I should probably go find a phone. I need to call my office. Thanks for letting me watch you work. Fascinating stuff!"

And then she popped from her chair and practically ran from the set to find someone—anyone—who might have a phone she could borrow.

CJ'S HEART WAS still racing from the intensity of the scene as the director called "Cut," signaling the end of the take. The rush of adrenaline was familiar, a testament to his immersion in the role, but as he stepped out of character, a different concern began to take shape. His eyes scanned the bustling set, searching for Erica. He hadn't noticed her departure during the filming; his focus had been total, consumed by the demands of the scene.

"CJ, you ready for another take?" Anna called out, waiting for his thumbs-up. He couldn't hold up production to go look for Erica, but it bothered him that she'd bailed. Had she found a ride back to base camp, eager to be rid of him?

Tension prickled at the back of his neck, a mix of disappointment and worry settling in his stomach. He'd wanted her to see him work, to perhaps understand a part of his life that was so crucial to him, but also to share more of himself, the thing about him that he cared most about.

And maybe his ego was in there, too. He wanted her to see him in his element. She might even be impressed enough to give him a second chance.

CJ reluctantly gave a thumbs-up and returned to his mark, settling back into character. He had no choice but to finish what he was doing and then try to find where Erica had gone.

Finally, after what felt like hours, the scene wrapped, and he was cleared to take a break. He immediately made his way through the throng of people, his stardom and purposeful stride parting the sea of crew members with ease.

He approached one of the production assistants. "Hey, have you seen Erica Pike, the woman from the resort who was with me earlier? The woman who was sitting with the director during the last scene?"

The assistant shook his head, apologetic. "Sorry, CJ, I haven't seen her. But I've been all over the place. Maybe she's around craft services. That's where I always find people."

CJ thanked him and continued his search. The set was a labyrinth of equipment, trailers and temporary structures, a daunting place for someone unfamiliar with its chaotic order.

In a stroke of luck, he found Erica near the AD's tent. She looked up when she saw CJ approaching.

"There you are. I thought maybe you bailed."

"I would have," she answered honestly. "But everyone's still too busy to take me back to base camp. How long are these shoots?"

CJ admitted, "Pretty long. I think we had a twelve-hour day scheduled, and that was before the wrangler didn't show up, so having to pivot has made the day even longer."

Erica groaned. "I'm tired, my feet hurt and I'm hungry."

"I can help with the hungry part. Let's swing by craft services and see what's cooking. I overheard someone say burgers were going on the grill tonight."

"I need to find a phone," she said, stressed. "I'm surprised Laura hasn't called Search and Rescue out on me yet."

"Why didn't you say something? You can borrow mine." He produced his cell from his back pocket. "It's almost dead, but it should have enough juice to make a call so no one worries."

"Are you sure?" Erica asked, unsure. "I don't want to use up all your power."

"I'll find a charger somewhere. Go ahead," he said, handing her his cell.

Erica accepted the phone with a grateful smile. "I really appreciate this. Thankfully I have the resort's number in my head, but heaven help me if I can remember anyone else's number without my phone."

He chuckled, stepping away to give her some privacy.

"Hi, this is Erica Pike. Can you transfer me to Laura, please?"

CJ could only faintly hear Erica's end of the conversation but caught the gist.

"I'm basically stranded until someone can take me back to base camp. I'm so sorry… Are you sure? I feel terrible… No, you have enough on your plate already. I'm fine. It's more of an inconvenience. I wish I could tell you what time I'll be back, but CJ says we're going to be here for a few more hours at least. Long night of shooting scheduled." Erica murmured something he didn't quite catch and then clicked off, handing him the phone with a chagrined expression. "I used up the last of your juice. I'm sorry."

He shook his head, feeling bad that she was trapped with him. "I'm sorry this day turned out so differently from what you might have expected. Is there anything I can do? Anything you need?"

The offer hung between them, an olive branch extending into the space of their complicated history.

"I…actually, I think I'll take you up on that offer to get something to eat. All I've eaten is a protein bar, and it didn't go quite that far."

CJ grinned, relieved that he could be useful. "Absolutely. Let's see what's available."

Erica's suddenly shy smile was like sunshine on his soul, even if it was gone in a flash. One thing he was learning about Erica: she held her feelings close to the chest and didn't trust easily, which explained why his actions had hurt her so much.

He couldn't understand why her opinion of him meant so

much to him, but it did. Maybe she'd give him a chance to prove that he wasn't a jerk. Nothing like a full belly to extend some much-needed goodwill.

Chapter Seven

As the production broke for dinner, Erica sat at a makeshift table with CJ and the director, their plates piled with grilled southwestern burgers. If there was one thing Erica couldn't pass up, it was an expertly grilled burger oozing with cheese and spicy jalapeños.

"Damn, girl, just one of those suckers would take me out," CJ joked as Erica ate her second pepper. "How do you have any taste buds left?"

Erica chuckled. "You can't grow up in Arizona without acquiring a taste for the good spicy stuff. Besides, as my dad used to say, 'Puts hair on your chest.'"

Anna laughed. "Ha! I haven't heard that saying in ages. My dad used to say it, too. But it was usually when he was eating ptcha, calf's foot jelly. I wouldn't touch the stuff, but my dad thought it was good eating."

Erica tried not to grimace. "I, uh, can't say that I've ever tried that dish."

"And if you're lucky, you never will. Like I said, I don't even like it, and it's part of my culture. I'll give anyone a pass to decline a dish of that stuff."

Having Anna as a buffer between her and CJ made dinner entertaining. CJ, for his part, seemed content to listen and enjoy his burger while Anna and Erica chattered about life in the movie business as opposed to running an upscale resort.

"Look, I know this is probably counterintuitive because of the business I'm in, but I can only imagine how exhausting it must be dealing with a bunch of over-privileged jerks," Anna said, biting into a fry. "I mean, the egos on set can be a real pain in the ass, but at the end of the day, I'm not seeing to their comfort, I'm doing a job, same as them. Catering to their bullshit? No, thanks. I'd rather eat a plate of ptcha."

Erica laughed. "It's actually not that bad," she said. "We've been really lucky in that most of our guests are well-mannered and just happy to have a relaxing time at a nice place."

"There has to be some nightmare stories you can share," CJ teased. "C'mon, we're all ears."

Erica blushed beneath the force of CJ's playful smile but shook her head. "Sorry. All of our guests have been wonderful."

Anna grinned at CJ. "This woman's a professional. Page Six couldn't pull the tea out of this woman. Good for you. I respect that. If you ever decide to get out of the hospitality business, I could use someone like you on my staff."

"Flattered, but I don't think I'm cut out for the movie business."

"Fair enough." Anna shrugged, accepting Erica's answer, and the conversation circled around to the film and the day's events. Anna praised CJ's performance in the day's tense scenes. They teased each other in good fun about one another's talents, and from Erica's point of view, it was fun to catch the behind-the-scenes.

However, it wasn't long before the topic shifted to the day's earlier disruption—the missing wrangler—and the vibe shifted.

"The wrangler, he's a local guy," Anna mentioned, picking

at her burger. "Came with good references. It's strange he'd just bail without any warning." Her gaze swiveled to Erica. "Any chance you know the guy? His name is Kyle Jefferson."

Erica shook her head. "Sorry—he doesn't ring a bell."

"So there's no word on him yet?" CJ asked. "He hasn't called in or anything?"

"Radio silence on his end, but when Caroline was trying to find him, she dug up something interesting."

Both Erica and CJ were all ears.

Anna hesitated, her fork pausing midair, as if unsure if she should share. "Well, I'm not one for gossip, but given the recent circumstances, I'd hate for there to be some kind of connection," she admitted, her tone lowering.

"Connection to what?" CJ asked.

"Allison Brewer—the girl Doug DeGraw is accused of murdering."

CJ stared, unsettled by the news. "How so?"

"It could be a rumor, but sounds like they were dating," Anna said, wiping her mouth. "The thing is the minute Allison died, a spotlight shone on everyone in her sphere. A murder is one of those situations that contaminate everything. Nothing is ever just a simple thing anymore. The notoriety of a murder follows everyone attached to the victim."

"That's terrible," Erica murmured. "I hope he's okay. Maybe he took a mental health day or something."

"Maybe, but a phone call would've been nice," Anna said, wadding up her napkin and tossing it to the paper plate. Before Anna could continue on that topic, a production assistant approached, whispering something into Anna's ear. She cursed beneath her breath, standing abruptly. "Sorry—have to handle another crisis. You two enjoy your dinner." With that, Anna was gone, leaving Erica and CJ alone.

After a moment of silence, Erica decided to broach the

sensitive subject. "I can't even imagine how it must feel for you with the whole murder situation. How are you coping?"

CJ sighed, setting down his burger. "I don't really want to talk about Doug," he admitted. "But yeah, it's been tough. His actions…they've made me question everything I thought I knew about him. I don't like to make it about me, but Doug was more than my manager, he was my friend…but it feels wrong to grieve over losing a friend when that friend turns out to be a murderer."

Erica got that. It was complicated, for sure, but the honesty in his voice revealed a vulnerability that resonated with her. She reached across the table, covering his hand with her own in support. "I can't imagine how that feels, but you're not responsible for his actions."

CJ looked at her, his eyes a mix of gratitude and sadness. "Thanks, Erica. It's just…it's a lot to process, you know?"

She nodded. Although she couldn't quite imagine the weight of that burden, she knew how it felt to feel alone in something. "Yeah, I do. But you'll get through this."

CJ smiled at her, his eyes shining. "I hope so," he said, then cleared his throat. "So, you up for dessert? I think I saw chocolate chip cookies."

Erica hesitated, then smiled. "Sure, why not? I never turn down an opportunity for something sweet."

"Good to know." CJ flashed a smile that made her stomach flip, and she wondered if she owed CJ a second chance or if she was just falling into the same routine as before.

THE NIGHT SCENES stretched on, each take blending into the next until CJ could barely remember his lines without a prompt. He was used to this, but he felt bad for Erica. She tried to put on a brave face, but he caught the surreptitious yawns as she sat beside Anna take after take.

It seemed forever before they were able to finally wrap, Anna's voice cutting through the desert night air like a beacon of relief. The set erupted into a flurry of activity and structured chaos only film crews could master. Everyone was beat, their movements sluggish yet efficient as they began the nightly ritual of wrapping up.

CJ, usually whisked away by a diligent production assistant, tonight felt a pull to do things differently. He managed to sweet-talk the assistant assigned to their ride, a wide-eyed kid who looked like he'd do anything CJ suggested, into letting him take the wheel of the golf cart meant to shuttle him and Erica back to base camp.

"Trust me—I've driven in worse conditions," CJ assured him with a grin, glossing over the fact that navigating a golf cart through a deserted movie set hardly qualified as challenging.

But fate, it seemed, had a sense of humor. As the set emptied and silence took over, CJ and Erica were the last to leave.

Erica shivered at the quiet set. "It's a lot different when it's not crawling with people," she said.

"Kinda spooky, huh?" CJ winked. "Don't worry—I'll protect you."

Erica rolled her eyes. "Just get me to base camp in one piece so I can get home. I feel like I've lived an entire life on this set in one day, and I need to sleep for a good twelve hours."

CJ chuckled. "Welcome to my life, baby," he said, climbing into the golf cart as she joined him. "Life moves at a different pace on set. It's always a little jarring to find your feet again in real life. Sleep helps."

CJ reached for the key that should've been in the ignition, but his fingers grasped nothing. He peered at the ignition and realized with a sinking feeling—the key hadn't been left behind.

"What's wrong?"

Damn, this was embarrassing. "Um, so, we have a bit of a situation…"

"A situation? What does that mean?"

"There's no key."

Erica's eyes bugged. "No key? What?"

He chuckled with chagrin. "Yeah… I guess someone forgot to leave the key in the ignition and then left without checking that our ride was…uh, rideable."

"What are you saying? Are you saying we're…freaking stranded?"

Did he want to say that? No. But was it true? Yeah.

He fished his phone from his back pocket and realized too late that he had forgotten to put it on the charger. "Okay, so…yeah, we're stranded."

"Nooo," Erica groaned, looking ready to cry. "What are we going to do?"

"A solution will come to me," he said, though his mind was terrifyingly blank. He'd never been in this position before. He was a freaking movie star. He hadn't had to troubleshoot a problem in ages—and he was out of practice. But he couldn't have Erica terrified, not on his watch.

He flashed her an apologetic smile that he hoped conveyed both *I'm sorry* and *We'll laugh about this later* and said decisively, "Well, we can't spend the night in this golf cart. Come on, let's find a place to hang out until someone realizes I'm not back at base camp and comes looking for me."

"Are you sure someone will come?" she asked, following him out of the golf cart and rubbing her shoulders at the chill in the air.

"I mean, I'm the star," he said, but when he said it out

loud, he was suddenly less sure that anyone would notice. It wasn't like he had a bodyguard who was in charge of his safety, and filming had gone on so much longer than anticipated. Everyone was probably exhausted and ready to go to bed. CJ Knight's whereabouts were the last thing anyone wanted to worry about.

"Stranded on a movie set in the middle of nowhere. Great." She shivered. "And likely to catch pneumonia by morning."

An idea came to CJ. "Actually, I think I have an idea. Follow me." He slipped his hand into hers and led her to another section of the set that hadn't been used that day because of the rearranging of the shooting schedule.

"Is this a…brothel?" Erica asked as he led her into the makeshift bedroom that was supposed to be above the saloon.

"Oldest job in the world and probably what made the Wild West…well, wild." He grinned, gesturing to the bed. "But that's a bed with real blankets, so not only are we sheltered from the elements, we actually have bedding. But we might need to, uh, cuddle to conserve body warmth."

Erica laughed despite the situation. "If I didn't know better, I'd say you did this on purpose."

"I didn't—I swear it," he said in earnest, but a part of him wasn't sorry it'd happened. "Hey, at least it beats the usual 'stuck in an elevator' scenario, right?"

Erica shook her head with silent mirth and climbed into the bed, snuggling into the blankets with a sigh. "This is the weirdest day of my life, but you're right—it's warm and surprisingly comfortable."

"All right, scoot over, bed hog," he teased, kicking his boots off and climbing into the bed beside her. Immediately, the warmth of her body brought up memories he had no trouble recalling.

Judging by the sudden silence between them, Erica remembered, too.

"We're just sharing the bed for warmth," she said in a trembling voice. "Nothing more than that."

"Of course not," he said. "One question, though…"

"Yeah?"

"Is cuddling out of the question?"

A beat passed between them before Erica grudgingly allowed, "I guess in the interest of keeping warm, some cuddling is fine."

CJ tried to keep the grin from his mouth as he gruffly agreed, "Yep. Just for warmth."

It was either going to be a long night or the best night of sleep he'd had in years.

Chapter Eight

As the Arizona night stretched on, cold and unyielding, Erica found herself nestled against CJ in a prop bed set up for a scene that never got shot that day.

The absurdity of their situation wasn't lost on her—a pair of adults, wrapped up in blankets on a movie set, pretending the chill didn't seep into their bones. Yet beneath the surface absurdity, a current of something more profound pulled at her, tugging at the threads of her resolve and her feelings for CJ.

Despite it being May, the wind outside whistled across the desert like a pack of hungry wolves, the echoes carried by the desolate landscape surrounding them.

"I never would've imagined a film set being creepy when everyone's gone," she said. "Feels like a completely different place when it's bustling with people."

"Do you believe in ghosts?" CJ asked playfully.

"No." Erica's quick answer was followed by another shiver, prompting her to add, "Well, I mean, I believe in *science* more than the supernatural, but I'm also not interested in challenging my belief structure. If ghosts exist, I'd rather not know. Besides, in my experience, the evil that exists in the world is most definitely human."

"No argument there," CJ murmured.

Shivering, Erica pulled the blankets tighter around her body as she rested her head on CJ's broad chest. She could feel his heartbeat beneath her ear, steady and strong. She breathed in deeply, taking in his woodsy scent that mingled with the dusty smell of the desert air. A sense of calm washed over her as she listened to the rustling of leaves in the nearby bushes and the distant creaking of metal contraptions used for filming.

"I remember this feeling," she whispered softly, her voice barely above a whisper. "Being next to you felt so natural, which is the exact opposite of how I usually feel."

"What do you mean?" CJ asked.

In the darkness, she felt safe to be more exposed and vulnerable than she ever had before.

"I'm not really the kind of person who lets people in. My circle of trust is very small, and it usually takes years to gain access, but somehow you managed to slip in beneath my radar, and I still haven't quite figured that out."

"And then I hurt you when I disappeared," he finished quietly.

She nodded, her throat closing. "Yeah."

He stroked her hair gently, a familiar gesture that sent warmth coursing through her veins despite the cold. They lay there in silence for a while, lost in their own thoughts and memories until Erica mustered up the courage to ask what had been on her mind all evening.

"Why did you ghost me?"

Her question hung in the air like a weighted balloon waiting to be popped, suspended between them like an elephant on a trapeze.

"I don't like to use it as an excuse, but it's true—it was the perfect storm of circumstances. The night we hooked up, I was scheduled to leave anyway, but I'd fully planned to invite you to come see me in LA. Except the news broke about Doug, and it blew my world apart. I know it sounds superficial, but my world isn't like yours. Losing a manager in this business is like losing a vital part of yourself. They hold your career in their hands, which is why it's so important to find the right one. I hate to say it, but Doug was magic for my career—which makes it doubly hard to stomach that he might've been magic for me but he was lethal to someone else. I mean, I can't even wrap my head around it. To be honest, when it all went down, you were the last thing I was thinking about, but when the haze cleared and I wanted to call you, it was too late. I knew that window had shut, and I moved on."

It made perfect sense. Her logical brain understood, but it stung to know that she'd been so easily forgotten, even in the face of a tragedy. But maybe that was unfair of her to think that.

"I would've understood if you'd given me the chance," she said, although a part of her questioned if that were true. She didn't usually grant second chances to people who'd hurt her.

"I should've called. I'm sorry."

Did he mean that? Was it possible she was holding too tightly to her hurt feelings and not listening to the truth he was offering?

"I'll just say it now—I've missed you. I know we haven't had much of a chance to really get to know each other, but… I'd love the chance to start over and do it right."

"Do you mean that?"

"I do," he answered solemnly.

"Never thought I'd end up spending the night on a movie set," Erica mused, her voice a whisper against the silence that enveloped them. The set, a ghost town under the moon's watchful eye, held them in a bubble of suspended reality.

"Stick with me, baby. I bring the excitement," CJ quipped.

A soft laugh bubbled up in her chest. "That you do," she agreed, meeting his gaze.

In the starlight everything seemed dreamy, more surreal. Was she lying in a prop bed with Hollywood's most eligible bachelor, or was she hallucinating some secret fantasy she hadn't even known existed in her heart of hearts?

Heat grew inside her, stoked by CJ's presence and the memories of their shared past. She closed her eyes, savoring the rhythm of his heartbeat underneath her ear, taking deep breaths to calm her nerves. *Just go to sleep—figure everything out in the morning.*

Great rational advice, but logic and reason had vacated the building, leaving behind growing need and a red haze of desire that was hard to ignore.

Her body trembled slightly as she tried to ignore the goose bumps rising on her arms and legs—a mix of cold and anticipation.

"You're shivering," CJ said, pulling the blankets closer around them. "Get closer—our combined body heat will warm you up."

But it wasn't the cold that was making her shake.

"CJ… I know what I said, and I meant it at the time. But… if we're going to start over…shouldn't we start with what got us all twisted up in the first place?"

Yeah, that was some shaky reasoning, but her brain wasn't in control anymore.

CJ stilled, catching her drift. "Are you sure?" he asked, his voice strained, as if he were fighting the need to be a gentleman and the desire to pin her to the bed.

And right now, she wanted to be pinned, devoured and reminded how toe-curling his moves were.

"I'm sure," she whispered before rising to press her lips against his.

As if in response to her request, the wind died down outside and even the distant creaking sounds faded away into oblivion. They were alone in their own little world, two souls intertwined amid the desolate landscape of illusions and movie magic.

CJ kissed her deeply, their tongues tangling as his hands traveled up and down her spine before cupping her backside possessively with a groan. "Only if you're sure, baby," he said as he helped her pull her clothes off in a feverish motion. Within moments, they were both naked and the chill of the night was forgotten.

"Girl, you've lived in my dreams since the last time we were together," he admitted, filling his palms with her breasts before rising up to suck each tightened nipple into his mouth in turn.

She gasped at the rough lave of his tongue across her sensitive tips, thrilling at the insistent press of his erection against her hot core.

This felt taboo—and yet so intensely hot.

She wouldn't dare admit that her erotic dreams and fantasies had featured CJ front and center, but it was her shameful secret that she'd take to the grave. She couldn't forget how he'd turned her inside and out both physically and emotionally, and now it was happening again.

The exquisite torture was a sensual explosion of the senses, heightened by their extreme circumstances.

Girl, you're playing with fire, the voice in her head cautioned, but Erica was beyond hearing anything resembling reason.

Right about now, going down in flames sounded like the most sublime way to go.

Erica's head fell back against the pillow as she moaned softly, her long brown hair spilling over the rough cotton sheets of the prop bed. The metal frame squeaked rhythmically in time with his thrusts.

Her body trembled under CJ's touch, her hips shifting against his hand in rhythm with his explorations. Her breathing grew deeper, and her eyes drifted shut, lost in the moment.

CJ couldn't believe how good it felt to be inside her—how right it felt. He slid his hand up her side and cupped her breast, his thumb brushing against the hardening nipple. She gasped, arching into his touch as he teased and twirled the tightened bud between his fingers. Her skin was warm and soft against his palm, her breasts full and heavy in his hand.

"You're so damn perfect," he murmured, trailing kisses down her neck, nipping lightly as he went. His lips found her collarbone and then lower still, until he reached the valley between her breasts where he paused for a moment to savor the taste of her skin.

The air was thick with the scent of their arousal, making CJ yearn for more. The sound of their skin slapping together filled the small room, growing louder as their pace quickened.

A bead of sweat trickled down his forehead, adding to the sheen on his skin that glistened in the dim light cast by the full moon and vast expanse of starlight outside the fake glass windowpane. The rustle of the sheets drowned out all other sounds as they moved together like two well-oiled machines. He smiled against her soft skin as her nails dug into his shoulders, no doubt leaving faint red marks that would soon turn to bruises. She gripped him tighter, pulling him closer to her core, urging him to go deeper.

Her legs wrapped around his waist, lifting her off the mattress slightly to meet each savage thrust, their hips meeting in perfect harmony with a desperate rhythm that left them both panting for breath.

His free hand trailed down her side, exploring every contour of her body before bracing himself against the metal frame, holding on for dear life.

He took advantage of this position to thrust even deeper against that velvet heat, groaning at the feel of their bodies joined so tightly together.

CJ's heart raced faster than he thought possible; his chest tightened with anticipation and desire as he buried himself so deep, they were nearly one.

When he climaxed, unleashing a torrent within her, he lost all sense of time and space.

He gasped her name, shuddering as he spent himself, rolling beside her, sucking air as his heart thundered in his chest.

It was several moments before he could collect himself enough to check on Erica—who was in a similar state.

A drowsy but satisfied smile found his lips, but as Erica cuddled up to him, a different feeling started to creep up on him, one that was unwelcome.

The feeling of being watched.

It was improbable that anyone was there with them.

But being alone with nothing to defend themselves with—not even the ability to call for help—made him feel vulnerable in a way he'd never truly experienced.

You're imagining things. Whatever this is, knock it off. Don't screw things up again.

He settled and tried to relax, but Erica caught the tensing of his body. "What's wrong?" she asked.

"Nothing…just a weird place to be stuck in," he said. "I—"

The sound of something banging outside interrupted him, and he bolted upright. CJ's heart thrummed against his chest as the noise outside jolted him back to reality. It was a sharp, sudden sound that sliced through the stillness of the night—a crack, perhaps, or a clatter that didn't belong amid the silence.

"What was that?" Erica asked, grabbing her shirt and pulling it on.

"Probably just a curious animal, but I think I should check it out."

"And do what if it is more than a raccoon? Hurl insults in the hope of hurting their feelings? I think we should just stay put and be quiet," Erica said, her voice a hushed whisper.

Wise, but not very gallant. "You want me to hide in the dark? Should I hand over my man card now or later?"

Erica persuaded him to return to her side. "I promise your man card is well and truly represented."

As much as he was tempted to return to cuddling, he couldn't rest until he knew they were safe. "Stay here. I'll be right back."

"CJ…" Erica called after him, frustrated. "Just—"

"Shhh. I just need to know no one's out there messing with shit."

Erica grabbed her pants and pulled them on. "Then I'm going with you. I'm not going to stay behind like a good little lady clutching her nightie. Besides, haven't you watched any horror films? You never separate."

"Fair point," he said, grinning. "Okay, Annie Oakley, let's do a perimeter search, then."

He slipped his hand into hers, and they went off to make sure no one was prowling the set. But he hoped to God it was just his imagination and not an actual threat because like, Erica had said…he had nothing but his sharp tongue to defend them.

Chapter Nine

CJ would've preferred Erica stay behind for safety reasons, but once he stepped outside, he was thankful for her hand in his. They moved together, a pair of shadows adrift in the enveloping darkness of the abandoned film set.

Despite the full moon, the pale light did little more than tease the edges of their path and create more menacing shadows. Every prop loomed like a specter, every flutter of wind felt like breath on the nape of his neck. But there was nothing—no sign of intrusion, no evidence of danger. Nothing but the rustle of leaves and the far-off hoot of an owl keeping vigil over the night.

"Probably just a raccoon," CJ concluded, though his voice lacked conviction and he felt a little foolish for being so jumpy. "I mean, what are the odds someone else is tromping around the set, too?"

"I'd hope the odds are small," she joked. "Otherwise that's creepy in a different way."

He agreed with a chuckle as they returned to their makeshift bedroom.

Back within the confines of the four walls they had claimed as their own, CJ caught Erica's gaze. There was a silent question there surrounding what'd unfolded between them once again. He didn't want to be just another scene in her life, a fleeting moment soon cut and edited out. Yet what was he hoping for? He didn't have an answer for himself, so he sure as hell hoped Erica didn't ask the question.

"People are always so surprised by how cold it gets in the desert," Erica shared as they climbed back into the creaky bed. "Laura said that we ought to consider having a boutique at the resort just for those times when guests come unprepared for the weather."

"Are you and your boss close?" he asked, curious about her personal life.

"Yeah, I guess so. I'm in charge of her bachelorette party, so I think she trusts me enough for that important job. She's a great boss, though. She doesn't micromanage, which is crucial for me. When people try to micromanage me, I get twitchy."

"You seem highly capable on your own. I can't see why anyone would feel the need."

"Thank you," she said, snuggling against him. "Right now this whole night feels unreal, like I'm going to wake up in my own bed and realize this was some fever dream."

"What? You mean you've never spent the night in a closed film set overnight? Girl, this is a typical Friday night."

She laughed at his joke, allowing the easy silence between them to settle. Why did it feel so natural to hold her in his arms? They barely knew each other. "Tell me something about yourself," he said, needing to know more than just the surface Erica that everyone else knew.

Erica yawned, her voice sleepy. "Hmm…what do you want to know?"

"Anything."

"I don't like artichokes."

The simple statement made him smile. "No artichokes. Is there a reason, or just in general?"

"If you must know, I choked on one when I was a kid. I accidentally got one of the thistles in my throat, and my throat seized up. Traumatized me. Haven't touched one since."

"Horses and artichokes—trauma central. Got it. Any other traumas lurking in your childhood I should know about?"

She chuckled. "None that I can think of offhand. How about you?"

"Nothing so dramatic or interesting. I'm allergic to pine nuts, though."

"Pine nuts? Not peanuts?"

"Nope—all good with peanuts, but give me a pine nut and I'll end up in the hospital."

"Good to know. No pesto sauce for you, then."

"Yeah, my love for Italian pasta has been forever shelved."

"There's always Alfredo," Erica murmured, nearly asleep.

He grinned when he heard her breathing change to slow and steady. He held her close, allowing himself to simply enjoy the moment—strange as it was—because he knew when the morning came, everything would change.

THE GENTLE INVASION of dawn's light heralded the return of reality. Erica's eyes fluttered open at the distant sounds of voices, the metallic clink of equipment being unloaded… the film crew had arrived, oblivious to the mini drama that had unfolded in their absence.

CJ awoke at the same moment, muttering, "Shit," and they scrambled, a flurry of limbs and fabrics as they wriggled into their clothes to slip from their temporary sanctuary before anyone caught them and started asking questions. "We need to find Caroline," he said, leading the way toward the AD's tent.

Erica appreciated CJ taking the lead, though she was embarrassed to be seen so disheveled. Even though she knew it was unlikely, she cringed at the thought that everyone who saw her would be able to see that they'd hooked up.

Talk about a walk of shame.

"Stranded? You two?" Caroline's voice climbed an octave, her professionalism dueling with concern as CJ shared their unfortunate unscheduled sleepover. "I'll find out who's responsible—"

"Hey, it's okay," CJ interjected quickly, shaking his head. "Everyone was running on fumes last night. Let's not make a mountain out of a molehill. Plus, if I'm being honest, it's more my fault than anyone's. If I hadn't persuaded the PA to let me drive back to base camp, this never would've happened."

Caroline hesitated, then nodded, her expression softening. "You're too kind, CJ."

Erica met his gaze, silently appreciating how he was willing to take the blame and save someone's job.

However, Erica felt compelled to add, "We did have to take shelter in the set with the bed because it was the only one with blankets. You might want to have your set team change out the bedding for sanitary purposes."

"Oh, yes, of course," Caroline agreed. "I'll have someone take care of that right now, but in the meantime, you both probably want to shower and get back to your routines."

"Much appreciated. Yes, a shower would be amazing right now...and a quick nap in my own bed. I'm thankful for the set bed, but the Old West wasn't big on comfort. I think I have a bruise from the metal springs," Erica joked, but then her cheeks flared at the unintended slip. She was bruised, all right...but not likely from the bed.

She glanced at CJ long enough to catch a smoking-hot look, and her breath caught in her chest. "Yes, anyway, I'd really love to get home," she said hurriedly.

A different production assistant approached, clipboard in hand, ready to shuttle them back to base camp. The return ride was quiet, professional, devoid of the closeness they'd found in the dark. Erica had felt the eyes of the crew on them, curious, speculative, which was an uncomfortable feeling for her.

CJ kept his distance from Erica, a bittersweet tug in her chest. She wanted to reach out, to steal one more moment, but the world was watching now, and she was no more interested in being the subject of everyone's gossip than he was.

Back at base camp, Erica and CJ exited the golf cart, and the production assistant confirmed he'd return in an hour to return him to set before he drove off.

"Wow, you really know how to show a girl a night worth remembering," she teased, pushing an errant lock away from her face as the slight breeze played havoc with her mussed hair.

He chuckled, cracking a short yawn. "You okay to drive back to your place?"

"Yes, I'm fine. I feel bad for you having to return to set for a full day of shooting after the night we had."

"No rest for the wicked."

"So they say," she mused, risking a look his way. Should they make plans to see each other again? What happened next? "Thanks for looking out for me last night…and sharing your body heat."

"My pleasure," he said in a silky tone that sent shivers down her spine. "I'd say let's do it again sometime, but I think we broke about ten different SAG and OSHA rules in one setting."

She laughed ruefully. "I think you might be right." Was it possible to hope that they truly could start fresh? Under ordinary circumstances she didn't believe in second chances, but CJ Knight was no ordinary guy. Maybe the situation warranted a little leeway.

She started to walk away, calling over her shoulder. "You have my number," she said, and let the innuendo fall where it might.

If CJ meant what he said, he'd call.

If not, she'd stick to her original plan and forget he'd ever existed.

Chapter Ten

"Okay, break for lunch. One hour," the AD called out on her bullhorn, and bells and whistles sounded throughout the set as everyone prepared to take a break from the grueling sun and grab a bite.

For CJ, he needed a minute to himself. There was too much on his mind—mostly Erica—but also there was something about last night that felt odd.

He used the time to call Landon and make sure his house was still standing.

"Hey, man, how's filming?" Landon asked. "I heard Arizona is heading for a heat wave. Not that it's not already the devil's armpit."

"Yeah, they're planning to erect some cooling stations here on location so people don't drop like flies. But other than that, it's business as usual. How's the house?"

"Everything's still standing," Landon quipped with a grin in his voice. "You know I treat it like my own. Ain't nothing gonna happen on my watch. Although you're going to need to throw some money on the house account because there's nothing to eat in this place."

"Buy your own damn groceries, you moocher," CJ shot back, but he was only kidding, and Landon knew it. "Fine,

I'll put some more money on the house account, but try not to spend it all on beer."

"Beer? Hard liquor, my friend—we're watching our waistlines." But Landon waited a beat before asking, "So, what's going on? What's the real reason you called?"

Landon knew him too well. "You're not going to believe what happened last night. Me and a friend had to spend the night on set. Had to spend the night curled up in a prop bed."

"You're kidding me. How'd that happen?"

"That's the thing—I'm sure it was an accident. The shooting schedule got all screwed up when the horse wrangler was a no-show, and everyone was running on fumes by the time we wrapped. But when I went to hop into the golf cart, there were no keys."

"Seriously? I've never heard of that happening. I mean, every production manager I've ever met is a bulldog and makes sure everyone's doing their job, or it's their ass."

"Same." He couldn't explain how he felt about what had happened last night both with Erica and being stranded, but it all felt unreal, and while being with Erica had been amazing, being stranded had not. "But a lot of weird things have been happening on this shoot. I could've sworn I heard someone walking around in the middle of the night even though I know we were the only ones there."

"Hey, hey, don't go there," Landon said with a chuckle, clearly trying to sound lighthearted. "It was probably just your imagination working overtime. The desert gets to everybody. Or maybe it was a ghost of productions past," he teased, before switching gears. "Now, why don't you tell me more about this friend of yours who stayed over? Are we talking sweaty production assistant or hot Sedona chick?"

CJ didn't like to kiss and tell, but he knew Landon would

figure it out somehow. “Yeah, it was Erica. Remember that girl I told you about before leaving?”

Landon whistled low. “Damn. How’d that go?”

“Good. I mean, I think we were able to hash out some things, clear the air, so to speak.”

“You like her?”

“Yeah, but she’s here, I’m in LA. Not really sure how much of a real future is there.”

“I hear you—best not to get too attached. That’s my motto every day.”

“You’re a commitment-phobe,” CJ said derisively. “We’re not the same.”

“Of course we aren’t,” Landon replied breezily, his words belying the ease with which he drew the parallel. CJ buttoned his lip; arguing about it only made him seem more suspect.

CJ switched gears, chatting about the minutiae of the film set and starting to relax. The real charm behind Landon was his ability to project some kind of inner calm even when his own life seemed steeped in chaos. The man didn’t have a stable address, couch surfed at various friends’ places and never worried a day in his life about where his next meal was coming from—yet rarely worked.

He could picture Landon sitting cross-legged on his couch with his phone pressed against his ear while he watched one of those reality home-makeover shows that always seemed to be on the television. Ironic, seeing as Landon would likely never own a home of his own.

CJ shook off his thoughts, realizing the time. “Break’s almost over, and I still need a ten-minute nap,” he said. “Thanks for holding down the fort.”

“No problem, man. You know I got you. Don’t get left behind. Get yourself a dedicated driver who doesn’t move a muscle unless he’s with you. That’ll solve that problem.”

CJ chuckled. "Thanks. I'll do that."

Landon clicked off, and CJ tossed his phone to the small table in his tent. On location, his private area wasn't much to look at, but at least it had a makeshift cot and a cooling fan. Good enough for a quick snooze before hitting the set again.

When he closed his eyes, all he saw was Erica, which made him wonder…should he pursue her? Or should he let that connection go?

He opened his eyes and stared up at the ceiling of his tent. The fan beside him whirred loudly as the air blew over him, providing some relief from the hot Arizona sun.

Maybe it was better if they didn't keep in touch. It would only complicate things and create unnecessary drama. Plus, what kind of future did they really have? She lived in Arizona and he lived in LA. They were in two completely different worlds.

But then again, CJ couldn't shake off the feeling that there was something special between them. Something worth holding on to. He couldn't remember the last time another person had dominated his thoughts like this. Most days his career took center stage—and he'd liked the simplicity of that single drive.

Maybe it was the whole situation with Doug that had him thinking of things in a different way. Or maybe he was just getting older and realizing there was supposed to be more to life than what he was doing.

His phone vibrated next to him and interrupted his thoughts. He grabbed it eagerly, hoping it was a message from Erica. But instead it was a quick text from the AD that shooting would resume in a half hour.

He sighed and tossed his phone back onto the table. This film project was consuming all of his time and energy, leaving him with little room for anything else.

Maybe that was a good thing.

He couldn't tell anymore.

ERICA'S STEPS CARRIED a lightness that only a combination of steaming water and a good hard nap could bestow. She breezed through the lobby of the resort, the clacking of her heels on the marble floor punctuating each determined stride toward Laura's sanctuary-like office.

"Hey," she said, pushing open the door without knocking. The familiarity between them rendered formalities unnecessary—besides, Erica knew Laura was anxious to hear all about her little adventure last night.

Laura looked up from a mountain of paperwork, her eyes widening in anticipation. "You're back! Tell me everything."

"Where do I even start?" Erica chuckled, sinking into the chair opposite Laura's desk. She recounted the surreal experience, omitting the scorching hookup with CJ, and instead painted vivid images of the deserted film set—props casting eerie shadows, the moonlight filtering through the skeletal structures of incomplete scenes.

"Wow, it's like you lived in a movie for a night," Laura said as she digested the cinematic adventure. "I have to admit it sounds pretty exciting, almost like an urban explorer or something. I'm a little jealous."

"Jealous?" I laughed. "Did you miss the part where I said we had to bunk down on a prop bed? Let me tell you—it wasn't a luxury bed, and it squeaked every time you breathed."

And when you did other things, she left out.

"And everything was chill between you and CJ?" Laura asked, curious. "Last I heard, you two were not exactly friends."

"Oh, it was totally fine," Erica assured Laura quickly.

"Nothing like a random stranding to put things into perspective. I was probably too hard on him. I mean, his manager was arrested for Allison's murder—that had to be hard to deal with."

Laura winced, murmuring, "It hurts my heart to even think of what happened to poor Allison. She was such a sweet girl. I still have nightmares about it."

Erica understood. It might've seemed like it was business as usual at Mariposa, but there was definitely a pall of sadness that clung to the darkened corners knowing that a young girl had died there. Laura had even considered having the place "cleansed," but Josh had thought that was a little extreme and shot down the idea.

Laura sighed, returning to Erica's story. "Maybe I'm not cut out for that level of adventure, but it might be nice to be without a phone for a night. I swear mine doesn't stop binging or chiming or yanking on my electronic tether for ten minutes."

"You could always silence your phone, Laura, if you need a minute to breathe," Erica suggested with a wry chuckle. "No need for anything as dramatic as being stranded in the desert."

"On the surface that sounds like a workable plan, but then I remember my family is so protective that if I was incommunicado for more than a few hours, they'd send a search and rescue team after me."

"Josh would definitely do that," Erica agreed, standing as she checked her watch. "On that note, I have to get moving."

Laura nodded, but her sudden "Oh!" as she reached into her desk told Erica that was more. "I almost forgot. I don't know where my brain is at, but I swear as soon as all this wedding prep is over, I'll be so relieved. There's one more person I absolutely need to have at my bachelorette party.

Her name is Willow Sanderson, and she was my absolute bestie in college. If I didn't invite her, she'd fly out from California just to put hair remover in my shampoo bottle and then leave again."

Erica frowned with alarm. "You *want* to invite her?"

But Laura laughed. "I'm kidding about the hair remover, but I'd definitely get an earful, and rightfully so—that woman got me through college. I can't count how many times she saved my ass from horrible dates. We had a system..." Laura remembered Erica was pressed for time, "Sorry—a story for another time. Here's her contact information."

Erica glanced over the paper. "She's in California? Isn't this a bit short notice for her to come to Arizona by next week?"

Laura waved off Erica's concern. "Her parents are loaded. She'll love the excuse to jump in a plane and stop whatever she's doing. Trust me. You'll love her. She's a hoot."

A "hoot" sounded like a headache, but it was Laura's party, so Erica wouldn't say no. "I'm on it," she said with a smile.

Laura winked. "You're the best."

Erica left Laura's office and headed to housekeeping to check in with staff, ensure that all was moving as it should, then met with the carpet installer, put out a few internal fires and set her office back to rights after her impromptu stay on set.

By the time Erica's day was finished, she felt confident everything was back on track, which was a nice feeling.

But what wasn't a nice feeling was the fact that CJ hadn't tried to text or call her since leaving her this morning. True, he was on set and he probably had a full shooting schedule, but how hard was it to send a quick text?

No fixating allowed, that voice reminded her. *People will show their true intention if you let them.* If CJ wanted to call, he would.

And if he didn't…well, she'd have her answer about that, too.

Erica perched on the edge of her neatly made bed, fingers dancing across the keyboard of her laptop as she typed out invitations for Laura's bachelorette party.

With every chime signaling an email sent, her thoughts intermittently drifted against her will, pulling her back to memories of CJ. Her heart fluttered a little with a mix of hope and doubt, the night they'd shared looping in her mind like a highlight reel that refused to stop playing.

She shook her head, trying to refocus on the task at hand, but the monotony of typing names and addresses left too much room for wandering thoughts.

The phone lay next to her, its screen blank and unyielding. She willed it to light up with a notification, any small sign that CJ hadn't just vanished after their intimate encounter.

"Come on, Erica, keep it together," she muttered to herself, her gaze inadvertently straying to the device again. The silence from CJ was louder than any message tone, a silent symphony of rejection that filled the spaces around her.

"Focus," she whispered, her fingers resuming their earlier rhythm. She breezed through a few more invitations until another pause allowed doubt to creep in once more. Wasn't this exactly what she had feared? That the connection she'd felt, the laughter and shared secrets under the guise of night, were nothing but a well-rehearsed act?

Which she'd fallen for *again*?

The clock on the wall ticked away the time, and the sinking feeling in her stomach grew heavier with each passing hour. It wasn't just that she was possibly being ghosted; it was the creeping realization that she might have willingly played the fool in CJ's performance not once but twice.

"Screw him, then," she muttered, the words hollow as they hung in the air. Yet despite her resolve, her eyes betrayed her, glancing one last time at the silent phone before she turned off the bedside lamp.

The darkness of the room seemed to echo the silence from CJ, wrapping around her like a shroud. As sleep eluded her, Erica lay there, grappling with the nagging question that gnawed at her pride: Was she really that much of a sucker?

Chapter Eleven

The dust swirled around CJ's boots as he made his way to Mariposa, the weight of the production's future pressing on his shoulders. Sure, one might say it wasn't his problem if the production failed, but he believed in this project, and he'd be damned if he'd let it fail without at least trying to help.

I have an idea, CJ had said to Anna as she'd stared up at the blue skies, the lingering of acridity of smoke still in the air.

But Anna had looked despondent. *I hate to say it, but this was the nail in the coffin. We can't recoup this loss*, she'd said, her eyes still red from the smoke. *I just don't understand how this happened. A set fire? I'm at a loss.*

It had supposedly been an accident—bad luck—but it seemed this production was having more than its fair share of that level of catastrophe.

And then a wild idea had come to him. *What the hell? What do we have to lose?* He'd pitched his scheme to the director, who likely had been envisioning her career on its deathbed for the production's failure.

Anna, clearly feeling it was hopeless anyway, had waved him on. *Sure. Knock yourself out, CJ. Lord knows we could use a damn miracle.*

With each step, he ran through the potential pitch in his

head now, aware that the entire project teetered on the brink of collapse. Under ordinary circumstances, he would've felt bad for the production but would've moved on without breaking a sweat. But this project had legs. He could feel it. It was more than just another Western in a crowded market—it had heart and grit.

He had to do whatever he could to save it from going under—and he knew just the person to ask for help.

Josh Colton, with his easy smile and lingering curiosity about the film industry, was sitting behind the reception desk when CJ walked into the cool lobby of the resort. The contrast between the calm interior and the chaotic set couldn't have been more pronounced. He knew it was a team effort, but he knew Erica helped keep this place running like a well-oiled machine.

"Hey, Josh," CJ began with an engaging smile. "Remember me?"

Josh smiled. "How could I forget? What brings you back? Need a room or something?"

"Actually, I'd like to ask a favor. I remember you mentioned an interest in the movie biz... Can we go to your office and talk a minute?"

"Hit me where I'm weak, why don't you?" Josh replied with an intrigued grin and motioned for CJ to follow him. As they walked into Josh's office, CJ caught Erica talking to staff, but she saw him right as Josh closed the door behind them.

"Okay, you got my attention. What's the favor?"

"I'll cut to the chase—a large portion of our set burned down last night. It was an accident, but the damage is catastrophic. This production has been hit with multiple whammies, and this one—well, the director doesn't think we can recover, but I do."

"How so?"

"By shifting locations while that portion of the set is rebuilt."

"As much as I'd love to help, I'm not really sure how I could. You're filming a Western, right?"

"True, but I recall you mentioning something about a piece of the Mariposa property that's closed for a remodel that just happens to have an old barn…"

"Yeah, that's true, but it's not safe out there, which is why we have it closed off."

"I wouldn't worry about that part. All we need is the façade, and the set team will have it looking like it's straight out of the history books," CJ assured quickly, preempting any concerns. "And if there's so much as a scratch on anything, it's on me. I'll foot the bill."

"Are you sure you want to take that on?" Josh asked.

"I'm probably reckless—and if my manager was still around, he'd make me stop—but I think that's why I want to do this. I need to do something good for other people, not just for myself, you know? And I've known Anna Wilson for a while, and she's the best of people. Her talent is next level, but it's taken her a while to get a project like this greenlit. I don't want to see it go down the toilet. Not if I can help."

Josh nodded quietly, seeming to feel the shadow of Allison's death just as surely as CJ did but likely for different reasons. "I'm happy to help. We'll find a way to make it work."

Relief washed over CJ. "That would be amazing, Josh. Truly. I mean, I know we don't know each other that well, but I mean it when I say that you're a good guy."

Josh chuckled, shaking his head. "Hey, don't go starting rumors. I've got a reputation to protect."

But Josh was a good man. CJ could see it. Not to mention

Erica was an excellent judge of character, and he couldn't imagine she'd work for a family that was trash.

"I'll set up a dinner with the director and producer so y'all can meet and hash out the details. I really appreciate this, man. You're saving a lot of jobs."

Josh smiled, remembering, "Hey, since we're talking, I heard you have a horse-wrangler issue. I know a guy. Good with horses, reliable. He could fill in."

CJ's excitement was barely containable as he shook Josh's hand. Not only had he secured a temporary shooting location but also a lifeline for the horse scenes. He couldn't wait to share the news with Erica, to see the spark of hope relight in her eyes. This was more than a win for the production; it was a personal victory for CJ, a chance to prove his worth beyond doubt.

"Now that we've got that settled, mind if I grab your executive assistant for a minute?"

Josh said, "I don't mind, but good luck trying to find her. She's never in the same spot for long. I'm pretty sure she portals from one place to the other."

He chuckled and let himself out, immediately heading in the direction he'd seen Erica last.

ERICA'S STEPS FALTERED as she turned the corner and spotted CJ, leaning casually against the wall with his hands buried in the pockets of his faded jeans.

The sight of him was a jolt to her system, like an unexpected storm breaking the stillness of a summer day. Why was he here? Her heart took off, wings beating erratically against the cage of her ribs. She swallowed, schooling her expression into one of friendly professionalism.

"Erica," he said, pushing off the wall with a grace that

made her stomach flip. His eyes locked onto hers, carrying that familiar spark of mischief she found so disarming.

"Why are you here?" she asked, her voice steady despite the fluttering within. "I thought your shooting schedule was tight."

"It was—it still is, but there's been a change in plans," he answered with a tone that seemed too casual for the concern knitting her brows together.

"A change? Like what kind of change?"

He ignored her question for a minute to gaze into her eyes. "Why do you get prettier each time I see you?" he murmured, as if perplexed by his own question.

She faltered, her voice catching in her throat as heat climbed her cheeks. How did he manage to make it feel like they were the only two people in the world?

But then she remembered. No calls, no texts…just silence. That unwelcome pattern crawled over her skin, leaving a trail of discomfort. She wasn't about to fall into his arms every time he found it convenient to be around her.

"Is everything okay?" Erica asked, trying for professionalism, even though her stomach muscles were trembling.

That seemed to shake CJ loose from the sensual fog, and he shook his head. "Actually, you're not going to believe this, but part of the set burnt down last night."

Erica's eyes bugged at the unexpected news. "Excuse me? Burnt down? Is everyone okay?"

"Everyone is fine aside from some scratchy throats and gritty eyes from the smoke. Thank God for the on-call fire engine. They were able to put it down pretty quick, but those facades go up fast. Doesn't take much to raze them to the ground, and *poof!* Millions of dollars gone."

"Oh God, that's awful," Erica said. "What part of the set went down?"

"The fire tore through the saloon," he answered, meeting her gaze. "It's all gone."

The saloon—their saloon—where beneath a pale moon, they'd crossed lines drawn in the sand of professionalism. Erica felt the sting of loss for a place that had become a private landmark in her memory.

"Wow, I…" She trailed off, her mind trying to piece together how this could have happened, especially considering how rigid safety protocols were on set. But then again, with everything else that had befallen the production, *safe* was perhaps not the right word.

"But there's a silver lining," CJ said, touching her elbow gently, grounding her back to the present. "Josh has agreed to allow filming to resume here while the set is rebuilt, so in a way, your resort is saving the production."

"He did what?" Erica repeated, shocked. "How'd you manage that?"

"When I was a guest, me and Josh started chitchatting, and he happened to mention that he'd always been fascinated by the movie business. So I capitalized on that fascination."

"I don't know how Laura is going to take that news," Erica said, shaking her head.

And speak of the devil.

"Oh my good gravy, Erica, brace yourself—my brother has volunteered the resort for a movie location." Laura's voice sliced through the low hum of resort activity as she approached, her expression a mix of bewilderment and burgeoning stress. Her hands fluttered to her chest, where her heart seemed to be pounding out an SOS. "Has he no idea how much strain that's going to put on the staff? On me?"

"Um, yes, CJ just told me," Erica replied, her voice soothing like a balm. "But don't worry, Laura. I'll handle everything." She laid a reassuring hand on her boss's arm, grounding her amid the swirl of unexpected news. "You just worry about your wedding stuff. Let me handle the resort extras."

Relief flooded Laura's expression even as she cast an apologetic look toward CJ. "I'm sorry. I'm sure it's terribly exciting to have a movie set on location, but right now, it's the last thing I can handle. This wedding prep is devouring every single one of my brain cells. If I had to juggle one more ball, I'd probably drop them all."

"I totally understand, and we appreciate your help more than you know. As I told Josh, Mariposa stepping up is definitely saving the production—and countless jobs."

That seemed to make Laura stand a little straighter with pride. "Well, I'm glad we can make it work." But to Erica, she said, "I'm sorry this is falling onto your plate. You already have so much."

"Well, you know what they say…if you want something done, give the task to a busy person," Erica said with a confident smile.

"True— Oh!" A sudden thought struck Laura like lightning, breaking through the overcast of her worries. "Willow RSVP'd! She'll be here for the bachelorette party. We'll need to arrange a room for her—one with a good view. She likes to watch the sunrise with her coffee."

"Of course. Willow will have a great room waiting," Erica promised, already mentally scanning the reservations to accommodate Laura's friend.

"Perfect—thanks!" And with a flutter of hands that mirrored the chaos of her mind, Laura dashed away to tackle some other emergent issue, leaving Erica and CJ alone once again.

"You're really the backbone of this place," CJ said with wonder in his voice.

Erica chuckled at his praise, but something still troubled her and she needed to talk about it.

"Come with me," Erica said to CJ, motioning with a tilt of her head toward the closed section of the resort.

The closed section, a forgotten corner of the resort that had seen better days, featured a large barn, broken-down stables and a rotting fence line that might've been built in the 1800s. Josh had plans to turn it into an outdoor amphitheater for outdoor concerts, but those plans were still in the early stages. In the meantime, it was cordoned off to guests for safety reasons.

She gestured to the area with a dubious look. "It's not much to look at. Are you sure the set department will be able to make it work?"

CJ surveyed the area with a critical eye, deciding. "It's perfect," he said, almost to himself. He turned back to her, a spark igniting in his gaze. "Our team can work wonders, Erica. You won't even recognize it in a few days."

"Camera-ready and safe?" She couldn't keep the skepticism from her voice, her brows knitting together as she imagined the scale of transformation required.

"Absolutely," he confirmed with a nod, his assurance as steady as the ground beneath their feet. "You'd be amazed what they can accomplish. An added bonus—Josh has a horse wrangler he can call in to replace the guy that was a no-show. Like I said, Mariposa is saving our production in more ways than one."

"Why are you so determined to make it work? I didn't think actors were this invested in the behind-the-scenes stuff."

"They aren't usually, but this production needs to get made and I have the means to make it happen. So I'm going to do what I can."

"Does that mean you need to renegotiate your contract to add producer credit?" she teased.

"Maybe if I still had a manager," he quipped, glancing away, reminding her that he was still dealing with the aftermath of Doug's actions. "But I'm good with being in the background for this. I believe in the production. The script is too good to let it die because of some bad luck."

"What if it's more than bad luck?" she ventured.

"Like someone is sabotaging the production?"

She nodded, but he didn't seem to believe it.

"No, this is just a case of coincidence gone bad. Nothing more. I'm sure of it, which is why I'm putting my money where my mouth's at. I've promised Josh that for any damages the production causes, I'll foot the bill."

Erica gasped. "CJ, that's financially reckless. I wouldn't make promises like that."

"I can afford it. It'll be okay," he assured her.

Erica watched him, noticing the way his confidence filled the space, as if he could already envision the final product. It was that vision, she realized, that made him so good at his job—and made him so damn sexy.

About that...

"CJ, if we're going to work side by side during this film shoot here, I need to say something, or it'll eat me alive."

Yet CJ had a different agenda. His gaze latched on to hers, his hand extending toward her. "I can't stop thinking about you," he confessed softly. "What spell has Erica Pike cast on me that turns me inside out and sidewise?"

Her eyes met his, her breath hitching in surprise, but she retorted smoothly, "Probably the same spell that has you forgetting how to use a phone for a quick text or call after hook-ing up with someone. You did it again, CJ—and I need to know what the hell is going on, or whatever this is between us…will have to be strictly professional going forward."

Chapter Twelve

CJ shifted uncomfortably, the Arizona sun casting long shadows that seemed to stretch out like accusatory fingers. Erica's expectant gaze held a blend of confusion and hurt, mirroring the tightness knotting his chest. "I've been swamped with the production," he started, the words tasting like ash on his tongue.

"Really?" Erica's eyebrow arched, skepticism etching her features. "Is that all there is to it? Because I'm a busy person, too, and I still manage to find time in my day to send a quick text if it's important."

He sighed, a hand raking through his hair as he met her probing gaze. Moments trickled by, each second heavy with an unspoken truth that he wasn't ready to share.

The fact was several times during a lull in production CJ had felt the lure of his phone, her number burning in his mind, but something—fear, perhaps, or a deeply ingrained sense of self-preservation—had stopped him every time.

But how was he supposed to say that without hurting her feelings?

Erica, sensing he was holding back, said, "Look, I'd rather an ugly truth than a pretty lie. Just be honest, please."

"You're right," he admitted, grappling with the unfamiliar weight of honesty. "I could've sent a quick text or made a short call, but I chose not to."

"Was it truly just about sex?" Erica asked.

"No," he answered quickly, "it was never just about sex. I like you, Erica. I mean, like, really like you."

"Okay, so why the radio silence after we hook up?" she asked, confused.

Yeah, CJ, why?

Frustration laced his tone, not only because of the awkward situation but because he couldn't really explain why he was acting like this.

"Here's the thing, I'm in LA and you're here. I can't do long-distance, and I would never expect you to leave what you have here just to follow me to California. So, I figure, why delay the inevitable, right? We had fun, it was great and I would be open to hanging out anytime I'm in town or vice versa. No strings, just good times. I mean, we're good together. Why not enjoy what we have when we have it?"

It sounded good in his head but felt hollow in his heart, and judging by the incredulous expression on Erica's face, she wasn't on board—and, worse, was insulted.

"Hang out?" Erica echoed, voice laced with disbelief. "You mean, be your 'Arizona girl'? Just a convenient hookup?" Her stance hardened, disappointment sharpening her words into knives. "Have you lost your mind? What gave you the impression that I would be open to such an arrangement?"

"I thought you might be open-minded to something a little unorthodox," he said stiffly, surprised at how red Erica's face had gotten.

"No, CJ. I won't settle for that—and frankly, I can't believe that you would even ask."

"Erica, I—" CJ began, but she cut him off.

"Thank you for letting me know where I stand. It helps

to clear up some confusion for me. Fool me once, shame on you…fool me twice, shame on me. I should've learned from the first time. From this moment forward, we'll keep it professional. That's all." With those final words, she turned away, leaving him standing there feeling like a jackass and wishing he'd said something different.

But he couldn't lie to her. She deserved better than dishonesty just so he could get what he wanted. He watched her walk away, leaving him behind like a bad habit, and he wanted to run after her but remained rooted in place.

Nobody ever shared how doing the right thing sometimes felt like crap.

He returned to base camp with good news, but his stride gave away his irritation. Why did Erica have to be so damn stubborn? The win with the resort's location approval was a thin bandage over the gash in his personal feelings over Erica's decision to cut him off.

He had no doubt Erica could handle being professionally detached—he'd already seen her do it once before—but he hadn't liked it nor had he enjoyed the feeling of being on the wrong side of Erica Pike.

"Anna, Caroline!" he called out as he approached the bustling cluster of trailers, catching the director and the AD talking with the production manager. Their heads swiveled his way, eyes alight with curiosity. "We got the green light for the resort location."

"Seriously? Don't get my hopes up if you're just messing around."

"I wouldn't joke about something this serious," CJ said without his usual sense of humor. "It's all legit. I suggested we meet for dinner to talk over the logistics, but Josh Colton gave the thumbs-up and we're clear to start whenever we're ready."

Realizing this was real, Anna's mouth fell open, her surprise giving way to swift efficiency. She whipped out her phone, punching in the numbers with unbridled excitement. "This is huge, CJ! Caroline, while I'm sharing the news with the executive producer, you set up dinner with the resort reps for tomorrow. I want to get this moving as quickly as possible before anyone comes to their senses and rescinds their offer."

"On it," Caroline said, clapping CJ on the shoulder. "Good work. You never cease to surprise me. Did your friend Erica have anything to do with this?"

His friend. For some reason that made him wince, but he shook his head. "No, I talked with one of the owners. Josh Colton has a latent desire to be involved with the movie business. I just capitalized on it, but make sure the crews know we're going to be on private property and they need to be respectful. I don't want the Coltons to regret saving our asses."

Caroline sobered. "Absolutely. I'll make sure everyone's on their best behavior."

"Great. I'll leave the rest of the details up to you guys. I need a nap."

CJ made his way back to his trailer, feeling drained and irritated. As he walked, he went over the conversation he'd had with Erica in his mind, still trying to figure out why she was so insistent on cutting him off entirely. She wasn't even open to being his *friend.*

When he reached his trailer, he kicked off his shoes and flopped onto the couch with a heavy sigh. He closed his eyes and let out a long breath, trying to calm himself down. But no matter how hard he tried, he couldn't shake off the lingering feeling that he'd just lost something worth keeping.

He reached for his phone on the coffee table and scrolled through his contacts until he found Erica's number. He stared at the number, wondering if he ought to walk back his disastrous verbal vomit, but he doubted Erica would take the call even if he tried.

He tossed the phone and dropped back onto the couch.

When he woke up hours later, it was already dark outside. He groaned and rubbed at his face, feeling disoriented from the long nap. His stomach grumbled loudly, reminding him that he hadn't eaten since breakfast.

CJ got up and headed toward the small kitchenette in the corner of the trailer. He rummaged through the cabinets until he found some instant noodles and heated them up in the microwave.

It was too late to go anywhere, and the rest of the base camp were off doing their own thing for the night. Flicking on the tiny television, he resigned himself to mindless TV shows to distract himself from the reality that he might've screwed up something worth exploring.

If he could only pull his own head out of his ass to figure it out.

ERICA STOOD BEFORE the full-length mirror, her reflection casting back an image of composure she didn't feel. The hurt still stung—a raw, uninvited guest lurking beneath the surface of her carefully applied makeup.

CJ's words echoed in her mind, a jarring note off-key from the reality of her professional life: "Like I would ever be his *Arizona* girl." She snorted indelicately. What the hell was he thinking?

What kind of woman did he take her for? Had she given off some kind of vibe that she'd be open to something so… *cheap*?

Ugh. Stop thinking about him.

She turned away, the hem of her short, slinky dress swishing against her thighs. Erica had chosen it not out of vanity but as armor, a declaration of her own self-worth in the face of someone who'd seen her as little more than a convenient diversion.

She was a woman of poise and intelligence, not just curves and legs—though the dress did accentuate them with a certain undeniable flair. *Eat your heart out, CJ Knight.*

Her phone buzzed on the dresser, a message from Josh lighting up the screen: Looking forward to tonight! It's going to be great having you there to finalize everything. Thanks!

Great was not the word she would have used. *Necessary*, perhaps. *Unavoidable*, definitely.

Josh was blissfully unaware of the undercurrents he was asking her to navigate—how could she explain to him or Laura the gravity of sitting across from CJ at dinner when she was working so hard to maintain the veneer that, indeed, everything was fine?

"Professionalism," she whispered to her reflection, a mantra to steel herself for the evening ahead. With one last glance, she ensured she was impenetrable to CJ's charm and determined to treat this as she would any business dinner with a VIP guest.

The restaurant's ambiance was impeccable, the kind of place where the lighting was always flattering and the waitstaff moved with an almost choreographed grace.

Personally, she would've preferred a burger joint, someplace where she could wear jeans and a T-shirt and eaten her weight in french fries, but Josh had wanted to make an impression, so Crimson Canyon Restaurant was the only choice.

As she entered, Erica felt eyes on her—not just CJ's, though his gaze was unavoidable. She drew in a breath and let the cool Sedona air settle her nerves.

"Erica, you look stunning," Josh greeted, all smiles and genuine appreciation. He guided her to the table with a hand at her back, utterly oblivious to the tension that knotted her stomach tight.

"Thank you, Josh," she replied, allowing a smile to grace her lips. It was easier with him because his intentions were clear and completely professional.

CJ's chair scraped against the terra-cotta tile as he rose to greet her, and Erica's pulse quickened against her will. Her entrance had drawn his attention immediately, his eyes tracing the silhouette of her dress—a subtle yet undeniable acknowledgment that she had, perhaps inadvertently, dressed to break his heart. She caught the brief hitch in his breath, a momentary lapse that betrayed his composure, and it gave her a private thrill.

"Erica," he began, the word hanging between them like a delicate thread.

"Good evening, CJ." Her voice was a cool drink of water, quenching any sparks before they could ignite.

CJ took the hint as Josh pulled Erica's seat out for her, and Erica sank gracefully into her chair with an appreciative smile.

"Right, so, introductions are in order—Josh Colton, I'm pleased to introduce our production's director, Anna Wilson, and our assistant director, Caroline Briggs."

"Pleasure," Josh said, grinning from ear to ear. "I gotta tell you—this is so exciting. My resort, immortalized in film… it's, well, pretty damn cool."

The table chuckled at Josh's unbridled enthusiasm, and Erica nodded, sharing a smile with Josh while wishing it wasn't CJ Knight's film that was making Josh's secret dream come true.

She shifted in her seat, the fabric of her dress clinging to her skin as if it, too, sensed the need to hold steady.

CJ's gaze darted to Erica as if pulled by a magnet, but he

quickly looked away as if he didn't trust his gaze not to linger too long. Was he remembering what every inch of her bare skin tasted like? She smothered a smug smile, hoping he was squirming beneath that strained smile.

From the corner of her eye, she noticed Anna observing the silent exchange, an unreadable expression etched onto her intelligent features. Anna said nothing, but the slight tilt of her head and the faint narrowing of her eyes suggested she perceived more than she let on.

"Shall we order wine to start?" Erica suggested, directing the conversation back to the safety of business, allowing her to breathe easier—for the moment. "Crimson Canyon is known to carry some of the best wines in the world."

"Great idea," Josh agreed, nodding. "Any preference?"

"Surprise us," Anna said.

The clink of fine cutlery against porcelain and the murmured symphony of negotiation provided a backdrop to Erica's strained composure. Across the table, CJ leaned slightly toward her, his eyes searching for an opening.

"Erica, you are—"

"Please, let's keep this professional." She cut him off with a brief smile, her voice a low whisper edged with steel. She ignored CJ and offered, "Let's start with the Puligny-Montrachet Premier Cru, one of my favorite French wines."

"Sounds exotic," Caroline said. "I'm always down to try new things."

CJ took the hint and swallowed whatever compliment he'd started to offer. His expression flickered with disappointment before settling into a resigned nod.

He turned away, his attention reluctantly reclaimed by the discussion at hand, leaving Erica to exhale a silent breath she hadn't realized she was holding.

As the dinner wore on, plans were etched into reality

with every stroke of a pen on a napkin, every handshake across the table.

The evening finally ended, everyone parted ways, their voices carrying promises of crews arriving with the first light, ready to transform the derelict section into a bustling film set for the next two weeks.

While Erica enjoyed seeing Josh so excited, she knew the filming would put a huge strain on the entire resort. Laura was more sensitive to the daily operations than Josh, but they'd make it work somehow.

And that included squashing her personal feelings about CJ.

In the solitude of her car, Erica allowed herself a moment to feel the pulse of pride for keeping her emotions under wrap, even when CJ looked like a delicious snack and smelled even better. She'd never considered herself prone to romantic whimsy, but CJ had a way of drawing out aspects of herself that she'd never known existed. She hadn't decided yet if that was a good thing or not.

But she held firm, clinging to her convictions like a shield.

This small victory was hers, a testament to her strength, yet it did nothing to soothe the hollow ache that lingered in her chest, a reminder that detachment came with its own cost.

Two weeks—that was all she needed to get through—and then she could get back to normal life.

Without CJ.

Chapter Thirteen

Days later, CJ stepped onto the set with a low whistle, his gaze sweeping across the landscape that had come alive under the meticulous hands of the set builders. The barn, once a skeletal relic, stood robust and proud. Granted, it wouldn't stand up to a certified inspection, but for a filming facade, it was damn good.

The sagging fence line now stood straight, like it must've when it had first been built. He could almost hear the jangle of spurs and the distant whinnying of horses as he walked through the resurrected 1800s Wild West set that was supposed to represent the Buford Homestead, where an integral character, Clarissa, had been killed.

His chest swelled with a sense of pride and purpose—this was the distraction he needed; this was his world, away from the complicated web of conflicting feelings that Erica spun around him.

"Looks good, huh?" One of the builders tipped his hat in CJ's direction, pulling him from his reverie.

"Better than good," CJ replied, his voice laced with genuine admiration. "It's like stepping back in time. Great job."

With a nod to the builder, CJ turned his attention back to the set. Every detail, from the weathered signs to the strategically placed water barrels and hanging tack, transported him into the heart of a story waiting to be told. He squared his shoulders, determined to pour himself into the work, to live in the scenes they were about to shoot, if only to push the thought of Erica to the furthest corner of his mind.

The energy on the set was electric as everyone prepared for the first take of the day. Cameras rolled into position, actors donned their costumes, dialogues whispered under breaths as the final touches were applied. Then, with the call of "Action!" the scene came alive, gunslingers and townsfolk moving with rehearsed precision.

But just as CJ was about to utter his first line, Anna yelled, "Cut!" It sliced through the action abruptly as the light rig started to flicker and buzz ominously until it shorted with a sharp snap and the lights went down.

Even though it was daytime, filming on location still required lights to make sure the scene was properly lit, and losing the light rig had the power to grind everything to a stop.

"Damn it! Not again," Anna muttered, rubbing her temples. Crew members scurried about while the rigging crew assessed the situation. "What's happening to the rig?"

The key gaffer jogged over to Anna with a perplexed expression. "Sorry, Anna. We're trying to assess the situation now. We just need a few minutes. It's probably a loose wire or connection."

"Let's hope," Anna said, shaking her head, looking worried.

"Got a surge here," called out one of the electricians, his hands buried in a mess of wires. "Gonna need a few hours to sort this out."

Anna swore under her breath and rose from her director's chair, removing herself. "I'll be in my room trying to convince the executive producer not to shut us down," she said, walking away.

Frustration simmered in CJ's chest as he watched the crew disperse, some seeking refuge in the shade while others tinkered with their respective equipment, hoping for a quick fix. The momentum they had built up seemed to evaporate under the midday sun, and CJ couldn't help but feel a growing sense of apprehension. Mishaps were part of the job, sure, but this felt like an omen. Was this production cursed? He wasn't a spiritual guy, but maybe they ought to have a priest come out and sprinkle holy water on everything, just to be on the safe side.

CJ leaned against a post, his gaze wandering over the set. This was supposed to be smooth sailing after all the hurdles they had faced, yet here they were, stuck again. With a quiet sigh, he glanced up at the sky, silently willing the universe to cut them some slack, to let them tell their story without further interruption. But as the sun continued its relentless march across the heavens, CJ knew better than to rely on wishes. They needed action, solutions—and fast.

The clatter of tools and hushed conversations of the crew echoed around him. A thin layer of sweat lined his brow, not just from the heat but from the weight of responsibility that now rested squarely on his shoulders. His name—once a golden ticket in the industry—was the adhesive holding this project together. He had leveraged his reputation to secure the location and even promised his own funds as collateral for any damages incurred during their stay at the resort.

His jaw clenched at the thought. Failure was a luxury he couldn't afford.

In the midst of his silent brooding, movement caught his eye. Erica stood a short distance away, her profile illuminated by the soft glow of the afternoon sun. She was talking with Caroline, her hands animatedly shaping the air between them. For a moment, CJ found himself rooted to the spot, captivated by the familiar cadence of her gentle laughter. Should he say hello? Wouldn't it be impolite to just keep walking?

Taking an involuntary step forward, he hesitated when their eyes locked. Her smile faltered, and she turned abruptly back to Caroline, dismissing him without a word. The sting of rejection lanced through him, and with a scowl etched deep into his features, he spun on his heel and stalked back toward the center of the set where his costar, Jenny Oliver, was going over lines.

"Are they shutting down production?" she asked, pulling her sides from a hidden pocket in her voluminous muslin dress to fan herself. "God, it's freaking hot here."

"Yeah, probably. Anna left to talk with the higher-ups about the additional setback, but we might be able to salvage the day if the gaffers are able to get the lights back up and running."

Jenny didn't share the same sense of urgency, yawning as she continued to fan herself. "I swear I'll fire my agent if he sends me another period piece anytime soon. I'm going to suffocate under all these layers."

He chuckled. "Well, you make it look good," he said. Jenny preened beneath his praise, taking a brief moment to twirl in her skirts for his benefit. "Well, at least this part is fun," she said, grinning.

Like him, Jenny Oliver was a hot commodity around Hollywood right now. She had all the right tangibles—young, beautiful and talented—a triple threat when a lot of actors only had one or two of those attributes to offer.

But when out of character, she looked bored out of her skull and less than enamored with their desert location. "Well, if we're done for the day, I'm getting out of this torture device. Catch you tomorrow, CJ."

He waved and watched her swish her way to the wardrobe trailer so she could change, leaving CJ to wonder why he hadn't done the same. There was no reason to hang around if the day was done, but he felt a different level of responsibility for the production than before, and for some reason, he just wanted to check with his own eyes that only the lights were mysteriously affected.

In hindsight, his mental health might've been better if he had just followed Jenny's example.

As if the day hadn't already taken enough out of him, another setback lay in wait. Approaching the props table, his keen eye immediately spotted the disarray. Leather holsters had been slashed, glass bottles shattered and vintage playing cards scattered and torn—all integral to the barn scene they were slated to film next.

"What the…?" He muttered, bracketing his hands on his hips as frustration chewed on his composure. "How in the hell did this happen?" He motioned to the prop master, a veteran with more years under his belt than CJ had been alive, hustled over with a tight-lipped expression. "Did you see this?"

"Yeah, right about the same time the lights blew. I was just about to let Caroline know."

"How'd it happen?"

"No idea. They were fine this morning—each one logged in perfect condition in the prop book."

"So, someone managed to ruin important props, and no one saw them do it?"

"Appears that way, but I'm asking around. I'll find out what happened."

CJ nodded, reluctantly letting it go because what else could he do? With a heavy sigh, CJ surveyed the damage, an uncomfortable suspicion nagging at his brain. Was someone sabotaging this production?

"Rough day, huh?" The voice belonged to the new horse wrangler, a rugged man with easy confidence that seemed alien to CJ at that moment. He swiveled to greet the man who offered his hand. "Rein Granger—pleasure."

"Rein…" CJ repeated with a small smile. "It's a good thing you turned out to like horses, or else you might've found that name a hard act to live up to."

Rein grinned, as if used to a little ribbing about his name. "Lucky for me my family is four generations deep in horseflesh and ranching. This stuff's in my blood. Not sure how well I'd fare as a lawyer. Can't handle being caged in four walls for longer than a minute, which is why I work so well with the animals. Plus, they don't make a fuss about dirt on your knees."

CJ chuckled, envious of those kinds of deep roots. His family had been more nomadic in nature. They'd bounced from place to place throughout his childhood, but he'd always longed for a place to call home for longer than a year. Probably the reason why he'd bought his house with his first big check. He'd paid up front so that no one could ever take it from him, no matter if his career dried up someday. Doug had given him hell at the time for not financing the house like most people, but he'd been adamant. He wanted something that would always be his until the time he decided to move on.

"You friends with the Coltons?" CJ asked.

"Yeah, me, Josh and Knox go way back. His old man was a bit of a jerk, but Josh is good stock. Hell, if I wasn't afraid that Josh might kick my ass from here to tomorrow for even looking sidewise, I might've tried shooting my shot with his sister Laura, but it wasn't meant to be, I guess."

CJ remembered a snippet of information from Erica, saying, "She's about to get married, I heard."

"Yeah, that door shut hard on my chances, but hey, what're ya gonna do, right? It is what it is."

CJ liked Rein's chill attitude. He could see why Josh had called him in. The man was a good fit. "Well, looks like we're down for the day," he said, dusting off the knees of his chaps. "What's there to do around town? Anything good?"

"Depends. Looking to wash the trail dust down with something stronger than whatever you've got stocked in that fancy room of yours?" The wrangler tilted his head toward the direction of Sedona. "I know a place that's good for toe-tapping music, good whiskey and a pretty girl or two."

CJ hesitated for a heartbeat. The rational part of his brain screamed to decline, to prepare for the next day's shoot, but rationality wasn't in the house any longer—not with Erica's obvious snub and the set's problems dogging him. "Sure," he found himself saying. "Why not?"

"Great. The place is called the Rattlesnake Pub. Don't let the name—or the look of it—scare you. It's where all the locals go to let off steam. Meet you there at nine tonight." But as Rein started to walk away, he spun on his heel to ask, "You ain't a sloppy drunk, right?"

CJ had to laugh at the bold question, but he answered, "Not that I can recall."

Rein grinned with approval. "Good. I hate babysitting grown men," he said before returning to finish up his duties.

The Rattlesnake Pub was a dive, its neon sign buzzing like an agitated hornet. Inside, the smell of stale beer and fried food contested for dominance, but the music was jumping, and it was filled wall-to-wall with people.

"What'd I tell ya?" Rein said, motioning for another round of whiskey. "This is where the real fun happens—not in those stuffy, gentrified places where a half-empty plate will run you a month's rent."

CJ downed the shot, elbows planting heavily on the sticky counter. The bartender, a woman with a no-nonsense look, slid a shot glass toward him without a word.

"Keep 'em coming," CJ said with a grin that he wasn't sure was real, the fiery gulp scalding his throat and offering a brief respite from his thoughts.

He didn't want to think about Erica, about the way she'd turned away from him, closing off whatever fragile connection they might have shared. So he drank. Each shot was a hammer blow to the barricade he'd built around her image in his mind, each one crumbling it further until he could no longer tell if he was trying to forget her or work up the courage to call her and beg for forgiveness.

"Slow down, Hollywood," Rein advised, downing his own shot. "I told you I ain't babysitting a grown man. If you fall on your face, that's where you stay."

"Fair enough," CJ said, though the floor was probably where he belonged. The booze loosened his tongue enough to ask, "You got a girl or something?"

"Naww, I had an old lady, but she split when she realized I was never gonna make enough money to buy her that fancy house she was dreaming about."

"I'm sorry, man. That's rough."

Rein waved away CJ's condolences. "Everything happens for a reason."

CJ internalized that sentiment, wondering if that were true. He didn't want to ruin the mood by sourly pointing out that sometimes bad things happened randomly to good people because a bad person crossed their path. *End of story.* Like what'd happened with Allison Brewer. *Ahh, hell, don't go there. Not tonight.* Shoving Doug from his thoughts, he simply nodded as if he agreed, and moved on. "Hey, any chance you might've known the original wrangler who went MIA?"

"Kyle Jefferson? Yeah, I've heard of him. Decent guy. Not known for being a flake, that's for sure," Rein said. "He just didn't show up for work?"

"Yeah, that's the story. Rumor has it he knew the girl, Allison Brewer. Like, they dated or something."

"Well, I didn't know him *that* well, but I remember the name Allison Brewer. She's that poor girl who got killed by that rich guy?"

CJ nodded, admitting, "My manager was that rich guy."

"No shit." Rein breathed in surprise. "That must've been a shock."

"You can say that again," he quipped darkly, motioning for another round. "You think you know someone until they go and do something like that. Makes you realize you don't know much about anything."

Rein whistled low and commiseratively. "Amen to that." Seeming to want to switch subjects quickly before the mood completely soured, Rein asked, "Well, how about you? Is there a Mrs. Hollywood waiting for you back in LA?"

CJ barked a short laugh. "No, not even close. Currently the only other person in my house is a professional moocher who house-sits for me when I go on location. He's a decent guy, but I think he's more interested in *saying* he's an actor than actually pursuing a gig. But I don't mean to make him sound all that bad. He's cool—and he's kinda like my best friend. I mean, when you have a career like mine...you have to keep the people you trust close to you and keep everyone else out."

Rein chuckled. "I know the type." He paused a minute

before asking, "What do you know about that hot executive assistant? I think her name's Erica..."

Red-hot territorial energy that he had no right to feel ripped through him. "What about her?" he asked, a little sharply.

"Chill, chill—I was just asking. She's probably too rich for my blood anyway. Are you two a thing?"

"Nope. I screwed that up. Big time. Twice." *Damn, enough alcohol.* At this rate he'd be giving away all his secrets by night's end. He knocked on the sticky bar with a derisive chuckle, admitting, "I think I ought to call it a night. I have an early call in the morning, and I can already tell it's going to be rough."

"Yeah, no problem. You need a ride?"

"No, I don't want you to leave on account of me. I'll catch an Uber or something."

"You sure?"

"Yeah, it's cool." CJ rose and the world swam, but he managed to walk stiff-legged out of the bar and into the cool night air. His vision blurred as he tried finding the Uber app, his fingers feeling fat and uncooperative. That whiskey must've been practically moonshine—and it was catching up to him faster than he realized.

He must've blacked out for a second because when he opened his eyes again, he'd definitely called someone to come and get him.

"I need a ride," he slurred, the world swaying in a nauseating dance. The chill of the night air slapped him but did little to sober his senses. There was no getting around the fact that he was drunk. "I'm outside the R-Rattlesnake Pub." He sat heavily on the curb before he fell down. "I'll be waiting."

He clicked off, fighting off the urge to barf his guts out.

It seemed like forever before he saw a car roll up, but as

he struggled to his feet, he realized with drunken embarrassment he hadn't called Uber.

He'd called Erica.

Chapter Fourteen

Erica's phone shattered the silence of the night with its insistent buzzing, a discordant sound that pulled her from the brink of sleep. Groggy eyes squinted at the screen, a name flashing in neon letters against the darkness: *CJ*. What on earth?

"I need—uh—ride," the voice slurred from the other end, words sloshing around like a dinghy in a storm. "Rattlesnake Pub."

Was he drunk?

She sat up, frowning. Rattlesnake Pub's background noise bled through the call, a cacophony of raucous music and laughter. Erica pinched the bridge of her nose, irritation sparking. Why was he calling her? Didn't he have an entourage of people at his beck and call for this kind of thing? It was on the tip of her tongue to hang up and go back to sleep, but she couldn't do it.

"All right, CJ. Stay put," she sighed, rolling out of bed and pulling on a pair of jeans. Duty gnawed at her conscience; no way could she leave him stranded. Anything could happen to the idiot, and then she'd feel like crap that she'd ignored his call.

The night air nipped at Erica's skin as she made her way to the pub. She found CJ slumped over the curb, a lone figure on the cold cement. If half the people knew they were walking past an A-list celebrity they'd whip out their phones and record his sorry state for cash or bragging rights.

Hauling him to his feet was like trying to lift a sack of wet sand, but she managed, half dragging, half supporting him to her car.

"Good service," he mumbled with a drunken grin. "And you smell good. Can I say that? Is that allowed? 'Cause you do. You smell like coconut and lemons. Like a lemon pie."

Erica ignored his ramblings, even though his praise made her warm all over. It wasn't the first time CJ had complimented the scent of her skin, though under different circumstances.

It was too late to drive to the resort, so she'd just have to take him back to her place and he could have the sofa.

Thankfully her little house wasn't far, but getting CJ from the car to the house was like wrangling a hundred-eighty-pound toddler who didn't want to take a nap.

Finally she managed to deposit him onto the couch, his body sprawling with the grace of a felled tree. As Erica fumbled with his shoes, a mumble escaped his lips, raw and unguarded.

"I'm such an idiot," he groaned, his head lolling back. "Always screwing things up...she's practically perfect."

Could he be talking about her? How embarrassing would it be if he was rambling about someone else? Maybe his co-star? Jenny Oliver was drop-dead gorgeous and younger than her by at least ten years.

His words stirred something in Erica, a memory of her grandmother's sage voice: *a drunk man's words are a sober man's thoughts.* The phrase hung in the air, heavy with truth. Was this remorse speaking? Her cheeks heated at the possibility that CJ felt a certain kind of way about her but, for whatever reasons, couldn't exactly act right.

She observed him, a mixture of exasperation and curiosity softening her features. The man had a knack for finding trouble, yet in this vulnerable state, it was hard not to feel a tug of empathy.

However, be that as it may, was she expected to simply absolve him each time he messed up just because he was stunted in the emotional-intelligence department?

"Forgive and forget?" she whispered to herself. No, that wasn't her style. *Say what you mean, mean what you say* was more her speed.

Yet as she watched him, a familiar ache twisted inside her, a reminder of what could have been. She'd be a liar if she didn't admit she'd imagined what life together might've looked like, even with their divergent career paths. Unlike CJ, she hadn't automatically assumed it would never work.

The night stretched on, punctuated by the uneven rhythm of his breathing and the restless turning of her own thoughts.

Erica padded over to the kitchen, the soft shuffle of her feet against the linoleum barely registering above CJ's rhythmic snoring. She filled a glass with water to the brim and grabbed two aspirin to head off the monster hangover that would be waiting for him when he woke up.

"Here, drink this," she coaxed, nudging the glass into his hands with a tenderness that surprised even her. "And take these."

"Wha...?" His voice was sandpaper on silk, words half-formed and slurred. Eyelids fluttered open, revealing bloodshot eyes that struggled to focus on the care she offered.

"Water. Aspirin. Trust me, you'll thank me later." Her tone brokered no argument, but it wasn't without warmth. She didn't envy him the migraine that awaited him.

He complied, the water spilling down his chin in his clumsy attempts. As he swallowed the pills, he muttered something indistinct, a mumble lost to the void between consciousness and oblivion. Erica retrieved the empty glass before it could slip from his grasp and end up a mess on her floor.

She draped a blanket over him, tucking the edges around his frame. His breaths came easier now, less like the gasps of a drowning man and more the steady tide of peaceful sleep.

Damn him for being a taboo snack she shouldn't want.

Still, she lingered, studying the way the moonlight danced across his features, casting shadows that played hide-and-seek with his stubble.

The corner of her mouth twitched upward—a reluctant smile for the drunken idiot who had somehow snuck into her heart despite every wall she put up. Even as her mind scolded her stupidity, her fingers brushed a lock of hair from his forehead, a silent concession to the feelings she fought so hard to deny.

"Good night, CJ," she whispered, the words spilling out like a secret meant only for the stars outside her window.

Once under her own covers, sleep proved elusive—her thoughts a jumbled mess, flipping endlessly between irritation and concern, frustration and something perilously close to longing.

Her dreams, when they finally claimed her, were a kaleidoscope of blurred faces and half-remembered touches, leaving her to wake in fits and starts, which only made the promise of morning something she wasn't looking forward to.

Sunlight invaded the room in sharp, accusing beams, prying Erica's eyelids open with the subtlety of a sledgehammer.

Despite feeling like dog poop, she rose, dressed in her

running gear and padded into the living room with her tennis shoes in hand to find CJ sitting up, an awkward figure on her sofa.

"Morning, sunshine," she said with a derisive smile in her tone. "Rough night?"

"Hey," he rasped, voice gravelly, as he struggled to straighten up. His hair, a wild mess of dishevelment, stood defiantly in every direction, declaring the chaos of the night before. And yet if the situation were different between them, she'd climb his body like a monkey shimmying up a tree because even a hot mess, CJ was…well, hot.

"Christ, my head…" CJ pinched the bridge of his nose between thumb and forefinger, squinting up at her. "I, uh… how did I…?"

"Mix up calling an Uber with dialing my number? One's an app, buddy." Erica crossed her arms, leaning against the wall which felt oddly supportive. "I'd love to know the mechanics of that one myself."

"God, did you pick me up?" Shame shadowed his features, an apology forming in his bleary eyes before his lips could catch up.

"Looks like it." She kept her tone light, but her insides twisted. To see him unraveled, apologetic—it tugged at something within her she wasn't ready to examine too closely.

"Sorry," he mumbled, and the word seemed to fall from him, heavy with a regret that reached beyond last night's bad decisions. It hung in the air between them that Erica was quick to push away.

"Apology accepted," she replied as if it was really not a big deal, even though it was. "It's my job to look over the VIP guests, though I've never had one call me personally to be their DD."

"Erica, I don't—" He shook his head, as if to clear the cobwebs, then winced again, recoiling from the pain that movement surely caused. "Hell, I don't even know where to start. I've never done anything like this before."

"Don't worry about it," she said, waving away his apology as she dropped into a chair to lace up her tennis shoes. "The shower is yours. I'm going for a run. It should take me about an hour. K-Cups are on the counter if you want coffee."

CJ nodded, wincing at the movement. "Have a good run," he managed, before falling back against the couch, closing his eyes against the invading sunlight.

Erica chuckled to herself and headed out, thankful she wasn't suffering like CJ was, but it probably served him right. What was he thinking going into a strange bar without a good wingman?

As she was finishing her run, her watch dinged with a text message from CJ.

Thanks for picking me up. This time, I ordered an actual Uber to take me back to the resort so I don't mess up your morning routine any more than I already have.

Was that sharp disappointment that he'd split before she returned or relief that they didn't have to dance around the inevitable awkwardness?

Kinda felt like disappointment, but where was the sense in admitting that?

No, this was a good thing. Now she could go about her business like normal, without CJ in the way.

Yeah. Much better.

So why did she feel like all of the endorphins from her run were suddenly swirling down the drain?

THE GLARING LIGHTS of the set felt like needles in CJ's skull, the aftermath of last night punishing him with every step he took. Embarrassment clung to him like a second skin, the memory of waking up in Erica's house after mistakenly dialing her instead of managing to open a damn app replayed on an endless loop behind his bloodshot eyes. She must've thought he was a complete idiot after last night.

It wasn't even an understandable mistake. It was as if his subconscious had deliberately sabotaged him with that move.

"Places, everyone!" The voice cut through the fog in his head as he emerged from the makeup-and-wardrobe trailer, transformed into his character.

His hangover receded to the wings, upstaged by the adrenaline that came with performance. Lines poured out of him, smooth and rehearsed, the morning's shoot unfolding with the precision of a well-oiled machine.

This was what he knew and understood—whatever was happening with Erica might as well have been in a foreign language for all he could figure out.

But the moment the director called "Cut!" and the crew dispersed like ants to a dropped sugar cube, the sanctuary of his focus crumbled.

Except something else caught his attention as everyone else rushed to craft services for lunch.

The smell of sawdust and hot wires mingled as voices carried—a hushed, urgent conference between Anna and Caroline.

"Can you believe it?" Anna's words were wrapped in disbelief. "Someone actually messed with the electrical line. I thought it was just a coincidence, but it looks like it was deliberate. What the hell is happening?"

CJ's heart lurched, his stomach following suit as he realized the import of Anna's revelation. This wasn't just about forgotten lines or a prop misplaced; this was someone playing with lives—and it pissed him off.

Lunch became an afterthought as CJ waited for Caroline to leave. He wanted to talk to Anna alone.

"Anna," he said, his voice low and edged with the gravity of the situation, "what's going on?"

Her eyes, usually sharp with command, swam with unshed tears. She sighed, the sound heavy with the burden of potential ruin hanging over them. "If one more thing goes wrong, CJ…the execs—they'll shut us down. They're scared, and I can't blame them."

"Hey, we'll figure it out," CJ tried to infuse confidence into his words, the same kind he summoned for a difficult scene, but it sounded hollow even to his ears. "It's probably just someone being petty. You know how people can get when they don't get their way or something. I doubt anyone's trying to actively shut us down."

"Yeah, maybe." She gave a shaky laugh, the sound brittle enough to crack. "I need to…" Her gaze darted away, landing on something unseen. "Handle something." With a swipe under her eyes, she excused herself, promising to return before it was time to roll cameras, but CJ got a bad feeling.

There were no rewrites in real life, no second takes to fix the dumpster-fire turn their production had taken. It wasn't fair. Anna had worked so hard to make this film happen, and now? It was falling apart faster than anyone could patch it back together.

CJ's gaze snagged on Jenny openly flirting with Rein.

Rein, the epitome of rural charm in denim and leather, caught CJ's eye across the lot and shot him a conspiratorial wink before his attention snapped back to Jenny.

Good for him, he thought. Though Rein ought to be careful—Jenny had a way of chewing men up and leaving them on the side of the road for dead.

Watching them was like peering through a window at a scene he wasn't part of, one where laughter came easy and regrets didn't linger like stale cigarette smoke.

A pang of something—a mix of envy and a wishful longing—twisted in his chest.

Why couldn't it be like that between him and Erica?

His tongue twisted into knots and his words tripped over themselves whenever she was close enough to touch. He wanted to say it out loud, to unravel the tangle of *I'm sorry* and *I can't help it* that knotted inside him, but history had taught him that he was more likely to choke on the truth than to speak it.

Shaking his head, he turned away from the duo. His still-sour stomach made the idea of lunch a queasy one. He bypassed the craft services table and went looking for the key gaffer. He had questions only the man in charge of the lighting department could answer.

He found him quickly enough, still working while everyone else was enjoying carne asada tacos.

"Hey," CJ started, his approach cautious. "I heard about the wires. What happened?"

The gaffer grunted, a noncommittal sound that hovered in the air between them. CJ could practically see the thoughts flicker behind the man's eyes—calculations and concerns etched deeper than the lines of age and experience.

"Your guess is as good as mine. Someone messed with the lines. Cut a few clean through."

"Any idea why someone would do that?" CJ asked, frowning.

"Kid," the gaffer began, his tone flat as the plains, "why people do this kind of stuff is above my pay grade."

"Right, sorry," CJ said, feeling like a trespasser and an annoyance, but he couldn't help himself. "Any clue who might—" CJ tried again, only to be cut off by a slicing hand gesture.

"Look, I lay cables, not traps. Got no business sniffing out sabotage," the man stated flatly. His gaze slid away, signaling the end of the conversation.

"Sure, sure," CJ said, backing off, but a different question needled his brain—was the key gaffer the one deliberately sabotaging the production? He didn't like to think that was possible, but suspicion clung to his thoughts even as he walked to the barn.

He needed a minute to regroup, get his head on straight. But the threat of potential sabotage hummed in his ears, a discordant sound that refused to be ignored. He was no detective, no hero in some gritty thriller—he was just an actor caught in a plot twist that felt far too real.

And it made him feel useless. All he could do was throw money at the problem, and that didn't seem to be solving it.

The script pages felt heavy in his pocket, a reminder of the work still ahead. But as he rounded the corner, he stopped dead, the wrinkles of concern smoothing out at the sight of Erica.

She sat alone on a bale of hay, munching a sandwich while the sun painted her in hues of gold and amber.

The sight of her was a jolt to his system, like coffee after a night of bad decisions. He hovered there, one foot half-turned toward her, the other itching to bolt. To join or not to join, that was the question hammering through his veins.

Hey, Erica, he could say and maybe this time get it right. Or maybe he'd just trip over his tongue again and add another layer of awkward to their already patchy history.

He watched her laugh at something only she knew, the

sound silent to him but loud in his imagination. It was a private moment, one he had no right to interrupt. Was she texting someone else? A different guy?

Not your business.

CJ spun on his heel, leaving Erica to her business.

"Lines," he whispered to himself, the word a feeble shield against the swell of emotions threatening to capsize him once again.

It was the script he needed to focus on—being someone else was about the only thing he understood these days.

Chapter Fifteen

The Buford Homestead loomed like a grizzled sentinel of the past, the setting sun casting long, eerie shadows through its weathered beams. The Colton barn had been transformed into something Erica hardly recognized, as real as if it'd been taken from a page of history and plunked down on the property, and she was stunned at the high production value of every detail.

When Anna had invited her to watch this particular scene, Erica had been tempted to decline with the excuse of too much work on her plate already poised on her tongue. But she'd accepted the offer with secret eagerness that should've been a red flag.

And now she was here. The set was alive with motion as everyone prepared for the big scene.

Erica, her mind muddled with lists and plans for Laura's bachelorette bash, stepped onto the film set, a buzz of anticipation zipping through her veins. She had told herself that this was just another task, another box to check—behind-the-scenes access, nothing more. Yet as the director shouted "Action!" and CJ burst into a brutal fight scene with his on-screen nemesis, her pulse quickened.

She watched, utterly absorbed, as CJ grappled and lunged with the ferocity of a warrior. The sound of their grunts as they strained against one another in a brutal dance of coordinated savagery was mesmerizing in a way she wasn't ashamed to admit had her enthralled.

Each calculated swing, each deft maneuver was poetry in motion, and the duality she'd once seen in him melted away, leaving only the artistry of his craft. Her heart hammered a rhythmic tribute to his every move—the clash of fists, the controlled aggression a ballet of bruising encounters. It took her breath away.

It wasn't hard to see why the man commanded the box office.

And then it was over.

"Cut!" The director's voice sliced through the charged air, and like waking from a trance, Erica blinked back into reality. The actors relaxed, shoulders drooping with fatigue but faces aglow with the thrill of the scene well done. They knew they'd nailed it, and their confidence was contagious. Erica jumped from her chair beside the director and ran up to CJ, gushing.

"Wow, CJ, that was…incredible," she found herself saying, the words tumbling out in a rush of admiration she hadn't anticipated. CJ turned toward her, a smile cracking the rugged facade of his character.

He wiped at the sweat dripping down his face, grinning. "There's nothing quite like getting your ass kicked for authenticity, right?" He chuckled, rubbing a hand along his jaw, where a darkening bruise bloomed like a storm cloud. He rolled up a sleeve, revealing a tapestry of scars like battle honors, each one a story etched in skin. "Months with the fight coordinator to make it look this good. But, man, the bruises were real."

Her laughter bubbled up, genuine and bright. "You wear them like medals."

"Only the brave get wounded in battle," he replied with a wink.

This was a world she couldn't fathom, but CJ made it look like it was just another day at the office. "Well, that was incredible," she said, unable to hide her enthusiasm. "To be honest, I've never been one for violence in movies, but seeing it from this angle… I have a newfound appreciation for all of the work that goes into making them."

"I'm glad you came," CJ said, holding her smile with one of his own. "I—"

Just then, the moment shattered as a loud crash boomed, a cacophony of splintering wood and chaos. Instinctively, Erica flinched, and the world tilted violently. She felt a solid body collide with hers, sending them both sprawling to the ground—a jarring thud that stole the air from her lungs.

"Erica!" CJ's voice was sharp with concern, close to her ear.

As the dust settled, she realized how narrowly disaster had missed her, an unkind game of chance played with falling timber. A shiver raced down her spine, her heart pounding a frenetic drumbeat against her rib cage.

"Are you okay?" CJ's eyes searched hers, the playful light extinguished, replaced by a flicker of something raw and protective.

"Y-Yeah," she stammered, her voice barely above a whisper, the brush with mortality still echoing in her bones. "I'm fine."

At least, she thought she was. She blinked against the plume of dust clogging the air from the shattered wood, coughing against the scratch in her lungs. "What happened?"

"Erica, you're bleeding!" The urgency in CJ's voice cut through the ringing in her ears as she tried to make sense of the chaos around them.

Shards of sunlight pierced the dust-laden air, revealing a scene punctuated by frantic movement and sharp shouts. Crew members darted about, their faces etched with concern, but none so viscerally alarmed as CJ, whose hands hovered over her, unsure where to touch without causing more harm.

"Let me see," he said, his tone softer now, guiding her gaze to her arm. Erica's eyes followed, and what she saw sucked the breath from her lungs—a splinter of wood, jagged and unyielding, protruding from her flesh. A bloom of crimson marred her skin, painting a vivid contrast against the pale fabric of her blouse.

"God, that looks bad." CJ's face was pale, a ghostly echo of his usual confidence.

"Doesn't feel great, either," she managed, shock weaving its numbing spell through her veins. Her voice sounded distant, like it belonged to someone else, someone watching this unfold from afar.

Had she really just been skewered like a cube of beef?

"Get a medic here—now!" someone bellowed, and within moments, the set's first aid team swarmed in, their practiced hands working with an efficiency that only amplified the gravity of the situation.

"Looks like we need to get you to a hospital," one of the medics announced after a cursory examination, his voice a calm anchor amid the storm.

"I'm going with her," CJ stated, the words falling like a decree. His hand found hers, a lifeline in the chaos, grip firm and unwavering.

"Thank you," she whispered, feeling the tremble in her fingers mirrored by his own.

As they loaded her onto a stretcher, the wail of approaching sirens crescendoed into the frenetic action, the ambulance emerging as some semblance of order. Laura and Josh appeared on its heels, their faces etched with worry.

"Erica!" Laura's voice broke as she caught sight of her, hooked to an IV and a bandage carefully wound around the bleeding wound.

"Hey, I'm all right," Erica tried to reassure her, words tumbling out brittle and hollow. But was she all right? She had a piece of wood in her arm.

"Move back, give her some space!" a paramedic instructed as they wheeled her toward the waiting ambulance, the urgency displacing comfort.

Laura reached for Erica's hand, squeezing it in a silent promise of solidarity. "I'm coming with you," she declared, eyes locked with Erica's in a fierce pact.

CJ stepped aside, the lines of his jaw tense, and nodded. "I'll follow behind."

Erica felt the world shrink to the space of her own heartbeat—fast, insistent, alive.

One minute she'd been riding a high, and the next she'd narrowly cheated being squashed like a bug and heading to the hospital to have what felt like a tree trunk removed from her arm.

Life was weird.

She pressed a hand to her forehead, trying to steady the swirl of dizziness that threatened to pull her under.

"Really, I'm fine," she insisted, her voice betraying her with a quiver as she fought against the wave of lightheadedness. The metallic taste of fear lingered at the back of her throat.

Laura was at her side in an instant, her presence like the steadfast push of a lighthouse beam through fog. "No way am I letting you go alone," Laura said firmly, edging CJ out with a protective maternal fire burning in her eyes. The strength in her voice was the kind that could part a sea of chaos.

CJ's face, etched with lines of concern, tightened, but he stepped aside. "All right," he conceded, the word dragged from him like a weight. He turned to the cluster of people gathered around, their faces a blur to Erica's strained focus. "Josh, can you—"

"Already on it," Josh cut in, his tone all business as he volunteered himself for duty, motioning to the others nursing their own wounds. "We'll follow the ambulance."

Erica watched through the ambulance's open doors as Josh rounded up the rest of the walking wounded, including CJ, who cast a last look back at her—the gleam of his eyes a silent vow to see her soon.

As the paramedics secured Erica for the journey, the chatter and chaos of the set became distant, like listening to the ocean from inside a shell. The barn, now a skeleton of danger, stood ominously quiet in the background.

"Let's call it a night," someone called out, their voice slicing through the murk of Erica's thoughts. "Shut everything down until we know it's safe."

One by one, lights snapped off, the glow of the day's filming fading into a stark reality. Actors, crew, everyone—their movements slowed, subdued by the near miss that hung over them all.

"Take care of her." CJ spoke softly to Laura, relinquishing his place beside Erica as if passing a baton in a race they were all running together.

"Like she's my own," Laura replied, her grip on Erica's hand a lifeline anchoring her to the moment.

The ambulance doors closed with a definitive thud, sealing away the outside world. The engine hummed to life, its rhythm syncing with Erica's racing pulse, a shared cadence as they pulled away from what might have been a final scene.

And only then did Erica blissfully pass out.

CJ'S HEART POUNDED a brutal rhythm against his rib cage, while his hands clutched the steering wheel until his knuckles whitened, each turn and stoplight a frustrating delay. He hadn't given Josh the option to drive, even though it was Josh's town and not his. He couldn't handle the thought of not being able to drive as fast as his anxiety demanded to get to Erica.

With each passing moment, Erica's pained face flashed behind his eyelids, a stark image that drowned out all thoughts of the chaotic film set he'd just torn away from.

"Damn it, move!" he muttered under his breath, urging the traffic to part like some petulant sea before his mounting desperation. He couldn't shake the image of Anna's face, either, pale with dread as she went to share the news with the higher-ups. The production was hemorrhaging money and trust, but none of it weighed on him now—not with Erica's well-being hanging in the balance.

The hospital loomed ahead, a beacon in the approaching dusk, its fluorescent lights harsh against the dimming day. CJ skidded into the parking lot, nearly colliding with a shopping cart left carelessly by the curb. The sting of his seat belt cutting across his chest went unnoticed as he bolted from the car, barely registering Josh's strained voice calling after him.

"Easy, CJ! She'll be okay," Josh said, but CJ was already threading through the sliding doors of the emergency room, his eyes scanning for any sign of her.

"Family only beyond this point," a stern-faced nurse blocked his path, but CJ's frantic gaze and the bandages peeking from beneath his sleeve spoke volumes. A flicker of sympathy crossed her face, and she stepped aside with a resigned sigh. "Make it quick."

Inside, the sterile scent of disinfectant mixed with the metallic tang of blood. The relentless beeping of monitors played counterpoint to the shuffle of shoes and low murmur of voices. There she was—Erica, his compass in the storm, laid out before him with medical staff orbiting her like planets around a sun. Her arm, marred by the jagged wood shard, seemed so small amid the white sheets.

Thankfully, it must've been a slow day in the ER because a doctor was already talking with Erica when he arrived.

"Hmm, that's quite a souvenir. What happened?"

"We're not sure. One minute everything was fine and the next, a portion of the barn had collapsed. When the dust and the shock settled, I saw this in my arm," Erica explained.

CJ walked in, going straight to Erica's side, daring anyone to tell him to leave. He shared additional information. "Hi, I'm CJ Knight. The accident happened while on set. She's right—a piece of the barn just collapsed, and we have no idea how it happened."

The doctor eyed CJ. "You look injured yourself."

"Just scrapes and bruises. There are a few people who got hit during the collapse, but Erica took the brunt of it."

The doctor nodded, returning to Erica. "Well, it's in there pretty deep. Given the nature of your injury, I'm going to recommend surgery to remove the debris," he explained, his voice clinical yet not unkind. "The nurses will go ahead and prep you. Once you're under, it shouldn't take long to patch you up."

"Sounds like a piece of cake," Erica said, but her voice trembled.

The doctor removed his gloves and threw them away, leaving to make room for the nurses to do their thing.

A kindly nurse appeared with a soft, round face and a gentle disposition. "Sounds like surgery is in order. The good news is it'll feel like you blinked and then it'll all be over. However, standard protocol requires us to ask—could you be pregnant?"

Erica blinked and shook her head. "No, I don't think so."

But the nurse made an apologetic expression as she said, "Well, we'll just run a quick test to be sure, and then we'll be able to prep you for surgery."

CJ's fingers threaded through Erica's, holding on, willing his heart to stop beating like a wild thing. He couldn't stop replaying the scene in his head or freaking out over how Erica could've died.

"Hey," she whispered, squeezing his hand back. "I'm tougher than I look. It'll be fine."

"Yeah, I know you are. I just… I'm so sorry, Erica," he said, feeling responsible for her injury. "I'm going to find out what happened, and I swear, if someone did this on purpose, there'll be hell to pay."

But Erica was less bloodthirsty, saying, "I'm sure it was just a freak accident. Don't work yourself into a lather over this."

The nurse returned then, her face etched with lines of concern. She hesitated, eyeing CJ before settling on Erica, the weight of unsaid words hanging between them. "Erica, there's something we need to discuss privately," she said, voice low and steady.

Perplexed, Erica looked to CJ in apology, saying, "Can you give us a minute?"

"Yeah, sure, of course," CJ said, releasing Erica's hand. Every instinct screamed for him to stay, yet he found himself stepping back, seeming to retreat to an area where he wasn't privy to the whispered secrets between patient and healer. But he could still hear the hushed tones of the conversation. Was it wrong? Probably. Did he care? Not really. He felt territorially protective over Erica in ways he couldn't explain and definitely couldn't fight.

"Um, well, seems you actually are pregnant, Miss Pike," the nurse said with a small, rueful chuckle. "I hope this is good, unexpected news, but it does change the plan to put you under general anesthesia."

CJ's breath caught in his chest. *Pregnant?*

Erica seemed just as shocked. "I'm sorry, I think I have dust in my ears… Did you say I'm pregnant? Are you sure?"

"Yes, the blood test is conclusive. Not far along but definitely pregnant. Due to this, we can't risk general anesthesia," the nurse continued, her words wrapped in professional warmth. "Local anesthetic—it's safer for a baby in the first trimester during the procedure. The danger of miscarriage is small, but the doctor won't want to risk it."

CJ's heart hammered against his rib cage, a frenzied drummer too loud in the quiet corridor. Pregnant? The world seemed to twist beneath him, reality skewing into a shape he couldn't recognize. He stumbled backward, the taut wire inside him snapping, sending his senses reeling.

Footsteps rang hollow on linoleum as he shuffled to the waiting room, the pulsing thrum of his pulse drowning out the world around him. Each step felt like wading through molasses, time stretching and bending like a surreal painting.

He collapsed onto the closest chair, the plastic cool and unforgiving beneath him. The weight of the revelation pressed down, each breath heavier than the last. Was the child his? A storm of possibility raged in his mind, every thought a flash of lightning with no thunder to follow.

Josh found him and immediately started asking questions. "How's Erica?"

CJ snapped out of his funk to nod, answering on autopilot. "She's good. They're going to use local anesthesia to pull the wood free and then sew up her injury."

Looking relieved, Josh said, "That's good. Everyone else seems okay, too. Erica's injury seems the most severe, but man, that scared the shit out of me."

"You and me both," he murmured.

"I need to head back to the resort, start the insurance paperwork. I'll catch an Uber so you can stay here if you want."

CJ nodded, appreciating Josh's willingness to catch a ride without him. He couldn't fathom leaving Erica's side, not when he knew she was pregnant.

The baby might not be yours—calm down. That voice of reason seemed almost defensive, but there was something in his gut that told him no, that baby was his. Erica didn't sleep around. He knew that much about her. Plus, the nurse said she was in her first trimester, which was early from what he understood about babies—which, admittedly, wasn't a lot.

So what did that mean for them?

He didn't have answers—only more questions.

And the only person who could help him answer those questions was about to go into surgery to have a big shard of wood removed from her body.

He slumped down in the hard plastic chair, feeling out of his element…and scared.

Chapter Sixteen

Erica's heart lurched, a tiny paper boat caught in a tempestuous sea—*pregnant.* The word echoed in her skull, bouncing off the insides like a rogue pinball. She barely had time to wrap her mind around the life-altering revelation before the sterile tang of the hospital nudged her back to the present.

"All right, Miss Pike, we're ready for you," a nurse said, her voice a calm contrast to the storm inside Erica.

She nodded mutely as she was wheeled down the antiseptic corridor, harsh lights flickering overhead like a staccato rhythm to the chaos in her chest. The operating room loomed, a frigid cave of clinical precision where her arm would be freed from the jagged invader that had punctured her skin. A part of her wished she'd been able to just go to sleep and wake up with all of this a weird dream, but the reality was far more jarring.

"Deep breaths, Erica," the doctor instructed, his tone professional yet oddly soothing. "We'll have that wood out in no time."

And true to his word, the procedure unfolded with a stark simplicity that belied the complexity of her thoughts. A few well-placed stitches, a whisper of relief as the offending wood was extracted—a minor victory overshadowed by the reality of a new life growing inside her. Before she could grapple with the magnitude of it all, she was being patched up, handed a prescription and sent on her way.

"Take it easy with this arm, avoid any heavy lifting and make sure to take your antibiotics as prescribed," the doctor advised, ticking off each point on his fingers.

"Thank you," Erica managed, forcing a smile through numb lips.

When she emerged into the lobby, the sight of CJ waiting, his posture radiating concern, seemed to anchor her. His eyes met hers, and without a word, he was at her side, handling her with the delicate care one might use for a precious, yet fragile, artifact.

"You didn't have to—"

"Hush," he said. "I'm driving you," he said in a tone brooking no argument, as if she were silly for suggesting otherwise. She didn't have the desire to argue and simply nodded.

He helped her gently into his car, the silence between them thick with the unsaid. Every glance he cast her way felt heavy with words they weren't ready to speak, every touch a silent vow of support she wasn't sure how to receive.

No less than three days ago, she'd tersely cut off any semblance of even friendship with CJ, drawing a professional boundary between them that he wasn't welcome to cross.

Now he was her baby daddy.

So much for keeping it professional, she thought wryly.

"When we get to your place, you're going to rest," CJ said, firmly in control. "I know that goes against your personality but… I mean, there are other things to consider now."

Dancing around the elephant. Fun times.

But CJ's hand found hers, tentative yet steady, a tangible connection amid the dizzying and rapidly changing reality between them and she clung to him.

"Thanks," she breathed—not just for the ride, but for the silent understanding, for the presence that didn't press or pry, only offered temporary sanctuary, which she sorely needed.

CJ's car rolled to a stop outside Erica's place, and CJ was already out and opening her door before she could gather her thoughts.

"Careful," he murmured, his hands ghosting around her as if she were a soap bubble ready to pop.

"CJ, I'm not made of glass," she murmured but stepped gingerly onto the pavement, her injured arm cradled protectively against her.

Inside, the living room greeted her with its familiar comfort, everything as she liked her environment to be after a long day at work. How would she fit a baby into her space? She had so many breakables and collectibles that weren't exactly baby-friendly.

CJ guided her to the sofa, piling cushions with an exactness that didn't match his usual easygoing nature. He moved through her space, straightening, adjusting, doing anything but standing still.

"Thanks," she managed, sinking into the pillowed cloud.

"Water? Food?" CJ asked, hovering close, his restlessness palpable.

Oh gosh, if he didn't stop hovering she'd lose what was left of her frayed sanity.

"Sit, please," Erica said, her voice thin but insistent. He obeyed, perching on the edge of an armchair like a bird too anxious to roost.

Silence stretched between them, filled only by the ticking clock and their shared unease. Erica took a shaky breath, feeling the weight of revelation balloon within her.

"We might as well get to the heart of the current situation. I didn't know," she started, her gaze locked on her hands, twisting in her lap. "About the…pregnancy." The word felt foreign on her tongue, like she was talking about someone else's situation instead of her own. "I mean, I…wasn't in the right time in my cycle and… I, well, I just…"

Frustration made her stumble on the truth of the matter until she finally blurted, "Okay, we should've been more careful, but neither of us were thinking clearly, obviously."

"So… I'm safe to assume…"

"Yes, CJ. It's yours," she said, the words brittle but true. "I haven't been with anyone else since—you know, before you left."

His expression shifted, the questions now replaced by a dawning comprehension that she caught at the same time. Good gravy, that meant she'd already been pregnant when they'd hooked up a second time on the movie set.

"Wow" was all he managed, the monosyllable heavy with a thousand unspoken thoughts.

"Wow," she echoed, a laugh bubbling up from her nerves like fizz in a shaken soda can.

The room seemed to breathe around them, the walls echoing back their astonishment as if to say, *Yes, this is really happening*, and neither knew what to say.

CJ's descent onto the sofa sent a plume of air rushing from beneath the cushions, a testament to the gravity of the situation that anchored him next to her. His mouth opened and closed, a fish gasping for comprehension in an ocean of responsibility.

"Guess we can't keep things professional now, huh?" Erica's voice, a frayed thread, tried to weave humor into the heavy fabric of reality.

He managed a strangled sound—half laugh, half sigh—before springing up as if the couch were a launchpad to fatherhood. "We'll need to schedule your checkups, get prenatal vitamins and—oh, foot rubs? Is that a thing? I've heard pregnant women have feet issues. Probably from carrying around another person all day. I'll have a masseuse brought in to rub your feet every day—"

"Stop," she pleaded, the word a hand raised against the barrage of his well-meaning torrent. "Just sit with me. Please."

Her plea reached him through the static of his panic, and he paused, the frenetic energy in his eyes softening. "Right. Sorry." He folded back down beside her, his presence a solid, reassuring weight. "I'm just out of my depth, and I don't want to keep screwing things up. I'm sorry, Erica. I—I don't even know what else to say."

Erica understood. "Can you hold me?" she asked.

CJ scooted forward and enveloped his arms around her, drawing her close. Erica's tension melted into the warmth between them. Her exhale filled the space, a sound rich with relief and the faintest echo of hope, even though she just wanted to shut her brain down for a bleeding second.

"Thank you," she whispered into the fabric of his shirt, the texture against her cheek grounding her in this new, shared existence. They didn't need to solve every problem right this second. What she needed right now was CJ and a quiet moment.

The rest could wait.

AFTER A LONG WHILE, Erica disentangled herself from CJ's arms and rose with an offer to make them something to eat, to which CJ could only stare with incredulity, returning with an adamant, "The hell you are. If anything, I'll order us something, because I'm not much of a cook, but you're not lifting a finger tonight."

"CJ, don't be ridiculous. I'm not broken—and before you

come back with 'But you're pregnant!' women have been having babies for a very long time, and I feel mostly fine, so stop worrying."

"Be that as it may, you're carrying my baby, and I don't feel comfortable with you overdoing it on my watch. At least wait until I leave," he added with a subtle return of his usual humor.

She chuckled with acquiescence. "Okay, that's fair. Tonight I will not lift a finger and you can handle everything. And if you're offering to order takeout, I'd love a burger with all of the trimmings. I'm actually starving."

Relieved to have a purpose, CJ jumped on her request, and within minutes, he'd placed two orders for the best burgers Sedona could offer and promised the delivery driver a ridiculous tip if he could get it here within thirty minutes or less. Being rich had its perks.

But now that he'd finished that one task, he was left to wonder what to do next. He was still a nervous ball of energy and yet feeling totally useless at the same time.

Erica sighed, sensing the tension inside him, though she must've misinterpreted his anxiety, saying, "CJ, I'm not expecting you to drop to your knee and promise me forever. We're both adults. We can handle this situation between us without placing any relationship expectations on the table, okay?"

But it wasn't okay and that wasn't why he was nervous. "What if I want a relationship with you, Erica?" he blurted before he could stop himself. At her widened stare, he rushed to clarify. "Okay, I know I'm being super erratic right now, but I like you…and I can't imagine anyone I'd rather have a baby with, but every time I try to say the right thing, somehow my foot ends up in my mouth and I screw it all up."

"CJ…" Erica's gaze darted away, as if uncomfortable with

his admission, and he felt like an idiot for blurting out something so raw. "I just think we should take things slow for now…we're both running on shock right now. Neither of us should be making big decisions in the wake of our discovery. Let's just…let it rest for a minute, okay?"

That made sense, even if it deflated his sails a bit. His grand gesture had fallen embarrassingly flat, but her advice was more logical, forcing him to nod glumly. "Yeah, of course," he said.

But Erica saw how her advice had landed and softened the blow, adding, "Let's just…take our time with this." Erica's fingers traced the fabric of the cushion, her gaze fixed on some distant point of contemplation. "I'm not saying no to figuring it out together. I just don't want us to do something rash because of… Well, because of this."

CJ blew out a short breath, taking a minute to settle his nerves. She was right. Nothing had to be solved or sorted out today. What mattered was that Erica was safe, the baby was safe and they had at least eight months, give or take, to figure out the rest.

The food arrived, and CJ enjoyed a good, solid meal that also helped settle his thoughts and put him back on track. As much as the news that Erica was pregnant was huge, he had another issue to deal with, and it couldn't wait.

"Are you sure you're going to be all right?" He double-checked with Erica as they cleaned up after dinner.

"I'm totally fine," she assured him. "I need to call Laura and let her know what's going on, but I plan to be at work tomorrow."

Even though CJ would rather she stay home and rest, he knew that was asking a lot. "Light duty, right?" he suggested.

"Yes, I'll take it easy."

"Okay, then I'll trust you to keep your word on that. I

have to talk to Anna about the production. Last I saw, she was heading to make a call to the execs, and I don't think it was going to be a good conversation after the barn practically fell on us."

Erica frowned. "CJ…there might be some truth to the suspicion that someone is trying to stop the production. I don't think you can chalk up all of these incidents to bad luck or coincidence."

CJ agreed. "The key gaffer admitted that someone had cut the wires to the lighting rig a few days ago. It was a miracle it didn't catch fire again."

"Do you think that's what happened to the saloon at the original location?"

"Seems likely. All it takes is a single spark, and everything goes up in flames."

Erica shuddered. "Why would someone want to sabotage a big production? That's a lot of jobs and a lot of money on the line."

"I don't know, but I think it's time to start asking different questions," he said, grabbing his keys. "I need to talk to Anna before she's an entire wine bottle deep in depression. This production was her baby."

At the mention of *baby*, they both paused, then laughed awkwardly as CJ admitted, "It's weird to think, huh?"

"Yeah," she nodded, smiling. "I guess we'll get used to it eventually."

He was struck by how incredibly beautiful she was, and he reached for her gently. "Can I kiss you good-night?" he asked.

Erica answered with a slow nod, her gaze meeting his boldly. He didn't waste a minute in pressing his lips against hers, his tongue darting to lightly taste, sending a thrill hurtling through his nerve endings. They were electric together—was it any wonder they'd made a baby?

He could've spent all night kissing her, but time was his enemy right now. Regretfully pulling away, CJ said his goodbyes and left for the resort, switching gears.

Time to figure out what the hell was going on and why someone was deliberately trying to kill any hope for the production.

Chapter Seventeen

CJ's hand hovered over the door, a sense of dread settling in his stomach like an unwanted guest as he knocked softly on Anna's room at Mariposa Resort. When the door creaked open, there she was: silhouette slumped against the sunset bleeding through the curtains, wine glass cradled like a fragile hope in her hand. Her eyes, usually sharp as sea glass, were now glassy and rimmed red, telling him more than words could about the day's toll.

"Anna?" His voice tiptoed into the room. "You okay?"

She managed a wobbly smile that didn't reach her eyes, shaking her head as she tipped the bottle, filling her glass. "Drink?" she asked, voice flat, the word hanging awkwardly between them.

"No, thanks," CJ declined, the weight of her gaze pulling him closer. "The execs—what did they say?"

There it was, the dam breaking behind her eyes as she swallowed hard, fresh tears pooling. "They've pulled the plug, CJ. It's over," she whispered, her voice a ghost of defeat. "Too many accidents…we've become an insurance nightmare."

His throat tightened, watching her crumble. Anna, the unshakable force behind their project, now reduced to this—a woman questioning her own resolve. Goddamn, if he got his hands on whoever was responsible for this mess, he'd catch a murder charge.

"Maybe they're right," she muttered, a tear betraying her and rolling down her cheek. "I can't… I don't want anyone else getting hurt because of me." Her hand paused mid-wipe, and her bleary eyes sought his. "Erica? How is she?"

"Erica's…" CJ started, then hesitated, the irony of the situation twisting his lips into a half smile. "She's fine. Actually, she's pregnant. And—I'm the father."

For a moment, Anna looked as if he'd slapped her with a dead fish. "Excuse me? What? You two? I didn't even realize…"

"Neither did we," CJ admitted, scratching the back of his neck with an uneasy chuckle. "I mean, it was nothing official between us, but I guess things have changed now."

Raising her glass in a trembling salute, Anna offered a watery "Mazel tov" before pushing herself up from the chair, her legs shaky as newborn foals. "Sorry, CJ, I'm terrible company right now. I have to find the courage to tell the rest of the cast and crew that we're done, and so far, it wasn't in the wine bottle and now all I want is to go to bed."

CJ understood. "Yeah, of course. But Anna, before you tell anyone, give me twenty-four hours, okay? Let me talk to someone…higher up."

Her laugh was bitter, devoid of humor. "You think you can turn this around? Be my guest."

"Promise me," he insisted, holding her gaze.

"Fine," she sighed, half-defeated. "Knock yourself out, hero. I'll be here, trying to sleep away this damn nightmare."

And with that, she turned away, leaving CJ grappling with the wreckage of their dreams and the new life forming amid the chaos.

SUNRISE FOUND CJ with his duffel slung over one shoulder, the crisp morning air biting at his cheeks as he strode across the dew-speckled grass of Mariposa Resort.

He squinted against the early light, a crease forming between his brows—a physical manifestation of the resolve hardening within him. It wasn't just about saving the production now; it was about proving himself, about stepping up when everything seemed to crumble.

He slid into the driver's seat of the rental car, the fabric cool and unwelcoming beneath him. The engine hummed to life, a soft, steady purr that seemed at odds with the turmoil churning in his gut. He had a quick flight to LA already booked, and he had a meeting slated for thirty minutes after he landed.

As the vehicle rolled out onto the open road, CJ's thumb hovered over his phone screen, a message drafted but not yet sent. The words felt heavy, each letter weighted with a significance he'd never dealt with before. With a flick of his thumb, the message shot through the digital ether:

Hey Erica, heading to LA to sort some things out. Back tomorrow. —CJ

It was simple, almost too simple, but beneath the surface, there was so much more going on. He wasn't just letting her know about his whereabouts; he was laying down the first brick on the path to reliability, to being present. He released a shaky breath, never before realizing how he'd always been the one to disappear first, laughing off conflict and adopting a "chill" attitude that often translated into the guy who couldn't be caught.

The car ate miles of asphalt as he drove to the airport.

His thoughts drifted to Erica, their unplanned intertwining of lives, and the small, budding existence that now linked them forever. He didn't voice it, didn't even shape the thought clearly in his mind, but somewhere deep inside, a silent vow formed—a whisper of commitment to the future and to the family he never knew he wanted until now.

But first, he had to figure out what the hell was going on with the people who signed the checks. If being an A-list celebrity didn't afford you the chance to champion a good cause, what good was it?

Time to make his celebrity status work for him, instead of working for his status.

THE PING OF Erica's phone was a welcome distraction, her thumb swiping the screen as CJ's text tumbled across it. Had she been holding her breath, wondering if he would text her before leaving town again? Maybe. The fact that he had felt like a step in the right direction, small though it was.

Grinning to herself, she pocketed the device and slipped through the back offices, her pace brisk and her mind focused with the news she knew she had to share.

But as she rounded the corner toward Laura's office, she halted mid-stride at the unexpected visitor chatting casually with both Laura and Josh.

Matthew Bennett? *Good lord, does that mean he accepted the wedding invitation?*

Matthew, a Colton stepcousin, with his sportsman physique and a head full of cropped dark brown hair that somehow managed to look effortlessly windswept, was a wild card in Erica's book. Unfortunately Matthew was connected to family drama. It wasn't his fault, but no one knew for sure where his true allegiances landed. Money always had a tendency to muddy the waters, in Erica's experience.

Golden-brown eyes flicked her way, a spark of recognition igniting within their depths.

"Erica!" Laura's voice, laced with something more than greeting, pulled Erica from her appraisal.

In an instant, professionalism cloaked her like a second skin, her smile stretching as she crossed the threshold into the buzzing office. She read the room—the subtle shifts, the tension riding on the undercurrents of conversation—and knew this was not the time for her news.

"Matthew, Josh," she greeted, nodding at each in turn.

Josh smiled with genuine relief. "I was so relieved when CJ let us know that you're okay. I can't believe the barn failed like that."

"What happened?" Matthew asked with a confused frown. "An accident at the resort?"

Josh looked reluctant to share, but answered, "There's a film shooting on location here. There was a small mishap. Thankfully everyone was okay, except for Erica. She took a piece of wood to the arm."

"Sounds terrible. Are you sure you're okay?" Matthew asked.

"Nothing a few stitches and a round of antibiotics can't handle," Erica replied with a quick smile.

Laura shared a look with Josh, just as Matthew said, "Hmm, that could be a liability issue. Have you had the lawyers look into the ramification of an accident like that caused by filming?"

"We don't know that it was caused by the filming," Laura clarified quickly. "It was the old barn in the closed section of the resort. It might've been unstable from the start. We're having it inspected to determine the cause of the accident."

Matthew nodded. "Good idea. In the meantime, I'm assuming filming is shut down until it's been deemed safe?"

Erica wanted to glare at Matthew for poking his nose where it didn't belong—they had the situation well in hand and didn't need Matthew's two cents—but her expression remained professionally neutral.

Laura offered a brief smile. "All in hand. Hey, Josh why don't you give Matthew a tour of the resort, show him some of our newest attractions."

"Great idea," Josh said, gesturing for Matthew to follow.

As the men exited, their footsteps a fading beat against the floor, Erica turned to Laura, with an incredulous expression. "Who appointed him the OSHA representative?" she joked.

Laura pursed her lips in annoyance. "Honestly, when I sent the invitation, I didn't expect him to accept. I only let him know about the wedding out of courtesy, and now he's here thinking he can have an opinion on how we run Mariposa."

"Stepcousin, right?" Erica said, affirming her memory.

"Yes," Laura said. "I mean, I'm sure he means well, but right now, I just want him to zip it. Anyway…" She shook off the last few minutes and returned to Erica, "How are you? Are you sure you're okay?"

"I'm totally fine," she assured Laura. "They didn't even have to knock me out to stitch me up. Honestly, I probably could've saved myself a trip to the hospital if I'd just pulled it out myself and smeared some antibacterial ointment on it."

"Good God, no. You absolutely needed to be seen by a doctor, but I'm glad you're okay. I was so worried."

The silence settled like a heavy blanket between them, the absent hum of office chatter leaving room for Erica's racing heart to fill the space.

"However," Erica said, taking a steadying breath. "Laura," she began, the words slipping out with a tremulous certainty, "something else was discovered while at the hospital."

"Something else?" Laura repeated with a confused frown. "What do you mean?"

"So, as it turns out… I'm eleven weeks pregnant."

Laura's face lost color as if the news had physically struck her, her lips parting in a silent gasp. "Eleven weeks?" Laura gasped.

"Yep."

"Eleven— Oh God, are you telling me…" Laura finally found her voice, a mix of disbelief and concern. "It's CJ's baby, isn't it?"

Erica nodded, her own surprise at the situation still fresh, "Yeah, sure is."

A groan escaped Laura, her hand flying up to her face. "How?" She dropped her hand to clarify at Erica's blush. "I mean, I know *how*, but you're the last person I'd ever suspect would find themselves pregnant from a one-night stand."

"You and me both, sister," Erica quipped, shaking her head. "But life has a way of humbling you when you least expect it."

"You can say that again." Laura took a minute, trying to find her footing in the conversation. "Okay, are you… I mean, do you feel—okay?"

"Okay? I don't know." Erica forced a laugh, attempting to slice through the tension. "Ask again in a few days." She flexed her fingers, the bandaged arm a visual reminder of her vulnerability.

"Yeah, I get that," Laura said but quickly switched gears as only Laura could. "Well, okay, it is what it is. No more lifting or—"

"Hey, I'm fine," Erica cut in, the firmness in her voice belying her inner turmoil. "Really. Just because I have to go easy on the arm doesn't mean I've turned into glass. You and CJ both are trying to put me in a padded bubble, and that's not necessary."

Laura studied her, the corners of her mouth twitching upward in a hesitant smile. "You'd hate that, wouldn't you? Being treated like you're fragile?"

"More than anything," Erica confirmed with a nod, grateful for the understanding that always seemed to anchor their friendship.

Laura's concern etched deeper lines into her forehead as she leaned forward, the creak of her chair breaking the tense silence. "You know, I could always pass on the bachelorette-party planning to someone else," she offered, her voice soft but insistent.

Erica shook her head with a determination that surprised even herself. "No way. The plans are set, everything's ticking along like clockwork. I'm not letting anyone snatch this from me—it's going to be epic."

Laura grinned. "It was probably a stupid offer."

"It kinda was," Erica said with a wink. "But your heart is in the right place." Back to business, Erica said, "Willow flies in tomorrow, right?"

"Yeah, and I should be psyched to see her, but..." Laura's voice trailed off, her eyes darting to the window, where chaos seemed just a pane away.

"Hey," Erica said, her tone firmer than she intended, "this storm will blow over. And your wedding? It's okay to be over the moon about it—no guilt allowed."

A smile flickered across Laura's face, the first genuine one since the bombshell news. It was moments like these that reminded Erica why she'd go to the ends of the earth for her friend.

"You're right," Laura said with a small, guilty snicker. "I'm super excited. And you know what—it's going to be fine. Everything is going to work out for you and for me. Do you hear that, universe?" She shook her finger at the ceiling as if chastising a listening deity. "I'm manifesting total bliss, and that's that."

Erica laughed, her voice bouncing off the office walls. "Well, there you have it, folks. But now I've got work to do." She paused, throwing a playful wink Laura's way. "Enjoy your time with the relatives."

With that, she exited Laura's office, leaving behind an echo of her laughter. Her heart felt oddly buoyant despite the looming life-altering shift ahead of her.

Was pregnant euphoria a thing?

Note to self: buy book on pregnancy.

Heading down the halls, her heels clicked sharply as she went.

When everything else was out of whack—routine always felt right.

Chapter Eighteen

CJ's sneakers slapped the sunbaked pavement as he hustled through a maze of trailers and cables, the LA heat clinging to him like a second skin. The studio lot buzzed with an undercurrent of tension, electric and alive, a far cry from the calm serenity of the resort.

Funny how he never really noticed how this environment was a recipe for anxiety. He'd always attributed that tension in his body as excitement, but now it felt different. Was this the impending "Dad Effect" happening? He'd have to untangle that later. For now, he had to focus on the situation facing the production.

"Mr. Knight?" A young PA with a headset that seemed too large for her head flagged him down, her eyes scanning a clipboard as if it held the secrets of the universe. "Mr. Greene is ready for you on the fourth floor."

"Thanks," CJ grunted, taking the stairs two at a time, the thud of his heartbeat keeping pace with his ascent. He was taking a huge chance, but he felt he had to do it.

The door to the executive's office swung open with a decisive push, revealing a space that screamed power—the kind of room where dreams were made or shattered on a whim. There, behind a desk that could double as a small aircraft carrier, sat the man himself: Harold Greene, the notorious executive whose fair handshake was as legendary as his ruthless business tactics.

The fact that Mr. Greene had taken CJ's request to meet spoke volumes about his star power, but CJ wasn't naive—Mr. Greene liked money, and he liked making it. And right now, that was CJ's superpower. The minute CJ stopped being box office gold, the man would forget he existed. So, with that knowledge, CJ figured he might as well "make hay while the sun shone" and use whatever advantage he had to save the production.

"Harold," CJ began, going straight to the point, "you can't just pull the plug over a couple of hiccups. *Waterworld* tanked—literally—and they still finished shooting."

"No chitchat first? Okay, I respect that." Greene leaned back, his chair creaking in protest. "CJ, unless you've got Costner's deep pockets and are willing to sink twenty-two mil into this sinking ship, I suggest you let it go," he said. "This production is going to turn into an albatross around your neck if you're not careful."

But CJ wasn't going to do that. Maybe it was his stubborn belief in the underdog or his sense of fair play, but he couldn't let it go. "Let's get down to brass tacks. I know for a fact you have a handful of pet projects that aren't going to make a dime domestically and you're not pulling the plug on them. So, why this production? This feels personal. You aren't giving Anna a fair chance. What's the real reason—because I smell a steaming pile of bull, and you can't convince me it's a bed of roses."

Harold's gaze narrowed. "Say it with your whole chest. What are you implying?"

"Not implying, I'm pointing out the obvious. Every film has its setbacks. Hell, what's happened so far on this production is literally small potatoes, but you've got Anna dancing on a wire, threatening to the pull the plug at every turn. You're being an ass, and I want to know why."

He was taking a risk. Harold Greene had the power to crush his career if he chose, but CJ was banking on the fact that he also knew that the man was a straight shooter and respected bold moves.

A moment passed between them until Greene sighed, shaking his head. "It's not personal, CJ. Maybe the project was just too damn ambitious, and maybe Anna wasn't the right call," Greene said, toying with a pen between his fingers. "And if it seems like I've been riding her throughout this production, it's because I actually want her to succeed. I think she's very talented and deserves a shot."

"So, why are you shutting down the movie?"

"Look, the insurance companies are getting real skittish about insuring productions with problems. Sure, no one was badly hurt, but there have been too many incidents that could've been bad. No one's going to rally behind a film shoot that someone died on. It's just facts. I'd rather cut my losses than deal with the potential of a tragedy."

Might as well go big and tell Greene what he suspected. "Someone's messing with us, Harold. The key gaffer found the wires cut to the main lighting rig, and I'm willing to bet that someone created the dangerous situation with the barn. The owner of the resort is having the structure examined as well as the set crew."

"Sabotage? Why?"

"Hell if I know, but it feels personal."

"But you don't have any proof of that, correct?"

"I mean, we have proof someone cut the wires," CJ said.

"That's not enough. Shit happens on a production. The wires could've been accidentally compromised. What's the motive? I know you want to find a reason to make this more than it is, but you don't have to. Look, if it's about your paycheck, don't sweat it. Doug might've been a twisted guy, but he negotiated a tight contract. You'll get your cash either way."

Just the mention of Doug was a trigger for CJ. "Damn it, Harold, it's not about the money!" CJ's words echoed off the walls, his frustration palpable.

"All right, all right." Greene raised his hands in a calming gesture, clearly mistaking CJ's passion for desperation. "Take it easy, CJ. We'll make sure you're taken care of."

CJ's stomach churned, acid bubbling like a caustic critique. The money talk? It was white noise, a static hum in the background of a much bigger picture. He wasn't some mercenary actor, flipping roles for a quick buck; this was about the art, the story that needed to be told.

"Listen to me," CJ said, his voice low and tight with urgency. "You think I'm here rattling cans for change? This is bigger than a paycheck."

Greene sat back, the chair creaking under the shift of his weight, eyes wide with a flicker of uncertainty. Maybe he hadn't seen this kind of fire before—not from someone like CJ.

"Anna's vision for this film…it's groundbreaking. And I won't stand by while you choke it with red tape." CJ's words were a punch, direct and unflinching.

"Groundbreaking?" Greene echoed, skepticism pulling down his mouth. But CJ could see it—the crack in the exec's smooth facade, the hint that maybe, just maybe, he got it. "C'mon, it's a Western period drama. Let's not make it to be more than it is."

"If that's all you see about Anna's vision, you've got it all wrong. The historical aspect of the film is just the vehicle for the theme of human grit required to shape new worlds and survive the violence of new beginnings. I'm telling you, this script has *Oscar-worthy* written all over it."

Greene chuckled wryly. "If I had a dollar for every time someone has pitched that to me… I wouldn't need my studio paycheck to pay for my next ex-wife."

"Yeah, well, when it's coming from me, it means something."

"Of course," Greene said, his tone placating. But CJ wasn't having it.

"If you don't have the stones to see this through, I'll do it. If it takes every dime I've got, I'll bankroll it myself." The words spilled out, a reckless promise, but they carried a weight of truth that anchored them firmly in the room.

Greene's face froze, his usual slick composure slipping like ice underfoot. "CJ, what are you doing? Are you serious?"

"Watch me." Without another word, CJ turned on his heel, strides eating up the plush carpet as he headed for the door.

Behind him, the silence was loud—a stunned quiet that felt like the aftermath of a scene well played. But this wasn't a performance. This was real, raw, and CJ was all in.

As the office door clicked shut behind him, CJ's pulse thrummed a victory beat. He might have shocked the big shot in the suit, but more importantly, he had just bet on the one thing he believed in more than anything: the movie, Anna's vision, their shared dream.

He might've just done the stupidest, most reckless thing in his life.

And he had a kid on the way.

ERICA WAS THREADING her way between the bustling halls when she sensed someone trailing her. She turned to find Matthew, his approach casual but his eyes intent.

"Erica!" he called out, a practiced smile spreading across his face as he quickened his pace to match hers. "I've been hoping to catch you for a moment."

"Matthew," she responded, her voice even but her mind racing. She didn't have time for idle chitchat, especially not with a Colton hanger-on. Still, politeness won over. "What can I do for you?"

Matthew leaned in, his eyes sparkling with intrigue. "I have to admit I'm fascinated by all this movie-business intrigue that's been going on here at the resort. What really happened at the barn?" he asked, his voice dropping to a conspiratorial whisper as if they were buddies and Erica was going to spill secrets.

Erica's guard went up immediately. For one, she wasn't going to share resort business with anyone, much less someone who was simply a stepcousin with a tentative claim to the family resort. And two, she wasn't the sort of person to gossip.

"There's really no intrigue. Just a minor issue with one of the set pieces," she replied evasively. "It was really nothing."

"Nothing? I heard you had to go to the hospital," Matthew returned with a quizzical expression. "Doesn't sound like nothing to me. What kind of safety protocols were in place?"

Erica forced a short laugh at his query. "It was nothing so dramatic. All I needed was a few stitches. It was more of a setback for the production than for me."

"So, they're going to keep filming?"

"I would assume so," Erica said with a short, pleasant smile that was her standard operating procedure for anyone difficult. "It was just bad luck," she offered with a dismissive wave. "These things happen sometimes in big productions." She hoped her explanation would end his probing.

"Sure, sure," Matthew said, nodding, though his brow remained furrowed with concern—or was it something else? He switched gears, sliding into even darker territory. "And Allison Brewer's murder…that must have been tough on everyone here."

The mention of Allison sent a prickling discomfort down Erica's spine. She forced a tight-lipped smile, the shadow of the tragedy too heavy to lift with pleasantries.

"Absolutely tragic, yes. But we're all trying to move forward." Her words came out more clipped than she intended, but Matthew's relentless digging was wearing thin on her patience.

"Of course, of course," he murmured, his gaze drifting past her as if trying to unearth secrets from the very air, which as far as she was concerned, weren't his business. She also knew Laura wouldn't appreciate him digging like this, either.

"Sorry, Matthew, I need to handle something," Erica cut in, seizing the chance to escape. "Excuse me."

As she walked away, her thoughts churned with suspicion. Matthew's intense interest didn't sit right. She couldn't shake the feeling that his inquiries were more than mere curiosity. *Talk to Laura*, she reminded herself mentally, already anticipating the next item on her never-ending list of tasks.

Later, finding a rare pocket of stillness in the outdoor spa area, Erica slumped into a chair. Enclosed by high hedges, the world seemed to fall away, leaving only the hum of distant activity. Exhaustion weighed her eyelids down like anchors.

Pregnant, she reminded herself, the word alien yet full of consequence. She placed a hand over her belly, the future stirring there as imperceptible as a whisper. Hard to believe a baby was growing in there when her pants weren't even tight yet.

"Life's curveball," she muttered, her heart thrumming with a mix of anxiety and wonder at what lay ahead.

Could CJ be part of this new chapter? The idea of integrating their wildly different worlds seemed as plausible as mixing oil with water. He belonged to the glitz and glamor; she to the quiet routine of her small-town life. And she liked her life, just as much as she was sure CJ liked his—so who had to be the one to give something up?

"Movie stars don't do diaper duty," she whispered, the reality pinching her heart.

A glance at her watch jolted her back to the present. With a resigned sigh, she straightened up and brushed off the invisible crumbs of fatigue. There was no time for rest, not when duty called. She pushed herself up, the promise of an early night's sleep dangling before her like a carrot on a stick. Dinner, then bed—that was the plan, and she intended to stick to it.

Chapter Nineteen

The crunch of gravel under tires announced CJ's return before he even killed the engine. Erica watched from the porch, arms wrapped tight around her midsection. The last rays of the setting sun caught on his wind-tousled hair as he stepped out of the car with a briskness that didn't quite reach his eyes.

Her instant joy at seeing him dimmed at the seriousness in his gaze.

"Hey." His voice carried across the yard like a pebble skimming water, all surface energy. "We need to talk."

She nodded, her own reply snagged in the dryness of her throat. Her gaze lingered on the lines of tension drawn tight across his forehead as they settled into the living room. He paced, then stopped abruptly, facing her.

"Is everything okay?" she asked.

CJ shook his head, frustrated. "Let's just say the meeting wasn't as productive as I'd hoped."

"What happened?"

They stepped inside the house before CJ admitted, "Harold Greene seemed pretty adamant that he had no choice but to shut down the production, but he's got to be lying to me," he started, scratching the back of his neck, going straight to the headline. "So, I did the only thing I felt I had to, and I took on the production financing myself."

The words hung between them as Erica visibly balked at the announcement. "I'm sorry, what? Financing? CJ, that's…" She hesitated, the walls of support she wanted to offer him cracking under the weight of her worry that he'd just done something incredibly brash. "Can you…afford that?"

CJ didn't shy away from the question. "Um, well, I don't know. I mean, I have money in accounts and whatnot, but Doug handled all that stuff with my accountant, so I guess I'll have to find out the details. Maybe use my house as collateral if need be, but I feel it had to be done. Besides, I think I'll make back my investment. Anna's film is Oscar-worthy. I believe in it."

"CJ, that's incredibly risky," she murmured, wondering how to handle this news. On one hand, it wasn't her business how he spent his money, but on the other, this could be an indication of future behavior that could prove problematic for a new father that made her feel uncomfortable. Was he going to do this kind of thing whenever things didn't go his way? He couldn't possibly think that throwing money at a problem was the only way to handle a situation that wasn't to his liking.

"I know, but the production's being shut down over such small things," he shot back as if that was enough to justify his action. "I mean, it's sabotage and it's not Anna's fault, but Greene is acting like everything that's happened is because she's not capable of handling the production. You've met Anna—does she seem incapable of handling the job?"

"No, not at all," she murmured, but she wasn't a fair judge of what made a good director. "But CJ, maybe you shouldn't have jumped into such deep waters before checking the depth. Taking on a movie production that could cost millions without even finding out if you could write a check that big? I… I mean, I can't even fathom doing something so rash."

"Good thing I can swim," he quipped darkly with a flicker of a smile, but Erica didn't think now was the time for flippant remarks.

The silence stretched, a taut string ready to snap. Erica breathed through her nose, forced calm into her lungs. *Okay, regroup. Take a minute to process before saying something you regret.* She reached out, fingers brushing his. An attempt to bridge the chasm yawning open in the room. There was no doubting his ambition, his drive. But at what cost?

"Let's just…sit on this for a night, okay? I ordered pizza, thought you might be hungry after jet-setting to Southern California and back in a day," she said, gesturing to the pie waiting for them.

A true smile replaced the tension in his jaw as he nodded, reaching for her. "I am hungry—for the pizza and for you," he said, pulling her to him. They hadn't exactly worked out what they were to each other yet, but Erica willingly went into his arms, sinking into the pleasure of his touch.

"Thanks for being there for me," he murmured, pressing a kiss against her forehead, the tension leaving his body. "Let's eat."

Erica didn't push back with her misgivings, choosing to let it go for now, but a part of her worried she was only kicking a can down the road. She would never bank her financial future on a decision made in the heat of the moment, but CJ just did.

CJ, as if moving on, gleefully grabbed a slice of pizza and bit into it with relish. "Oh yeah, that's good stuff. Good call, Erica. Good call."

She smiled and grabbed a slice, but her smile felt pasted

on. Sometimes love felt like a leap into a void, and tonight, the ground beneath them seemed perilously thin.

By the time they were finished with the pizza and cleaned up, Erica felt CJ's hope that she might invite him to stay the night, but she couldn't bring herself to do it. She could only pretend for so long before she said what was bothering her, and that would probably ruin the night. Instead she kissed him soundly and sent him on his way with a promise to see him tomorrow.

CJ, obviously perplexed by her decision to send him back to his own room at the resort, left without pressing the issue, and Erica was grateful.

The door closed behind him with soft click, a quiet thunder in her chest. She stood alone, surrounded by the aftermath of their conversation, the pizza sitting heavily in her stomach.

A past lover had once accused her of being too rigid in her own ways, too set in her belief that her way was always the right way. Was she doing it again? Or was she right to question CJ's actions when a baby was in their future?

In bed, the sheets were cold, and it took a minute to warm up, reminding her that she'd practically kicked CJ out when he could've been there wrapping her in his warmth. The clock ticked away the seconds, each one a heartbeat of doubt. Erica turned onto her side, then her back, then her side again, a restless dance with the shadows. She hated not having the answers.

Was she being too rigid? It wasn't her decision to make about his finances, but they were a team, weren't they? A partnership meant diving together, not watching one plunge while the other stood safely on solid ground.

She could manage on her own; her independence was not a question. Yet the notion of CJ's recklessness, the ease with which he gambled their future on a roll of dice gnawed at her. Trust was a fragile thing, and tonight it felt as if he'd tossed it into the wind, leaving her to catch the pieces.

With a sigh, she punched the pillow, seeking comfort in its softness. Sleep would come eventually, but peace was another matter—a puzzle whose pieces didn't quite fit in the darkness of the room.

THE FOLLOWING DAY, Erica rose and rushed to get to the resort, eager to cling to her routine. Sunlight filtered through the office blinds, casting long stripes across the floor as she shuffled papers on her desk with a mechanical rhythm, trying to immerse herself in the mundane tasks at hand. But the echoes of last night's conversation with CJ reverberated in her mind, each note of his voice a reminder of the rift growing between them that he had no clue was forming because she didn't speak up.

"Erica? You got a minute?" Josh's voice, usually the epitome of calm, held an edge that cut through her concentration.

"Sure," she responded, pushing aside her concerns as she rose from the chair. Her footsteps were silent against the carpet as she followed Josh into Laura's office.

Laura sat behind her desk, her athletic frame rigid, the tension in her posture telegraphing the seriousness of the moment. The usual warmth in her blue eyes was replaced by a stormier hue.

"Close the door, please," Laura said, her fingers drumming an anxious beat on the wooden surface.

Erica did as asked, the soft snick of the latch amplifying the knot in her stomach. Josh leaned against the wall, arms crossed, his expression grave. She took a seat, bracing herself for the impending disclosure.

"We just got word from the investigator," Josh began, his gaze fixed on Erica. "About the barn collapse."

"Okay..." Erica prompted, her heart picking up speed.

"Two support beams were tampered with," he continued, the words dropping like stones into the silence. "Deliberately weakened."

"Damn it," Erica breathed, wishing for different news. "Who would do such a thing?" she managed to ask.

"That's what we need to figure out," Laura said, worry etching lines around her eyes. "We can't let this get out. Not yet. We don't want to cause a panic."

"Of course," Erica agreed, feeling the weight of the secret settle on her shoulders. "Are you going to allow the production to continue on the property?"

"That's the question. I want to help, but it seems the production has a bigger problem than their location. Someone could've been seriously hurt," Laura said. "As it is, I hate that you were collateral damage in whatever beef this person has against the film crew or the production itself."

"I'm fine, Laura," she assured her boss, but this news only deepened her concern that CJ had taken on more than he could chew.

However, given this new information, Erica felt it prudent to share her own concerns. "There's something else," Erica ventured, the image of Matthew's intense golden-brown eyes flashing before her. "Matthew has been asking questions. About the resort, the accident. It made me uneasy. I feel he deliberately waited until I was alone to ask me questions that he should've been asking you or Josh."

"Matthew?" Laura's tone sharpened with surprise. "Why would he—"

"Family drama." Josh's interruption was clipped. "You know how it is with the Bennetts. Always some undercurrents."

"Maybe I shouldn't have invited him to the wedding?" Laura's expression was troubled. "I just hadn't wanted to seem rude, but honestly, the whole situation with Glenna and Dad…and now Matthew…it's another thing that seems more like a burden than anything else."

"I mean, you had to invite Dad and Glenna. Like it or not, they're family, which means Glenna's nephew is family, too. Maybe his questions were just part of a curious mind and nothing more."

"Maybe," Laura agreed, but her frown remained. "Thanks for telling us. I'm sorry he made you uncomfortable. We'll talk to him about going to other people about resort issues."

"I don't want to create more drama, but it seemed prudent to share," Erica said. At Laura's nod, she felt okay to switch gears since she was there. "Everything is set for the bachelorette party. Willow is arriving tonight, and her room is ready. Was there anything else you needed me to put on my calendar for today?"

"No—you've been amazing, my rock, as always," Laura said, smiling with genuine appreciation. "Thank you, Erica."

Erica smiled and let herself out, leaving Laura and Josh to work out the problem with Matthew. Even though she should probably keep the information to herself, she felt compelled to share with CJ what the investigator had discovered, especially since he'd just agreed to take on the production.

It was one thing to suspect foul play, another entirely to confirm it with cut beams and obvious evil intent.

But was she betraying Laura and Josh's confidence by sharing that information? Was it her place?

"Can't keep secrets," she muttered to herself. The words came out gritty, like sand against her teeth. She knew what she had to do, no matter how much it twisted her insides. She reached for her phone, thumb hovering over CJ's contact.

Hey, she typed, then paused. Her thumb hesitated, then pressed with determination. We need to talk. It's urgent.

The message sent. There was no taking it back now. Erica sat there, her heart drumming a frantic beat, waiting for CJ's response.

This felt like a big move, a momentous decision to share information that wasn't exactly hers to share but could affect CJ's future.

And hers, by proxy.

She'd never been a rule-breaker by nature, and doing it now didn't give her a thrill. If anything, she felt sick to her stomach, but she couldn't in good conscience let CJ leverage everything he had on something that could end up costing him everything.

Maybe even his life.

Chapter Twenty

CJ knocked sharply on the door of Anna's bungalow, his thoughts churning from the news Erica had just shared with him in confidence.

Anna, looking better than the last time he'd seen her, was on her laptop when he entered. "We have to talk," he said, getting straight to the point. "I've got information that you're going to want to hear, and you'd better stay sitting down because it's a doozy."

"What's going on?" Anna asked.

"Someone's trying to tank the movie, Anna." CJ's words were like flint striking steel, ready to ignite. "And if that wasn't a big enough pile of bullshit to shovel, the fact that they nearly took out Erica makes me see red."

"What do you mean? How do you know this? I haven't heard from the loss and mitigation team doing the report."

"The Coltons ran a private investigation and found two support beams had been deliberately cut, which means none of the shit that's been happening has been accidental."

Anna's hand flew to her mouth, her breath hitching. "You're serious?"

"Deadly, but there's more." He recounted the confrontation at Harold Greene's office and how he'd thrown caution to the wind, vowing to keep the production afloat with his own funds when Greene refused to back down.

"Oh, CJ!" Anna gasped, her shock reverberating in the small room. "You did what?"

"Maybe I've lost it," CJ admitted, his hands flexing as if grasping for solutions that weren't there. "But I can't let it go under. Not now."

"God, CJ," she breathed, shaking her head. Her disbelief was a punch to the gut, but there was no turning back.

CJ searched Anna's gaze, needing pure honesty. "Tell me, do we pack it up? Or do you want to keep going? Because I'm in it for the long haul if you are."

"Are you sure?" Anna asked, uncertain. "We're talking a lot of money on the line. Can you…afford it?"

He chuckled ruefully, shaking his head. "I guess we'll find out. But I need to know this is what you want, too. This is your project Anna—I'm just trying to see it through."

Anna held his gaze, seeming to waver, but when determination replaced her anxiety, he knew they were going for it. "If you're in, I'm in. Thank you for believing in the project, CJ."

"Then it's settled." CJ nodded, the weight of his decision settling on his shoulders like a mantle. "But before we do anything, we find the bastard behind this. Let me take care of that part. You handle getting the crew back in working order. We're behind schedule, and we need to make up the deficit."

"Look at you—you're a natural producer," she teased with a smile as he let himself out.

Exiting the bungalow, CJ didn't pause as he dialed his accountant. The ring sounded like a countdown to a bomb going off.

"Hey, it's CJ. Look, I need to free up some capital. Put my Malibu place up as collateral."

"Are you insane?" The accountant's voice crackled through the phone, incredulous and sharp.

"Completely," CJ shot back, a wry grin tugging at his lips despite the gravity of the situation.

His accountant launched into a tirade of reasons why this was financially irresponsible, but CJ cut him off. "Just prep the paperwork. I'll be in touch."

Hey, it's only money, right?

Ending the call, CJ immediately dialed his attorney next, the numbers familiar under his touch.

"Draw up the contracts. I'm stepping in for Harold Greene for the Anna Wilson project."

"Christ, CJ, that'll ruffle feathers. What are you doing? This could be professional suicide. Think this through."

"Let 'em ruffle." CJ's response was curt, final. Greene wanted to see how far he'd go to see this project through? *Watch and learn, buddy.* CJ had stubbornness in spades.

He ended the call and stared out across the resort, the sprawling landscape a testament to grandeur and ambition. His heart raced, adrenaline and resolve fueling him. He'd made his play, laid his life's work on the line, and now he needed to talk to Erica.

CJ's stride was purposeful as he closed the distance between himself and Erica, who he found doing her usual rounds, being the busy bee that he'd come to recognize as part of her personality.

"Hey," he breathed out, his voice tinged with the remnants of chaos from the morning's revelations. "Thanks for digging into that barn mess. I appreciate you sharing the information. I needed to let Anna know. We've got to clean house before we move forward."

"CJ, about that… I'm happy to help however I can, but I have to tell you that I'm intensely uncomfortable with how recklessly you've jumped into this new role as producer. Do you even know the first thing about being a producer?"

"No, but I've always been more of a trial-by-fire kind of learner. I'll figure it out."

"Before you lose your damn shirt?" she countered with a touch of exasperation.

CJ shifted, pushing his hand through his hair, irritated that Erica was being a giant wet blanket when he needed her support. "It'll be fine. The movie's half-shot anyway. All I'm doing is ensuring it gets finished. Besides, once I find out who the clown is that's been sabotaging the production, it'll be smooth sailing."

"Has any movie in the history of moviemaking ever been 'smooth sailing,' as you put it? C'mon, CJ, I feel you need to take a step back and think this through."

CJ stiffened. "I thought you'd be more supportive. I'm doing what's right, not just what's right for me."

She recoiled slightly, words catching in her throat. "I am supporting you," she said, softer now. "But I'm also worried. You're playing a dangerous game with…well, a future that includes more than just you."

That last part jabbed him hard. Was she implying that he wouldn't be a good dad because of this? He needed space before he said something he regretted.

"Got it. Thanks." His response came out sharper than he'd intended. When she blinked at his tone, he tried to soften his delivery with a noncommittal, "Let's talk later? Dinner?"

"Sure," she agreed, but her smile didn't quite reach her eyes. He turned on his heel, leaving her standing there with her concerns hanging like a heavy curtain between them.

He couldn't think about that right now. He had a long list of people to interview if he was going to figure out who was responsible for the sabotage.

The day aged, the sun climbing to its peak and then bowing gracefully toward the horizon as CJ sat across from crew member after crew member with each team lead. Questions fired, answers dissected. Then he met a production assistant—a guy with shifty eyes and a story that didn't add up.

"Name?" CJ demanded, not bothering with pleasantries.

"Rick Dennies," the PA mumbled, shifting uncomfortably under the scrutiny.

The production manager checked his roster, frowning. "Who brought you on, Rick?" he asked. "I don't see you on my list of new hires."

"Can't say. Hired over the phone." Rick's gaze darted away, then back again, a flicker of guilt passing through his expression.

"Cut the crap," CJ insisted. "How the hell did you end up on this production?"

"I..." he stuttered, clearly no criminal mastermind as he blanked on a convincing lie before admitting, "I mean, I got hired over the phone and was told when to show up. My credentials showed up in the mail with a wad of cash."

The production manager balked. "Are you kidding me? That's not how we hire people. What the hell?"

CJ knew he was looking at the problem. "Ever work on a movie set before?"

"No, but I got skills—handyman stuff."

"Skill enough to cut a wire, but not enough to know that you're cutting through a support beam, I'm guessing."

Rick started to deny the implication, but he wasn't smart enough to come up with anything that quick. A look of defiance hardened his features as he shrugged as if he didn't care if he was caught or not. "Whatever."

"Yeah, whatever. You could've killed a woman when your stupid stunt nearly brought the barn down on her head."

At that, Rick shifted his gaze. “Look, I needed the work, and this seemed easy enough. Besides, y’all got enough money to spare with all your rich cars and houses. No one needs your Hollywood bullshit anyway. But no one was supposed to get hurt. I was just supposed to mess things up a bit.”

“Yeah, well, you nearly got someone killed.” CJ glared, barely able to throttle down the white-hot rage that burned up his throat. “And you burnt down an entire set.”

“Didn’t mean for any harm,” Rick stammered, hands fumbling. “Just some trouble is all. Got paid cash to stir things up.”

“By who?” The question hung heavy, loaded with the threat of unspoken consequences. Both the production manager and CJ pressed for details, but Rick wasn’t exactly a fount of information.

“Like I said, never saw a face. Just instructions, cash and when to show up for work. Once I was on set, no one asked me any questions. It was easy to go unnoticed.”

“Jesus.” CJ scrubbed his face with both hands, feeling the edges of control fray. “Remind me to beef up security. I want everyone to get new ID badges and lock this set down. No one is present unless they’ve been cleared to be there.”

The production manager nodded, grabbing Rick. “You’re coming with me until the police can come and get you.”

Rick jerked his arm out of the production manager’s grip, but when CJ jumped up with a snarl, just begging him for a reason, Rick wisely backed down and agreed to go quietly.

But CJ’s adrenaline was pumping through his veins, needing an outlet. They might’ve found the gun but not the person behind the trigger. Who the hell was going to such lengths to sabotage the film? Was it Harold Greene?

As much as he wanted to pin this on Harold, it didn't seem his style.

But if not him, who?

Was he supposed to wear the hat of actor, producer and now detective?

So be it.

He wasn't stopping until he had answers, a finished film and the satisfaction of knowing he hadn't quit—for any reason.

AS THE SUN dipped below the horizon, casting a fiery glow upon the resort, Erica's phone buzzed against the smooth marble countertop. She snatched it up, heart lurching before she registered CJ's name on the screen. A breath she hadn't realized she'd been holding escaped in a rush when his message popped up, a simple: Can't make dinner. Rain check?

Oh, thank God. She was a coward to avoid the conversation they needed to have, but a complex knot of frustration and relief tightened in her chest.

CJ's reckless decision to fund a sinking ship of a production gave her stomach a queasy feeling that had nothing to do with the tiny fluttering human growing there.

"None of my business," she muttered to herself, even as the murmur felt like a lie. The truth was that everything CJ did was her business now, whether she liked it or not. But dwelling on it wouldn't solve anything. Instead she craved the comfort of logistics and lists—things she could manage, things she could control.

"Erica! Look who's here!" Laura's voice, vibrant and clear, cut through Erica's brooding.

Willow burst into the lobby, her arrival a spectacle of energy that seemed to make the air buzz. Laura enveloped her friend in a boisterous embrace that made Willow's luggage topple forgotten to the side. Their laughter echoed, bouncing off the walls and filling the space with warmth.

"Finally, the party can start!" Willow declared, grinning from ear to ear.

"Wouldn't dream of starting without you," Laura shot back, her blue eyes twinkling. "Oh my God, please tell me you are ready for an epic night of catching up because you are not sleeping a wink until I've completely caught you up to the events in my life."

"Babe, it's what I live for. Let's do this. I'm yours for approximately two weeks and then I have to regretfully return to my life, but until then…let's pretend we're back in college and have the metabolisms of our college selves."

"Deal." Laura and Willow hooked pinky fingers in a secret handshake that looked like something teenagers would do and then pealed into laugher at their shared inside joke.

The sight of them, so carefree and excited, acted like a balm to Erica's frayed nerves. For a moment she allowed herself to bask in their joy, letting the tension seep out of her shoulders. The bachelorette-party preparations—a tangled web of decorations and schedules—flashed through her mind. It was just the kind of distraction she needed, a project to immerse herself in fully.

"All right, you two, let's get you settled in," Erica chimed in, stepping forward to help Willow with her bags. "We've got a bachelorette party to throw and only forty-eight hours to do it."

"Lead the way, party queen," Willow teased, looping her arm through Laura's as they headed toward the accommodations.

"Trust me," Laura replied, beaming at Erica, "we're in good hands with Erica in charge."

She smiled with appreciation for the sweet vote of confidence and made for the party zone, her steps quick and purposeful. The balloon arch mocked her with its limpness, half-inflated balloons sagging like the worries she tried to keep at bay.

She snapped instructions at the decorators, her hands deftly twisting a stray balloon into place. With each pump of the helium tank, her confidence swelled. This was her realm, the orderly world where shades of pink and gold obeyed her command.

"Make sure those balloons are smiling by the time guests arrive," Erica directed, her tone leaving no room for anything less than perfection. The party coordinator, a clipboard clutched in her arms, scurried over to Erica, rattling off updates.

"Got it. Check on the cake…chocolate, not vanilla. Confirm the caterer's menu…no shellfish—Laura's allergic. And the punch…make sure they are clearly marked *alcoholic* and *nonalcoholic*." Erica recited the list as if it were the litany that kept chaos at bay. "This bachelorette bash must go down without a hitch. Laura deserves the best."

"Absolutely," the coordinator affirmed, her pen flying across the checklist with each of Erica's crisp confirmations.

Satisfied, Erica surveyed the space, noting the twinkle lights woven through the trellises that promised an evening of enchantment. It was all coming together—every detail crafted with care, every corner curated for celebration. This was control, something painfully absent when it came to CJ and how he handled his life. Here she could shape the outcome, mold it with her own two hands.

"Thank you," she said, offering a rare smile to the team. "You're making magic happen."

Flushed with the success of a plan in motion, Erica gathered her things, ready to call it a night. As she strode toward the exit, a hushed urgency from a nearby hallway tugged at her attention. She slowed her pace, ears straining to catch the fragmented whispers that bounced off the walls.

"The merger with Sharpe Enterprises—not likely," a male voice grumbled, the words sharp and clipped with tension.

Erica leaned against the wall, frowning at the unknown voice. "It's a bad investment...murder and accidents...insurance nightmare," another muttered, the weight of concern heavy in his tone.

Erica's pulse hammered a frantic rhythm in against her wrist. Whoever it was must've been talking about Allison's murder, for sure. She didn't know anything about a merger, though. She melted into the shadows, hoping to catch another fragment but whoever had been talking was gone.

A merger? Erica knew a little bit about the Colton family issues—a tangled mess that had started with Laura and Josh's father, Clive, and involved a lot of money disagreements—but Erica made it a point to stay out of that side of the Colton business.

However, that phone call...didn't sound good. Not only were they referencing Allison's murder but the more recent accidents on the set, which made Erica wonder if someone was capitalizing on the resort's bad luck or creating bad luck for their own purpose.

She checked her watch. Laura was likely already gone with Willow to party like they were back in college, and she hated to ruin the night with something like this. Perhaps it could wait until after the bachelorette party.

Yes, she decided, settling her nerves, whatever that was... could wait. It wasn't as if she had much more than a snippet of conversation to share, which honestly could end up being nothing.

Which was an excellent reason why eavesdropping was a bad idea, and she didn't know what was wrong with her.

This situation with CJ had her running backward for the first time in her life, and she didn't like it.

Not one bit.

Chapter Twenty-One

CJ leaned against the sun-warmed terra-cotta railing that bordered Mariposa's main courtyard, his gaze tracking the flurry of crew members dismantling the final shot of the day.

The golden hour light dripped over the scene like warm honey, casting long shadows that swayed in rhythm with the palm fronds above. He exhaled a sigh of relief, his chest unclenching for what felt like the first time in weeks. With the bad apple in custody, the air seemed lighter, almost effervescent with newfound optimism.

And it felt good.

"Cut! That's a wrap!" he heard the director call out, the words sounding in his heart like a victory chant.

"Finally," CJ murmured to himself, a smile tugging at the corners of his mouth. Hard to remember when his biggest challenge had been learning his lines. Now he had an entire production on his shoulders, on top of his usual performance.

He pushed off the railing and walked toward the resort's main building, where Erica would be immersed in her own brand of chaos. As he navigated through the labyrinth of hibiscus bushes and trickling fountains, he rehearsed the lines in his head, planning to dissolve any lingering doubts she harbored about his new role as producer now that he felt more secure in the production.

"Erica, hey," he called out, entering the whirlwind of the impending party that looked lavish enough to host a celebrity.

She was a vision of efficiency, her fingers flying over a tablet screen while simultaneously barking orders to the staff swirling around her. Her focus was laser sharp, not a single detail slipping past her vigilant eyes. Erica was a marvel to watch in action. He ought to pick her brain about how to make his production more efficient, he thought with a private chuckle.

"Can it wait, CJ?" Erica didn't look up, her voice clipped with the stress of imminent celebration.

"Actually, I just wanted to—"

"Listen, I'm drowning in party prep here," she interrupted, finally glancing up, her eyes reflecting the storm of responsibility on her shoulders. "There's a mountain of things to sort, and I've got half an hour to move Everest."

"Sure, sure," CJ conceded, taking in her frazzled state. He knew better than to add to her burden. "Just wanted to let you know today on set went smooth. Like, baby-bottom smooth. Not a single mishap."

"Thank heavens for small miracles," she sighed, a ghost of a smile flickering across her face.

"I think I make a pretty good detective, actually," he teased, coaxing a small smile from Erica before she returned to her tablet.

"Hey, want to be my plus-one tonight?" Erica asked, not looking up from her device. "It's a bachelorette party, but it's co-ed."

"Me? Hanging with my baby mama at Arizona's hottest party?" He raised an eyebrow, his mouth curving into an unexpected grin. "Wouldn't miss it for the world."

But Erica blanched and immediately shushed him with a

panicked look. "*Ixnay* on the *abybay* stuff," she said, dropping adorably into Pig Latin, which oddly delighted him.

"You never cease to amaze me, Erica Pike," he murmured, reaching out to snatch her close, ignoring her protest and enjoying the immediate blush in her cheeks. "I don't care who knows that you're carrying my *abybay.* I'll shout it to the world if you give me half the chance."

She melted against him. "That's not fair," she said breathlessly as his mouth hovered dangerously close to hers. "The hormones are playing Ping-Pong with my brain."

"Good," he returned with a silky chuckle. "Just the way I like you," he said before sealing his mouth to hers. He reluctantly released her, loving the way she softened against him like her bones suddenly evaporated. "See you tonight, boss lady," CJ said with a grin, leaving her to her business.

But even as he walked to his room, each step took him further away from that happy place he'd been basking in. Was Erica working too hard? Should pregnant women be pushing themselves with such a punishing schedule? Or was he worrying about nothing and creating one more thing for them to argue about?

Frowning, he muttered to himself. "I need to trust her." If Erica needed a break, she'd take one. She wouldn't do anything to hurt the baby. Besides, it wasn't his place to dictate how she ran her life, even if she was carrying his precious cargo.

A baby. His baby. A whole body shiver followed the thought. *Wild how things turn out...*

After showering and changing, CJ returned to the section of the resort cordoned off for the private party and whistled low and appreciatively at the stunning view. The sun dipped lower, splashing the sky with hues of tangerine and lavender, shadows lengthening across the manicured grass. The guests began to arrive, their laughter and chatter mingling with the soft strains of music floating on the breeze. Laura Colton emerged from her private bungalow, radiant in an off-white summer dress that swayed with her every step.

But it was Erica who stole his breath.

Her elegant frame was sheathed in a pale lavender dress that dusted her knees and hung on her shoulders with thin spaghetti straps. Her beautiful dark hair tumbled down her back in loose waves that made him want to bury his nose in the thick mass of it. His mouth hungered for the taste of her lips and his fingers itched to palm her belly and hold her close.

Erica saw him and quickly joined him with a radiant smile. "What do you think?"

"I think it might be rude to outshine the bride-to-be at her own party," he said, bending down to brush a soft kiss across her lips. "But you're a vision."

"Oh gosh," Erica gasped softly, blushing beneath the compliment, but she recovered with an appreciative "You look pretty good yourself," as she smoothed his silk tie.

"Well, I will say this—if you ever leave Mariposa, you have a career in celebrity parties. This is better than any Hollywood party I've ever been to."

Erica grinned. "I actually do enjoy party planning. It's stressful but relaxing at the same time. I don't know…it's hard to explain, but I really enjoy this part."

The party, much like the woman it celebrated, seemed to shimmer with an effortless charm. Within an hour the party was in full swing, everyone laughing and having a great time.

But just when the caterers brought out a huge cake, a ripple went through the crowd, a discordant murmur that CJ felt somehow in his bones.

The atmosphere had shifted—subtly at first, like the soft encroachment of a shadow before darkness falls. CJ's senses pricked as laughter soured into confusion, the clinks of glasses halting mid-toast. The first guest staggered, hand clutching their stomach as if an invisible fist had landed and then another. More people started to moan and look sickly, clinging to tables and chairs, some barfing their guts out.

What was happening?

"Erica?" CJ called out, scanning the crowd for her familiar form. His voice cut through the growing murmur, sharp with concern.

She was doubled over, one hand pressed to her stomach, the other supporting herself against a table. Her face was ghostly pale, a stark contrast to the vibrant colors of the party around her. CJ's heart plummeted, dread coiling in his gut as he rushed to her side, sidestepping a man who crumpled to the grass like a puppet with its strings cut.

"What's wrong?" he asked, the urgency of the situation dawning. There were too many people sick at once for this to be an accident.

"Someone call an ambulance!" The command was torn from his throat as he reached Erica, his hands hovering, afraid that touching her might somehow make it worse.

"Oh my God, the baby," she gasped out, eyes wide and brimming with shared fear.

"It's going to be okay, Erica," he promised, but a thin sheen of sweat had popped along his forehead at the realization that someone had poisoned either the food or the punch, something that could reach the most amount of people at this party.

And Erica had ingested something contaminated…

Around them, the party descended into chaos. Bodies slumped onto tables or lay writhing on the ground, the sound of coughing and retching punctuating the air. Staff scrambled to help, their faces masks of terror and uncertainty.

"Help's on the way," someone shouted, a disembodied voice amid the cacophony as he held Erica, refusing to let her go until a medical professional wrenched her from his hands.

Sirens wailed in the distance, the sound slicing through the pandemonium.

The paramedics arrived, a flurry of motion and urgency. Erica was lifted onto a stretcher, her form small and vulnerable beneath the stark lights. CJ followed, feet numb, every step an echo of the fear pounding through him.

"Will she be okay? She's pregnant," he said, his voice a stranger's in his ears—strained, raw.

"Sir, we'll do everything we can," a paramedic answered, not unkind but distant, focused.

The ambulance doors closed behind Erica with a thud that resounded like a verdict. CJ watched as the vehicle lurched into motion and Erica was trundled off to the hospital for the second time since knowing her. If the situation were different, it might even be funny, but there was nothing to laugh about right now.

His mind raced, images of the day's successful shoot dissolving into the horror of the present. Was it connected? Another sabotage attempt? His jaw clenched at the thought, anger and worry a tangled knot in his chest.

Laura's friend Willow was one of the people who was also transported, along with a handful of other guests, but Laura found CJ with an offer to ride with her to the hospital.

At the hospital, their party overwhelmed the emergency room as the staff put a rush on the toxicology report, and it wasn't long before doctors discovered the culprit: ipecac syrup.

Both CJ and Laura breathed a sigh of relief as the attending doctor took a minute to explain.

"In most cases, not lethal, but definitely enough to make people very sick. Most of the patients in your party will be released as soon as they finish a round of electrolytes, but we'd like to keep Miss Pike a little longer to make sure nothing affected her pregnancy."

Laura nodded vigorously. "Yes, of course. Thank you, Doctor." She waited a beat for the doctor to go on his way before turning to CJ, tears brimming in her eyes. "I don't understand why this is happening. First the barn and now this? Why?"

Maybe it was a rhetorical question and her last nerve had just frayed beneath the strain, but CJ felt compelled to share what he knew so far. "I don't know if this is related to the stuff happening on the set, but we caught the person who sabotaged the barn and he's currently still in custody. I'm sorry about your party. It was truly beautiful before all the throwing up started."

Laura stared for a minute before a bubble of near hysterical laughter follow. "It was, wasn't it? Oh God, I don't know if this is a sign or—"

She was cut off by the sound of the man Erica had previously whispered into his ear was Laura's fiancé, and Laura sank into his arms, openly sobbing as he held her, crooning softly.

The man took a minute to calm his bride and then briefly introduced himself to CJ. "Noah Steele. Can someone tell me what the hell is going on?"

Laura hiccuped and wiped at her eyes, offering a watery introduction. "Noah, this is CJ Knight, Erica's…uh, friend. I don't know what you guys are—I'm sorry. My brain isn't working right now," she said, apologizing. "He's here for Erica."

CJ shook Noah's hand. "The doc said someone dosed something with ipecac syrup. My money's on the punch. I doubt anyone would've noticed, and judging by how many people were sick, it was the easiest way to get to as many people as possible."

"Sounds about right." To his lady, Noah said, "I'm going to have everything bagged and tagged and have it tested. Are you okay?"

Laura nodded, her lip trembling. "I never drank any of the punch. I was still nursing a hangover from last night with Willow, and my stomach wasn't up to anything that sugary. I was sticking to water until it was time to do the champagne toast."

"That decision may have saved your guts," CJ quipped. "Some of your guests got hit harder than others. You're going to need to call in a professional cleaning team to get the smell out of your courtyard."

Laura's gaze flew to Noah. "This is the worst timing, and I'm not talking about my bachelorette party."

"I know, honey. We'll talk about it later. Let's get you home," he said, wrapping an arm protectively around Laura, but she stopped, putting her keys in CJ's hands with a simple "I trust you" before leaving with her fiancé.

CJ found Erica lying in an emergency room bed in a plain cotton gown, hooked to an IV just as a nurse was running a Doppler over her stomach. The quick flutter of a fast heartbeat filled the room.

"All good in there," the nurse announced with a smile. "Mama might feel like dog dirt, but baby is snug and safe and none the wiser for your little adventure."

Erica gave a wan but relieved smile. "Thank God."

The nurse looked to CJ in question. "Are you Daddy?"

"Yes," he answered, going to hold Erica's hand. "Everything… Nothing's wrong with the baby after all that?"

"Nope. Babies are surprisingly resilient. Mama just needs a little rest and some extra fluids. Then the doctor will probably release you."

The nurse rolled up her Doppler unit and stuck it into her pocket before leaving them alone, pulling the curtain for privacy.

"Hey," Erica murmured, voice hoarse but fierce. "Is everyone okay?"

Still thinking of others even when she's laid up worse than the rest. God, he loved this woman. He smoothed her hair. "Everyone is fine. Toxicology came back as ipecac syrup. Nonlethal, but definitely going to make you miserable."

Erica frowned. "Ipecac? Why? I can't understand why anyone would do that."

"I don't know, but her fiancé—I'm taking it he's a cop or something? He's going to collect everything and have it tested, though he's pretty sure it was in the punch."

Erica blanched in distress. "I thought it tasted funny, but I figured it was just my taste buds being weird because of the baby. I didn't even think to have it thrown out and made fresh. Damn it," she muttered, looking frustrated with herself.

"Hey, don't you do dare do that. This is not your fault, and I won't let you take that on," he said firmly. "Someone was a royal dick and poisoned an entire party. You can't plan for that kind of contingency."

Erica blinked back the shine in her eyes, nodding. "You're right. I just feel bad for Laura."

"Yeah, me, too, but she seems like she can rally and she's got a good support system. Honestly, I'm more worried about you. This is the second time you've landed in the hospital and I'm afraid what a third might look like."

"Fair point. My insurance hasn't even crunched the numbers on the first visit yet," she tossed out with a dry chuckle. Her smile faded rapidly as she continued, "I'm not one to believe in omens or anything, but since Allison... Well, Mariposa just hasn't felt right. It's like there's this dark fog hanging over the resort. I can't shake off this nagging thought...could it somehow be connected?"

CJ didn't believe in ghosts, but he knew bad energy existed. However, he had a feeling whatever was happening had less to do with the supernatural and more to do with someone working on their own agenda.

The question was...who was it and what did they want?

Chapter Twenty-Two

The sterile scent of the hospital still clung to Erica's skin as she shuffled through the sliding doors, her arm looped gently through CJ's. He'd insisted on driving her home in Laura's car, a sturdy SUV that smelled faintly of citrus and expensive perfume.

"Home sweet home," CJ announced with a forced cheerfulness as he guided her inside her quiet house.

"I can take it from here," Erica murmured, but CJ's expression left no room for argument.

"Like hell you can. I'm not leaving you alone. Doc said to rest, and I'm here to enforce it."

"Are you sure?" Erica asked. "I feel the bulk of our relationship has been punctuated by you having to take care of me, and honestly, I don't know how I feel about that. I'm not used to being the one needing care. I've always been self-sufficient and independent. This whole 'damsel in distress' gig is outside of my comfort zone, and I don't know how to act."

That was probably the most honest statement she'd made to CJ about herself, and it made her feel vulnerable but it was par for the course. Nothing between them had been typical for her relationships, and maybe that was why he made her feel things she'd never felt before.

Still, all that raw emotion was hard to manage when

you were used to compartmentalizing everything into neat, tidy boxes.

CJ's gaze softened with understanding as he gently knuckled her cheek. "I like that you give me the opportunity to take care of you. I've never been the one who was riding in on a white horse to save the day, but I like when it's you I'm saving."

Erica's heart swelled with absolute love for this man even though she couldn't quite explain how she'd fallen so quickly and so hard. Maybe it had something to do with the tiny human growing inside her, but she wanted to fall asleep in CJ's arms and wake up every morning seeing his sleepy face. But how would that work given their completely different lifestyles?

Tonight was not the night to solve that dilemma. She sank into his arms, loving how safe and secure she felt within the cove of his embrace and simply enjoyed the pleasure of his touch.

"I'm tired," she admitted against his chest.

"Then it's time to tuck you into bed," CJ decided, grasping her hand and walking toward her bedroom. She flicked her bedside lamp, bathing the room in a soft glow as she undressed and slid into the sheets, thankful to be home.

Within moments, CJ had stripped and joined her.

Erica had never felt comfortable inviting men over to stay at her place. She'd had her share of noncommittal hookups, but she'd never invited them to sleep over and cuddle. If anything, the idea of seeing them again in the morning had made her want to run away.

Except with CJ, she wanted him to stay. She felt safe with him, but there was so much they still needed to figure out.

"You have the loudest silence," he murmured, as if feeling the questions in her head roll off her skin and bounce off his forehead as he held her. "What are you thinking?"

She sighed. "Too many browsers to share right now. All I do know is that right here, right now, I feel safe and content, and that's enough."

CJ's arms tightened around her. "Good."

The twilight hours passed in a blur of soft pillows and even softer silences, their bodies entwined in the sanctuary of Erica's bed.

"When I thought I might lose you…and the baby…" The words cracked, heavy with unspoken fears. "I couldn't think straight. It scared me."

She turned to face him, the moonlight casting a silver glow across his features. "Everything turned out okay," she said, aiming for reassurance, but her voice wavered, betraying her. She'd been scared, too.

"This time. But look at what just happened. Poisoned, for Christ's sake." CJ propped himself up on one elbow, his gaze searching hers. "I mean, this is like something out of a movie—which feels totally weird for someone like me to say, but it's true. I've never known an actual person who's been poisoned before because it just doesn't happen."

"Yeah, tell me about it," she agreed, the admission tasting bitter on her tongue. It should've been a sick joke, but reality bore down on her with all its weight. Who would do such a thing? "I still can't wrap my head around it. I don't know who would want to hurt the Coltons. As far as I know, the community loves the family and the resort. I mean, the family always pours so much into the community, and they take pride in offering something of value to the area. It doesn't make sense to me why anyone would target them."

"Do you think someone was targeting Laura specifically?" CJ asked.

Erica frowned, perplexed. "I can't imagine why or who would do that. Laura is an absolute sweetheart, and I'm not just saying that because she's my boss. She's genuinely nice."

CJ wondered out loud, "If it's not targeted toward the family, maybe it was connected to the movie? I mean, it feels like a stretch, but I've never been on a movie like this where everything that can and will go wrong has, only to find out that someone was actively sabotaging the production."

"Yeah, but didn't you say the guy responsible for all the mishaps was in custody?" Erica asked.

"Yes, but we still don't know who hired him to do all that crap. We found the gun, not the person behind the trigger, and that's what worries me."

"It seems unlikely the two events are connected, though," Erica said. "I mean, the first incident happened out in the desert, not at the resort."

"That's what keeps tripping me up, too," he admitted, releasing a long sigh. "Hell, one thing this situation has shown me is that I wasn't cut out to be a detective."

"I don't know…you've done pretty well so far," she said with admiration in her tone.

He chuckled. "Well, I'll be happy to return to what I'm really good at. Although I'm not going to lie, I actually enjoy the producing gig. The level of control is something I've never had in a production, and it's been refreshing."

"Do you think you might want to do more producing?"

"I don't know—maybe. We'll see when this production finally wraps without a body count."

She smiled, enjoying the quiet conversation that finally felt real between them. Maybe there was a future together if they could hold on to this moment and turn it into something worth keeping.

THE STACCATO CLAP of the slateboard pierced the air, and CJ nodded to the director. "Action!" Anna shouted, setting the scene in motion. It felt good to return to his character without the burden of worrying about the lights getting shut off because some corporate dickhead wanted to play games.

Everything was going smoothly, all scenes working as they should, and it looked as if they might be able to break for lunch early if they kept this pace, but just as they were knee-deep in the next scene, Anna's voice cut through the action like a hot knife through butter. CJ looked up in surprise only to see Harold Greene standing beside Anna, her expression pensive.

CJ's hand curled into a tight fist at his side, a visceral reminder that this intrusion was unwelcome as Anna waved him over.

"CJ, Mr. Greene would like to have a quick word with you," Anna said, civil but annoyed at the disruption when they'd been doing so well. CJ didn't blame her, and seeing as he was the one paying the bill, he wasn't interested in interrupting their flow.

"Harold," CJ greeted coolly, his voice betraying none of the irritation that buzzed under his skin like a live wire.

"Let's talk." Harold's tone brooked no argument, yet CJ stood his ground.

"Sorry—we're on a tight schedule and can't break just yet. I'll catch up with you during lunch." CJ turned his back on Harold, signaling the end of their exchange—for now.

As the crew resumed their orchestrated dance around the set, CJ's thoughts churned with wary curiosity. What the hell was Greene doing here?

Lunchtime descended upon the set like a curtain call, and CJ found himself face-to-face with Harold once more, the midday sun casting sharp shadows on the ground between them. He folded his arms across his chest, an unspoken barrier erected against whatever onslaught Harold had planned.

"Look, CJ," Harold began, leaning forward as if to press his words physically onto CJ. "You've made your point. I get it. You want to be taken seriously and this project seems like the perfect vehicle to make that happen, but you're in over your head. Get out before the legal sharks come circling. It's not just about signing checks. The studio will bury this production so deep, it'll never have a chance at picking up a distributor if you hold this line."

"And why would they do that, Harold?" CJ countered with a calm he didn't feel. "Unless you made it that way? Which would fly in the face of your claims that this wasn't personal, it was business."

"And I stand by that—there's nothing personal about my decision to cut the funding. This set was a liability, and someone was going to get hurt. Sometimes you have to cut your losses. If you're truly serious about wanting to produce, you'll learn that."

CJ's jaw tightened, his resolve hardening like concrete. "You're wrong."

"Wrong about what?"

"This production. You're so hung up on the numbers you haven't taken the time to think about why this film needs to be made. It tells a story that hasn't been told yet, and if you don't have the balls to see it made, I will. Pretty simple."

"Is it worth losing everything?" Harold's challenge hung in the air, weighted with threat and condescension. "Because that's where you're headed. You think you're being all noble, but your cause is flimsy. Look, there will be other movies, better movies than this one, but if you burn your bridges, that ain't gonna happen. You hear me?"

Harold's eyes narrowed, but CJ didn't flinch. This was a

battle of wills, and CJ was not about to surrender the field. He couldn't explain it—he couldn't back down. He knew what was at stake, but he couldn't let it go.

CJ tilted his head, scrutinizing Harold's rigid stance, the man's fingers drumming an impatient tattoo on the aluminum table. The tension in those digits fascinated CJ, a silent metronome to their standoff.

"Here's some news for you," CJ said, his words slicing through the hum of lunchtime banter and clinking utensils. "We caught the jerk creating all the problems on set—and since he's been gone, it's been smooth sailing."

Harold's rhythm faltered, his forehead crinkling. "What are you talking about?"

"Someone's been causing trouble on set. Deliberately," CJ clarified, the corners of his mouth lifting just so, savoring the flicker of bewilderment that danced across Harold's face. "And guess what? They were paid for it. The bigger question is who paid him? But I don't have to figure that out. I'm sure the detective on the case will dig into the *why*s and *how*s."

"Paid?" Harold echoed, his voice hollow, disbelief etching lines around his eyes deep as canyons. "I had no idea..."

Something about that raw surprise gnawed at CJ's certainty, like a gust of wind threatening to snuff out a flame. A part of him didn't want to believe Harold was involved, but then another part had questioned simply because he'd been so quick to shut the production down, almost as if he'd planned it that way.

But Harold's genuine shock was something of a surprise and he looked concerned about the information. "You're sure?"

"Without a doubt. The guy confessed—down to the dollar amount he was paid in cash to make trouble. You didn't know anything about that, right?"

Harold scowled. "That's a stupid question—of course not. I'm not a criminal, and I don't hire criminals to do my dirty work."

CJ sensed truth in that statement. Harold Greene was known as a hard-ass but never a shady guy, which was why he'd been surprised at how seemingly eager Harold had been to shut down the production for petty reasons.

Maybe Harold was just a tight-fisted investor and not a villain, which made him wonder all over again who might have cause to get their hands dirty on this. "Do you know anyone who might gain from the production getting shut down?"

"Not off-hand, but you can bet your ass I'm going to find out," Harold said, and CJ believed him. "Look, when I say it isn't personal, I mean it. But I may have pulled the trigger too fast, and I'm willing to concede that point."

"Thanks," CJ said grudgingly accepting Harold's version of an apology, but he didn't want to relinquish his producer spot now that he'd experienced how it felt to have some control of a project he believed in. "I appreciate that."

"With that said, listen when I say you don't want to tangle with the suits over this project. However, before you get that look in your eye, let me talk to the studio and see what we can do together, okay? I like that you've got balls, even if you're willing to put them in a vise just to make a point."

"What are you proposing?"

"I can bring you on as an official producer—not the executive producer, though. But you'll still have a seat at the table when major decisions are being made without having to throw your career and livelihood in the chipper to see it done. Sound fair?"

It did sound fair, but was he ready to give up the seat at the head of the table? Was his ego driving the train, or was he leveling up in his career?

With a baby on the way, he needed to figure it out before he made a decision that affected his future family in a bad way.

Chapter Twenty-Three

Erica's fingers danced across the keyboard with a vigor that had been absent for far too long. The soft clack of keys was a welcome sound after days of rest at home, punctuated only by the occasional concerned call from friends and colleagues.

The only saving grace had been CJ's solid form curled against her every night. She felt safe with him beside her and enjoyed some of the best sleep of her life, which was interesting, considering she'd never been much of a cuddler.

However, happy to be back to her routine, even if everyone had balked at her announcement that she was returning only a few days after being poisoned. They meant well, but the walls closed in on her if she stayed still for too long. She needed the resort's pulse, the hum of activity to ground her—to remind her life was moving forward.

Besides, when it was quiet the questions that didn't have answers started to crowd her brain and panic followed.

"Erica." Laura's voice sliced through the rhythm, carrying a note of reproach. "I really wish you would've taken at least a week off."

Shaking her head, Erica swiveled in her chair to face Laura. "Rest is a cage," she declared, the intensity of her gaze saying more than words could. “I need to work, need to feel useful.”

Laura sighed, the lines of worry that were etched around her eyes deepening. But Erica wouldn’t be argued with when her mind was made up.

“Fine,” Laura conceded, “but you’re taking a lunch break. Dani’s in town. You haven’t seen her since she arrived, have you?”

“No, not yet. How’s she doing?”

“Great! Of course, she missed all of the excitement—and by *excitement* I mean when someone tried to kill everyone at my bachelorette party.”

“To be fair, the doc said ipecac syrup isn’t lethal,” Erica countered trying to lighten the reality. “Do you have any disgruntled boyfriends we should know about?”

Laura barked a short laugh, shaking her head. “Not that I’m aware of, but who knows?” She motioned for Erica to finish up. “Let’s go. I’m starving and teetering on the edge of a low blood sugar attack where I turn into an entirely different person.”

While she didn’t want to break her pace, the thought of fresh air and friendly faces was appealing. “Well, we can’t have that,” Erica replied with a fake shudder, already saving her document and logging off her computer. “I’m ready when you are.”

The bistro was a riot of smells and sounds, a kaleidoscope of life buzzing around them as they sat at a wrought-iron table under the shade of a sprawling elm. Dani’s laughter, light and carefree, wove through the conversation like a bright ribbon.

“Glenna’s coming to the wedding, then?” Erica asked, spearing a cherry tomato with her fork. It burst with flavor as she popped it into her mouth. “That’s unfortunate.”

"Tell me about it," Laura grimaced, swirling her iced tea with a straw. "But Clive would throw a fit if we didn't invite her."

The fact that Laura called her father by his given name spoke volumes about how she felt about him, but she still felt obligated to observe certain social expectations. If it were Erica, she'd tell the old fart to pound sand. Clive Colton wasn't exactly vying for humanitarian of the year, and Erica was glad none of his kids seemed to inherit his personality deficits.

"Have you ever considered doing a DNA test to make sure you're even related?" Erica said, half-joking. "Your mother must've been a saint to put up with him."

"Trust me, the thought has occurred to me." Laura sighed. "But yeah, my mom, may she rest in peace, had to have been serving some kind of spiritual penance to put up with that man." She shared a short look with Dani, even though they had different mothers. "Clive has a knack for tricking people into believing he's a decent human being."

"So what happened with Glenna?" Dani quipped. "She's not exactly Mother Teresa."

"That's karma in action, I think," Laura answered with a small laugh. "Either way, they're peas in a pod, and I hope they live a long and unhappy life together."

"Laura, that's not like you to be so salty," Dani chided, although it was tongue-in-cheek. No one was up for championing either Clive or Glenna.

"What can I say? The well is almost bone dry for sympathy and magnanimity for people who don't deserve. But I'm not about to create more gossip by not inviting them. I'll just try to pretend they aren't there."

Dani nodded, her brow creasing ever so slightly. "Keeping up appearances is such an emotional drain."

"Speaking of appearances—" Erica leaned in, her voice dropping an octave "—did you ever find out why Matthew Bennett was so interested in what's happening at the resort?"

Dani's eyes widened, a spark of concern igniting within their dark depths. "Matthew? Glenna's son? What was he asking about?"

"He was just real interested in stuff that I felt was none of his business," Erica said. "It made me uncomfortable, like he wanted me to share inner financial workings of the resort just because he's peripherally related to the Coltons."

Laura's expression of distaste mirrored Erica's. "Yeah, I'm not sharing that information with anyone who isn't on legal paperwork—and even then, it's on a need-to-know basis."

"Maybe he's just curious," Dani offered, trying to lighten the mood, though her light brown eyes betrayed her unease. "I've never gotten the vibe from Matthew that he was cut from the same cloth as his aunt."

"Maybe," Erica allowed, but her gut told her there was more to it than mere curiosity. "But with everything that's been happening...seems prudent to circle the wagons."

"Amen to that," Lauren agreed with an exhale, shoulders slumped as she toyed with the rim of her glass. "We need this merger. Sharpe Enterprises could turn things around for Mariposa."

"Is it really that bad?" Dani asked, concerned.

A furrow dug deep between Laura's brows, etching worry into her skin like a map of all the resort's troubles. Erica reached across the table, a silent offer of solidarity that Laura grasped like a lifeline. "Negotiations have been brutal," Laura continued, the words spilling out heavier than lead. "And now this most recent situation has made the investors twitchy. I just don't know how this turns in our favor, and it scares me."

"Hey." Erica squeezed Laura's hand. "I wish there was more I could do." Helplessness gnawed at her, a hungry rat in the cellar of her capabilities. This was a game played in boardrooms and on balance sheets, far from her expertise.

Dani bit her lip, the line of her jaw taut as a bowstring. "Is there *anything* we can do?" she asked.

"Right now, it's a waiting game," Laura replied with a resigned shrug.

The conversation paused, a momentary ceasefire in their battle against worry, and Laura straightened up, armor back in place. "Enough about stuff that makes us sad," she announced, turning to Erica. "And how about you and CJ? How are things on that front?"

Heat crept into Erica's cheeks, unbidden and undeniable. "I'm…falling for him," she confessed, the words tumbling out in a rush. "Harder and faster than I ever expected, and I don't know how I feel about that, honestly."

"Is it because of the distance?" Laura asked.

"I want to say no, but it's definitely a consideration. I'm not about to start jetting off to LA every other weekend when the life I love is here."

"But a baby changes things, right?" Laura countered.

"Yeah, it does."

"I would imagine compromise is key," Laura offered with a knowing look.

"Compromise," Erica echoed, tasting the word, finding it both sweet and sour. The future unfurled before her, a path forked and formidable. One thing was clear: standing still wasn't an option, but picking the wrong path…would be devastating.

CJ'S BOOTS CRUNCHED on the gravel path leading to Anna's bungalow as dusk painted the sky in strokes of burnt orange and fading blue. He'd been turning over the day's events like a well-worn coin in his pocket, the edges blurred from too much handling. The weight of Harold's offer and the future of the film balanced precariously on his mind's edge.

"Hey," he said, rapping a knuckle against her door frame.

Anna appeared, waving him in. "CJ," she greeted, a smile touching her lips, but she looked preoccupied. "After today's shoot, I'd half expect you to be dead asleep. Great emotional depth, though. I just saw the dailies, and you never fail to impress me with your performance."

"Thanks," he said, appreciating her praise, but he needed to talk about the business end of the production. "Do you have a minute? I've got some stuff to hash out."

Her expression sobered as she nodded. "Of course." She stepped aside, granting him entry into the sanctuary of her temporary home. "What's going on?"

"Harold wants to come back on board, but it means I have to step down, though he offered me a producer credit. I don't know what the right decision is. Things have been going pretty good, and I like to think I had something to do with that. But it could also be coincidence and more a consequence of kicking out the bad apple."

"Which happened because of you," she reminded him. "Don't sell yourself short, CJ. You've really stepped up in ways I never could've imagined."

CJ cracked a smile, needing to hear the outside validation. He never imagined his sense of self might be as fragile as it seemed these days, but he really felt the weight of every decision like never before. "Do you think I should take the deal? Let Harold back in even when he'd been willing to trash everything we've worked so hard to create?"

Anna perched on the edge of the coffee table, her fingers laced together, a portrait of poise. Yet something flickered behind her eyes—a fleeting storm cloud skimming across a clear sky. "I don't know, CJ," she said, the words smooth but her voice betraying a tremor, like a violin string quivering after the note has died. "I've been so grateful for your help in keeping us going, but I can't deny I worried we might be kicking a bigger problem down the road without the studio's backing."

The distribution dilemma. CJ nodded. "Yeah, I know what you mean. I'd hoped a solution would just magically present itself, but something tells me that's not likely to happen."

She shook her head. "No, not likely," she agreed.

CJ looked to Anna. "Harold looked shocked when I told him about the sabotage, and I think it was genuine—which then got me to thinking...if not Harold, who would want to shut us down? Could it be personal? Some beef someone has with you?"

Anna hesitated, a mere second, but enough for him to catch it—the look, quick as a thief in the night, that dashed through her gaze. "Personal?" she echoed, a practiced innocence to her question.

"Maybe something over a different production?" CJ ventured, treading lightly on the edge of her privacy. He wasn't one to pry into locked chests, but the stakes were high, and trust was the currency they were short on.

But the moment passed, and Anna shook her head, baffled, assuring him, "No enemies that I know of. Your guess is as good as mine."

"You're right—it could be totally random. Some crackpot with too much money and an active imagination. Lord knows the movie business draws them out like bees to honey," CJ said, though his gut twisted with doubt, intuition gnawing at him. He could push, but instead he chose to let it go.

Sometimes the unsaid spoke volumes, and he was learning to listen.

"CJ, Harold has the connections," Anna started, returning to the real issue at hand. "Fighting the studio now…it's like trying to swim upstream. It might feel noble, but you'll just tire yourself out. If Harold is willing to come back, I think you should let him."

He nodded slowly, the weight of her logic settling over him like a heavy cloak.

"Sometimes I forget it's not just about the art," he admitted, dragging a hand down his face. The reality of it all made his head throb. "Erica's expecting, and I can't—"

"Play the high-stakes game?" Anna interjected with understanding.

"Exactly." CJ straightened, a rueful smile tugging at the corners of his mouth. "You're right. As much as it galls me to admit it, Harold's got the clout we need. But taking a step down after I made such a big decision, feels like…failure."

"No, that's your ego talking. Don't let pride sour a good thing," she advised. "Besides, it's not that simple anymore, right? Having a child…it shifts your universe. Trust me."

CJ couldn't help but chuckle, the sound more baffled than amused. "Yeah, I'm starting to realize that. The little bugger isn't even here yet, and I feel like every decision has to be made with a different level of diligence, which is way out outside of my comfort zone."

Anna nodded. "The decisions you make now? They'll ripple outward, touch everything and everyone you care about, which is why I think it's not a good idea to hold the course if Harold is willing to step back in play."

"You're probably right." CJ exhaled, a silent acknowledgment of the truth in her caution. "Guess it's time to start thinking long-term, huh?"

"Long-term," she echoed, her lips curving in a knowing smile.

With a final nod, CJ pushed away from the door frame, feeling the gravity of the moment settle into his bones.

Stepping out into the cool evening air, CJ felt the weight of his conversation with Anna cling to him like a second skin. The crunch of gravel under his boots seemed unusually loud in the quiet that enveloped Mariposa's bungalow-lined path. Each step was deliberate, a staccato rhythm to the beat of his troubled thoughts.

The sky hung heavy with stars, something he appreciated about the Arizona nights that he never got to enjoy back home with the LA smog.

Once upon a time, he'd ribbed Landon mercilessly for his lackadaisical approach to life, but now the mirror turned its unforgiving gaze onto him. What had he been doing all these years if not dressing up fear as freedom?

Change meant risk, and risk was a language he'd thought he spoke fluently. Yet there it was—the potential cost laid bare by Anna's gentle wisdom. It wasn't just about the film anymore; it was about Erica, their unborn child and the kind of life he wanted to carve out for them.

A chuckle escaped him, dissipating into the night. "Commitment," he murmured, rolling the concept around in his mind like a foreign coin. This was no longer just about contracts and deals—it was about the heartbeats that would rely on his decisions.

"Scared, CJ?" he challenged the darkness, daring it to answer. The silence was his reply, an uncomfortable truth settling in his chest. Perhaps he had been chasing shadows when all this time, what he truly needed was shining right in front of him.

"Damn." He breathed out, stopping mid-stride. Was he

really contemplating diving headfirst into the biggest role of his life? Father. Partner. Steadfast anchor.

"Or maybe it's damn time," he declared, louder this time, a decisive edge to his tone. With that, CJ spun on his heel to ride with Erica back to her place. He was ready to rewrite the script of his own life.

Which meant giving Harold his decision.

Chapter Twenty-Four

The morning sun had barely crested the horizon when Erica's pulse spiked at the sight of police cars reflecting off the terra-cotta walls of Mariposa Resort.

As she and CJ pulled into the drive, their arrival was swallowed by the commotion—a cluster of police officers, a pair of agitated resort managers, Josh and Laura, and on the fringes, a vulture-like reporter snapping photos and scribbling furiously in a notepad.

"Something's wrong," Erica muttered, her gaze darting to her bosses, speaking in hushed tones, their expressions strained as they talked with police.

CJ reached for her hand, his own grip tight with concern. "Should I stay?"

"No, it's okay," she assured him, motioning him on. "You'll be late for set."

He hesitated, his brows knitting together in that way that said he wanted to argue, but she squeezed his hand, a silent plea. "It's probably nothing. I'll fill you in at lunch, okay?"

"Okay," he relented, reluctance etched across his face as he turned toward the growing daylight and the promise of work, leaving her to deal with whatever this mess was.

Erica approached the scene, her heart thudding erratically, each beat a question mark pulsating through her veins. She caught Laura's eye just as the latter finally managed to peel away from an officer's questioning gaze.

"Erica," Laura breathed, the edges of her usually poised demeanor fraying like worn fabric. "It's bad."

"What's going on?" Erica asked, almost afraid to know.

"A guest was attacked." Laura's words tumbled out in a hurried torrent. "Someone hid in her closet, tried to—Well, she fought them off. They ran, but she left at four this morning—couldn't stay another minute—and I can't blame her, but I just can't believe it happened at all. We've never had a security breach like this before."

"What about the security footage?" Erica asked, her mind already racing through protocols and contingencies.

"Malfunctioned. Nothing recorded." Laura's hands were shaking, the tremors of responsibility and fear intermingling in a visible dance. "Can you believe that luck? Of all days for it to go on the fritz!"

"Damn it," Erica swore, unable to process the absurdly bad luck.

"And that's not all. More guests are checking out. They're scared," Laura continued, her voice quivering on the edge of tears. "And that stupid reporter over there is writing all of this down, like we need one goddamn more brick to fall on us right now."

"Hey," Erica said, her tone softening as she reached out to steady Laura's trembling shoulders. "These things, they happen. We'll get through it."

Laura nodded, her eyes glassy with unshed tears. "I've never felt so helpless."

"Neither have I," Erica admitted, her gaze drifting over the tranquil grounds that now harbored an undercurrent of menace. "But we won't let this break us. Not now, not ever."

"But this feels like the nail in the coffin for the Sharpe

merger. As if people getting poisoned on our watch wasn't bad enough, now this? We might as well close the damn doors."

"No, we'll find a way out of this," Erica assured Laura, but the words tasted hollow. If it looked pretty bleak from Erica's point of view, she could only imagine how it looked from Laura's.

By the time the officers finished taking statements, photographing the room for evidence and collecting any trace evidence that might've been left behind, it was noon and Erica was ready for a break. Her nerves were stretched tight, and she wanted nothing more than to fall into CJ's arms and forget everything for a minute.

But then he said something completely aggravating, and her raw nerves couldn't handle the additional stress.

"Excuse me?" Erica said, hoping her strident tone communicated that he better rephrase his statement before she bit his head off like a female praying mantis during mating season.

"I don't want you here alone after dark anymore," CJ stated firmly as they sat across from each other in the resort's secluded garden, the scent of flowering flora doing little to sweeten his sour mood.

Erica stiffened at his words, her spine a rigid line against the ironwork chair. "I can take care of myself, CJ," she said, her voice edged with a frost that belied the warm desert air. "I don't need anyone treating me like I need protecting."

CJ ran a hand through his hair, a gesture of exasperation that did not go unnoticed. "It's not about that, Erica. It's just—what if this guy is still out there? Waiting?"

"Then we'll handle it," Erica replied curtly, unwilling to let fear dictate her movements, even as an involuntary shiver traced her spine.

"Handle it? Erica, come on! What's the plan? Hurt his

feelings with harsh words?" CJ leaned forward, the muscles in his jaw ticking. "This isn't some script we can rewrite. This is real life. LA might be a jungle, but at least there you know where the danger lurks."

"LA, safer than here? That's rich." The scoff slipped out before she could catch it, her arms crossing over her chest in defiance.

"Damn it, I'm serious!" he barked, his cheeks flaring. "I can't… If anything happened to you or—" His voice cracked, the unfinished thought hanging heavy between them like the thick desert heat. "I'm not okay with you taking unnecessary risks for a dumb job. It's not worth it."

"A dumb job?" she repeated, insulted. "You think my job is dumb just because I don't make millions like you? Is that how you feel?"

"No, I'm not saying that," he said, shaking his head. But she wasn't convinced and frankly, she wanted to slap a knot on his entitled head for even thinking it.

Their gazes locked, a silent battle of wills, until Erica finally broke away, looking out over the sunlit grounds. She hated the feeling of being caged, of having decisions made for her.

CJ checked his phone, swearing beneath his breath. "I have to get back to set. We'll talk more about this later."

"Well, I don't know what else needs to be said," Erica said, rising stiffly and walking away.

Yet as she walked the familiar paths later that day, her senses were heightened, betraying her inner turmoil. The rustle of palm fronds, the whisper of sand beneath her shoes—every sound had her head snapping around in search of shadows that danced just beyond sight.

"Pull yourself together," she muttered under her breath,

chiding herself for the adrenaline that quickened her pulse. She was jumpier than a jack rabbit in a room full of coyotes.

By the end of the long day, Erica was ready to put the events behind her. She was mentally and physically exhausted and just wanted to soak in a warm bath.

The dimming light cast long shadows across the path, turning benign shapes into lurking threats. She quickened her pace, the soft scrape of her shoes against gravel seeming to echo like something out of a horror movie.

A sudden flicker of movement caught her eye—a blur at the edge of her vision—and her heart leapt into her throat. With a start, she twisted around, the keys now a cold lump in her clenched fist.

"Easy there," came a low voice as Roland Hargreaves, the square-jawed head of security, stepped out from the twilight's embrace, hands raised in a calming gesture. "Just me, making sure everything's locked down tight."

"Roland," she exhaled, relief flooding through her, though it couldn't wash away the lingering disquiet. "You nearly gave me a heart attack."

"Sorry 'bout that." His eyes, a steady presence, scanned the area. "Can't be too careful, not after today."

Erica nodded, her gaze drifting over the tranquil facade of the resort, a stark contrast to the turmoil inside her. "Never thought we'd see more trouble like this here," she murmured, more to herself than to Roland.

"First time for everything, I guess," he said, though he seemed just as troubled as everyone else, perhaps more so as head of security.

"Let's hope it's the last," she said, forcing a hopeful smile.

Before heading for the parking lot, she paused by a Saguaro cactus, a shiver tickling her spine as she glanced around. Not one for superstition, Erica still found herself muttering, "Allison, if you're the one causing all this trouble, please stop." But then she realized how stupid she was being, talking to thin air and was thankful no one saw her. *Come on, Erica, ghosts and goblins? Grow up.*

"Ready?" CJ's voice cut through her reverie, firm yet laced with concern. He stood there, resolute in the fading light, his presence both an anchor and a reminder of their earlier spat.

Even as she wanted to tell him he ought to stay at his own bungalow tonight, her insides softened at the sight of him, rippling with protective energy, brooking no argument. His hand reached for hers, fingers intertwining in with hers, a silent vow that her safety wasn't an option.

They walked to the car together, his steps shadowing hers, and despite the tension that hummed between them like a live wire, Erica was silently awed by the tender feelings spreading throughout her body at the knowledge that CJ wasn't going anywhere.

Even if she wasn't being the easiest person to be around.

And that meant something—more than she realized.

Her entire life she'd spent cultivating a persona that was efficient, easy to get along with—a problem solver.

And if you were always the one with the solution, you couldn't afford being the problem, which meant her feelings were often shelved for the sake of calming tempers.

She didn't have to hide her feelings with CJ—and he didn't expect her to fix everything.

For tonight, she could let someone else take care of things.

Starting with, "I'd really love to soak in a warm bath and forget this day happened," she said, meeting his gaze.

CJ's expression softened as the tension between them broke. "Then a bath is exactly what you shall have."

CJ's FINGERS DRUMMED an impatient beat on his thigh, the sound inaudible over the clamor of the crew dismantling the barn set. Sawdust and the smell of fresh paint hung heavy in the air as they worked to erase any sign that they had ever been there. The resort shimmered with the last golden rays of the setting sun, a serene backdrop to the controlled chaos before him.

"Watch it with that beam!" he snapped more harshly than he'd intended as a couple of grips navigated a large piece of scenery past him.

"Sorry, Mr. Knight," one mumbled, ducking his head.

"Damn it," CJ muttered under his breath, raking a hand through his hair. He hadn't meant to bark; it was the gnawing concern for Erica nipping at his conscience that made him short-tempered.

He ought to be excited that they were able to return to their original location, but he couldn't focus when all he could think about was Erica being left at the resort without him.

The police were still clueless about the attacker, and every shadow seemed suspect. Yet Erica's pride wouldn't hear of any suggestions that removed her from the resort. So, he said nothing, even though concern twisted his guts and left him on edge.

"Hey, CJ, you heading out with us tonight?" Caroline called out, snapping CJ from his thoughts, her clipboard in hand.

"Not tonight. Got a flight to catch back to LA," he said with a half-hearted smile. "Tying up loose ends with the studio."

"All right, we'll see you when you get back."

He nodded, watching as the final pieces of the set were carted off, leaving nothing but memories and dust motes dancing in the waning light.

Hours later, CJ sat across from Harold in the latter's sleek Los Angeles office, the city lights a glittering mosaic far below. He tried to ignore the tightness in his chest as he listened to Harold lay out the terms of his new position. Associate Producer. It felt like a demotion, but the paycheck that came with it was anything but.

"Your accountant can breathe easy now, huh?" Harold joked, a smile playing on his lips.

"Guess I won't be joining the ranks of the houseless in Malibu," CJ quipped back, but he hadn't been worried.

Harold's expression softened, picking up on the dissonance. "Look, CJ," he began, leaning forward earnestly, "sometimes, holding out for the right shot is worth more than a quick jump at a big win. You're sharp. You'll get your chance to shine, and when you do, I want to be there, seeing you do it the right way."

CJ absorbed the words, their unexpected weight grounding some of the tension inside him. Maybe this wasn't surrender but a strategic retreat. Harold wasn't just handing down orders; he was offering wisdom.

"Thanks, Harold. I'll remember that," he said, a genuine note of gratitude threading through his voice. But even as Harold seemed in a general good mood, there was something that seemed to preoccupy him as he fidgeted with his gold-plated pen, spinning it between his fingers. "Was there something else?" he asked.

Harold sighed and set the pen down, meeting CJ's gaze with a hint of sheepishness. "It's about Anna," he confessed, the words coming out almost reluctantly. "Got some chatter in my ear a while back. Should've known better than to listen to that crap."

"Someone was badmouthing Anna?" CJ raised an eyebrow, feeling a protective twinge. "What'd they say?"

He waved away the details. "Doesn't matter. I usually toss that stuff straight into the trash bin in my mind. But this time… I don't know, it got to me. I think that's why I wasn't willing to listen to what you were saying about the production."

"Who was doing the chirping?" CJ asked, his curiosity piqued. He couldn't help but wonder if there was a connection to their earlier problems on set.

"It's not a good idea to name names in this business," Harold said, frowning. "But it's got me to thinking."

"Is it possible that whoever was doing the talking might've had motive to sabotage the set?"

Harold tapped his chin, considering. "Seems unlikely, but I suppose anything is possible."

"Would you look into it?" CJ pressed, needing an answer. "They might've thought it wasn't a big deal tampering with the set, but Erica was hurt—she could've been killed when that barn collapsed."

"I agree," Harold affirmed, his tone final. "No one's pulling that crap on my set and getting away with it."

CJ stepped out of Harold's sleek office, the polished chrome door clicking shut behind him. Relief was a cool shadow slipping across his mind, knowing Harold would dig into the underbelly of their troubles.

But as he strode down the corridor, lined with movie posters boasting bold titles and brighter stars, a nagging concern twisted in his gut.

Erica.

Her image flashed before him—those fierce eyes that didn't just look at you but through you, seeing past the facade.

"Damn it," CJ muttered, raking a hand through his hair

as he pushed through the exit, sunlight glaring down like an interrogation lamp.

Was she tucked away safely between the manicured hedges and blossoming bougainvillea? Or was there someone watching her every move, waiting for the moment to strike?

Outside, CJ slid into his car, the leather seat hugging him like a promise of control he wasn't sure he had. He fired up the engine, the purr a low growl that usually set his pulse thrumming with power. Today it was just noise.

"Erica, you'd better stay safe," he muttered, a plea to the universe to keep his baby mama from harm while he was away.

Honestly, he couldn't get back to Arizona fast enough—back to the woman he'd fallen for at some point when he hadn't been paying attention.

Chapter Twenty-Five

Erica spotted her first. The slender figure of Glenna Bennett Colton wound through the hazy midmorning light across Mariposa Resort's manicured lawn. The air was thick with the scent of blooming jasmine, but Erica's nose wrinkled as if she could already catch a whiff of the tension that followed Glenna like a second shadow.

"Looks like trouble," Erica murmured under her breath, her gaze tracking Glenna's determined stride toward the main office. Laura, standing beside Erica at the reception desk, stiffened visibly, her fingers tightening around a stack of brochures.

"Of all the times I do not need this," Laura said with a heavy sigh. "All right, time to put my professional face on and see what we owe to the *pleasure* of this unexpected visit."

Erica followed Laura as they caught up with Glenna as she paused to inspect a rose bush as if she had a degree in botany and it was her job to police everyone's garden. "Good morning, Glenna. This is a surprise," Laura said, forcing a smile.

"Surprises keep life interesting, don't you think?" Glenna said. "Darling, your roses look a little wilty. Have the gardener water morning and night to combat this arid desert climate. Poor things are positively droopy. I'm sure your guests aren't keen to pay VIP prices for hostel-level greenery."

Laura forced a tight smile. "I'll mention it to the groundskeeper."

"Excellent." Glenna's gaze was sharp, and she had that look about her—the one that said she'd come for more than idle chitchat—and Erica wasn't wrong. "I heard about the... incident," she began, her voice dipped in concern that felt as real as fool's gold.

"The incident?" Laura repeated, playing dumb. "What incident would that be?"

"Well, how many have there been that you can't recall which one I'm referencing? Obviously I'm talking about the assault on a guest. It was all over the newspaper. Front page, even. So embarrassing for the family. How did that happen?"

You nasty old windbag, Erica thought privately but kept her mouth shut. Glenna was purposefully poking at Laura to create a reaction.

"Yes, that was unfortunate, but we're trying to move forward," Laura said quickly, a practiced smile plastered on her face. Her blue eyes, however, shot daggers that didn't quite match the diplomacy of her tone.

"Unfortunate?" Glenna echoed, arching an eyebrow so perfectly sculpted it could have been drawn on by a master artist. "I'd hardly call a brutal assault on a guest as simply *unfortunate*—and from what I read, the papers seemed to agree. Have they found the assailant yet?"

"Not yet but they're still looking," Laura answered, clasping her hands in front of her, probably to stop herself from punching her snotty stepmother in the mouth. "I'm sure they'll find who did it, and we'll move forward with pressing charges."

"Newspapers tend to exaggerate," Erica interjected, unable to help herself. "It's how they sell copies."

"Or perhaps they're reporting genuine concerns." Glenna's voice took on a weighted quality as her gaze flicked past Erica with annoyance before returning to Laura. "Your father is worried, you know. He thinks—"

"Clive needn't worry," Laura interjected, her words clipped. "Everything is under control."

"Darling," Glenna said reproachfully, "must you insist on calling him by his name? He's your father, not the janitor."

Laura responded with a tight-lipped smile—which, judging by the subtle twist of Glenna's lips, had the desired effect. Glenna knew full well of the strained relationship between her husband and all of his children, which should say something about the man's character, but Glenna was cut from the same cloth.

"Still," Glenna continued, undeterred, "safety isn't something we can afford to be lax about. It's bad for business. Bad for the family name." Her lips curved into a smile that didn't quite reach her eyes—a smile that seemed to carry a heavier message than mere familial concern.

Laura nodded, her expression schooled into one of polite acknowledgment. "Of course, Glenna. We're all committed to safety here at Mariposa."

"Are we?" Glenna asked, her tone light but her implication heavy as lead. "Because I'd hate for any more...unpleasantness to affect your big day."

"Thank you for your concern," Laura said finally, her voice steady despite the storm raging in her eyes. "We'll make sure everything is up to standard."

"Good." Glenna gave a curt nod, her message delivered, the battle lines drawn without a single shot fired. "That's all I wanted to hear."

Josh appeared, as if summoned by an emotional bat signal sent up by Laura and Erica was glad for the intervention.

"Glenna, what a surprise," he began, the timbre of his voice threading through the tense atmosphere. "If we'd known you were coming we would've planned for lunch."

"Oh, I can't stay…just stopping in after reading that terrible article about the assault to show my support. Honestly, I was just telling Laura that situations like that should've never happened here. There's a standard, a reputation to uphold, and all it takes is a few bad slips and everything goes down the tubes. I'd hate to see that happen."

"Rest assured, we've not only increased our security personnel but replaced the faulty camera. It seems a rodent gnawed through the wiring—an unfortunate mishap, but not something we could've foreseen."

Glenna's nod was slow, her green eyes scrutinizing as she briefly examined a manicured nail. "I see. Though it does make one wonder—how often are these equipment checks done? With vermin being a concern, perhaps regular inspections should be more…meticulous."

"We don't have vermin," Laura retorted, a flash of temper showing.

Erica clenched her jaw, the muscles twitching as she bit back a retort. Her role here was support, not confrontation, no matter how much Glenna's honeyed barbs made her want to start swinging. She sucked in a breath through her nose, letting the scent of the resort's flowering jasmine calm the storm within.

"Your input is noted," Josh replied with an unflappable smile. His stance remained relaxed, yet there was something in his gaze—a glint of steel—that suggested he was no pushover.

"Right then, so happy to know that someone capable is

at the helm. Laura, darling," she said, her voice wrapped in velvet concern. "You look absolutely exhausted. It's simply not flattering for a bride-to-be to appear so...worn."

Laura's blue eyes narrowed just a fraction. She forced a neutral expression, her athletic frame tense. "Thank you for thinking of me, Glenna, but I'm fine."

"Nonetheless," Glenna persisted, digging through her designer bag with bony fingers, "I must insist. Here—" she said, finally producing a crisp business card. "My nutritionist. A vitamin infusion works wonders. You should give it a try."

Erica could barely suppress the snort that threatened to escape her; Glenna's suggestion was almost comical, considering the woman looked more in need of a solid meal than anyone else in the room.

"Can't wait for the wedding. It will be quite the event to see." Glenna's laughter tinkled like glass about to shatter, and with that, her heels were clicking a staccato farewell down the path to her car.

"That woman," Laura growled, "is the devil in designer clothes. She's practically gleefully rubbing her hands at the thought of us failing."

"Don't let her get to you," Josh murmured, placing a hand lightly on Laura's shoulder. "If the Sharpe merger falls through, we'll find something else. She's not getting her hands on Mariposa, okay?"

Laura's gaze met his, a silent acknowledgment passing between them. The weight of his words seemed to settle her, the rigidity in her stance easing ever so slightly. Erica watched, her own fists unclenching, the battle lines drawn yet again in the sand of their desert rose.

"I know. You're right," Laura said with a resolute nod. "She just caught me off my game with everything going on."

"Hey, we're all in this together, right?" Erica finally found her voice, though it sounded thin even to her own ears. Her gaze flitted between Laura and Josh, seeking some sign of assurance that wasn't reflected in the tight lines of Laura's posture.

The silence stretched, taut as a bowstring, before Laura managed a tighter nod, though it seemed more for her own benefit than anyone else's. "Absolutely," she said, but the word lacked its usual conviction.

But a different worry infiltrated her thoughts. Was it possible things were worse off at the resort than Erica knew?

Her job. Her livelihood. It wasn't just a paycheck—it was the sun-soaked mornings greeting guests, the laughter echoing from the poolside, the scent of salt and citrus that permeated the air. To lose that… Her heart skipped a beat at the thought.

Laura drew a deep breath and forced a smile, returning to business. "Erica, did you manage to get the police report from the bachelorette party?"

"It's on your desk," Erica said, watching as Laura left to handle the insurance claim for the people affected by the incident, leaving Josh and Erica behind.

Josh seemed to sense Erica's disquiet and said cheerfully, "Don't worry—it's going to work out," and then went on his way, leaving Erica to wonder if everyone was in a state of denial or they were deliberately trying to keep everyone in the dark.

For the first time, the possibility of being jobless gnawed at Erica's gut.

CJ SLUMPED INTO the producer's chair, the weight of endless days pressing down on his shoulders like a leaden shroud.

His scenes were finished, and he was just waiting for his production assistant to take him back to base camp for the day.

The desert sun beat down mercilessly, but its searing touch was a mere whisper compared to the fatigue that clawed at his insides. Every muscle in his body screamed for rest, for the sweet surrender to sleep that seemed as elusive as a mirage in the vast Arizona landscape.

"Hey," Anna said, her voice slicing through the haze of exhaustion. She plopped down beside him, concern etching lines into her normally smooth forehead. "You're looking more beat than an old rug. You okay?"

He forced a grin that felt more like a grimace. "Burning the candle at both ends takes its toll, but nothing a good night's sleep won't fix." The lie tasted bitter on his tongue, but admitting weakness wasn't in CJ's script. Besides, this was all temporary. Soon enough the shoot would be finished, and he could take a break, though he wasn't sure in which zip code he'd land.

Anna's gaze lingered on him, sharp and assessing. She leaned in, close enough that he could catch the faint scent of lavender from her hair. "You can't keep doing this to yourself. You're human, not some machine. Caroline tells me that you're driving out to Sedona every night after the set wraps instead of returning to base camp."

There was no denying it. "Erica needs me. Can't have her alone in Sedona—not now. Not to mention the woman seems to be a magnet for accidents. Two emergency room visits—and I'm sure as hell not going to let a third happen. I'm half tempted to hire an on-call doctor just to follow her around and make sure she doesn't trip and fall down a well or something."

Anna chuckled. "I've never seen you so protective before. I like it. It's a nice change."

Tired as he was, he shared a smile. He was changing and while it right, it was still a challenge not to fall back on old habits but he supposed that was normal.

"Ever thought about bringing her here? Your trailer is pretty nice," Anna suggested. "Switch it up a bit. Might do you both some good."

"Maybe," he said, wondering if Erica would be open to "glamping" in his trailer, though he rather enjoyed getting away from everything associated with the movie business at the end of the night. Cuddling up with Erica at the end of a long night was the most normal he'd felt in ages, and he wasn't sure he was ready to give that up just yet for the convenience of a shorter commute to work.

Anna paused, her energy shifting as she said, "I need to talk to you about something."

"What's wrong?" he asked.

"I've been thinking about the question you asked me a few days ago, about who might want to screw with the film and if it might be personal against me."

"Yeah?"

"At first I dismissed it, but then something happened, and I had to wonder if maybe… I should say something."

"Is everything okay?" CJ asked.

"Yes, it's just not something I'd like everyone to know." She exhaled, as if the words were reluctant prisoners escaping her mouth. "A while back, I…had a thing with someone. A producer. And he was married," she added, her gaze dropping to her boots.

"Doesn't sound like you," CJ said, not a judgment, just a fact.

"It wasn't." Anna glanced away, heat rising in her cheeks. "And when I came to my senses, I ended it. Badly."

"Bad enough to mess with your work?" CJ asked.

"Maybe." Anna met his eyes again. "I got this text, out of nowhere, asking to meet, asking if I needed any help with the production. I shut it down, but…the timing is off. It's got me thinking—maybe he orchestrated all of this to get me to come back to him, like he was going to swoop in and save the day."

"Could be a coincidence," CJ offered, but they both knew better. Coincidences didn't run rampant in their world. "But I think I should tell Harold."

"I hate naming names in this business because it always has the potential of biting you in the ass later, but given how Erica had been inadvertently hurt during the last incident, I don't see how I can withhold my concerns if there's even a hint of bad behavior happening because of me. His name is Bob Wendell."

"Thanks for telling me," CJ said, the gears in his head already turning. Harold would definitely want to hear if there was someone willing to go to such lengths to get even over something personal.

"Okay, then." Anna squared her shoulders, the confession's weight visibly lifted. "That's all I've got for now. See you tomorrow."

CJ's production assistant popped up, and CJ climbed into the golf cart, ready to rinse off the trail dust and make a quick call to Harold to share what Anna had told him.

Wrapping early meant he could actually sneak in a nap before heading off to Erica's for the night, which was sorely needed.

Once back at his trailer, he wasted no time in calling Harold to share the information with the caveat that it was pure speculation and that it would be best to handle this discreetly. But Harold's tone told CJ that he had reason to believe there might be merit to the theory.

"Bob Wendell has a reputation for a wandering eye—that much isn't speculation, but it doesn't surprise me that he might try to orchestrate something to shift a situation to his advantage. I've caught him in the past doing shady shit and I chose to overlook it, but this is going too far."

"We don't have proof," CJ reminded Harold, but the wheels had already been set in motion. "Just make sure he's actually guilty before you potentially destroy a career."

Harold chuckled as if CJ's warning was cute. "You just worry about your end of things. I'll handle this situation. Thanks for letting me know."

CJ clicked off, wondering if he'd just made a big mistake or if he'd rectified one. Time would tell.

Later that night, CJ didn't have time to worry about Bob Wendell because Erica was agitated from the moment he stepped into the house.

"Is everything okay?" he asked in alarm when he caught Erica pacing. "What's going on?"

"I don't even know where to start," Erica said, stopping to stare at CJ in distress. "Glenna the Bad Witch showed up and started stirring all sorts of trouble—which is on brand for her, and normally no one pays attention, but now it's different. I think the resort's in real trouble and no one wants to admit it—and if that's true, then I think my job is in jeopardy."

"Hey." CJ's voice was a gentle interruption, warm and steady. He patted the seat beside him on the sofa, beckoning her to sit. "I don't think wearing a hole in your carpet is going to solve anything."

She complied, a frazzled sigh escaping her as she sank down next to him. He could feel the tension radiating off her, see the worry creasing her brow.

"Talk to me," he urged, his tone wrapping her in an embrace as his arm followed, drawing her in close.

"Bookings are down, cancellations are up, and I know it's because of all the bad publicity the resort has suffered as of late, which is unprecedented, honestly, but..." Erica started, her voice warbling. "Laura's doing all she can, but...if this keeps up, I might be out of a job. And with the baby on the way, I—" She broke off, biting her lip.

CJ absorbed her fears, choosing silence over empty reassurances. He could assure her that she had nothing to worry about, that he could easily take care of her and the baby, but that would do nothing but poke at a fiercely independent woman like Erica, so he just stroked her arm and listened.

"Feels like I'm staring down the barrel of a loaded gun," she whispered, leaning into his chest.

"Whatever happens, you're not alone." His words were simple, but they carried the weight of his conviction. CJ's heart ached with the urge to whisk her away from all this, to wrap her up in the safety of his world back in LA. Yet he held back, understanding that her independence was not his to take.

When he didn't offer to snap his fingers and solve everything, she actually seemed relieved, which seemed counterintuitive, but he was starting to understand Erica's complicated brain and knew she had to find a solution that worked for her.

"Thanks, CJ." Her breath hitched, and she seemed to draw strength from his presence. "Just having you here—it means everything."

He pressed a kiss to the top of her head, breathing in the scent of her shampoo. In that moment, he was her fortress against the chaos, even as his own walls threatened to crumble.

He didn't know how or when it'd happened, but he was

desperately, hopelessly and possible ridiculously in love with Erica Pike.

So how the hell was he supposed to tell her that without sending her sprinting for the hills?

Chapter Twenty-Six

Erica's heels clicked a steady rhythm on the polished tile as she navigated the familiar halls of Mariposa. The scent of fresh lilies, strategically placed to welcome and soothe, mingled with the undercurrent of anxiety that had settled over the resort since the assault. She pushed open the door to Laura's office with a tap of her knuckle, her practiced smile wilting at the sight of her boss.

Laura stood motionless, her gaze lost beyond the windowpane, where the relentless sun carved sharp shadows across the courtyard. "You okay?" Erica ventured, the words slicing through the hush that clung to the room like cobwebs.

"Thinking about axing Clive and Glenna from the wedding guest list." Laura's voice was flat, but the muscles in her jaw twitched.

"Seriously?" Erica's brows shot up. "What brought this on?"

"I've just been thinking… I think Glenna fed the story to the press about the assault, and if that's the case, I don't want her anywhere near what is supposed to be the happiest day of my life."

"Not that I don't support your decision, but why would she do that?"

"She wants to smear the resort's reputation when she knows it's imperative for us to shine."

"How would she even know about the assault to tell the press anything?" Erica asked, confused.

"If she had someone on the inside whispering into her ear, she'd have everything she needs."

"Do you really think anyone here would be willing to do that?" Erica asked, horrified.

"I don't want to, but it's the only thing that makes any sense."

"Okay, even if that were true—and I sincerely hope it's not—what's in it for Glenna and Clive to ruin the resort?" Erica asked.

"The family has chosen to keep a certain situation regarding the resort very private, keeping it strictly within a tight circle because we didn't want to alarm anyone. Plus, frankly, it's no one's business what goes on behind closed doors."

"What's happening?" Erica asked, afraid of the answer. "Is the resort bankrupt?"

"No, not at all," Laura assured Erica, creating a wave of relief that nearly weakened her knees. "The resort is doing very well. It's a land ownership issue that has my father threatening to get his grubby hands on the resort for the cash. He wants to liquidate all assets, but we as a family stood against his wishes, which is why it's so important that Sharpe Enterprises agrees to the merger."

Erica's heart hammered against her rib cage, a drumbeat of anxiety as she absorbed the gravity in Laura's gaze.

"We're banking on the merger. Without it..." Laura let the sentence drift, unfinished yet understood.

"Without it, Clive wins?" Erica ventured, recalling the man's hawkish eyes and the way his presence seemed to linger like a storm cloud over their every move. She'd never liked the man, which now seemed warranted.

Laura nodded. "Exactly. He's circling the resort, waiting for a slip. The land dispute has given him an opening, and the sharks—" Her hands cut through the air, mimicking the feeding frenzy of lawyers that had descended upon them.

"God, Laura." Erica's mind reeled. "I didn't realize things were this dire."

"Few do, and that was by design. Appearances are everything. We can't have people thinking the resort is in any trouble or we'll lose even more bookings, which we sorely need right now."

"Is my job...?" Erica couldn't finish the sentence, her throat constricting around the fear of the unknown.

"Everyone's is." The words were blunt as Laura's gaze met Erica's. "Even mine. But we're doing everything to keep this place in our control."

The room seemed to shrink, the walls closing in with the weight of their shared burden. And yet amid the encroaching darkness, Erica felt a flicker of something defiant kindle within her. She loved Mariposa and the Coltons; she'd do whatever possible to help.

"Then count me in the fight. I'm not about to watch Mariposa get squeezed to death by your greedy father and his bony-crony wife."

Laura cracked a reluctant smile at the dig. "So you think I should uninvite them to the wedding?"

"Why in the world would you keep Clive and Glenna on the wedding guest list after all this?"

"I guess to keep up appearances? Foster some sort of goodwill? Maybe appeal to my father's nearly nonexistent kernel of familial loyalty? I don't know."

"I think that kernel is damn near microscopic at this point."

"Yeah, you're probably right." Laura rubbed at her forehead, her shoulders dragging beneath the weight of everything happening. "God, what a mess."

Erica leaned against the edge of Laura's desk, her fingers tracing the grain of the wood as if seeking answers in its swirls and knots. The office was quiet, the tension between them palpable, like the charged air before a storm.

"I appreciate your loyalty, Erica," Laura said. "But if you need to leave, to be with CJ and start something new… I'd understand."

Startled, Erica straightened, her gaze snapping to Laura's. "Resign? Now?" Her words came out sharper than intended, a defensive edge to them. "That's not even on my radar, Laura."

"You're so loyal. I know you'd probably be willing to go down with the ship if need be, but I don't want that for you. You need to do what's right for you, not just what's right for the resort."

"Mariposa is more than just a job," Erica said finally, her voice steady. "It's home. And you…you're not just my boss." She let the words hang, a testament to the bond they'd forged.

"Thank you," Laura whispered, gratitude and respect woven through the simple phrase. "I feel the same way about you."

Erica nodded, a silent vow passing between them. Uncertainty might cloud her personal horizon, but here in the heart of Mariposa, her course was clear. Whatever the future held, she'd face it head-on, with the resort's soil beneath her feet and its fight coursing through her veins.

Now if only it was as easy to figure out her future with CJ.

CJ UNFOLDED THE checkered tablecloth with a flourish, masking his nerves with a practiced smile. The Crescent

Moon Ranch sprawled before them, an expanse of tranquility far removed from the chaos of movie sets and flashing cameras.

Now that the production had wrapped, he was free to actually spend some quality time with Erica that didn't revolve around their hectic schedules. Today it was all about enjoying each other's company.

He watched Erica's face light up as she took in the rolling hills and the distant silhouette of horses grazing, her delight more soothing than the gentle Arizona breeze.

"Wow, CJ, this is…it's beautiful," she breathed out, the stress lines that had taken residence on her forehead seeming to smooth away with each passing second. "It's wild how you can live near someplace and yet still be a tourist. I can't believe I've never been here before now."

"Only the best for you," he replied, arranging the picnic with precision—a spread of her favorite fruits, artisanal cheeses and a jar of the marinated artichoke hearts she'd been craving endlessly since the pregnancy had started.

Erica laughed, a sound he'd come to cherish, as she popped a strawberry into her mouth. "You're spoiling me rotten, but I don't mind. Please feel free to continue. God, I needed this. How'd you know?"

"We've both been under a lot of stress. I needed this just as much as you," he admitted. "I've never in my life been under so much pressure than I have with this production. I'm glad it's wrapped, but also, I'm proud of the work. They say nothing worth having comes easy, so hopefully all this drama will translate to a film that makes it all worth it."

"I'm sure it'll be amazing. From what I could see, it's an amazing story."

"Thank you," he said with genuine pleasure at her assessment, settling across from her at the weathered picnic table.

Their conversation meandered through comfortable territory until, bolstered by the serene setting, CJ broached the subject that had been gnawing at him.

"Erica, can you ever picture settling down in LA?" he asked, trying to keep his voice light.

Her expression shifted, the hint of a frown marring her features. "LA?" She shook her head, auburn hair catching the sunlight. "I… No, I can't. It's not the place I imagine raising our child. I mean, it's not exactly a place I picture as a place with solid values. When I think of LA, I think of shallow people and transient moral values, which is the last place I'd want to raise a family."

The words hit CJ like an unexpected punch, deflating his buoyant mood. "LA has some good people," he said, offended. "Every place has its good and bad points. I wouldn't say that one place is inherently better than another. It all depends on where you live. I, for one, live in a very nice and safe neighborhood with great neighbors."

Erica shrugged. "Well, you asked me and I told you. No, LA has never been on my radar as a desirable place to live, much less raise a family."

"But my career—it's there. I need to be seen, available. You know how this works. My career isn't like most people's and requires a certain flexibility."

"Sure, but Arizona is where I feel at home and where I have the most support," Erica countered. "The only person I would know in LA is you."

"Am I chopped liver?" he quipped, but there was something else behind his words that he couldn't quite hide. Most women would happily relocate if they were in Erica's position. But then, he hadn't fallen in love with those women. He wanted Erica—but he wanted Erica to follow him to LA.

"Of course not, but that's not how I operate. I need more," she said simply, stunning him with her brutal honesty.

But wasn't that what he appreciated most about Erica? The way she didn't pull punches, the way he always knew that she'd give it to him straight, no matter if he didn't like what she had to say?

Yeah, but right now, he'd love a little less of that blunt honesty. However, if that was how she wanted to play it… "Erica, let's be real, I can take care of us in a way that you can't. It doesn't make sense for you to stay here. Come to LA with me, and you'll never want for anything. I promise."

Her gaze narrowed. "Except autonomy. When did I give the impression that I wanted to be a kept woman, like some pretty bird in a golden cage? I am capable of taking care of myself and this baby, even if it's not to a Hollywood Hills standard—and frankly, CJ, it's offensive for you to even say something like that to me."

Heat flashed through CJ as regret tasted bitter in his mouth, but his pride wouldn't let him apologize. A part of him felt he was right, even if he wasn't.

"You're being stubborn and short-sighted," he bit out. "C'mon, Erica, think it through. Don't let your mouth overload your ass. I'm offering you the world on a plate. If you want to get a job or something in LA, I won't stand in your way—I'm just saying you don't have to. Take up a hobby or something. That's what most of the wives do anyway."

Erica rose, her nostrils flaring. "CJ Knight, I am not a 'woman who lunches' or whatever you're trying to make me enjoy. I have a career I love, and I'm good at it. How dare you imply that I don't deserve the same consideration in a decision that should hold equal weight? I need a minute to calm down before I say something I truly regret—though, lord knows, you're choking on your whole damn foot!"

He watched her walk away, her figure growing smaller, feeling the rift between them widen with each step she took. The thought of spending a few more days wallowing in the aftermath made his skin itch. Decision made, he packed away the uneaten food, the silence around him now oppressive.

The drive back to Erica's place was excruciatingly silent, but the tension in the air was enough to choke a horse.

"I think I'll go back to LA," he announced, his voice devoid of the warmth he so desperately wanted to offer.

"Okay," she said simply, without turning to look at him.

By the time they reached her place, it was a done deal. The hurt between them was a chasm that couldn't be jumped without falling to their death a mangled mess.

Swallowing the lump in his throat, CJ packed up his bag and left without saying much more of anything else. What else could he say? He wasn't entirely sure if he was truly in the wrong and she was being stubbornly prideful, or he was woefully out of line and ought to beg for forgiveness.

He should've said something about calling later, but he didn't because, frankly, he didn't know what could be said. Neither were willing to budge and both felt solidly they were in the right.

An impasse.

By the time he landed in LA and caught an Uber back to his place, he was tied in knots but numb at the same time.

He walked into his place and found Landon in the kitchen making a cheesy panini. "Hey, man, you're back! How was filming?"

"Eventful," CJ admitted, feeling a weariness that permeated his soul as he sank down onto the stool at the kitchen counter. "How were things here?"

"All good," Landon promised, hefting his gooey sandwich, offering, "Want me to make you one? I picked up some of the good gouda from that cute mom-and-pop in Santa Barbara we found that time we were hungover following that wild Golden Globes after party. You remember, that time you—"

"Yeah, I remember," CJ cut him off, the trip down debauchery lane not needed. "But no, thanks. I'm good. I'm mostly exhausted. I feel like I could sleep for days and still need a few more winks."

"Sleep's important, man," Landon agreed, crunching into his sandwich with a groan of appreciation. "Mmm, that's criminal. Damn, it's going to kill my stomach later, but for now, I'm in heaven."

CJ smiled, rubbing at his gritty eyes. "Anything else going on?"

"Oh yeah," Landon said, recalling as he chewed. "Have you heard about Bob Wendell?"

CJ perked up with wary interest. "What about him?"

"The guy's been playing puppet master with people's lives. It's real sinister movie-plot type stuff. I mean, honestly, if it were on paper, I'd say it was a little over the top, but this shit's real. He's probably going to jail. It's wild what people think they can get away with in the digital age. Receipts are everywhere, man."

"Seriously?" CJ said.

"Yep. He's toast," Landon said, taking a huge bite. "Turns out he's been strong-arming women for…favors, if you catch my drift. And if they didn't play ball? Career sabotage."

"Damn." CJ shook his head, the news stirring a bitter sense of justice within him. "That's messed up."

"Understatement of the year, buddy." Landon finished his sandwich and wiped his mouth before tossing his balled-up napkin into the trash like he was an NBA player. "Nothing but net, baby."

CJ realized Harold had really pulled no punches, chasing down a lead that had turned out to be the jackpot. He mostly felt vindicated for Anna. She'd been carrying that secret shame for too long, and now she could let it go.

He released a pent-up breath, relieved on that score, at the very least. Too bad his situation with Erica wasn't so easily solved.

As if reading his mind, Landon asked, "So, what's the deal with Erica and the kid?"

Hell, if I know. He could only shrug. "Things are kind of…up in the air right now."

"Look, CJ," Landon said, his tone unusually serious. "Far be it from me to dispense life advice, but don't be a jackass, all right? Chase your bliss. Because this place?" He gestured to the clustered cityscape beneath his sprawling estate. "It's nothing but a recipe for heartbreak."

"Easy for you to say," CJ muttered, but the truth of Landon's words stung. Still, he shot back, "When have you ever taken anything seriously?"

Landon's gaze turned somber for the briefest second. "Not soon enough, man." He flashed a lopsided grin as he shouldered his duffel bag. "Anyway, got a new gig lined up. I'll keep you posted."

As the sound of Landon's Uber faded away, CJ stood alone, the silence echoing loudly in the empty house. He tried to picture a kid running amok this place but couldn't manage it. His house was gorgeous and everything he'd thought he'd wanted when he'd purchased.

Now it felt hollow, like a movie facade. He didn't have anything in this house that felt distinctly representative of him as a person. Sure, it was decorated with style and class, but nothing stood out as his. By comparison, Erica's place was ten times smaller but was packed with warmth and personality. Photos lined the walls, knickknacks representing adventures and holding memories were sprinkled throughout her house, and a cozy night spent in her little house felt more inviting than a lifetime spent in this cold place.

Was this what he wanted to bring a child into?

CJ slumped against the door frame, hating how morose he felt. The air felt thicker somehow, charged with a truth too raw for the glitzy veneer of LA. Landon's words clung to him, a tattoo on his conscience.

"Chase your bliss," he muttered under his breath, the syllables tasting like a dare.

He shook his head, trying to dislodge the knot in his stomach. Landon, the eternal drifter, had lobbed a grenade of insight that left CJ's defenses in shambles. A guy who couldn't hold down a job to save his soul, yet there he was, doling out life lessons that rang with an uncomfortable clarity.

"Damn it, Landon," he said to the empty room, feeling the fissures in his well-constructed facade.

Had he screwed things up with Erica? Was she right? Was it better to raise a family outside of LA? Of course he'd seen the effects of privilege and wealth in this town—useless nepotism was a constant reality—the drug use, the moral decay of youth gone wild without any guardrails. But he'd raise his kid differently, he wanted to protest.

Except he didn't know the first thing about raising a kid, much less raising a kid with the kid of guidance it would need to avoid the pitfalls common to movie-star kids.

He hated that term, along with *A-list* and *celebrity*, but it was the reality of his life.

CJ's phone buzzed, a jarring intrusion. He glanced at the screen—another meeting, another chance to be seen. It should've spurred him into action. Instead a weary sigh slipped from him, the allure of the spotlight dimming.

With a final glance at the city below, he grabbed his keys, decision hardening like cement in his veins.

"Time to find some damn bliss," he grunted, determination etching itself across his features. He flicked off the lights, stepping out into the night, a man on a mission to rediscover what mattered most.

Chapter Twenty-Seven

CJ watched the moonlight drape like a sheer curtain across Erica's bare shoulders, her skin shimmering with an ethereal glow.

She lay beside him, her hand delicately poised on her collarbone, the new wedding ring catching slivers of silvery light. How had he gotten so lucky? His heartbeat echoed *forever* with each pulse as he committed to memory the way her chest rose and fell in gentle rhythm.

"Beautiful," he murmured, not solely for the modest band adorning her finger but for the entirety of the moment—their moment.

"Thank you," she said softly, her eyes lifting to meet his, brimming with shared dreams and silent promises. "For this, for everything."

He reached out, brushing a stray lock of hair from her forehead. The familiar rush of being impossibly blessed to have her swelled within him in the private moment.

Erica shared a smile in the quiet of their bedroom before a small frown pulled on her brow. "Whatever happened with that production assistant that got busted for sabotaging your set?"

"Ahh, in the excitement of making you my bride, I forgot to tell you. Have you ever heard of a producer named Bob Wendell?"

"Vaguely? What about him?"

"As it turns out, he was blackmailing women in the business. It was vile—career advancements traded for…for favors." His jaw clenched at the thought, disgust souring his tongue.

"Blackmailing? How did you—"

"Anna Wilson," CJ answered, still amazed at how things unfolded. "Apparently she had a fling with him, but when she ended things, he snapped. Hired someone to ruin her film, figuring she'd be desperate enough to go back to him. But it all unraveled when I stepped in."

Erica sat up, blankets pooling around her waist, her eyes wide with shock. "You stopped him?"

"More like inadvertently exposed him. The assistant he used flipped on him, handed over texts that led right back to Wendell. And then…the floodgates opened. Other women came forward, stories worse than the last."

Erica reached for his hand, squeezing it tight. "God, CJ. That's horrific, but… I'm so proud of what you did," she said.

"Thanks, babe." CJ smiled, appreciating her support. "It feels good to be on the right side of a story. Oh, and you know our missing wrangler? Turns out it was simply a case of a family emergency. The guy had to leave town, and he was out of cell range wherever he was at, so he couldn't let the production manager know what was happening."

"Are there places on the planet that don't have cell service?" Erica asked.

"Apparently."

"Well, I'm glad it wasn't anything related to Allison," she said quietly, as if even mentioning the poor girl's name had the power to draw bad energy their way. "Okay, no sad talk allowed tonight. Let's talk about brighter things."

He chuckled, the mood in the room lifting. "Like baby names? What do you think about Arizona?"

"Arizona?" Erica laughed, the sound dancing in the air. "Absolutely not," she teased, though her smile hinted at the possibility that she might consider it.

"Ah, well, you make me work for every victory," he said, grinning. "And that's just one of the many reasons I love you."

"Good," she replied, snuggling closer. "Because with me, life will never be boring."

"Wouldn't have it any other way," CJ whispered, pulling her into his arms as they settled back into the embrace of the night.

CJ watched the play of moonlight on Erica's face, her features softened by shadows. Her fingers were still entwined with his, a lifeline in the quiet aftermath of their conversation.

"Harold Greene," she murmured, breaking the silence. "Never thought I'd say this, but I've got to hand it to him. He did the right thing in the end."

"Agreed." CJ nodded, the image of the usually stern-faced executive softening in his mind. "There's talk about another project he wants me on board with. Early days, though."

"Another project?" Erica's brow quirked up, curiosity alight in her eyes. "That could be something."

"Could be," CJ echoed, cautious hope threading through his response.

A pause settled, their breathing the only sound until CJ broke it with a question that had been gnawing at him. "Any news on the person behind the assault at the resort?"

Her sigh was a soft gust as she shared, "Trail's gone cold.

I'd hoped they could at least solve that mystery, just so everyone could feel less jumpy at every shadow. It would've been nice to have some good news to cling to. The Sharpe merger's looking shaky."

"Damn," CJ muttered, thinking of the sprawling resort that had become more than just a place to them. Mariposa would always have a soft place in his heart because of Erica.

"But you know me," Erica continued with a chuckle. "I'm not going anywhere. I'll stand with the Coltons, come hell or high water."

"Then so will I," CJ declared. "Whatever it takes, Erica. We're in this together."

"Always," Erica whispered, her eyes meeting his.

In the way she challenged him, made him strive for every little win, CJ found a thrill he'd never known. In this room, with her by his side, he could see the stretch of years ahead—unpredictable, demanding but utterly irresistible. And as he pulled her closer, feeling the warmth of her skin against his, CJ knew without a doubt that with Erica, the word *boredom* would forever remain uncharted territory.

"Whatever the future holds," he murmured into the space between them, "I know it's going to be one hell of an adventure with you."

"Wouldn't have it any other way," Erica whispered back.

And CJ finally understood what he'd been missing all this time—the thing that money couldn't buy but his heart had recognized immediately—the love of a woman worth building a life with.

* * * * *

Afterglow Books is a trend-led, trope-filled list of books with diverse, authentic and relatable characters, a wide array of voices and representations, plus real world trials and tribulations. Featuring all the tropes you could possibly want (think small-town settings, fake relationships, grumpy vs sunshine, enemies to lovers) and all with a generous dose of spice in every story.